The Sun

the SUMMER FIELDS

LP FERGUSSON

CANELO

First published in the United Kingdom in 2020 by Canelo

Canelo Digital Publishing Limited
31 Helen Road
Oxford OX2 0DF
United Kingdom

A CIP catalogue record for this book is available from the British Library.

Print ISBN 978 1 80032 004 8
Ebook ISBN 978 1 78863 368 0

This book is a work of fiction. Names, characters, businesses, organizations, places and events are either the product of the author's imagination or are used fictitiously. Any resemblance to actual persons, living or dead, events or locales is entirely coincidental.

Look for more great books at www.canelo.co

Printed and bound in Great Britain by Clays Ltd, Elcograf S.p.A.

For Ben

Historical Note

This story is set in 1704. Queen Anne, the last of the Stuarts, is on the throne. England and her allies are at war with France, determined to stop the relentless expansion of King Louis XIV. The man chosen to command the allies is John Churchill, the 1st Duke of Marlborough. In August this year he wins a resounding victory in Bavaria near a small village called Blindheim (anglicised to Blenheim), which saves Vienna from invasion and destroys the Continent's belief in the invincibility of the French.

Part I

The Red Plague

Chapter 1

It is a freezing night, a month into the new year. Elen Griffiths sprawls in front of the embers of the kitchen fire, a book cranked towards the glow. She longs to fetch a rushlight, but her father is sleeping in his chair on the other side of the hearth. If he wakes, he will tell her to leave the book and go upstairs. Instead she gathers up a handful of twigs and pushes them into the embers. Her father stirs. One of the dogs out by the dairy barks and falls silent. The twigs flare, lighting the strange woodcuts on the page of her book: poor St Agatha showing her dreadful wounds. The dog barks a second time. Others take up the cry, baying louder out in the yard.

Elen frowns, gets up from the floor and crosses to the window. She draws the curtains aside and looks out. The dogs are already at the gate. She can just see them, moving backwards with the violence of their barks, regrouping like wolves guarding the entrance to their den. They have heard something bad – not the screech of an owl out in the woods or the cry of a fox across the lake. They have heard people approaching. Men abroad at this time of night spells danger.

She darts over to her father and shakes him by the shoulder. He wakes with a start, momentarily clumsy with sleep. 'Why are you not in bed?' he says.

'I can hear someone coming.' Her tone makes him struggle to his feet, snatching up the stick he keeps by the fire. He goes to the window, one arm held behind to keep her away, putting his body forward to protect her.

Imagination is worse than fear and she twists round him, squeezing next to him. Through the gaps in the casement she hears the rattle of wheel-spokes in the distance, bouncing between the ruts of the track.

'Upstairs,' her father says. 'Quick with you.'

'Is it a carriage?' she says. 'It sounds bigger than a trap. It is a carriage, a carriage is coming.'

She looks at her father for reassurance, but senses fear. A glow out in the darkness sweeps across his face, the blaze of the carriage's flambeaux lighting the underside of the overarching trees. A vehicle bursts into view, pulled by a team of horses, vapour jetting from their muzzles. The coachman leans back on the reins. The horses plunge and slow, the farm dogs snapping and scattering in front of the clattering hooves.

A servant jumps from the back, hastens round to pluck open the carriage door. The coach tips, disgorging a figure, small and hunched against the cold. He yells up to the coachman, 'Turn it round. We depart directly.' Before kicking aside one of the dogs, sending it off with a cowering yelp. 'Bring that light. Follow me.' The man and servant stride towards the cottage.

'Upstairs I say,' her father says, propelling Elen towards the foot of the stairs just as a fist begins to hammer on the door.

'Open the door. Open up this instant,' a voice calls.

Elen scuttles up the stairs. Despite the clutch of tightness she feels at her throat, her curiosity overcomes her fear. She pauses, sinking down onto a step, hidden in the shadows. Below, her father snatches a lighted twig from the fire, clatters with the lamp as he tries to light it. He sets it down on the ground and opens the door no further than a slit, his stout boot braced against the sweep. She can see the fingers of his hand working on the stick at his side. He straightens, snatches up the lantern and pushes out past the servant who hovers on the threshold. Elen feels the cold night air creep up the stairs and surround her,

3

squeezing the warmth from her body, making the skin shiver between her shoulder blades.

'Dr Argyll?' her father says, holding the lantern high and peering into the dark.

'I need to see your daughter,' a voice replies.

'Elen? Elen's not sick.'

Dr Argyll steps into the pool of light, pulling his hands free of his gloves. 'Let me in, Griffiths. It's bitter out here,' he says, and then to the servant, 'wait there. This will take no more than a minute.'

The farmer stands to one side, allowing the doctor to pass before closing the door and bolting it behind him. Elen slips carefully down to a lower step in order to hear better.

'Fetch your daughter, Griffiths,' Dr Argyll says.

'She's upstairs, asleep.'

'Call her.'

'It's gone ten o'clock. She'll be dead to the world. She must rise before dawn for the milking.'

'That cannot be helped. She is needed for a more pressing duty.'

Elen shrinks further into the shadows. She doesn't want to be caught as an eavesdropper. She hears a creak behind her, and turning, she sees her brother Rhodri standing in the corridor above. 'What's happening?' he whispers.

She creeps up towards him, beckons at him to kneel down and grasps his shoulders. 'The doctor is here,' she whispers.

'Is Tad ill?'

Elen crosses her finger on her lips. 'Hush, you'll wake the others. No one is ill. Get back to bed. He asks for me.'

'Why?'

'If you hold your tongue we'll find out soon enough.'

Beneath them they hear their father sigh, then the sound of him coming to the foot of the stairs. Rhodri creeps away, back towards the bedroom.

'Elen?' her father calls softly.

'I'm here, Tad. I'm on my way down.'

Dr Argyll is pacing around in front of the fire, silhouetted against the flames. When he hears her step, he swings round, acknowledging her with a slight dip of the head. His expression is grave. He is a small man, probably about the same age as her father, but he has the polish and neatness of a gentleman, which makes him seem more youthful.

'Miss Griffiths, good evening to you. I need you to fetch your cloak and sufficient articles to see you through a few days. Do it quickly. You are to come with me.'

'What's that you say?' her father demands, but the doctor raises a hand to quiet him.

'Hold your tongue Griffiths. Viscount Mordiford is very sick.'

'That's bad news indeed, but what has it to do with Elen?'

'It is the smallpox.'

'The red plague?'

'Call it what you will, she must accompany me to Duntis-bourne Hall directly.'

Excitement nips at Elen's diaphragm. She has always wanted to know what lies behind the walls of that great edifice of towers and gables. And if she goes with the doctor, she won't have to rise at dawn to begin her daily drudge. The viscount is sick. She will be expected to sit with him.

She frowns. A small worm of anxiety taints her excitement as she turns to fetch her things. Her father shoots out a hand and grasps her by the wrist. 'You shall not go, Elen,' he says. 'I will not allow a circumstance such as this to put your life at risk.'

'My life, Tad?'

The doctor begins to tap his tricorn against his leg. 'You know perfectly well she will be in no danger, Griffiths,' he says.

'From the plague perhaps not,' her father replies.

'And what other dangers are you suggesting await her at the hall? Come on man, speak up.'

Instead of answering, her father blusters, 'I need Elen here, at the dairy.'

'Her brothers and sisters can take the load until the sickness has run its course. If things go badly, she may be back sooner than you think.' Dr Argyll pauses. She sees his gaze shift sideways. 'Heaven help us all if that proves to be the outcome.'

'For the love of God, let me bring her over in the morning,' her father says.

'I need her tonight. There is no time to waste.'

The doctor's pebble-grey eyes give her a quick, undecided look. She takes this as a veiled invitation to voice her opinion. 'I am quite willing to go tonight, Tad,' she says.

'You shall not,' her father barks.

'Hold your peace,' says the physician, cracking the sideboard with his hat, shuddering the crockery. 'Do you think I would have ridden out on this black and frozen night if it was not a matter of life or death? Have you any idea what is at stake? What do you imagine will happen if the viscount dies?'

'It'll be a tragedy.'

'A tragedy? It will be a tragedy for your family, make no mistake. A message has been sent to London informing the viscount's father, the earl that I have secured a suitable girl to help me.'

'There are other girls in the village who have had the pox.'

'Not with your daughter's education.'

Elen's eyes widen, she lifts her chin. She feels a swell of pride. She has been singled out. All the learning her mother gave her before she died has not gone to waste. Her name has been put forward and she has been summoned.

'So we are to be doubly cursed,' her father says.

'Come on now, Griffiths – you are surely doubly blessed. I have chosen Elen because she cannot get the pox and the earl is delighted with my choice because your dear departed wife, God bless her soul, gave Elen an education to rival any girl on the estate.'

'I wish she had not.'

'Then you should not have stolen the heart of Lady Ludlow's governess, Griffiths.'

Her father gave a bark of exasperation. 'You had no right to recommend Elen without consulting me,' he says.

Elen is quite old enough to decide for herself but she holds her tongue. Her father is not the sort of man to listen but he has met his match in the doctor. As she watches the two of them quarrel, she holds the insides of her cheek between her teeth to stop herself from smiling.

'I have every right,' Dr Argyll says.

'And if I refuse?'

'You cannot refuse – not if you wish to keep your tenancy.'

A deep unease fills Elen, stifling her humour. What would happen to them if they lost the dairy? She has known no other home, her father has known no other trade. Every field and barn is filled with memories of her childhood, every room in the cottage is filled with the spirit of her mother.

'You hope to press your case with threats?' her father says.

'This is no threat, this is a reality.' The doctor pauses, drops his head momentarily. He continues in a more conciliatory tone, 'Look man, the earl is sure to reward you.'

Elen moves closer and says, 'A reward of any sort could change our lives, Father.'

'We manage very well,' he says with angry pride.

The doctor gives a great sigh. 'Then I shall lay it out in starker terms, Griffiths. If you refuse to let your daughter come, life will go very badly indeed for you and your family. The earl is not a man to be trifled with and today we are all in hell together.'

'You mean I have no choice.'

'None of us do. Now hurry.'

Chapter 2

Every soul in the cottage is now awake, tumbling around in the rush and panic. Little Judy mewls in the bed. Her younger brother Marc stares at Elen with eyes as big as saucers as Elen snatches at clothes to pack. Libby stands forlornly in the doorway, shivering in her nightclothes. Rhodri pulls on his boots, insisting he should accompany his sister.

Elen clatters down the stairs to where her father awaits with her cloak. He looks furiously at her, but she knows he is worried. He tosses the cloak across her shoulders, tries clumsily to hug her to him. She pulls away, impatient to follow the doctor.

Out into the yard they go, the doctor's cloak cutting a path through the mist ahead. Clouds of steam from the horses' hot, wet bodies rise into the light of the flambeaux. Elen lifts her hems high above her boots to pick through the mire, anxious not to sweep manure into the waiting carriage. The footman opens the door and helps her up the steps. She places her feet carefully. Everything is slippery with the mud and ice.

The doctor squeezes in behind her, shuffling around awkwardly, twisting so as not to brush himself against her. Her father runs around to the other side, tapping on the window and pointing at the sash to urge her to drop it. The coach pitches as the footman climbs up beside the driver, the reins crack and she is flung back in her seat as the horses bound away.

The carriage lurches and shudders through the darkness, the blazing torches on the top of the coach bend in the wind, intermittently licking a ripped flame past the outside of the window. She glimpses the doctor in the flickering light. He stares into the middle distance, preoccupied.

The space inside the carriage is cramped. Elen has to turn sideways to stop her knees knocking against the doctor's. The neck of her cloak is still undone, but she dare not release her grip on the damp leather of the seat to secure it. After one particularly bruising jolt of the carriage, which pumps an audible grunt from the doctor, he says, 'The track will improve presently.'

They pass through the deep shadow of the forest that hugs the northern margin of the lake, where the mist sucks up the smell of winter vegetation, rotting and black around the edge of the water.

After several further minutes of silence, the doctor says, 'I did not wish to cause you or your family alarm by coming so late to the farm. I would have gladly waited until the morning had there been a choice. I have little stomach for these roads at this time of year.'

'Is Viscount Mordiford very ill indeed, sir?'

'He is. He arrived back last night from London. They thought he had the influenza – that vile disease is ravaging the city this winter – and packed him off in a carriage. At least the steward had the wit to ensure I was at the hall for Mordiford's arrival. The instant I looked at him, I saw the first marks of the pox had already appeared on his face and hands.' The doctor sighs heavily. 'He should never have been brought across the country. Any number of people could have been infected. The footmen and driver have all been isolated at the old saw mill in Nash Wood. The earl, thank God, is at Court.'

'And the viscount, sir?'

'I have managed to quarantine him in a sealed chamber above the hall but, apart from myself, I cannot risk exposing any more of the servants to the disease and I cannot attend him day and night.'

'I don't understand what I can do, sir.'

'You must not be concerned, my dear. You will not have to deal with any indelicate treatments.'

'Treatments?'

The light of the flambeaux flickers across the doctor's face, momentarily illuminating him. She knows he carries bone-handled knives, a little bowl to catch the blood. Her mother had been spared the indignities of modern medicine in her final days. Her father railed that she might have lived if they had been moneyed. Elen was glad they were not. It was only the wealthy that had to submit to emesis and purging. She shudders at the thought of having to help a man through those humiliations.

'Treatments?' the doctor says. 'Of course. I usually depend on my daughter to help me – she survived this terrible illness a few years ago.' Elen's mother used to say it was a good thing the doctor's daughter had found a husband before she fell ill. Her skin had been left scarred and dull, ruining her looks. 'But she's with child at the moment,' the doctor continues, 'the baby is due in the next few weeks. I cannot have her exposed to the stress of nursing during her confinement.'

'Nursing? I cannot nurse.'

'Perhaps nursing is too specific a term for it. There is very little I can do for Mordiford apart from keeping him comfortable. At the moment there is no one at the hall who can even take the poor man a fresh drink.'

They reach the edge of the forest. The moon casts a cold glow between the thinning trees, penetrating the blackness of the interior of the carriage. Elen steals another look at the doctor. His features are small but pleasantly symmetrical. His eyes are neither too far apart nor too close together, his nose is rather more neat than distinguished, and his lips, although on the thin side, tip up at the corners of the mouth, giving him a cordial expression even in repose. The single feature that robs him of the sophistication of the wealthy is his skin, which is pockmarked as heavily as her father's is weather-beaten. Aware of her scrutiny, he smiles quizzically at her and says, 'You are very quiet. Is it the pox that frightens you?'

'A little, sir.'

'You understand that you cannot contract it?' The road on which they travel has improved and the doctor takes the risk of leaning forward in his seat, his elbows on his knees. 'You remember when your fingers blistered and your father was terrified that you had the pox?'

'I remember. And you went to see our cows and two of them had blisters on their udders,' Elen says.

'The cows gave you a precious gift. Although I know you were not at all well for several weeks, your malady had a weaker distemper.'

'I still bear some scars on my hands.'

'Be thankful for them. For some reason known only to God Almighty, if you have the cowpox you will never have the smallpox. If I see a girl out and about in Presteigne market and her skin is as smooth as a baby's, the chances are she is a milkmaid. You can be sure, the red plague will never scar and twist your face.'

'I understand that,' she says.

'Something else troubles you. Do not be afraid to speak up.'

'I was too young to remember when it took my brother and sister, but I remember how my mother suffered.'

'Ah, is it the suffering that frightens you?' Dr Argyll says.

She nods. She remembers it keenly along with the drudgery of caring for her siblings during a long, hot summer. She remembers the daily grind of milking the herd and her father's baffled anger at the world. She remembers how the disease bubbled and crusted her mother's beautiful face. When her mother was too sick to talk, Elen prayed to God to let her mother's sickness flow into her so that she could fight it instead. When her prayers weren't answered she cursed the cows for giving her the gift of cowpox. She wanted to be with her mother in Heaven, not stuck here on earth, crushed with sadness.

'It's terrible to see another person suffer, sir.'

'It is difficult, I grant you but it is ignorance that makes us afraid. When you understand the disease, you will focus on being able to help in the most relieving way. You will know that the patient is suffering less because you are there.'

After her mam died, Elen was haunted by the image of her face covered with the pox, but as the months passed, earlier memories of her mother crept back in – the long walks the girls took together with her, up to Mam's favourite part of the estate, Maes yr Haf, the pretty stone house nestling in a vale of fields. As they walked Mam told her and Libby tales of Greek Gods and stories of Twm Sion Cati (Libby was in love with Twm Sion Cati, never mind he'd been dead for over a century). Now when she closes her eyes at night, Elen remembers her mam with her lovely skin and her naughty laugh, her hair blowing free. She is afraid that nursing the viscount will bring back memories of her mother, sick and dying.

The trap breaks from the copse. The doctor pulls a hand free of his glove and begins scraping at the frost on the inside of the window with a fingernail, until he has cleared the glass sufficiently to assess their progress.

Elen sees the moon riding high above the mist, lightening the sky. The hall's castellations rise up from the horizon like a conjurer's castle, the shape as flat as if cut from a single sheet of black paper.

'We shall make swifter progress now we have entered the park,' Dr Argyll says, pulling his glove back on, blowing into his cupped hands and vigorously rubbing them together. She feels him watching her again as if he is uncertain he has reassured her. 'There is something else that worries you still?' he says.

'There is, sir. I am afraid that the viscount may die,' she says. As the words leave her mouth, the cold pinches at her, stealing in around her neck and creeping deep into her chest.

She imagines her father loading their possessions onto the handcart, hitching Judy and Marc up on top because they're too young to walk, Rhodri and Libby trailing behind. In the summer they could live like the hop pickers, moving from farm to farm, but the summer is half a year away. If the viscount dies, they will have to face a frozen countryside and treacherous roads. They could be mistaken as vagrants, whipped and imprisoned.

'We must hope that he does not – but you should not fear death itself, Miss Griffiths.' She looks directly at him, wonders if she should tell him her fears. However, she has learned that one should never look for long at people and slowly she lets her eyes drift away as he warms to his theme. 'I have seen many men die,' he says. Elen wishes he would stop. 'Many women and children too. There is peace for everyone at the end, even for the few who cling to life in terror. I have witnessed enough people die to know that however dreadful the prelude, the point of surrender is the final great moment of life. It is as if, even the ungodly rush to the arms of the Almighty with peace in their hearts.'

The doctor smiles at her then his gaze slides over to the window, the smile melting. He gives a heavy sigh, his breath forming a dense cloud that fogs the glass. 'Let us not dwell on such a sad conclusion,' he says. 'I have every confidence, Miss Griffiths, that you will make the next few weeks pass for that wretched young man with a sweetness that I could certainly never bring. There really is nothing for you to fear.'

Chapter 3

The carriage plunges into the blackness of an arched tunnel, the clatter of hooves echoing around the stone walls, before it thunders across the vast courtyard of Duntisbourne Hall and shudders to a halt.

Elen presses herself back into the seat, turning her head to one side, for the doctor is on his feet, bent double in the confined space. He struggles to loosen the sash, letting the window drop with a crash. A blast of paralysing frost gusts into the carriage.

'Hurry, man,' Dr Argyll yells up to the footman. 'Climb down and release this door.'

Elen follows the doctor out of the carriage and as she steps down onto the frozen gravel, she gazes upwards. The whole building is in darkness apart from the wing to their left, towards which the doctor heads. A small door opens, throwing a patch of light across the mist, hovering ankle deep above the ground. A figure carrying a lantern hurries towards them.

'God's blood. What took you so long?' someone calls out in the darkness.

'Language, Harley. I have Miss Griffiths with me.'

'Miss Griffiths be damned, the house is in uproar. The viscount has been bellowing so loud he can be heard from the servants' quarters.'

'Come, my dear,' the doctor says, holding a hand out towards her and flicking his fingers to encourage her to hurry. 'Leave your bag. Mr Harley will take it.'

She stands away from the carriage door to let the fellow reach inside. 'Do you mean this sack?' Mr Harley says, holding it up.

As she tries to snatch it from him, the light of the lamp falls across his face. Elen starts. The valet is not yet thirty and his face is a great deal more pleasant than his manner. He doesn't wear a periwig. Instead his tough hair, springing from his forehead, is pulled from his face, plaited at the back into a neat queue.

He seems equally surprised. His left eyebrow begins to rise and the corner of his mouth follows as if he struggles to stop himself from grinning. 'Begging your pardon, miss,' he says with a mock bow. 'I imagine you were obliged to pack in haste.'

The doctor comes to a halt and shouts back, 'And you, Mr Harley, judged in haste. Miss Griffiths, here, is the angel the viscount has prayed for.'

'If he ever prays,' Mr Harley says.

'Indeed,' the doctor says. 'Now bring the bag and hurry.'

Elen follows but before she passes into the building, she pauses. She has seen the hall from the estate many times but now it seems as if she stands in a vast outdoor room, all the windows black around her, except for there, high above the front door at the centre of the building, a faint light burning out into the night. Is that where the heir to this enormous estate lies, racked with disease with no one bold enough to help him except Dr Argyll and now herself?

'Come along, Miss Griffiths,' the doctor calls. 'We have taken too long as it is.'

–

The servants' entrance to the hall takes them down into an undercroft. The air is colder here than outside. Elen's footsteps echo around the lofty underground tunnel as she hurries to keep up with the guttering flame of the lantern ahead. She tries not to stride. She is too tall to be called delicate, too wiry to feel womanly.

The light jumps in the draughts that swirl around them, throwing the shadows of her companions onto the walls where they seem to dance, distorting into lowering fiends before flitting away as the next gigantic demon rises from the floor. Elen is aware of dark corridors snaking off to her left and right. She hardly dares to look down them as she passes, for fear of seeing something crouching in the shadows.

The valet hurries up a set of stairs, the doctor following, his cloak billowing out behind him. As they reach the top, a heavy door opens and a weak light spills down the steps. She hesitates. Have they reached the sick chamber so soon?

Catching her breath, she enters the room. It is poorly lit but mercifully warmed by a fire beside which several comfortable chairs have been drawn. Elen looks around, now and again lowering her eyes so as not to appear too curious. No, she thinks, this cannot be the sick chamber. The walls are lined with shelves stacked with bowls, flasks, baskets and glasses. A large Welsh dresser dominates another wall. She recognises the earl's crest on the china.

A thick-set fellow in his late forties, with the pale doughy face of a man who enjoys his food, gets to his feet, buttoning up his waistcoat. She can see from his livery that he is the steward.

'Ah, Mr Antrobus,' Dr Argyll says, moving into the room.

Elen stays by the door, unsure where she is meant to stand. Mr Harley, the young valet, beckons her forward to wait beside him. That is kind of him, she thinks. He places her bag at their feet, looking up at her from beneath his brow, then stands to attention, his hands folded behind his back.

Elen wonders what he makes of her. She still expects people to think her tall, as she was as a child. By the age of twelve she towered over her elder brothers. Mr Harley is stocky and almost as tall her, which she finds pleasing.

Mr Antrobus points to a tray on the large table in the middle of the room. 'I have put out the jugs of small beer and a tankard as you requested,' he says to the doctor.

Elen frowns. After all this rush and bustle, she is surprised the doctor has time to take refreshment, but instead he studies the tray, nods his approval and says, 'Thank you, Mr Antrobus. Could you also furnish me with a handful of candles?'

Mr Antrobus retrieves a large bunch of keys from the table by the fire, singles one out and beckons to Mr Harley. The valet dips his head towards Elen to indicate she should stay where she stands, before taking the keys and unlocking a tall cupboard at the back of the room.

'How many, sir?' he calls over his shoulder.

'A dozen should see us through, if you would be so kind. And send up another basket of wood. We must keep the sickroom as warm as possible throughout the night.'

Mr Harley places the candles on the tray, and as he turns to take up his position beside her, Elen sees the corner of one eye momentarily close with the faintest of winks.

The doctor lifts the tray, jangling the jugs against one another.

'I will carry this, Miss Griffiths. It is too heavy for you to manage.' She feels a flash of irritation. Her slenderness makes people underestimate her strength. 'Bring your bag and follow me, please. Bring the lamp also.'

Mr Harley moves across the room to open the door for the doctor. After he has passed through, the valet leans forward and says quietly to her, 'I will see you shortly I hope, Miss Griffiths.'

She smiles at him and turns to follow the doctor. She is not used to catching a man's eye. They leave the warmth and comfort of the steward's pantry behind and start up a second flight of stairs. As they climb into the gloom, the doctor says, 'It is not safe for the viscount to drink water while the fever has him in its grip. I have told Mr Antrobus he will need at least twelve pints of small beer every twenty-four hours. You must make sure he takes it. As the boils develop in his mouth and throat, the hops will keep his saliva clean.'

They reach the top and the doctor pushes his shoulder against the baize of a door. As they step out onto a gallery, Elen is aware, even in the darkness, that there is a vast drop beside them on the right. She clutches momentarily at a handrail to steady herself.

'We are above the great hall now,' the doctor says, his voice hushed.

Elen gazes down into the void. The very edge of the pool of light thrown by her lantern illuminates part of a huge staircase sweeping up towards them, the shadows of banners shifting gently in the icy breeze that moves through the great space.

A muffled cry of fury from above echoes around the hall. The doctor, his hands busy with the tray, cocks his head and widens his eyes to indicate she needs to follow him. She hurries along the gallery until her lantern shines on a small oak door studded in metal where the doctor waits, nodding at the latch for Elen to open it.

Dropping her bag to the ground, she struggles with the handle. It frees with a clunk that echoes and dies away. As she pulls the door open, the shouting increases in intensity. The doctor begins to ascend a narrow spiral staircase. She snatches up her belongings and follows, her bag pinioned to her side to leave a free hand to support herself against the central column of stone as she climbs.

'Keep close to me,' the doctor calls back to her. 'You plunge me into darkness if I am more than a turn ahead.'

Elen has to stoop to fit beneath the fan of steps above her head and by the time they make the first twist, the narrow treads behind her have spiralled out of sight. She has the terrible sense she is trapped in a column of rock.

Up and up they clamber, round and round, the doctor's breathing becoming heavier with the exertion, the soles of his boots crunching the pieces of grit on the steps. Another bellow of profanity funnels down from above, the sound reverberating around the stone, causing the doctor to pause for a moment. 'Close your ears, Miss Griffiths, I beg you,' he says.

Chapter 4

When they eventually reach the top the doctor presses himself against the wall, clutching the tray of beer to enable Elen to struggle by to reach the door handle. The doctor's laboured breath is hot on her cheek, tainted with the smell of alcohol and tobacco. She opens the door and he hurries in to set the tray on a low table in the centre of the room. Elen hesitates in the doorway. The stifling air within stinks of male sweat – not the pleasant musk of fresh exercise but a sour smell, like fox or tomcat.

The room is large and low ceilinged, several candles gutter in alcoves around the walls. Elen strains her eyes into the gloom. A faint russet glow comes from a fire that has all but burned itself out. A feather of smoke leans into the room and is gathered up into the draught. As the shadows move and clot, she notices a bed on the far side of the room, draped with faded fabric. On top of it, she sees the pale shape of a bed shirt and can just make out the prostrate body of the man who wears it.

The doctor takes the lantern and together they approach the bed. His patient lies face down, his head turned towards them. By the dim light, she sees his eyes are tight closed. She is struck by his youth and exhaustion. Perhaps all the bellowing has worn him out. As the doctor holds the lantern to his face, he stirs but barely has the strength to lift his head.

The doctor puts the lantern on the table and squats at the side of the bed, peering into the young man's face. Satisfied he is still alive, he stands. 'Miss Griffiths, I need more light. Fetch the candles from the tray and fill the sconces by the bed.'

The doctor hooks the hangings out of the way. 'You will find a candelabrum in the vestibule through there. Bring it also.'

Glad of the industry, Elen lights the extra candles until the part of the room around the bed is bright with flame. The doctor reaches for the viscount's shoulders, struggling to pull him onto his back. 'Miss Griffiths,' he calls over his shoulder, 'a hand, if you would be so kind. Gather the pillows up in such a fashion as to allow me to place him in a sitting position.'

The doctor struggles to haul him up the bed then turns to her, needing help. She doesn't want to grasp the viscount, to feel the sweat that stains his shirt. Instead she picks up some pillows, moves them to the top of the bed. The linen is fine and smooth but she can see dark stains blooming across the white.

'Put those down,' the doctor says, grunting with effort. 'Kneel on that side of the bed. Help me. He has quite swooned away.'

Elen hitches her skirts up and wriggles across the wide bed until she reaches the patient. She can feel the heat pouring from his body as she grasps his upper arm. The crescent of sweat under the sleeve isn't wet. It's dry and crisp. She splays her knees, braces her body and hauls the viscount up the bed. The doctor looks across at her and says, 'Well done, Miss Griffiths. You have a deal of strength in those limbs after all.'

She purses her lips and nods. The doctor touches the viscount's forehead and shakes his head. 'Too dry. That is not a good sign, not a good sign at all. A wet fever heals, but a dry fever kills.'

He leans forward and lays the back of his hand against the viscount's chest where his shirt has fallen open. The marks of the pox are clearly visible in the bright candlelight. Elen counts ten spots by the doctor's hand, a shower across the collarbone, more up the neck and into the face, as if someone has taken a handful of red dust and flung it across him. The blemishes are small and flat, but she knows that within a matter of days, each one of them will bubble and fill.

The doctor goes over to the tray of beer. She sits back on her heels and continues her study. She has never been this close to the viscount before. His hair is blue-black in the candlelight. He has a broad brow and straight nose but none of the refinement she expected. His lips are well defined but already beginning to blister along the margins. Sometimes she caught sight of him riding on the estate but her imagination must have embellished the impression he made, cantering past in the distance. Now she thinks him a rather ordinary young man.

At that moment his lids spring open and she starts back, surprised not so much by his abrupt return to consciousness as by the colour of his eyes. They are an extraordinary blue and shine with the lustre of sapphires, the pupils as wide as an opium user. He stares at her with unblinking ferocity until she edges away and drops to the floor. Yet still they gaze upon each other.

The doctor hurries back to the bed with a tankard of small beer and slips an arm behind the young man's head, raising the tankard to his lips. The patient drinks with difficulty, flinching as he swallows – the pox is in his mouth and throat already.

The fierce, tremendous eyes alight again on Elen. 'What's that draggle tail?' he says, his voice weak but disdainful.

'This is Miss Griffiths, my lord. She will be here to serve you through your sickness.'

The viscount grasps the doctor by the edge of his coat and pulls him close. 'I do not want her, damn you,' he hisses. 'This is men's business.'

The doctor sighs. 'If I could spend every hour at your side, my lord, you know I would.'

'Send me Harley,' he says. 'He can be my valet.'

'I cannot. He has never had the pox.'

'The pox? I cannot have the pox. I must take up my commission. The army leaves for the Continent within weeks.'

'I know they do, my lord. But you are far too sick at present to join your regiment.'

'I have measles, nothing more than measles.'

'You had that as a child. I attended you myself. It is impossible for it to visit you again.'

'Get me my steward. Send for Antrobus.'

'I cannot. You have the red plague, my lord.'

'I do not,' he says vehemently, setting off a fit of coughing.

Elen backs away, afraid of the spittle flying from his lips. The doctor gestures to the bowl at the side of the bed and she shoves it at him, shielding her mouth and swallowing hard as the viscount hacks and spits into it. He lies back, exhausted and says, 'Damn you, Argyll. Bring a man to attend me.'

'There is no one else,' the doctor says. 'Miss Griffiths is a very capable country girl who nursed her mother during the same affliction. Here, Miss Griffiths, take this.' Dr Argyll holds the bowl towards her.

Elen recoils. The doctor gives her a sharp look, snatches up a napkin from the table and throws it across the top of the bowl. 'Are you able to take it now?' he says.

Viscount Mordiford grasps at the doctor, pulling him close and hissing in his ear, 'She cannot even stand the sight of spit. What use is she to me? Send her away, I tell you.'

'I can assure you,' the doctor says, 'that for the time being, I alone will attend to any...' the doctor clears his throat, adding in a quieter tone, '...intimate duties.'

'Fates preserve me,' Viscount Mordiford says, closing his eyes. The doctor watches for a moment then gets to his feet.

'He will sleep now,' he says to Elen. 'Hurry along. Empty that bowl and clean it up.'

She scurries behind the screen where she finds a washstand and a table on which stands piles of napkins and a jar of glowing lavender stalks. The resinous smoke rising from them does not counteract the smell coming from a large bucket, standing in one corner and covered by a wooden lid.

Elen slips the toe of her boot underneath the handle to lift it and, looking away, kicks it aside. A sharp smell of ammonia and excrement rises into her nostrils. She tries to breathe through her mouth but the tang is sufficiently strong for her to taste it. Staring at the wall above the bucket, she tips the bowl.

The doctor appears, arms folded. 'You are going to have to modify your sensibilities young woman if you are going to be any help at all.'

'I don't like pus.' She gulps several times to quell her nausea.

'You had better get used to it. You will be dealing with quantities of laudable pus before the week's out. Imagine what that poor young man is suffering.'

Elen doesn't want to.

'Anyway,' the doctor says, 'I must leave you now.'

'Surely not,' she says. She drops the bowl onto the washstand with a clang. 'You cannot leave me here alone. My father would not allow it. This is not decent, sir.'

'What a nonsense,' the doctor says. 'You must be able to see with your own eyes that you are quite safe. Look at that poor wretch. He can do you no harm.'

'It is not proper for me to spend a night here alone with the viscount.'

'Proper? Oh, put your foolish scruples aside. Do you think the servants tittle tattle about what goes on at the hall?'

'I know they do, sir.'

'In this situation I assure you they will not.' The doctor checks his watch. He snaps it closed again. 'Anyway, you will have to get used to it. You heard the viscount mention just now his desire to leave with the army. He must delay but I cannot.'

'You intend leaving?'

'I must travel to The Hague in the next few weeks, by which time, if the viscount is not fully recovered, you will be in sole charge of his care. You must see, the situation cannot be helped.'

She stares back at him with mute defiance.

'Come now,' the doctor says, indicating a chaise longue in the corner of the room beside the fire. 'There is a comfortable and warm spot where you can sleep and keep an ear and eye on your patient. A servant will rap on the lower door when the wood arrives and you can go down and collect it.'

'And later on in the night, I am expected to avail myself of that earth bucket, am I sir?'

'Miss Griffiths. I do not care for your tone. At the risk of repeating myself, you have no choice. Accept it, for I shall not retract. If you need to carry out any personal ablutions you will find a selection of handy and practical notions here, in the vestibule.'

Elen maintains her sullen expression even though she knows the battle is lost. Presently she sighs and says, 'What should I do if he wakes again and discovers you are not here?'

'You must give him beer, as much as he can drink.' As he turns to leave he hesitates and touches her on the arm. 'Your selfless aid, my dear, will not go unnoticed nor unrewarded, of that I am sure.' The doctor guides Elen back into the sickroom and says quietly, 'Make sure the covers are placed no higher on his body than the waist. Now that the rash has started to appear, his fever should abate. I will visit the apothecary in the morning and collect some tansy to bring out the sweats.'

'And if he complains a deal about the itching? I remember my mother's agony as the spots began to fill.'

'Yes, indeed. I may encourage him to take some yarrow or pennyroyal. Tomorrow we must begin to sponge the skin regularly with burdock root. Whatever we do, we must not stop the evil humours breaking from the body. This is nature's way of dispelling the distemper.' The doctor gives her arm a hearty pat of comradeship, swirls his cloak onto his shoulders and is gone.

Elen is about to close the upper door when she hears a discreet tapping from below. Glancing over her shoulder to make sure that her patient is still asleep, she makes her way down several turns of the staircase and calls out in a loud whisper, 'Who is it?'

'Ned Harley,' the reply floats up. 'I have wood for your fire.'

24

She looks down at the steps receding into the darkness. She needs her lantern. 'Leave it there,' she calls out quietly. 'I will fetch it shortly,' and she makes her way back up the stairs to the chamber. Grasping the lantern from the table, she holds it above the viscount for a few moments before setting off down the spiral stairs. She rests the lantern on the final step and opens the gallery door.

A wall of blackness greets her, as dense as a velvet curtain, hung across her face. The lamp lights the edge of a basket of wood and, as she reaches forward to take some logs, she sees the glint of an eye in the darkness. She jumps back, her hand stifling a cry.

Chapter 5

'Why, Miss Griffiths, I never meant to startle you,' Ned Harley says, stepping from the shadows.

'Oh, my goodness,' Elen says, catching her breath. 'I'm glad to see a familiar face.'

And she certainly is. The valet stands before her with an expression of polite concern, which makes his face boyish and pleasant.

'Did you think me some kind of phantom?' he says. 'It can be strange out in the main house at night in winter. I sometimes fancy these portraits watch me as I move along the gallery.' The wind moans and Ned lifts a finger to his ear and smiles. 'But wait until the spring when the earl begins to entertain again. Then you will find us merrier company, I'm sure.'

'My duties will be despatched long before the spring comes,' she says.

'That'll be a pity – not for his lordship, of course, because I wish him a speedy recovery, but certainly for me.'

She looks away. 'Does the earl not entertain during the winter?' she says.

'Hardly ever. It's a hopeless task to heat this great mausoleum. Most of the time it's just us servants here. Since the coronation of dear Queen Anne, the earl spends most of his winters at Court where he can keep warm for next to nothing, no doubt generating a deal of hot air with his compliments to Her Majesty.' He gives her a warm smile and says, 'Now, let me help you with this wood.' He lifts the basket from the ground and stands, awaiting her instruction.

'I cannot allow it,' she says. 'It's not safe for you to come up unless you've had the pox.'

'I've been saved that misfortune, I'm happy to say, but if that's your concern, I need not enter the room. I will merely carry the basket to the top for you.'

'Are you not worried the miasmas may funnel down the stairs from the room above?'

'Not particularly,' he says.

'You are either very brave or very foolish.'

'I am neither.' He smiles with a roguish vigour and leans forward as far as the basket of wood allows. The willow handles creak as he bends. 'I am protected from a great many afflictions by an accident of birth.'

Elen frowns, certain he is teasing her. 'Whatever can you mean?'

'Well, Miss Griffiths, as this is the first evening I've made your acquaintance and the accident of which I speak is of a — how shall I phrase it? — a mildly personal nature, I think I may maintain an air of mystery for a little longer, at least until we're more familiar with one another.'

She feels a blush of heat rising. Did she pry? No, Ned volunteered the confidence. 'But suffice it to say,' he continues, 'I have no concerns whatsoever about the pox, whether I enter the room or not. My only worry is that you may well be razed by fear should you have to journey into this cold and dark place to fetch more wood later on tonight.' He gives her a warm and encompassing smile. 'Imagine my horror were I to find you tomorrow morning, ice cold in death with your face twisted into a mask of stark and staring terror.'

'Now I know you're teasing me,' she says, but she smiles despite herself.

'I sincerely hope so. Now come, hold the door open for me and I will take the logs to the highest step you will allow.'

Up they climb, Ned striding in front with a lithe motion, carrying the heavy load as if it were a nothing. When he reaches the top landing, again Elen is forced to squeeze around to reach the door. This time, the experience is not at all unpleasant and he gives her a jaunty smile as she brushes past. For the few moments that they share the air within this confined space, she catches a clean smell coming off his body that reminds her of fresh laundry and crushed cloves. How she wishes the man on the other side of the door smelt as clean and healthy as the valet.

'Thank you,' she whispers, her hand on the latch of the door.

'Are you sure there's nothing else I can help you with?' he says. 'Have you eaten? I could fetch something from the kitchens if you wished.'

'Please don't trouble yourself. I have little appetite at this time of night.'

'Well then...' he hesitates and she wishes he would linger. 'I'm sure I'll see you tomorrow, Miss Griffiths, and remember, if there's anything, anything at all, you only have to come down to the undercroft and find me.'

'I will, sir.'

'Please call me Ned. Goodnight, Miss Griffiths,' he says, setting off down the stairs. Just before he disappears around the first turn, he looks back at her, nods and drops out of sight into the darkness.

She waits until she hears the door into the gallery close, then sighs and gathers up an armful of logs before letting herself into the sick chamber. The air is stuffy and she wrinkles her nose at the tang of sweat.

Viscount Mordiford lies in the same position as when she left. She goes over to the hearth, kneels down in front of the fire and takes up the poker. She likes building fires. She bares the embers and breaks up some of the twigs, gently blowing into the ash until they catch. Once they are burning merrily, she makes a tripod of smaller logs, sitting back on her haunches and watching the flames dance higher. The warmth and light lift her spirits, and she gets to her feet, brushing the smuts off her hands.

When she turns, she starts back. Viscount Mordiford is staring at her from the bed, his eyes burning with fever. 'Who's there?' he says.

'It's Miss Griffiths, your lordship.' He doesn't respond. 'My name is Elen,' she adds, taking a few steps towards him.

His gaze remains focused on the spot where she has been. He is not looking at her at all but at the shadows thrown up by the fire. As she watches, he begins rocking his head on the pillows as if trying to tear his eyes away from what he sees. 'Not us,' he shouts out. 'Forgive ourselves. Everyone forgive ourselves...' His expression melts into despair and a sigh catches in his throat.

Elen hurries to the vestibule and fills a basin with water. Grasping up a napkin, she soaks it and returns to the sickbed. She squeezes the cloth and places it across his forehead. Immediately his hand comes up to strike it away but weakness prevails and he lets it be.

And so the long night continues. Between stoking the fire, cooling her patient and feeding him hourly with beer, she wonders if she will ever find a moment to sleep. Then she wonders if she should sleep at all. Perhaps the doctor expects her to stay awake. She cannot seem to keep the room warm enough, however much she banks the fire. She sits close to the flames, her face burning hot, the back of her arms chilled from a draught that has found its way under the eaves. She watches Viscount Mordiford as she used to keep watch when a cow was labouring.

At times he thrashes around, flinging the covers away and tearing at his clothing. Then he lies so still and white she thinks him dead and creeps across the room, peering down at him, watching for the rise and fall of his chest.

She has a terrible feeling that her presence here will not be enough to save her family. The viscount must live. His death could bring greater hardship to her than even the death of her poor, dear mother. The novelty of her arrival at the hall has lost all its gloss. The night is cold, uncomfortable and interminable.

Eventually she notices a patch of grey, low in the wall near the bed. It is a window, small and leaded, perhaps the one she saw, burning high above the portico, when she first arrived.

The discovery makes her ridiculously happy. She crosses the room and presses her nose against the panes. The courtyard is a patchwork of greys and black shadows, the lake white beyond where the mist rises. Dawn is here. At last, morning has broken.

The fresh supply of candles has almost burned away and, eager to be ready for the doctor's arrival, she goes into the vestibule to see if she can find more. She notices another weak glow, this time at the foot of the wall some feet away. In the half-light she realises it is not a wall at all but a hanging made of heavy fabric.

It is threadbare and worn, but she can make out the faint shapes of huntsmen and hounds, a white hart, his mouth open in terror, rearing up on a carpet of delicate fronds and flowers. Three of the hounds have him by the flanks, their teeth sinking into his flesh. The hanging moves gently in a draught, lifting and sinking back like the side of a giant creature. She presses her hands against it, feels a wall a few feet behind it and, curious to know why it moves, she feels for the edge of the tapestry and slips behind.

She finds herself between the back of the heavy tapestry and a rough stone wall. Up ahead she sees light spilling out from an alcove. She begins to inch her way towards it, dipping her head beneath the sheets of cobweb, heavy with dust, which hang from the ceiling. She presses them aside and hears the patter of loosened dust fall to the floor. She comes to a door of blackened pine, light spilling out around the frame. The simple latch is made of iron but beneath it a beam of light shines out through a large keyhole.

'It will be locked,' she says to herself as she reaches for the latch. It lifts easily.

Chapter 6

'Miss Griffiths!' Dr Argyll says from the other side of the tapestry. He sounds angry. Elen eases the latch down and hurries back behind the hanging. 'Miss Griffiths?' The doctor's voice is close, just the other side. She reaches the corner and tumbles out.

The doctor is staring at the hanging, frowning, trying to follow her progress. He makes a little noise when he sees her, then draws himself up and expands his chest. 'What on earth are doing behind there?' he says. 'You are meant to be with the patient.'

'I am sorry sir. I saw a light and went to see what it was.'

'A light? What sort of a light?'

'There's a room back there. I think there must be a window.'

The doctor frowns, shakes his head at her. 'Very likely. There are storage rooms throughout this part of the hall, but it is not your place to go poking around looking into them.' He glares at her the way her father does when he's displeased. Then he sighs. 'Well, never mind. You gave me a turn. I arrived and found the sickroom empty except for the viscount. I was alarmed.'

'I was gone for barely a minute.'

'I was not to know that. Viscount Mordiford is restless. I imagined that you had run off back home.'

'Not at all, sir. I have sat with him all night.'

'Have you now?'

She comes towards him, brushing the dust from her apron. The doctor frowns, reaches out towards her hair but snatches

31

his hand back at the last minute and wags his fingers towards the side of his periwig.

'There's something stuck… caught in your hair,' he says. She reaches up, feels sticky cobwebs and pulls them clear.

'Thank you, sir,' she says. His awkwardness has swept away his anger.

'Well, I admit you look tired. How did the patient fare?'

'His night has been divided between hours of deep sleep and high agitation, but I made sure that he had his beer and that he was not fully covered with bedding when asleep. There were times when he seemed to imagine things.'

'Imagine things?'

'He was troubled. He stared and shouted.'

'At you?'

'No, I don't think so.'

'What was he shouting about?'

'The words he said made no sense.'

'It is not unusual for a man with a high fever to have hallucinations. But come, we have work to do.'

The light from the small window has been joined by the dawn creeping in around gaps below the eaves. Many more spots have appeared on the viscount's face during the night. The doctor places his hand on Mordiford's forehead but he does not stir.

'I think he is cooler this morning' he says, giving her a tight smile. 'You have done your job well.'

'Is his fever over, sir?'

'For the time being. I have studied this disease closely and noticed that when the rash spreads, the fever abates. See here…' and he peels open the shirt. 'The rash is spreading quickly.'

'So the danger is passed?'

'No, I am afraid not. Look, the blemishes that first erupted on his forehead are already becoming raised.' She moves nearer and the doctor reaches out to the table, takes up a candle and holds it up. 'Soon they will fill with a thick, opaque fluid.'

'Every single one of these marks will fill?'

'Unfortunately, yes.'

'But there are so many.' Many more than she remembers on her mother – and her mother died.

'And more blooming all the time. See here,' the doctor says, 'in the hairline. This one has a dimple in the centre.'

She cranes forward. There is something uncomfortable about studying this poor man as he sleeps, like spying on someone who doesn't know they're being watched, but as the light catches the pock her curiosity gets the better of her and she peers at the deep pit.

'It looks like the button on a belly.'

'Indeed. As they rise up, it is possible to feel a sharpness beneath the skin. Place your finger upon it, Miss Griffiths.'

She hesitates. She trusts the doctor, but she feels a residual anxiety about contact with such scrofulous skin. Remembering Dr Argyll's admonishment of the previous night, she fights her reluctance and reaches out.

'What do you feel?' Dr Argyll says.

'A lump. It is as if a piece of lead shot lies beneath the skin.'

The doctor nods. 'The fever will rise again soon and remain high until scabs form over the bumps.'

'Is it possible to squeeze the lump out?' she says, remembering the queasy pleasure of milking the core out of the boils that periodically appeared on her brother's back.

'No. It is seated deep in the tissues beneath and, besides, that is the purpose of the boils, to bring the evil humours to the surface and shed them later with the scabs.'

'Will you bleed him?'

The doctor releases the edge of the nightshirt and moves a little way from the bed. 'I know that is the usual course of treatment but I have noted that excessive bleeding weakens a patient.'

'You intend to purge him?'

'A clyster is of little use here.' She feels a wave of relief. She cannot stand the notion of helping the doctor administer an enema. 'No,' Argyll says, 'I intend soaking him.'

'Soaking him? In what?'

The doctor takes her by the elbow and leads her away from the patient. 'We shall talk over here in order not to waken him.'

He sits down on the chaise longue and indicates that she should join him. 'I came across an extraordinary account of two sufferers in some God-forsaken part of the world who were near to death.'

'From smallpox?'

'Yes. In despair, these wretched men dragged themselves down to a lake. They intended soothing their skin in the water but as they tried to submerge themselves, they bobbed to the surface as if they were made of cork.' She frowns, trying to imagine the scene. 'Nevertheless,' the doctor continues, 'the feeling was pleasant and they floated around for a full day and a night.'

'Did they not get cold?'

'They were hot with fever. It must have been extremely calming. By the following morning both men were feeling greatly recovered. They left the lake and made a full recovery.'

'Was it a miracle?'

'Indeed it was. A miracle that God led them to the lake, but the manner of their cure, I believe, has a more worldly explanation. This lake was known to be exceedingly salty, far more briny than the ocean itself. The salt was so fierce that local people knew no fish could live beneath its waters. I have a theory that the salt, which choked the life from the fish, stifled the disease itself.'

She thinks about the pig they slaughter every autumn, the huge pink slabs of flesh, frosted with salt, the beads of moisture oozing out of the skin as it hangs, drying in the game larder.

'How can a substance used to cure meat help a man?'

'Salt has been used down the centuries for rubbing into wounds.'

Elen shivers. She has read of sailors subjected to this terrible practice.

'But surely that was to increase the punishment after flogging?'

'Yes and no. I believe it prevented infection following the beatings, even if that was not the intended purpose.'

'The viscount will suffer terribly.'

'I think not. My plan is to fill a receptacle with strong brine and lower him into it as the pustules fill. There will be no abrasive property to the treatment. The water will be soothing as long as the lesions are still protected and not open.'

She shudders at the thought, but when she looks into the eyes of the physician she sees they burn with zeal. He is convinced that his treatment will work.

'Anyway, we have a few days to get things ready for this,' the doctor continues. 'I shall sit with his lordship for the moment. You are to go down to the south wing and find yourself some breakfast. While you are there, make some enquiries. I will need a bath of some kind but one which we can manoeuvre up the spiral staircase together.'

'Is the spiral staircase the only way up here?' Elen asks.

'It is now. There was another staircase that could be accessed from the undercroft beneath the private apartments but a fire, many years ago, weakened it and they tore it down.'

'So all the furniture here and in the storerooms is marooned up here?'

'It is – but unfortunately, nothing that we can use as a bath.'

Elen puzzled the problem before saying, 'Ned can help.'

'The valet? But he hasn't had the disease.'

'He told me last night that he is protected.'

'Oh, that nonsense. Yes, I know he believes he is, but it's not true.'

'Do you know why he thinks that he is?'

'I do as a matter of fact.' The doctor's eyes twinkle with amusement and a certain amount of indecision. Instead of continuing, he nods towards the commode. 'Take that down with you.' Now the doctor has taken her into his confidence she does not mean to show disgust in her expression, but he narrows his eyes and says, 'For a country girl you are surprisingly squeamish.'

'Animals are different.'

'They urinate and defecate the same as us, or has your father protected you from the uglier side of life?'

'My mother made no secret of wanting a different life for me. My father has never gone against her wishes.'

'And what life would that be, pray?'

'She wanted me to teach.'

'In order to fulfil her own thwarted aspiration, I suppose.'

'I wouldn't know.'

'Well, your mother turned her back on a comfortable life when she married a farmer. She wouldn't have done that unless she was made of stern stuff. Shame she didn't pass that on to you.'

'She taught me plenty.'

'Is that so? It is of no matter. Take the slops down anyway and give them to Joan to sluice for you if your stomach still feels weak.'

Chapter 7

Elen descends the spiral staircase, the horrible bucket clanking at her ankles. The stench of ammonia is magnified by the confined space. She pauses for a moment by a small window halfway down and breathes in a lungful of the frosty air that percolates through the casement.

The window does not offer her a view out across the estate. Instead she finds herself peering at other windows in the walls surrounding an interior courtyard. These must be servants' rooms because unlike the windows she saw last night on the east facade, they are small and tightly packed. The ceilings on those floors must be very low indeed. The rooms would not get the sun at any time of the day.

She stands on tiptoe and, looking down, she can just about see the basement level. It is filled with old crates and boxes, a dumping ground for the servants' quarters. As she watches, a maid comes out of one of the doors and empties a chamber pot into an open rill that runs in a shallow channel through the yard.

Elen hurries on down the stairs, eager to despatch the bucket of effluent, but when she steps out onto the minstrels' gallery, she stops. The ghostly shapes she saw the night before are bathed in a hard light. Above her head, a wooden roof of exquisite beauty spans the space. The beams and struts create squares and between each of these, the plaster is highly decorated with beautiful images and motifs. Awestruck, her eyes are drawn down into the hall. The low winter sun is shining through the glass and picking up the motes of dust. The dark oak of the staircase is embellished with carvings, the steps covered with thick carpeting, blood red, and bearing the crest of the Duntisbournes. All around the walls, portraits of earls, their countesses and children stare down in mute solemnity, their clothes luscious, their hands and faces delicate. One group of children have a tiny dog at their feet, so small it looks like a cat. Above the huge front doors on the opposite side of the hall, hangs the earl's banner covered with heraldic symbols, and ships and scallop shells.

The rank smell from the bucket invades her reverie and sighing, she picks it up and heads towards the baize door at the opposite end of the gallery. She finds the top of the service staircase and makes her way down. When she reaches the undercroft she can hear crockery being stacked and, following the sound, eventually comes to the room where the servants are finishing their breakfast.

All eyes turn towards her, some of them none too welcoming. She stands straight and tall. She looks along the bench of faces and sees Ned at the same time as he spots her. He drops his spoon and jumps to his feet.

'Miss Griffiths,' he says. 'What have you there?' Some of the servants chuckle. 'Leave it outside, for the love of Heaven and come and sit. Joan, kindly relieve Miss Griffiths of her load.'

Joan is a slatternly looking girl with a sallow and scarred skin. She crosses the room and takes the bucket, clanking out of a door and into the yard.

'Come and sit down,' Ned says.

'If I could please wash my hands.'

'There is a pitcher and bowl on the side there,' Ned says, hopping off the bench and offering her a napkin to dry her hands. He then announces to the room, 'This is Miss Griffiths. She has come to take care of the viscount.'

The breakfasters continue to eat.

'We know who she is, Ned,' Mr Antrobus says without looking up. 'Get on with your breakfast.'

Ned leads her around the table and gestures to a lad to move along to make space. Joan returns, wiping her hands on her soiled apron.

'Joan,' Mr Antrobus says, 'fetch Miss Griffiths a bowl of gruel and make sure it has a good splash. She'll need her strength.'

Joan drops a dollop of boiled oatmeal into a bowl then washes it with a clear liquid from a terracotta flask on the sideboard.

'Thank you, Joan,' Ned says as she puts the dish in front of Elen. Immediately the girl's surly expression lifts. She bobs a small curtsey at Ned before retreating back to the serving table, a crooked smile lighting up her face.

'Good old Joan here,' he says, nodding in her direction, 'has to brave the long walk back and forth from the kitchens so that none of us get our feet wet, eh, Joan?' The girl makes an odd sort of noise, as if she's trying to clear phlegm, and puts a hand to her mouth, covering her large brown teeth. Elen thinks she must be laughing.

Mr Antrobus gives Joan a severe look and brandishes his spoon at her. The moment he resumes his breakfast, Joan gazes back at Ned with a bovine regard.

The gruel is lukewarm, and heady with alcohol, but Elen is hungry. As she eats, other servants join the table, but apart from the steward who asks after the viscount's progress, Ned is the only person who goes out of his way to talk to her.

'Bit different from life at home, I would imagine,' Ned says. 'It is.'

'We never get a hot meal down here. The kitchen's way over by the stables on the other side of the courtyard. Mind you, we get it hotter than the family when they're at home.' He eats in huge mouthfuls. She can hear his teeth meeting as he chews. A man of appetite, she thinks to herself, smiling at the contrast between his enthusiasm and the viscount's trembling distaste for anything she raises to his lips.

'I bet you all eat in a cosy kitchen, with your mother cooking at the range,' Ned says between mouthfuls.

'We used to, but my mother died a few years ago. The family will have to do with my younger sister's cooking until I return.'

'I'm sorry to hear your mam has passed. What took her?'

'The pox.'

'Oh, that's harsh indeed and here you are having to relive every grisly detail.'

Elen is touched by his sympathy. She remembers worrying that nursing the viscount would remind her of her mam's sickness but it has not.

'I'm sure I have Dr Argyll to guide me.'

'I think you're very brave. I wouldn't like to spend the night locked away up there with the viscount as he gets more and more plooky by the day.'

'It isn't very pleasant.'

'Has he quite lost his looks yet?' he says with a sly smile.

'I wouldn't know.' She drops her voice, leans towards him and says, 'for I thought him a rather ordinary man to begin with.'

Ned throws his head back and gives a great bellow of laughter.

'What is so amusing, Ned?' the steward says.

'A nothing, sir.'

'Miss Griffiths?'

'A passing remark, sir.' They continue to eat in silence, heads down. Ned turns his face imperceptibly at the same time as her and they share a conspiratorial glance. She finishes her food and remembers the task the doctor has set her.

'Excuse me, sir,' she says to Mr Antrobus. All eyes turn towards her. 'Dr Argyll has asked me to enquire if it would be possible for a bath to be taken up to the sealed chamber?'

'A bath?' says Mr Antrobus with as much astonishment as if she had requested taking a coach and horses up there. 'It's barely possible to climb the stairs with a tray in your hands. How on earth does he imagine we can navigate a tin tub up there?'

'Perhaps the blacksmith could fashion one the shape of a horseshoe,' Ned says. Joan makes her choking noise and Mr Antrobus looks annoyed.

'I believe the doctor is planning to use it for one of the viscount's treatments,' Elen says.

'Then he will have to think again,' Mr Antrobus says, his tone leaving Elen in no doubt that further discussion would be useless.

Ned finishes his oatmeal, sits back from the table and wipes his mouth on a grubby kerchief before returning it to his pocket. 'Miss Griffiths,' he says, 'since the good doctor has released you for half an hour, why don't you let me show you around the house to familiarise yourself? Would that meet with your approval, sir?' he says to Mr Antrobus.

'The doctor's a busy man, Ned. He has his morning rounds to do and will need Miss Griffiths back now that she has finished with her breakfast.'

Elen feels a wave of disappointment that her moment of freedom is coming to an end, but Ned leans towards the steward and says: 'I'm sure the doctor would allow Miss Griffiths a breath of fresh air. I promise to have her back up those stairs within ten minutes.'

She looks at Mr Antrobus, expecting another reprimand. Instead he gives the slightest of nods and winks at Ned who is already on his feet. She gets up so rapidly that the legs of the bench scrape across the floor. She is aware of Joan watching her as she leaves the room so she gives her a pleasant smile. It is not returned.

Ned retraces the route they took the night before. Although the undercroft is poorly lit and has no natural light coming in apart from through the hopper windows at floor level, the passageway does not hold the same horrors. She peers into the corridors that disappear to the left and right of them.

'What's down there?' she asks.

'All sorts of places, wine cellars and storage rooms,' he calls over his shoulder as he strides ahead. 'The undercroft runs right under the whole building. It is like a rabbit warren. They say a boy was sent down here once on an errand and didn't come back for a whole week. He'd been wandering in circles, round and round. They only found him because a gardener saw his little fingers reaching out through a grill round on the northern side.'

'I don't believe you.'

'You have a very suspicious nature, Miss Griffiths. Here we are.' They ascend a short, stone staircase. Ned struggles with the keys until he opens the door and a welcome rush of cold air sweeps in towards them.

'How lovely,' she says, stepping out onto the flagstones. The winter sun has broken free of the Black Mountains in the distance and is beginning to burn away the mist rising up from the lake.

'Looks as if it will be a fine day,' he says. 'What a pity you have got to spend it locked away in a sickroom.'

'It is only for a few weeks.'

'Maybe less if all goes well.'

'Surely you mean if all goes badly?'

'I suppose I do.' Ned tucks his thumbs into the pockets of his waistcoat and stands full square, looking out on the view. 'So, has the good doctor expressed an opinion as to when you will be freed from your duties?'

'I don't think he can tell yet.'

'It would not be good if you were locked away up there for too long.'

'For me or the viscount?'

'For all of us,' he turns towards her, that cheeky eyebrow of his rising up, 'but never mind. Have you had enough fresh air? I should be getting you back or Mr Antrobus will have my guts for garters.'

With a gallant sweep of his arm, Ned invites her to return to the undercroft. She pauses longingly for a moment. How she would love to run out into that crisp morning instead of returning to the gloom of the sealed chamber. The cows will be milked by now and lumbering out across the fields, their hooves cracking the ice on the puddles. She wishes she were walking behind them, her switch in her hands, the cold morning air like pepper in her nostrils.

Ned clears his throat behind her and with a sigh she turns. As she passes him, he smiles at her with such warmth she feels emboldened and says, 'I told Dr Argyll that you had offered to help.'

'Did you now? And what did the good doctor say?'

'He said he could not risk you getting the disease. I told him you believed you were protected but he says,' and here she drops her voice and leans in towards him, 'he did not believe for a moment that something of that nature made any difference.'

Ned frowns. 'He told you?' She gives him a look to imply that he had. She knows it is sly but her curiosity has got the better of her. 'I suppose you want to see?' he challenges her.

She starts back. Does she? He has said it is of a personal nature. In sudden panic she knows she should call a halt on her trick but Ned is too canny for her. He laughs softly and says, 'Ah, Miss Griffiths, you have one of those faces that cannot hide a thought. Here's a thing. If you're going to dupe a fellow into giving up a secret, you're going to have to learn to control your expression. I can read you like the clouds. Come on then, inside. I'll show you.'

'You must not,' she says, her alarm overwhelming her curiosity.

'Don't worry. It may be personal but it's not improper.'

Chapter 8

Ned locks the door and, as he descends the steps, he grasps Elen by the hand and guides her into the shadows near the entrance to the undercroft. As he begins to undo the buttons of his waistcoat, she draws away from him.

'What are you doing?' she says.

'I thought you wanted me to reveal my secret.' She gives him a guilty smile. He begins to pull his undershirt up, twisting his body slightly to release the fabric before hooking his thumb over the waistband of his breeches, pushing it down.

She feels the heat of embarrassment warming her neck as his well-muscled abdomen appears. Her eyes flick away and then down. Her curiosity overcomes her modesty and she moves towards him, bending slightly to get a better view. A line of dark hairs mark the middle of his torso, swirling and thickening at his waist, but the skin beneath is as smooth as the palm of her hand.

'Oh, my word,' she says, 'you don't have a navel.'

'Indeed I do not. It is almost as if I was never born of woman.' She gasps and moves back a step. 'But don't worry, I'm no demon. It was an accident of my birth.'

'How could that ever happen?' she says, her eyes wide, staring at the smooth skin of his stomach, still as a cat.

'The night I was born,' he says, letting go of the waistband and running his palm across his skin, 'the family were camped out by Upper Radnor woods for the autumn coppicing and there were no women folk to help. My father was deep in the woods working, and I came fast.'

She tries to think of the woods in autumn and a woman in a makeshift camp crying out in labour, but the image of his hand running across his stomach, pushing a ridge of silken skin ahead of his fingers, has distracted her. She shakes her head to realign her thoughts.

'And your poor mother had none to help her?' she says, leaning back on the wall, turning her palms towards the stone to cool them.

'She was not alone. My brothers were there and helped as best they could. The eldest ran up into the forest to try to find Tad but when I shot out into this world, Dewi was on his own with Mam. She was exhausted and told him to cut the cord but he was only ten years old and woodcutter's tools are not precise. When he cut me free, he cut me close, much too close.'

Elen winces. She imagines the knife crunching through the cord, rooted deeply in the centre of the tiny stomach. 'Why did you not bleed to death?'

'I almost did, but the story is that when Tad saw what had happened, he swaddled me around the belly as tight as can be, almost squeezing out the few precious breaths of life I had managed to snatch. Then he slung me across his back and rode down to Dr Argyll and begged him to save my life.'

'Which clearly he did.'

'In a way. In fact, the doctor seemed to think Tad had stumbled upon an excellent treatment. Apart from adjusting the swaddling to allow me to breathe and feed, he left it undisturbed. By the time the dressings dried and fell away, the two sides of the wound had closed with such accuracy it was as if I had never been attached to Mam. You can feel where it should have been though, just to prove that I am not a fiend.'

Ned reaches out and, taking Elen's hand, he draws it towards the spot. Again she hesitates. Again she submits. Her fingers feel his warm skin slip over the muscles underneath and there, right in the centre of the whorl of hair, she finds a lump, no larger than a pea. His muscles tremble under her touch and she hears him draw in his breath.

'My fingers are too cold,' she says.

'No, not too cold,' and he looks at her with such intensity, she feels a ripple beneath her diaphragm. Then he smiles and begins to push the fabric of his undershirt back into his breeches. 'And that,' he says, buttoning up his waistcoat and straightening it with a tug, 'is why I can never be licked by the pox.' She leans back, feeling a little winded.

'I don't understand why that protects you,' she says.

'Why, surely you've heard of draping the bed with scarlet curtains to keep scarlet fever away or eating yellow spice to banish the jaundice?'

'Some of those I know.'

'Well, the pox before it scabs has a dent in the middle.'

'I have seen the very thing you refer to. It looks just like a navel.'

'It does. So it stands to reason that as I do not have one, I cannot get the pox.' She follows his reasoning but is not convinced.

'If the doctor agreed with you,' she says, 'surely you would be tending the viscount instead of myself.'

'Pah! The doctor thinks himself an individualist but even he does not know everything. Both my brothers had the fever and I never caught it once.' An agreeable smile spreads across Ned's face and, pushing himself away from the wall he whispers in her ear, 'Now you know my secret, what will you give me in return?' Before she has a chance to answer, he tenses, listening.

'What is it?' she says.

'I can hear a carriage approaching.' Sure enough a crunch of gravel is followed by the shouts of a driver. 'Quick,' Ned says, 'we must not be caught here.' He clasps her by the hand, pulling her through a door on the opposite side of the corridor and into a large vestibule, the walls lined with hunting prints and maps. Along one wall is a row of hooks hung with oilskins and outdoor capes, pairs of muddied riding boots standing beneath.

Ned doesn't completely close the door. He presses his eye to the gap to see who has arrived and Elen bobs beneath his arm until the undercroft comes into view. There is a muffle of voices, the sound of the outside door opening and boots descending, then the undercroft fills with capes as three gentlemen, with powdered wigs beneath their hats, stride ahead of the servants who struggle behind with trunks, grunting under their weight.

As the footsteps and voices recede a draught, heavy with the taint of rosewater mixed with tobacco, slinks through the crack in the door. Ned closes it, steps away from Elen. His eyes slide sideways, distracted.

'Who were they?' she says.

'I have no idea.' The spell of intimacy is broken and she wishes it were not so.

'Were they family?' she says.

'No.'

Elen wants to regain their earlier companionship, but Ned has turned half away from her, listening at the door. He is more interested in where the guests have gone than he is with her. She moves into his line of vision and watches his face, trying to gauge his mood, understand this disconnection.

After a minute or so she says, 'They cannot be guests of the earl if they have been brought in down here, can they?'

Ned shrugs. 'Who knows? I am just a servant. We had better get you back or the doctor is going to be sending out a search party.' He opens the door again and peers out. She catches the distant murmur of conversation. 'We'll have to find another way upstairs,' he says, setting off towards a set of steps that disappear around a corner.

'What is this place?' she says, quickening her pace to keep up with him.

'Mordiford comes in this way if he is been out hunting,' he says over his shoulder as he hurries on. 'It leads up to his study. The earl takes a rum view of him coming in and out of the servants' door. Still, it keeps him out of my way most of the time.'

'You don't like him very much, do you?'

'He's a hard master to like.'

'What's wrong with him?'

Ned turns to her and she sees a flash of exasperation in his face but then he smiles and says, 'Oh, not very much, apart from his wealth and entitlement. I find it rankles somewhat. But there'll be plenty wrong with me if I don't get you back upstairs. Come along, we must hurry.'

Chapter 9

Elen has no desire to get back to the monotony and unpleasantness of the sickroom. She watches Ned's back as he navigates his way through the private apartments, longing for him to turn and take her hand. She feels such an emptiness inside her, such a sadness that their intimate conversation has come to an abrupt end. She wants to bask in his gaze again, feel the thrill of his attention.

She completely loses her sense of direction and is astonished when Ned pushes open the green baize door onto the minstrels' gallery. Now she can hear the doctor's voice echoing around the hall.

'He is shouting with a deal of spleen,' Ned says. 'You'd better shift your bob.' And he is gone.

'Miss Griffiths!' the doctor says, hurrying towards her, impatience in his voice. 'There you are at last.' He is wearing his outdoor cloak. 'I have been waiting this half hour for your return. Where on earth have you been?'

She tries to think of an explanation that will not increase his irritation, but he doesn't wait for her to speak. 'I have been forced to leave the patient,' he says crossly. 'He has fallen into a fitful slumber. You must make haste. He could wake at any minute. I have to go or I will never complete my visits in time to return this evening.'

'Do you have any instructions for me, sir?'

'I have no time any more, you will have to use your wits and manage on your own. This is very tiresome indeed.' He exhales an impatient breath. 'What of the bath? Did you remember to enquire about the bath?'

'Mr Antrobus says it would not be possible.'

'Not be possible? Oh, for pity's sake. Do I have to do everything myself?' He purses his lips, looking at her with a stern expression as if she is to blame for this also. 'I will be back but it will be exceedingly late in the day.' He sweeps past her, disappearing through the door at the end of the gallery.

Elen glares at the door through which he has departed. She has been here for less than twenty-four hours and in that time, despite striving to carry out her duties with as good a will as possible, she has been criticised, reprimanded and shut away, forced to help a sullen ingrate with a series of humiliating and unpleasant services. And what thanks has she had for it? None. The doctor constantly goads her about her squeamishness. The servants ignore her, apart from Ned, and even he has cooled for no apparent reason. Her mother warned her that bettering oneself was never popular. Perhaps they all mean to bring her a branch lower and the doctor contrives to do it by pushing her towards a point where he imagines her spirit will be broken. Well, it will not. She will prove him wrong.

As she climbs the stairs, she resolves to show the doctor that she is made of very stern stuff indeed. If he wants her to nurse Viscount Mordiford, then nurse him she shall. She will bathe his sores and purge his bowels if necessary and she will sweeten the unpleasantness by daydreaming about Ned Harley. But why that sudden cooling towards her? Could it be that he was anxious about being caught with her? Mr Antrobus was a gruff man. Perhaps the arrival of those gentlemen would have sent the servants looking for Ned. That must be the reason for his sudden change. The next time she sees him things will be back to normal.

The emptied earth closet bucket is on the landing at the top of the spiral stairs. The smell momentarily makes her frown but then shakes her head back as if to clear it, puts a studied smile on her face to greet her patient, and lets herself into the chamber. She stops. Her patient is nowhere to be seen.

Irritation grips her and she drops the bucket with a clatter, stumping across to the bed. Although it is patently empty, she flings the covers back. The palliasse is still warm. She goes around to the opposite side of the bed, wondering if the idiot has rolled in his sleep and landed on the floor. All she finds are bare floorboards.

Feeling rather foolish, she drops to her hands and knees and peers beneath the bed. It is barely high enough for a man to conceal himself beneath and besides, it might feel as if she's nursing a truculent five-year-old but surely he is too sick to divert himself by hiding from her.

She sits back on her heels and looks around. Her anger is subsiding and now she's worried. Is it possible that he's left the sickroom and is, at this very moment, stumbling around the corridors of the hall, spreading the plague as he goes? She breathes out a raggedy sigh. There is only one person who'll get the blame if that's the case.

She goes to push herself up from the floor and feels a stab of pain in her hand. She has struck her palm on a splinter, driving it into the flesh. She brings her hand up to her mouth and sucks the wound, trying to quell the sting. She struggles to her feet to inspect the damage by the light of a nearby candle. The splinter has gone deep. She can see the dark shadow in the muscle at the base of her thumb and try as she might, she cannot grasp the tip with her teeth, the skin has quite closed across it.

Her concentration is interrupted by the distant sound of a chair falling. Snapping her head round to listen, other sounds come to her from behind the screen and, quite forgetting the pain in her hand, she hurries into the vestibule.

The thick wall covering shivers in the draught, but the light that drew her in before, now glows powerfully from beneath the hanging. The door into the other room is open.

She dives behind the tapestry, working her way along until she reaches the door that, sure enough, stands ajar. She enters a long, low room jumbled high with furniture, some of the larger pieces shrouded with dustsheets, sprinkled with dirt and bat droppings. Smaller items tilt and lean, stacked at odd angles, and splattered with the white smears left by roosting birds. Straw from ancient nesting material lies across the floor. The furniture forms a hectic corridor that leads through to a large casement window at the far end of the room.

There, silhouetted against the light, is Viscount Mordiford, crouching on the floorboards, surrounded by a collection of junk, as if he has been turning the cupboards out. There are clay pipes and abandoned squares of linen, a spilled pile of books and a handful of quills, pewter jars and dishes. He has his back to her and is leaning over something, studying it intently. She can hear his harsh breathing. Every now and then he emits a low and desperate groan.

With great trepidation Elen approaches him. As she nears, he glances back at her, hunching to conceal whatever it is that he holds. In the raw light streaming in through the windows, his face looks shockingly altered. The red marks of the night before are raised and plentiful, his forehead and cheeks distorted as if a thousand tiny pebbles have been pressed beneath his skin. Despite his wild stare, she feels a wave of pity sweep over her, extinguishing her anger.

'Oh, you poor man,' she says, approaching him.

'Do not pity me,' he growls. As he turns away, a light flashes from the object he holds in his hand. It is a looking glass.

'Let me take that, sir,' she says. 'You do yourself no service.'

'Who the hell are you to tell me what I can and cannot do?' he says, his voice cracking with anguish.

She kneels down and reaches out to take the looking glass. At first he raises a petulant shoulder to block her but then he turns his head away and to her surprise, he lets her slide it from his grasp. She lays it face down on the floor and, slipping a hand beneath his arm, encourages him to his feet.

As he tries to stand, he sways. She steadies him, her hand on his chest. Through his shirt she can feel the heat of his fever and the trembling of his muscles. He makes a weak attempt to shake her off, but then submits, allowing her by degrees to lead him back through to the sick room and lay him on the bed. He turns away, weakly drawing the covers across his body.

'Let me fetch you beer, my lord.'

'Leave me be,' he says, his voice muffled by the pillows into which he burrows his face. She stands for a few moments more, wondering if she should insist he take a draught but then with a sigh, she turns away, taking up her post on the chaise longue where she can watch him.

Mordiford stays rolled in a tight ball with his back to her for a good half an hour. Bit by bit his hands release their frantic hold on the bedding and his breathing falls into the steady rhythm of sleep. She gets to her feet and tiptoes round to the other side of the bed. One of his hands flutter, the fingers twitching as he slips deeper into sleep and as she watches, he rolls onto his back with a sigh, flopping his arm out across the palliasse. Where his undershirt falls open, the pocks on his chest give him the appearance of some lichen-covered spirit of the woods. Elen eases the bed curtain across to cut out the light from the window and leaves him to slumber.

She goes back to the storeroom to tidy away the things that he has scattered across the floor. Was he hunting for a looking glass or did he come across it as he searched for something else? It lies over by the large casement window now and, before stooping to pick it up, she gazes out across the estate. A mercury glint between the trees marks the course of the River Lugg as it twists and turns through the woodland, bare of leaves save for the copses of evergreens that punctuate the landscape. She wonders if her family are missing her as much as she misses them.

Turning back to the room, Elen rights a fallen chair and replaces it beside a dressing table, exposed when Mordiford tore the dustsheet back and toppled the chair. She tucks the things away in the open drawers and is about to replace the looking glass when a flash of white catches her eye. She pulls the drawer further out and frowns. It is full of feathers. When she tries to lift one out, the feathers move altogether to form a shape, a mask constructed entirely of quills.

Lifting the thing out, she turns it in her hands. The feathers are too large to be from a goose. The tiniest stitches hold them in place on a rich, white brocade. Most of the feathers are of the purest white except where a widow's peak of black quills point down between the eyes, mimicking the shape of a swan's beak. A ribbon of the deepest black is fastened to each side. The longer feathers form the top of the head and around the eyes they have been expertly graded to create a velvet of down.

She glances momentarily over her shoulder and then, raising the looking glass, she presses the mask to her face. The feathers prick and tickle her skin, catching on the moisture of her lips. She blows them free with a soft puff.

She moves her head from left to right to see the effect in the looking glass. The image that gazes back at her is a fairy princess, masked in pure white swan's feathers. Perhaps that is what Ned meant about the place being merrier in the spring. How wonderful it would be to see a masked ball here at Duntisbourne.

Chapter 10

Elen busies herself throughout the morning, tidying and straightening the sickroom. Whenever her patient stirs, she goes over to his bedside, but the moment she comes into view, Mordiford covers his face and turns away.

Periodically he struggles to swing his feet over the edge of the bed, waiting sullenly for her to help him over to the commode. Each time she gets him to his feet, she is struck by his height and as she helps him across the floor, she slots neatly underneath his arm without the need to bend. She seldom stands next to a man who is substantially taller than her and his stature adds a poignancy to his helplessness.

With little else to do, she begins to feel bored. How she wishes she had had the foresight to pack a piece of sewing to fill these idle hours. She wonders if she could steal back to the storeroom and fetch one of the books. Instead she pokes away at the splinter under her skin, making it sore.

By midday, her thoughts turn to food. She begins to wonder if she's been quite forgotten and finds herself listening out intently for a tap on the lower door to let her know that a tray of food is waiting downstairs for her to collect.

Around three o'clock, her hunger begins to lessen, as it always does when the hour to eat passes. Boredom and warmth from the fire make her eyes heavy. Perhaps she can fill the afternoon by sleeping, but just as she starts to drop off, she hears footsteps.

She gets to her feet and hurries to the door, opens it and listens. Someone is coming up the stairs with great care, as if they are carrying something. It must be Ned. He has not forgotten her, for who else would risk bringing her a tray of food in person? She leans against the doorjamb aware that her heart is beating a little faster, but to her surprise and disappointment it is not Ned who appears, but the doctor.

'Dr Argyll,' she says, stepping down to relieve him of the tray, the contents of which are rattling, threatening to topple over. 'I was not expecting to see you until this evening.'

She takes the tray into the chamber and places it on the table.

'No, indeed,' he says with some unease, 'and I cannot stay long.' He doesn't remove his cloak and stands in the doorway as if intent on leaving immediately. 'I came back,' he continues, 'because I felt that in my haste this morning I spoke out of turn.'

'Not at all, sir. I am sure I was wrong to have been gone for so long,' she says, conscious that she needs to control her tang of sarcasm.

'No, I am the one in the wrong. I have been distracted all morning because of my thoughtlessness, which has been sitting heavily on my mind.' He begins to pace a little across the floor, his hands behind his back. 'In my anxiety last night, I plucked you from your comfortable hearth and brought you here without thinking the matter through. Of course you cannot be imprisoned up here, day in and day out, without a breath of fresh air or a few minutes of congenial company. Your health, if not your mind, will begin to suffer. It was unreasonable of me to expect you to hurry back this morning after such a short period of freedom.' In response to the doctor's genuinely conciliatory manner, Elen feels a wave of guilt for her earlier surliness.

'I understand,' she says. 'But I really—'

'I have been speaking to Mr Antrobus to see what we can do to alleviate your situation.'

'Really, sir, there is no need.'

The doctor raises a hand to quiet her. 'At first Mr Antrobus was at a loss. All members of the household have their duties and can hardly be spared, but to my great relief the valet…'

'Ned?' Elen says with enthusiasm before she checks herself.

'Yes,' the doctor brushes her with a quizzical look. Then his face lightens and he smiles saying, 'It was him, to be sure. He informed me that a lowly scullery maid, a girl called Joan, had survived the pox as a baby. I remembered the girl for she had been left in a sorry state indeed.'

'She was downstairs this morning at breakfast. I met her.'

'Yes, she would be hard to miss. Her face was badly scarred and she lost the sight in one of her eyes, as I recall. Mr Antrobus had not thought it pertinent to mention her to me as she is a girl of no education and scant intelligence. The earl would not normally entertain such a lowborn girl serving the viscount, but Mr Antrobus suggested she could sit with the viscount occasionally and give you a modicum of freedom.'

'Why, thank you, Dr Argyll,' Elen says, and this time her enthusiasm is genuine. 'This is most thoughtful of you. I would indeed enjoy a few breaks in the day.' To spend a little more time in Ned's company, she thinks.

'That is decided then. I will confirm it with Mr Antrobus on my way out. Now to the patient. I cannot imagine the poor man is taxing you greatly at present, being in such a moribund state. How has he been today?'

Elen hesitates. She wonders whether giving a true account to the doctor might change his mind, but the fancy passes in a moment. She has always tried to be an honest girl even if her courage falters occasionally when the consequences of truth put her at a disadvantage.

Checking over her shoulder to make sure they cannot be overheard, she drops her voice and says, 'I'm afraid that when I came back to the chamber, the viscount was in the storage room behind the vestibule.'

'Indeed? I am surprised he had the strength,' the doctor says.

'He found a looking glass. He was very distressed.'

'Oh dear. That is not good at all. If his appearance distresses him now, I am afraid there is far worse to come.'

'He's slept for some of the time since,' Elen says. 'But when awake I have been unable to engage him in any sort of conversation.'

'His spirits are bound to be depressed. What young man of that age does not value his good looks?' The doctor sighs and adds, 'Life brings hardships to us all.'

Chapter 11

The routine that punctuates Elen's days and nights is established. An hour before dawn she hears the mouse-like tappings of the scullery maid. When she opens the door, Joan slithers into the room without a word. Sometimes, the girl struggles up the spiral staircase with a load of wood or fresh bedding, but once these are deposited she takes up her post, standing as far away from the sickbed as possible.

At first Elen urges her to take a seat, but with little more than a sullen grunt, she shakes her head. After breakfasting, Elen returns to the room to find Joan still hunched in her corner. Initially she tries to engage her in conversation but Joan refuses to look in her direction. Elen wonders if embarrassment causes this evasion – one of Joan's eyes is milky and sightless – but even the good eye darts around as if she seeks a route by which to escape. All the while Joan's mouth hangs open, slack-jawed as if the inside of her nose has been scarred by the pox and she is unable to breathe through it. Elen would have preferred a more congenial partner with whom to share her duties, but she enjoys eating with the other servants and listening to the gossip.

It is rumoured that the earl is expected back before the middle of the month to entertain a group of important guests. Much surprise is expressed that he intends coming when the threat of smallpox is still present. Clearly the earl has great faith in the doctor and believes the sickness has been contained.

Elen's chief pleasure in having a few hours of freedom each day is the opportunity to see Ned who regularly accompanies her on an early morning stroll down to the lake.

'What is he like, the earl?' Elen says one morning as they walk. The air is still but the sky leaden and overcast. There has been a light fall of snow in the night, making it bitterly cold. How she longs to thread her hand into the crook of Ned's arm as they walk.

'The earl is very tall and distinguished,' Ned says.

'It is strange then that he never remarried.'

'Is it? The countess was such a sickly woman, he may not be in such a hurry to repeat the experience.'

'What was wrong with her?'

'Ah, well. There you have it. There are many rumours but it seems to me that women of high station are often sickly. Look at our poor dear Queen Anne. There's none higher in the land and none sicker by all accounts. She is so crippled with the gout that she had to be carried into her coronation on a sedan chair, the back cut away so that her train could trail out behind her.'

'Did the earl attend the coronation?'

'Of course he did.'

A group of ducks out on the lake begin to squabble, their quacking and flapping echoing through the still air.

'And the earl,' Elen says, 'what of his other children? Are there many?'

Ned comes to a halt and turns to her. 'There are none. There again the countess aped the habits of the Queen.'

'Which are what?'

'You must know, the Queen lost the lot – sixteen or seven-teen children they say. The only one to survive was the Duke of Gloucester, and he's dead now. And as for the earl, I know of six children for certain that were lost before they drew breath. They say one she bore was a monster with a nose like a rabbit but it died within a few days, which was a mercy.'

There is a casual indifference to his words, but she excuses him. Perhaps sympathy for his master is easier if he doesn't dwell on the suffering.

'It is a mercy the viscount was born at all, then,' she says.

'He was the firstborn. The dead ones all came after him. The rumour is that while the countess was lying-in down here for the month after the birth, the earl caught the eye of another young woman in London.'

'Really?'

'Unfortunately, it was not all he caught, if you get my drift.' Elen shook her head, frowning. Ned leans close to her ear and says, 'He also caught himself a hearty dose of the French disease, which he was generous enough to pass on to his wife.' All Elen knows about 'the French disease' is that it should not be discussed in polite company so doesn't ask Ned for further explanation. Besides, he has resumed walking and adds, 'Other less charitable folk say Mordiford poisoned his mother's womb before he left it. I am inclined to prefer that explanation.'

'Have you no good words to say about Viscount Mordiford?'

'Well, let me think,' he says and smiles at her, which lifts her heart. 'I hope he does not succumb to the pox.'

'That's unusually charitable of you,' she says.

'Not particularly. Should he perish, I would lose the pleasure of your company. If he survives, his recovery may well be slow and it'll keep you here for a while longer.'

He bends to recover a flat stone from the ground, skimming it across the ice until it drops over the edge, making a hollow gloop before disappearing into the water. Elen watches the ripples spreading out across the lake, expecting him to press his compliment, but he turns away from her and saunters on, back towards the hall, his hands thrust deep into the pockets of his coat.

–

As she makes her way back to the sickroom, she wishes Ned would take advantage of the time they spend together, alone and unobserved. She smiles to herself. She worried at first he was a rogue, and yet now he behaves as a gentleman, she is sad.

She must be happy she has his companionship and that he will be waiting for her again tomorrow.

She is about to open the door up to the chamber when she sees a glint of light in the shadows. A shaft of morning sun has crept into the dark space behind the column of stone that houses the spiral staircase, illuminating a small ribbed box she has never noticed before.

She looks around the gallery, but she is alone. She peers at the box, tries to open the latches but they are locked. She stands up, her hands on her hips. She sees that one of the struts is fractured. Then she remembers. She saw this very box a few days ago up in the storeroom beyond the vestibule.

'Joan,' she says when she enters the chamber. The girl is standing in her usual spot. 'Did someone tell you to take that box downstairs?'

The girl's eye slides away. 'No, miss.'

'A box from the room behind the hangings has been moved downstairs to the gallery. Did someone ask you to put it there?'

'I ain't touched nothing, miss.' She begins to move crabwise along the wall towards the door.

'No, wait a minute. It doesn't matter if you were asked to do it. I was only going to see if you needed help moving anything else downstairs. I would imagine several things may be needed for the entertainments if the earl is coming back.'

A sly smile spreads across the girl's face. She begins to mutter to herself in a manner so disconcerting that Elen comes forward, holds out her hand to calm her, but with a sudden and unexpected movement, Joan slides past and scurries out of the door.

Chapter 12

The scuffle wakes Mordiford. 'Miss Griffiths,' he says, his voice weak and rasping. Elen hurries over and looks down on him. When she first saw him, she thought him a rather ordinary-looking fellow. He certainly doesn't look ordinary now. The lumps on his skin are so numerous and inflamed, his face is stiff with swelling. His arms and legs are equally affected.

She should feel disgust, but she finds instead, she feels sympathy and has a powerful wish to scour the lesions off his skin. She longs to soothe his face with cold water until the swelling subsides and return him to normality. He may have little energy left to be disagreeable, but she would prefer a return of the angry man who tried to drive her away on that first night.

'What can I fetch for you, my lord?'

'Is it the bath?'

'I beg your pardon?' He turns his head sideways as if to use the direction of his eyes to point towards the door.

'The thing the girl was moving. Is it the bath?' So Joan was not truthful, she thinks, but she also realises that Mordiford must have heard the doctor discussing his treatment plan that first day.

'The bath?' she says. 'I do not think so, sir. It was mentioned but now seems quite forgot.' His gaze drifts away, a lost and frightened look in his eyes. 'Why?' she says. 'Do you feel anxious about the treatment?'

She is surprised that this familiarity comes so easily to her. She has been brought up to revere breeding and has a natural admiration for elegance and gallantry, even though she has had little first-hand experience of either during her life. Up until now, had she come across these qualities in a person, she would have known instinctively that they shared nothing in common. In fact, she would have avoided a man of such culture, as one might avoid the brilliance of lightning or anything else that is bright and alarming.

If Mordiford had begun their association with the normal politeness that a man of rank usually used towards a servant, she would carry out her duties automatically and with little emotional involvement, but ironically the roughness of his manner towards her at that first meeting has smoothed the differences between them.

Mordiford peers up at her from beneath his swollen lids, not with his usual dismissive glance but with a look of steady concentration. 'It is not natural to be submerged in water,' he says.

'It is when you are swimming. Did you not swim as a boy, sir?'

He runs his tongue over his swollen lips. 'I have a horrible taste in my mouth,' he says.

'I will fetch you a draught.'

'No, wait,' and his hand comes out and grasps her, pulling her down with a weak force to sit beside him. 'I hear that even the King of France does not submerge his body in a bath more than twice a year.'

'But I also read he can indulge both himself and his body by changing his undershirt four times a day,' she says. Mordiford almost smiles, but then he winces, the cracks around his lips opening.

'How does a girl like you know a thing like that?'

'I had a mother who was full of knowledge and learning.'

'She taught you to read and write?'

'She did. Reading is one of my greatest pleasures. Perhaps you would like me to read to you as you rest.'

'Perhaps.' He holds her gaze for a moment longer then looks away. 'I can hardly stand you to look upon my face,' he says.

'How can you bear to watch my body bubbling up as if I have been burned with fire?'

'I am here to nurse you, sir. It holds no fear for me.'

'I have become a monster.'

'You will heal.'

'If I live.' He shifts in the bed and turns his extraordinary blue eyes on her with a look of entreaty as if he longs to believe her. The rims are red and swollen. As she watches, the well of moisture, hovering along the bottom lid, rises and drops down his face, trickling between the raised boils. 'If I die, shall I be locked in this monstrous body for eternity?'

'When we die, we leave all earthly suffering behind,' she says, reaching to the side table to take up a flannel. She blots the tear from his cheek being careful not to disturb the pocks. 'But you will not die. You have Dr Argyll to take care of you.'

'And I have you. You and your pity.'

She hesitates but she cannot lie. 'How could I not pity you?' she says, dropping her voice to soften it.

'I no longer mind. I pity myself more than I ever imagined possible. I have become a freak. That gruesome girl cannot help but stare at me when you are not here as if I was some fiendish exhibit in a travelling show.'

'Does she?'

'I close my eyes and pretend to sleep but I can hear her close by, breathing through her mouth. Sometimes she bends so low over me, I can smell the taint of her breath.'

'She means no harm.'

He shifts restlessly again, one hand working its way beneath his hips. 'God's teeth, how my back aches.'

'Come, let me make you more comfortable,' she says. 'If you are able to sit for a few minutes, I can change the linen on your bed and return you to it once it is fresh and smooth. Perhaps a little movement would relieve the tension in your back.'

He meekly submits to her suggestion and, throwing a shawl around his shoulders, she guides him over to the chaise longue, lifting his long legs up so that they are supported along the seat.

As she makes his bed more comfortable, she marvels at his obedience. A few days ago, he refused to be served by her, but sickness has brought dependency and humility. It will not last, she thinks. Once recovered we will resume our allotted positions in life. She finishes her task and crosses the room to where Mordiford lies, moribund beside the fire.

'I have been thinking,' she says, 'if submersion in water is of concern to you, I could suggest to the doctor that the same benefits may result from bathing your lesions with the salted water instead. The pain of the salt on the open wounds would be easier to bear if it did not come all at once.'

'It is not the pain that makes me fearful. Surely if my body is allowed to soak in water, the disease will rush back in and I will surely die.'

'You must trust the physician.'

'Why? When the poor get sick it is said they are more likely to survive than the rich.'

'Perhaps it's God's way of balancing out the hardship visited on the poor.' Mordiford is not too sick to shoot a look at her at a perceived insult.

'You think it divine justice that the poor are mercifully saved?' Mordiford says. 'Does God mock us because we can afford to pay for the very doctors whose treatments cause more harm than good?'

'Come,' she says, as one does to a difficult child. 'Let me get you back into bed.' She helps him across the room, his scabbed arm heavy across her shoulders, and lays him down on the smoothed linen, arranging the covers neatly across his legs. 'Is that not cool and refreshing?'

'It is,' he says. She sits down on the edge of the mattress and takes up the subject once more.

'Dr Argyll seems quite the medical pioneer,' she says. 'His resistance to current thinking will benefit you. He does not want to bleed you, nor does he agree in constant cleansing or the purgative clyster.'

'Thank the Lord. I have been humiliated enough.'

'Some of his draughts are based on the same herbs the women in the village use to bring down fever and his theories on the goodness of salt are founded on strong evidence. I am quite sure you are in the best possible hands and that, if we follow his advice, you will make a full recovery.'

'I am not sure that I want to,' he says, turning his head away from her.

'Come now, this is the sickness talking.'

'The Duke of Marlborough will not want a monster of a man like me beside him when he rides out to defeat the French.'

'Your scars will not make you a monster. They will be a permanent reminder to all who see you of the suffering you have courageously endured. What better way to forge the face of a soldier?'

He reaches out a weak hand towards her but, perhaps thinking better of it, he allows it to drop before casting his eyes to the ground. 'You are kind,' he says.

Taking the candle from the side table, she leaves him to his dark thoughts, but as she busies herself tidying the sickroom, she offers up a silent prayer to God to bring the poor man a little comfort.

Chapter 13

The following day the hall is thrown into a state of panic by the news that the earl is due to arrive late in the afternoon.

'I am sure he will call for you, Miss Griffiths,' the doctor says, 'he will want to make sure his son is in good hands.'

Elen is bending over Viscount Mordiford, dabbing salted water on the pocks on his chest. Mordiford is not looking at her, he is braced for pain, his full attention on her hands. The doctor stands behind her, arms folded, watching the proceedings and chattering to Elen as she works. 'Let us hope this notion of yours proves successful, Miss Griffiths.'

The viscount flinches and gasps as she presses the cold brine onto a new lesion.

'Be careful not to knock it open,' the doctor says, leaning forward as he cautions her. 'Exposing them before they're ready will leave a deeper scar.' Mordiford gives a groan of despair and rolls his eyes. The doctor straightens up and says, 'Good work, Miss Griffiths. Now my lord, those should begin to feel more comfortable in a minute or two when the moisture has dried away.'

'That water makes my skin itch so damnably I am quite maddened by it,' Mordiford says, pushing himself higher on his pillows and curling his fingers in readiness to scratch the bathed area.

'No!' the doctor barks, pushing in front of Elen, knocking the bowl and spilling brine into her lap. As she pushes her chair back to give him more room, the doctor grabs the viscount by both hands.

'Get off me, man,' Mordiford says.

'I will not,' the doctor says with some vigour. 'Miss Griffiths,' he calls over his shoulder as they struggle. 'Fetch me those scissors and pare the nails while I hold him.'

Elen goes through to the vestibule, brushing the water off her apron. She finds the scissors and returns to the struggle, grasping Mordiford's finger and trying to position the blades over the nail. His hand writhes and bucks so violently she dare not take a snip.

'For pity's sake, woman. Leave me be,' Mordiford says. 'I'm not a child.'

'You're behaving like one,' the doctor says. 'A child cannot be expected to understand the consequence of his action. You, on the other hand, can.'

'The irritation is killing me.'

If anything kills him, she thinks, it'll be the smallpox.

It is impossible to use her scissors. She lets go of his finger, straightens up and waits, watching the two men struggle.

'I cannot stand it,' Mordiford says, desperately trying to wrench his hands free from the doctor's grip.

'You must,' the doctor says. 'Should you tear at these lumps whenever they irritate you, at best you will ensure your skin is pocked as densely as the face of the moon. At worst, you will inflame and anger the wounds, corrupting the flesh. Can you not use your self-control for once?'

Mordiford is suddenly still. Elen knows a storm is coming.

'What can you mean, "for once"?' Mordiford says. The doctor stares down at him, an impatient expression on his face. 'I lie here, deformed and humiliated as this girl...' Mordiford wags a dismissive finger towards Elen. '...strips away one dignity after another. Am I now to be spoken to as if everyone in the whole world has forgotten their place?'

Elen sees the doctor's face redden, all except for the tip of his chin, which blanches as the muscles around his mouth pinch with fury.

'Forgotten my place, your lordship?' Dr Argyll utters the address with the vehemence of an insult. 'At the present moment I am on a far higher plane than you have ever been to me.'

Elen backs away from the two men, fascinated and a little thrilled to observe the tussle.

'How dare you,' Mordiford says.

'I dare,' the doctor says, his face now an inch or two away from Mordiford's, 'because I have determined to give you your single most sporting chance to survive. I can just as easily choose not to, sir.'

The doctor straightens up and tugs his waistcoat down by the lapels. 'As for Miss Griffiths,' he says, 'a man's station in life does not give him the right to treat anyone with such contempt.' Elen bites her lips softly between her teeth to hide her smile. An argument is always enjoyable when one has a champion. The doctor continues, 'Miss Griffiths has left her family to come and take care of you. When I drove her here on that first night, she was full of dread. She controlled that fear and distress. In fact, she showed the stoicism and dignity that you, as heir to the Duntisbourne estates, are sadly lacking.'

The palliasse rustles as Mordiford shifts his weight, apparently struck dumb. Presently he raises his eyes, which fizz electric blue, and says, 'I have never been spoken to like that in my life.'

'You would undoubtedly be a better man if you had,' the doctor says.

The two men look fixedly at one another for what seems like minutes but is probably only seconds. Mordiford is the first to break the stare, looking down to draw the edges of his shirt closed across his chest.

'When does my father arrive?' he says in a low tone. Ah, Elen thinks, he pretends the conversation of the past few minutes never happened.

'Sometime this afternoon,' Dr Argyll replies lightly, knowing he has won the duel.

The doctor sniffs and turns away, preparing to take his leave. Once he has donned his outdoor cloak, he touches Elen on the elbow and draws her towards the door.

'Accompany me down to the gallery, if you would be so obliged,' he says. 'I have a few instructions to give you out of earshot. His lordship will come to no harm in the next five minutes.'

When they reach the gallery, the doctor places his bag on the ground and pulls on his gloves. He arranges his tricorn over his periwig and says, 'I do not imagine you will have trouble with him today.' He pauses momentarily and then gives her a broad and rather boyish smile, which lights up his face and makes him appear more youthful. 'Do not put up with any nonsense from him,' he says, then he shakes his head and purses his lips as if re-running the scene in his mind's eye. 'I will not have you spoken to in such a manner. I am confident I made my point quite plainly, but I do not completely trust him to hold his tongue when I am not there.'

Suddenly the doctor tosses back his head and laughs, clapping his hand across his mouth to stifle it. He controls himself, and pushes the back of his hand against his eyes. 'But upon my word,' he says, 'I rather enjoyed that. I have been wanting to give that young man a piece of my mind for years.'

Elen smiles at his glee, but part of her still feels sympathy for Mordiford. 'He was abrupt but surely that's because he's sick and afraid,' she says.

'Perhaps. But you did not know him when his mother was alive.' The doctor glances around the gallery, drops his voice and says, 'Follow me. There is a sketch over in the private side that will show you what I mean.' Leaving his bag where it lies, he slips down a short passage to the right of the baize door, opens a heavy oak door at the end and stands aside to let her through.

The air beyond is warm and smells sweetly of wood smoke. When she steps over the threshold, her foot sinks into the rug on the floor, as springy as moss. They appear to be in a kind of backwater of the private apartments, a place that people pass through. Even so, it has an air of comfortable softness, as if every wall, window and floorboard has been padded, the sounds muffled unlike the staterooms, which are all noise and echo. The doctor beckons her over to where a small picture hangs on the wall, a sketch in charcoal and chalk mounted in a simple frame of pine.

'The viscount was seventeen when this sketch was done,' the doctor says, his voice barely a whisper. 'His mother fancied having a bust made of him. She died before it was commissioned but this is how I remember him.' The doctor's tone leaves Elen in little doubt that he sees an entitled and indulged young man, but she sees something else. Yes, there is a lift of the head which may seem proud, but as she gazes at the clear eyes, the handsome line of the jaw and the broad symmetry of the face, she detects a tension in the shoulders and neck. This is not a proud young man at all. This is a hesitant man, hiding his anxieties beneath a mask of superiority.

'He was an insufferable young man when last we met,' the doctor says.

'How long ago was this?'

'Goodness, let me see. The countess has been dead for seven years now.'

'A man can change a great deal in that time,' Elen says, gazing at the portrait.

'Perhaps you are right, Miss Griffiths. My judgement was made on a young man indulged by his mother, who treated those around him with an unpleasant disdain. I felt he reached adulthood with a misguided notion of entitlement.'

'But he is entitled – he is a viscount.'

'Aha! You mean to be quarrelsome, Miss Griffiths,' the doctor says with good cheer. 'Yes, he has a title, but I felt that had he been less indulged, he might have understood earlier that privilege and duty go hand in hand. But perhaps you are right. I must admit that when I heard he had purchased himself a commission, I was beside myself with hope for him. Perhaps he truly meant to make something of himself.'

'But this sickness has snatched that away.'

'Indeed it has. The red plague has no respect for rank. It robbed you of two of your brothers and took your poor dear mother. It killed the Queen's sister, then two of her own children. It nearly took Queen Anne herself. And now the viscount is facing the same bleak reality and no amount of money can help him.'

'Is he bound to be disfigured?' she says.

'Oh yes, to a greater or lesser extent. He will bear the same pockmarks as a street urchin or...' Dr Argyll runs his hand across his own pitted face and smiles, '...a country doctor. However passionately he longs for a complexion as clear and as pure as yours, he cannot have it. But who knows, perhaps this hardship will be the making of him. Suffering is often the hammer, and misfortune the chisel, when God fashions a man's character.'

Chapter 14

Elen is making her way back along the gallery when she hears the noise of scraping furniture. She looks over the balcony to the hall below and sees four of the servants struggling to move a heavy marble table across the tiles. As she watches, Ned appears from underneath the balcony, directing them as they work. He moves across the hall, removing dustsheets as he goes.

'Ned!' she calls. He looks up and waves.

'Come down,' he says.

'I cannot, I must return to the patient.'

'Wait there then.'

He drops the bundle of sheets from beneath his arms and bounds up the wide staircase towards her. He has been working hard for, despite the chill, he has removed most of his livery except for his shirt, which clings to his body where the sweat has sprung from his back. He is such a picture of health and vitality, his skin glowing and his hair glossy, it is a relief to look on him and be reminded that the human body is a wonderful thing.

'Is this all in preparation for the earl?' she says when he reaches the gallery.

'It is.'

'But I thought he did not use the main rooms during the winter.'

'Usually he would not but there is to be a meeting of the Order of the Knights of St Sebastian in a few days' time.'

'The Knights of St Sebastian?'

Ned leans on the rail, pushing a handful of hair from his face. 'It is a group of important men who come from the four corners of Europe to gather here. They have politics and government in common with the earl.'

'That sounds wearisome.'

'Oh, they are not the dull lot you would imagine.' He climbs a step nearer to her and wraps his arm around the heavy carving on top of the newel post. 'They enjoy a fine dinner and good company.'

'Duntisbourne is a long way to come, particularly in these winter months. Why on earth do they not meet in London?'

'They would, but the Queen leads a pious life, and expects her politicians to do the same.' The fingers of his other hand begin to trace the head of the lion, following the curve of its mane, the contours of the tongue that projects from the wooden muzzle. 'What you and I would regard as natural high spirits, the Queen sees as licentiousness.'

'Is that so?' She feels a frisson of excitement to know someone who understands life at Court.

'It is. Any politician brought to her attention for immoral behaviour pays the price. She listens to her favourites at Court. A word from one of them has ended many a career.'

'You seem to know a great deal about it.'

'I do. The earl often takes me into his confidence.' A slight cloud comes across Ned's face and with sudden seriousness he adds, 'As I am taking you into mine.'

'But none of this is secret, surely?'

Ned shifts his weight, looks away from her, studying the carved lion's head. 'Of course not, not really, but I would be grateful if you didn't go tittle-tattling to the good doctor about it,' he says.

'Why ever not?'

'I told you, the earl and his friends have to be careful that gossip about their merry making doesn't reach Court. I'm sure the doctor would disapprove of their gaiety.'

'Would he? He seems an open-minded man.'

'Oh, you know these medical men. If something's fun, it's unquestionably bad for you.'

Elen frowns at him. 'With all this preparation,' she says, 'Dr Argyll is bound to see something is afoot, is he not?' She nods at the industry in the hall beneath them. 'He already knows the earl is returning this afternoon.'

'Yes, but the doctor will assume it is to be a general dinner. I simply meant it would be better if you didn't mention the Knights of St Sebastian. When they have their special dinner in a few days' time, they dine late, long after the doctor has concluded his evening visit.' Ned gives her a swift smile. 'Anyway, I must get back downstairs or that lazy crew will slither away and I will never find them again.'

He starts off down the staircase but pauses and turns. 'Actually,' he says, 'perhaps I have been a little indiscreet. It really would be better for me if you didn't talk about this to the doctor or to the viscount for that matter.'

'The viscount? Has he not attended these dinners in the past?'

'No. Politics has never interested him, much to the disappointment of his father.' Ned reaches up the bannister until his fingers meet with hers. His look is intense and open again. 'I think I have been a little foolish.'

'In what way?'

'I could not quite resist bragging to you, I suppose.'

His expression is so appealing it makes her smile. 'You are proud to have the ear of the earl?'

'I am.'

'And so you should be. Of course I won't pass on what you have told me.'

'Bless you.'

He hurries back down, turns at the foot of the stairs, touching his fingers on his lips and throws a kiss up to her.

76

Mordiford is in the same position as when she left the sickroom, propped up on a bank of pillows. He shifts restlessly, working his hands behind his back. Talk of the Knights' Order makes her think that Mordiford looks like the suffering martyr of St Sebastian, his hands pinioned behind him, his muscles straining against his bonds, his skin pierced with arrows. She has the fanciful thought that she is to be his St Irene, the woman who had the courage to draw each arrow from the martyr's flesh and nurse him back to health. Cautiously she approaches the bed.

'Do you think you will be able to manage a little luncheon later on, sir?' she says.

Mordiford moves his head weakly from side to side, his eyes closed. She comes nearer and lays the back of her hand on his forehead to gauge his fever. Even though her fingers are chilled from her time on the gallery, his skin feels a deal hotter than the last time she felt it. Her carefree conversations of the past half hour have made her forget how vital his recovery is to her and her family.

A terrible anxiety sweeps through her, a realisation that in the half hour she has been gone, he has deteriorated rapidly. How can that be? Has squabbling and fighting with the doctor worn him out or are these swings from lucidity to confusion part of the disease.

'Can you hear me, my lord?'

He rolls his head towards her and opens his eyes. He stares at her face but doesn't seem to see her, as if he is looking through her head to the wall beyond. His forehead puckers as much as the swelling allows. His eyes focus on her and he gives her such a look, that a terrible fear grips her heart as if she is about to lose Mordiford.

'What troubles you, my lord?' she says, desperately trying to keep a fearful tone from her voice.

Mordiford draws his parched lip between his teeth. 'I know not,' he says.

'How does the skin feel across your chest?'

'I cannot stand to touch it. The pain in my back is so fierce. Your hands are cold. Cold as the grave. Have pity on me. Lay your iced fingers on me, I beg you.'

Elen hesitates, but he seems to be in such discomfort, she draws the pillows out from behind his head and rolls him onto his side. She sees his crusted fingers working at his spine. She gently lifts his hand aside and lays her hands on the base of his back through the fabric of his bed shirt.

'I beg you, lay your hands on my skin,' he says, his voice muffled by the bedding. 'Or is my flesh too hideous for you to touch?'

'No, sir,' she says. She doubts he will recall these ramblings should he recover and she has, after all, been privy to far more degrading moments with him during their short acquaintance. Even so, before she pulls the bed shirt free, she draws the coverlet up to his waist to protect his modesty and preserve her own. It is one thing to steady him upon the commode, quite another to gaze down on him as he lies naked from the waist down.

Within a few minutes her hands have taken on the heat of his back. She slides the bed shirt back into place. Mordiford stirs but does not move. Very gently she draws his hair aside to study the skin on the back of his neck. The pocks are joining, much as the doctor feared.

She knows he is sickening fast, but is unsure of what to do. She needs the doctor's opinion. She thinks of quitting the room and calling down to Ned in the hall to fetch him with all haste but knows it is foolish to panic. She must hold her nerve and stay with her patient.

She busies herself tidying, stoking the fire and scattering a fresh scoopful of earth over the contents of the commode. Her mind cannot rest. When she can find no further tasks, she washes her hands in the ewer, opens the door into the stairwell and listens out to see if she can hear the doctor's approach. She cannot.

She sits down in a chair beside her patient. His breathing comes in swift, shallow pants. She whispers, 'Viscount Mordiford?' He does not stir. She watches him as if the strength of her concentration will keep him from slipping deeper into sickness.

The doctor had said Mordiford would begin to rally once the scabs began to form. This morning it seemed to be true. Now he is sicker than ever. She cannot imagine how uncomfortable he must feel. In the silence of the room, her mind leaps from worry to catastrophe. Fresh anxieties cram into her head. The doctor may be her staunch defender, but if Mordiford dies, no amount of championing from him will save her father's livelihood from the earl's wrath. What then would happen to Rhodri, Libby, Marc and her little sister Judy if the family lose their living and their home? The earl is the only employer for leagues around and without his beneficence, the Griffiths family would be destitute.

Finally, she hears the gallery door. She leaves her seat beside the sick bed and hurries over to the staircase. Yes, she can hear someone coming, the steady footsteps of the doctor and another climbing behind him. It will be Joan. But Mordiford is too sick to be left with Joan.

'Dr Argyll,' she says. The doctor stands on the threshold, turning to start back down. Joan shrinks in around him and scuttles across the room to her usual spot.

'Miss Griffiths,' the doctor says. 'You must come now. We have been summoned by the earl. He is most eager to meet you.'

'No, sir. Before we go down I urge you to...'

'Come on, off with that apron. Right now. You cannot afford to keep the earl waiting.'

'Sir, I beg you, would you please take a look at the viscount?'

'Later. Hurry now.' The doctor starts down the stairs, disappearing from sight before she can persuade him further.

She unties her apron, flings it down, shoots a look at Joan who hasn't even glanced at the patient. Elen opens her mouth to urge her to be vigilant but knows it is useless. Instead she follows the doctor. When she reaches the gallery she calls out to him, 'A moment, sir. I beg you.'

The urgency of her appeal stops him and he turns. 'Can it not wait? The earl is expecting us.'

'I am sure it cannot.'

The doctor pauses. 'Very well, but be quick.'

'It is the viscount. Although he seemed alert this morning, he has been sickening all afternoon.'

The doctor takes a deep breath and says, 'And I did not have time to take a look at him just now.' He pushes his fingers beneath his periwig and scratches the top of his forehead. 'Come, let me have your fears.'

'He complains of aching all down his back.'

'Ah, that should have passed by now.'

'And I noticed that many of the pocks are joining together and forming scabs, some as large as pennies.'

'Usually scabbing heralds an improvement.' The doctor knits his brows and pulls at his lower lip.

'These have lifted free of the skin,' Elen says, 'and have formed ulcers around their edges.'

'This is bad, very bad indeed.' The doctor takes a few paces away from her, his head bent, his hands folded behind his back. He retraces his steps and says, 'Let us despatch our duty with the earl with as much haste as possible. Twenty minutes will make little difference to that poor wretch upstairs. We'll go down through the private apartments. It will be quicker that way.'

—

Elen follows the doctor down the short passage, but before he opens the oak door he says, 'I need to think further on this. Until I have assessed the situation, we will tell the earl that his son is making good progress.'

'But he is not.'

'There will be no benefit in alarming his father at this stage. The earl is an unpredictable man with a muscular temper. The very last thing I want is for him to send for some physician from London.'

They hurry along the passage, past the sketch where they stood a short while ago and into a wider upstairs corridor, thickly carpeted. Quantities of fabric cover the walls and swathe the large window at the end, which frames a panorama of wet trees.

After the stark stone and wooden floorboards of the sick-room, the colours seem to stretch her eyes: rich swags of burgundy scrolled with golden threads, festoons of brilliant blue, brighter than the feathers of a peacock, tassels of acid yellow, singing against braids of emerald green.

As she tries to keep pace with the doctor, she glimpses lofty bedrooms, high and faint in the rainy afternoon light. In each stands a magnificent bed swathed densely in silks finer than those at the windows. The hangings are richly decorated with crewel work, the velvet valances stiff with embroidery. In one room, a maid is closing the shutters against the dank and darkening afternoon; in another an under-footman is setting the fire.

The doctor leads her on to the main staircase, smaller than the one in the great hall, but fine nonetheless. When he begins to descend, she hesitates on the landing and says, 'Dr Argyll?'

The doctor stops and turns. 'What's that you say?'

'Why do you not want a physician brought from London, sir?'

The doctor narrows his eyes and climbs a step nearer. 'Miss Griffiths, there is a tang to your question that I do not care for. I have not lost faith in my theories. Perhaps you have.' He drums his fingers on the bannister as he awaits her answer.

'I only wondered, sir,' she says, dropping her voice. 'If a physician at Court would have news of a remedy that has perhaps not reached this far west.'

The doctor studies the step on which he stands for a moment and then says without looking up, 'When King Charles lay dying, his physicians bled him of many pints of blood. They made him vomit. They fed him purgatives to clear his bowels. They administered enemas of antimony, rock salt, sacred bitters, beet root, mallow leaves, violet, camomile flowers, aloes, fennel seed, linseed, cardamom seed, cinnamon, saffron and cochineal. They shaved his scalp. They raised blisters. They applied poultices of burgundy pitch and pigeon dung. They tried extract of human skull, slippery elm, black cherry water, dissolved pearls. When he failed to rally, they forced ammonia down his throat and powdered bezoar stone. After a night of this first-rate treatment by the best physicians in the land, the king, by now utterly exhausted, died.' Dr Argyll leans towards her and, from his lower step, looks up into her face, his left eyebrow raised to emphasise his point. 'I would never let pride come between myself and the survival of my patient,' he says quietly.

Elen swallows and looks away. A clock somewhere nearby begins to whirr followed by a crisp and merry chime. In the pause between the chime and the strikes, she knows the doctor stares fixedly at her and she feels ashamed. She counts: one, two, three, four...

'Come,' the doctor says. 'We must not keep the earl waiting.'

They reach the lower landing, the doctor says, 'Stay here, Miss Griffiths, I will let Mr Antrobus know you are waiting, he will take you down to the smoking room.'

'You are coming with me?' she says, anxious that she has angered him so much he will abandon her.

'Of course, but we cannot burst in on the earl without being announced.'

Mr Antrobus appears, hurriedly pulling on his livery and leads them down yet another corridor. Elen watches the shoulders of the doctor as he strides ahead of her. She bitterly regrets speaking out. He is her ally. She cannot afford to lose his good opinion.

She catches the scent of tobacco drifting in the air. When they reach a set of double doors, Mr Antrobus throws them open and stands silhouetted against the muted light.

'Dr Argyll, my lord – and Miss Griffiths,' Mr Antrobus says before departing, closing the door soundlessly behind them.

Chapter 15

The first thing to strike Elen as she enters the smoking room is the enormous tapestry, covering the opposite wall. The image in the centre makes her catch her breath.

It shows a voluptuous woman, quite naked, sprawled in an Elysian bower. At first Elen thinks a swan is attacking the woman, but then she sees that the bird has climbed onto her lap, draping himself between her legs, his webbed foot lying delicately across her thigh. The woman's limbs writhe against the bird but her head bends forward with an expression of studied ecstasy as she takes the swan's beak between her lips.

Elen is a country girl and knows more than many of her age and sex that a bird is equipped in much the same way as a man. It leaves her in no doubt that this piece of art is a depiction of a shameless act of lust. The colour rises in her face and she looks down, trying to concentrate instead on the elaborate patterns of the rugs, but she cannot help glancing back at the arresting image, dominating the room.

The earl is sitting in a deep button-backed chair. Elen feels him watching her. She risks a glance at him and wishes she hadn't. He is smiling most lasciviously. He rises to his feet, changing his expression to one of welcome as the doctor approaches. She moves behind Dr Argyll to stay within his protection.

'Argyll,' the earl says. 'Thank you for taking time away from your patient.'

The earl is a tall man who must have been lithe in his youth, although now he carries too much weight around his middle.

He wears an elaborate wig, powdered white, the curls of which tumble across his shoulders and down his back. He is certainly not handsome, yet he is unmistakably refined. He has a long face and high forehead, deeply creased above the eyebrows, which are angled in a perpetual expression of disdain. His long, straight nose is faintly hooked at the tip, giving him the air of a bird of prey and beneath the nose, the lips have a looseness she associates with strong drink. He looks directly at her with the confidence of high station and the doctor steps aside to enable her to come forward.

'May I introduce Miss Griffiths?' the doctor says.

'Ah, the dairymaid,' the earl says as she drops him a shallow curtsy. 'You are a tall thing. All that milk and cheese as a child, I'll be bound, eh doctor?' The doctor bows his head to indicate agreement. 'I understand you work for your father, over at the farm.'

'I do, sir,' Elen says, lifting her head and looking back at the earl. His eyes are the palest blue, but cold, like a shadow on the snow.

'The doctor tells me we have been most fortunate to have you here. Your departed mother was a governess for Lady Ludlow, was she not?'

'For a very brief while, my lord.'

'I am told she gave up her position because her head was quite turned by one of my stockmen.' The tip of the earl's tongue flashes momentarily as he moistens his lips.

'That is the story, my lord,' she says. She narrows her eyes for she cannot quite read the earl's expression, but she senses his question has a lewdness to it.

'She taught at our little village school after her marriage,' the earl says.

'She did, my lord.'

The earl takes a step towards her and, unable to move without appearing rude, she leans back to increase the space between them.

'I hope that your father has not missed you too greatly,' the earl says, dropping his voice. His nostrils flare imperceptibly as if he is scenting the air around her, like a wolf.

'I would not know, my lord as I have neither seen nor spoken to him since my arrival. He is a capable man. I am sure he has found a way to manage.'

There is a pause. Elen looks away, aware that the earl is running his eyes down her body. When she looks up again, his gaze has returned to her face and he watches her with a lazy blink of the eyes before turning and making his way over to the fireplace where a lively fire is burning. He looks down at the flames, his back turned towards them, and says, 'I have been thinking through our last communication, Argyll. I am of course delighted to hear that Crispin is, in your opinion, over the worst of the illness.'

The doctor throws a warning glance towards Elen and replies, 'As are we, my lord.'

'My concerns now are the after-effects of the disease.' The earl turns and speaks directly to Elen. 'Do you think my son a handsome man, Miss Griffiths?'

She doesn't know how to answer. She has only known him swollen with the pox.

'I cannot say, my lord.'

'Oh, come now, you must have an opinion. Is he not fine featured, does he not have a head full of youthful hair and the body of an athlete? Why, you have had an opportunity to judge my son's physical attributes better than any woman in this county.' For the second time in as many minutes, she feels herself beginning to blush under the intense and amused gaze of the earl.

The doctor intervenes. 'It is hard to tell at present if the viscount will carry the scars of his affliction or not.'

'Hmm.' The earl is thoughtful for a moment, then says, 'The difficulty is that Lady Ludlow is eager to know how her daughter's intended is recovering. What am I supposed to tell her?'

'That the viscount will recover and shall bear any scars that remain with fortitude, my lord,' the doctor says.

'Do you believe that?'

The doctor doesn't reply.

'I see you do not.'

The earl leaves the hearth and paces around the carpet. 'This is all very tiresome. That boy has caused me no end of trouble in his short life. If he must join the army and get himself killed, the least he could do, before departing, is make a good marriage.'

'And I am sure he will.'

'I do not share your confidence. His cousin Arabella is a sophisticated and cultured girl and her mother, Lady Ludlow, puts great value on appearance. I cannot imagine either will look kindly on Crispin if this disease leaves him disfigured.' The earl turns to the doctor and adds with surprising cruelty. 'As disfigured as you, for example.'

Elen can bear it no longer. 'If the viscount recovers sufficiently to own a countenance as noble as the doctor's, he will be a lucky man,' she says.

The earl swings round. 'What's that you say, girl?'

She is saved from defending herself by a knock on the door. 'Your visitors have arrived, my lord,' Mr Antrobus says.

'Good. I am quite finished here,' the earl says, making an impatient gesture for the doctor to take his leave.

Dr Argyll glares at Elen and nods his head towards the door to encourage her to move. They pass Mr Antrobus and as they round the corner into the corridor, two men and a woman are waiting to be announced. The men are deep in conversation with the woman whose dress and presentation surprise Elen. Unlike the gentlemen, who are clearly well bred, she seems over-dressed, her face coloured and bright, her wig fanciful. The men watch Elen with a crafty gaze as she passes. Had they been younger she may have been flattered for they are clearly men of culture, but their seniority makes their interest unpleasant.

She hears one of them speak to the other although she cannot catch what he says. The laugh his remark produces in his audience leaves her in little doubt that they are talking about her and that their observations are not polite.

The moment they reach the stairs, Dr Argyll turns on her and says, 'What on earth possessed you to say such a thing to the earl?' His voice is tight with exasperation.

'I could not stand there and let him insult you so.'

'As you insulted me but ten minutes earlier?' He glares at her but she doesn't respond. Presently the doctor continues, 'It is up to me to deal with any perceived insult from the earl. The man has every right to be distressed about his son.'

'He would be exceedingly distressed if you told him the severity of the viscount's condition.'

'Be very careful, Miss Griffiths. You have too sharp a tongue. I cannot seem to convince you that the earl will not take a sanguine view of failure in the matter of his son's health.'

'He did not seem overly sympathetic to his plight.'

'That is not for us to say. I am sure he is concerned.'

'He was more concerned with how his son would look than how he would recover.'

'Miss Griffiths, that is enough. That spirit of yours will land you in all sorts of trouble if you cannot learn to hold your tongue. Now come along, I had better get you back to the sick room before you do any more damage.'

She is sorry she has made him angry – it was not her intention. However, once they reach the door into the gallery he turns and says, 'Perhaps you were attempting to make amends for your earlier remarks. It was valiant of you to come to my defence, but you must understand the earl has become extremely changeable of late. It is dangerous to speak out to such a man. Our situation here is precarious in the extreme.' She opens her mouth to justify herself but the doctor raises a hand to quiet her. 'No, I do not want to hear any more about it. Now, come along, I need to assess the patient.'

Chapter 16

'How do you feel, sir?' Dr Argyll says, seating himself on a chair beside the bed where Mordiford lies. He stirs and his lids flutter as he tries to open them, but a yellow rheum has built up, fusing his eyelashes together.

'Let me bathe his eyes,' Elen says. 'I think he battles to open them.'

'Very well.'

She goes over to the iron pot that stands on the hearth and scoops warmed water into a bowl. She dissolves a pinch of salt in the water; tears are salty, she thinks, this will be more comfortable than plain water.

When she returns to the bed, the doctor has taken hold of Mordiford's arm and is studying the pocks. Even the palms of his hand are now thick with scabs. She moistens a piece of cotton, squeezes it out and rests it on Mordiford's lids. His cracked lips move. She is certain he mouths the words, 'Thank you.' His lids open and she sees that the whites of his eyes are as red as a coot's.

'How do you feel, sir?' the doctor repeats.

'My life,' he whispers, 'is being pulled from me like a tooth.'

The doctor rises slowly to his feet. He stares down at Mordiford then beckons Elen away from the bed. She follows him over to the shadows on the far side of the room where they cannot be heard. A single candle gutters and dips in the stone alcove, throwing a sickly light onto the doctor's face. He is very pale.

'He has taken a severe turn for the worse,' he says, his voice almost a stammer. 'The fever has a putrid quality.' He moves nearer to her and whispers, 'I cannot see how he will survive the night.' Elen looks back at the poor wretch lying prone on the bed and does not believe him. His heart still beats, his lips still move, his eyes still open. The possibility of such a catastrophe has been with her all the time but still she is not prepared.

'Surely there is something we can do?' she says.

The doctor blinks rapidly, his eyes darting around the room. With a sense of rising alarm, she sees his panic. His breathing quickens. Beads of sweat ooze from his forehead. His hand goes up to his mouth and he brushes his fingers firmly across his lips. Elen grips him by the sleeve and gives his arm a shake to get his attention.

'We must soak him. Doctor, listen to me. You told me the story of the salted lake. Those men were close to death and yet by morning they were well.'

'It is impossible,' he says, his eyes staring past her, watching first the candle, then jumping across the room to the body of Mordiford. 'The steward says it is impossible. We cannot. Cannot.'

'Cannot what?'

'Do it. We cannot take him out of here. We would risk the lives of everyone in the house, in the county. We are incarcerated up here – and up here, we cannot submerge him. Mr Antrobus has said. It is impossible to get any kind of receptacle up that wretched spiral of a staircase. The earl will find out I have lied, think me a quack and a charlatan. We are trapped. Trapped up here and all we can do is watch him die. Watch him die, do you hear me?'

'We shall not watch him die. We must find a way to submerge him.'

'We cannot. All is lost.'

'Hush!' she says, looking over towards Mordiford. 'He will hear you.'

The doctor tucks his chin in and scowls at her, but she carries on. 'Doctor, listen to me. We must think of a way. It is his only hope.' She pulls the doctor over towards the fire and pushes him into the chair beside it. She pours a glass of beer, presses it into his hands and kneels in front of him.

When he stares at the flames, she rouses him by lifting the base of the glass towards his mouth until he takes a sip and then a draught. Finally, he gives a great sigh that shakes his whole frame. 'Yes, I am calmer. Thank you, Miss Griffiths. I am calmer now.'

All the while she watches his struggle, her mind is planning, skimming through ideas and solutions. One idea flashes brighter than the others and she grips him by the knee. 'We need canvas,' she says, 'a waterproofed canvas.'

'What? What for?'

'Canvas holds water.'

'I know canvas holds water,' the doctor says impatiently, puckering his forehead.

'We can bring a sheet of canvas up the stairs quite easily and sling it between the ceiling joists like a hammock in the bowels of a ship.'

'Why? What are you babbling on about?' and he claps a hand to his ear as if he wants to block out her voice.

'It is this that we will fill with brine. It is this in which we will soak him.'

The doctor's face creases, then the muscles relax with under-standing. He looks fixedly at her. Another thought seems to strike him and he frowns again, shakes his head. 'You and I will never be able to lift him,' he says. 'And I will not ask that scullion wench to help. She will not hold her tongue. The earl will know I am failing even before the viscount slips off this mortal coil.'

'You are not failing. We shall *not* fail. We can lay him on it before we raise it. We will fill it after it is raised.' The doctor shakes his head more emphatically, flaps his hand at her. He may wish she would leave him in peace, but she perseveres. 'We can do this, you and I. My father and I have raised the weight of a whole cow using nothing but a block.'

'A block?'

'Yes. A block. There is bound to be one here at the hall. For hauling grain or feed. We secure one end of the hammock to a beam and raise the other end from the floor with pulleys.'

'The weight of the water alone will bring the whole thing down.'

'Then we shall make it strong.'

'The water will chill him. The man will die of exposure.'

She nearly pinches him in exasperation. She presses her lips together to compose herself, and says, 'His fever is so high he will heat the water himself.' The doctor looks at her with some surprise. 'And we shall sling the hammock close to the fire,' she says. 'I shall keep the water topped up from the hot pot throughout the night and if, by morning, all has failed, at least we would have tried.'

'But it is madness to try...'

'It is madness not to, sir.'

Chapter 17

The last light of the afternoon is bleeding away when Elen reaches the minstrels' gallery. She peers into the great hall below. All was quiet. She takes the service stairs to the under-croft. She can hear the servants moving around in the common parlour and stands for a few moments listening out for Ned's voice.

Just then a pot boy comes out and she says, 'I have a message for the valet. Do you know where I can find him?'

'He's up in the steward's pantry, miss,' the lad says.

She finds Ned quite alone, cleaning boots. He glances up with an expression of indifference when she opens the door. Then his eyes widen and a huge smile spreads and opens his face.

He flings the cloth aside and jumps to his feet. 'Why, Miss Griffiths,' he says, his face tinged with a faint glow as if caught out by his own lack of guile. 'What a welcome sight you are on a dreary afternoon filled with drudgery.'

The pantry has a cheerful fire burning in the grate and is filled with the heady scent of beeswax and tallow. Closing the door as much as she dares without raising the suspicions of the rest of the staff, she goes and sits down next to him at the table.

'I'm afraid I have more work for you, if you will help me with a task.'

'Help you? Of course. How mysterious you are. What can it be?'

'Can you keep a secret? Oh, I know you can.'

'You have promised to keep my secret. How can I deny you the same privilege?' he says, drawing his chair closer to hers so that their knees almost touch. He wears a canvas apron over his shirt, the sleeves of which are rolled up to his elbows. She glances down at his forearms, at the silken hairs lying close and flat to his skin. She longs to reach out and lay her hand on his arm, to touch someone healthy and strong. Instead she leans a little nearer to him and says, 'You remember the doctor's request for a bath?'

'I do – and Mr Antrobus's opinion of the notion.'

'I have thought of a way to achieve it.'

Ned frowns. 'Why?'

She drops her voice and says, 'The viscount has taken a very bad turn for the worse.'

'Oh, I am sorry to hear that.'

'You do not sound it.'

'Do I not? You must let me have my little jest.' He lifts her hand and clasps it between both of his. She knows she should withdraw it but the dry warmth of his palms is comforting. 'So, how is this bath going to help the viscount?'

'The doctor believes that soaking him in brine will alleviate his symptoms.'

Ned drops her hand, throws his head back and gives a great bellow of laughter. 'These quacks. They have the most preposterous ideas.'

'Dr Argyll is no quack. He is well read and knows accounts of this treatment working.'

Ned shrugs. 'Very well. Who am I to disagree?'

'Will you help?'

'Of course. Haven't I said I shall?' He smiles at her with such warmth she cannot be cross with him for long. 'Tell me what you need,' he says.

'I believe that we can achieve everything the doctor requires by suspending a hammock between the beams of the chamber upstairs and filling it with water.'

Ned pulls a face of agreement and says, 'Yes. That would work, I am sure. There is a quantity of oilcloth down in the undercroft, rope too.'

'And a block and tackle?'

'A block and tackle? Great heavens, what is that man building up there? Noah's Ark?'

She pinches Ned on the thigh. 'Stop your teasing.'

Ned shrugs his shoulders and raises his palms in mock bafflement. 'A perfectly understandable observation,' he says.

'We shall need to lift the hammock, the water and the viscount. The doctor and I cannot do it alone.'

'Then let me assist. I can haul like a Black Horse.'

'I'm sure you can, but you know you cannot enter the sickroom. The doctor will not allow it.' She gives an impatient sigh and says with as much gravity as she can muster, 'You can help by finding me the things I need.'

'How serious you are.'

She nods. Ned watches her for a moment longer, still smiling. When she doesn't respond, he slaps his hands on his knees and pushes his chair away from her. 'For speed,' he says, 'I suggest we attack a different task each.'

He gets to his feet and unties his apron. 'I will take you down to the storeroom in the undercroft. While you hunt through the oilcloths to find one that is sound and of the right size, I shall hurry over to the stables and acquire a handful of stout pulleys.'

She gets to her feet and this time she reaches out and takes him by the arm. 'Oh, Ned,' she says, 'thank you so, so much. I don't know how I can repay you.'

'I will think of something,' he says, giving her a broad grin and a wink.

—

By the time Elen has scavenged all that is required, activities are increasing in the servants' quarters. The time of the evening dinner is drawing close. Despite this, Ned continues tirelessly to help. First he carries buckets of water up the spiral staircase and leaves them on the landing for Elen to take in and place in front of the fire. Next he hauls baskets of wood up so that the fire could be kept high throughout the night. He goes over to the kitchen yard and begs a tub of salt so heavy, Elen and the doctor have to drag it across the floor.

'Load the water with salt now, Miss Griffiths,' the doctor says. 'It can dissolve as we work.'

'How much should I add, sir?'

'We must make it stronger than sea water. Keep adding and stirring. When crystals sit in the base of the bucket and no longer dissolve, then the solution will take no more.'

Between charging and stirring the buckets, she works with the doctor, securing one end of the oilcloth to a low beam near the fire. Ned calls through the door that he is going over to the stables. He returns half an hour later with two stout pulleys and a length of chain. Elen hears the clatter of metal as he drops them on the landing outside.

'Tell that boy to get back downstairs,' the doctor says. 'He will be missed if he goes on helping. Questions will be asked.'

Elen slips out of the room. She can hear Ned making his way back down the spiral stairs and calls his name.

'I'm here,' he answers.

She finds him waiting a turn below, next to the alcove window where she placed a candle earlier in the evening. He looks tired and his shirt sleeves are grubby.

'You must be exhausted,' she says.

He pushes his hair off his face and laughs softly. 'Not as tired as you shall be by the end of the night. Are you sure the doctor won't let me into the chamber to help haul the hammock up?'

'He will not let you risk it. You have done more than enough for the viscount this evening.'

The flame of the candle beside them flares momentarily, throwing a warm light across his face. He leans a little nearer to her and says, 'You must know, I have done it all for you.'

'I know and I thank you, Ned.'

The air between them thrums with promise. Her nostrils detect the honeysuckle scent of cloves rising from his skin, mixed with the leathery musk of fresh exercise. She thinks for a moment that he means to kiss her and knows she will not be sorry if he does.

A latch clunks below. The door into the minstrels' gallery has opened. Joan's nasal voice calls, 'Ned? Are you up there, sir? The steward shouts for you.'

Ned rolls his eyes and sighs. 'Shall I return later?' he whispers.

'No,' she says. 'That would not be wise. I shall see you in the morning.'

'By which time we shall know.'

'One way or the other.'

'Good luck.' He touches his finger to his lips and is gone.

With a weary tread, she retraces her steps back up to the chamber. She feels utterly exhausted but knows there will be no rest for her tonight. When she opens the door, the heat of the room pushes out around her. Thick and foetid, it is heavy with the resinous smoke from the fire and tainted with the smell of sweat and sickness.

The doctor, who has discarded his wig and stripped down to his waistcoat and shirt sleeves, is standing on a bench, securing the pulleys to a beam on the other side of the fire. 'You are a country girl, Miss Griffiths,' he says. 'Tell me, have I understood the principle here?'

'No, sir. You have not.'

The doctor looks down on her in surprise. 'I have not?'

'No, sir. We must secure one of the pulleys to the hammock, fix a rope to the beam, bring it down to the hammock, round the first pulley and back up to the second one suspended on the beam. That way, we should be able to lift both hammock and the viscount off the floor.'

'Well, I can only be guided by your experience,' Dr Argyll says, untying his handiwork with an ill-concealed air of irritation.

Throughout their hours of preparation, Mordiford lies inert on the other side of the room, his eyes closed, his breathing coming in shallow pants. Periodically, Elen goes over to him and lifts a draught to his lips. Obediently he sips at the rim of the cup before letting his head drop to one side as if the effort exhausts him. She wishes they could let him lie undisturbed but she knows they cannot. His breathing is more laboured by the hour, his disorientation more pronounced. He may not live to see the dawn.

—

Eventually all is ready. The doctor checks his timepiece.

'It is ten minutes past six. We must complete the task before the earl dines in the hall below or the noise may alert him to the severity of the viscount's condition.'

'He will know that soon enough, sir.'

'Not if this treatment works.' The doctor hesitates, pulling on his earlobe as if he were milking a tiny udder. 'You are sure none but the valet knows of our intention.'

'None, sir.'

'Then let that remain the case. We must proceed with as much stealth as possible.'

She follows the doctor as he makes his way across to Mordiford's bed. She looks down on him and says, 'He is almost too sick to move.'

'Then we must get him to his feet and lay him on the hammock before he sinks deeper.'

Resentful of the disturbance, Mordiford makes a feeble effort to push them aside.

'Come along, my lord,' Dr Argyll says with sympathetic heartiness. 'Time to get you into the healing water.'

'Leave me, I beg you. You will kill me.'

'Quite the reverse. Up you come.'

Elen pulls his shoulders away from the pillows as the doctor takes his arms. They haul him into a sitting position. The doctor grasps him by the knees and swings his legs over the edge of the bed. Elen supports his back with the flat of her hand.

'A moment,' the doctor says. 'We must remove the bed shirt. It is easier to strip him here. Avert your gaze, Miss Griffiths.'

She puffs her irritation. 'You scold me one minute then try to protect my sensibilities the next, sir.'

'Oh, very well,' the doctor says.

Mordiford rouses himself. 'No. I beg you,' he says, flailing at the shirt as the doctor tries to draw it up and over his head.

Eventually Elen says, 'Tie the shirt around his waist at least, Dr Argyll. Save his modesty.'

'Nothing must lessen the strength of the salt on the skin,' the doctor replies irritably.

'Leave me be, you quack. You villain,' Mordiford bleats, although he's too sick to defend himself.

'Work the shirt down,' she says. 'You can slide it off when he's submerged.'

The doctor gives a nod of tacit agreement and helps her to lower the shirt over Mordiford's shoulders to his waist where she ties the sleeves to keep it in place.

Taking a side each, they prepare to heave him up. 'On my count of three,' the doctor says. 'One, two, three...' They haul him to his feet.

Mordiford's arm clenches involuntarily at her, his fevered skin is hot against her side where she is forced to press against him. Her back aches as she pulls. As his body rises beside her, she wraps her arm around his waist, feeling the flutter of his muscles as he tries to keep his balance.

Mordiford takes a faltering step forward. Then he stops and sways. Elen senses his weight rocking backwards, feels her own muscles hurt from the effort of keeping him upright. She thinks for a few seconds that he will swoon, taking them both down with him. His head lolls forward. The change of weight propels him onwards.

With the next step, he pinions the trailing bed shirt with his foot. The arms unravel and it flutters to the ground. Groaning feebly, he tries to bring a hand forward to cover himself but he is too weak to lift his arm from her shoulders.

She does, however, look away as she pulls him forward but in truth, she is certain that his skin is so stiffened and deformed by the pocks, any feature that may have intrigued or shocked her would be rendered quite neutral. She hears the doctor cursing under his breath as he kicks the shirt to one side.

Step by agonising step they make their way across the room. The fire is stoked so high that the heat in the room is unbearable, weakening her as she struggles. Her shoulder is drenched with Mordiford's sweat where his arm lies heavily across her.

Eventually they reach the oilcloth, spread across the boards in readiness. Carefully she helps to lower him. The doctor puffs and groans on the other side, bracing himself against the dead weight. Finally, they get him on the ground. Exhausted, she presses her hands on her knees to push herself up.

She can hardly bear to look down at the poor creature, twisting and squirming on the hard floor. She must remember that this is Mordiford, the man who squeezed her heart when he wept, the man she comforted when he was afraid. She must not allow the disease to make him less than human and steal away her compassion. The tall man she used to see cantering across the estate is still within that writhing body and no man deserves humiliation such as this.

She collects the bed shirt from the floor and drapes it across his hips, reaching out for the thickened hands that paw the air. He kicks weakly with his legs, threatening to rock himself onto the floorboards before they have a chance to haul him from the ground.

'Hurry,' the doctor says, waiting by the rope.

She rolls Mordiford back onto the oilcloth and steadies his shoulders. She dashes across to join the doctor, whipping the rope through the pulleys to take up the slack.

The end of the hammock leaves the floor. The ropes begin to creak under the strain. Together they pull, the chains above their heads swinging and clanking. She feels a sudden resistance – they are hauling the weight of the patient. A cry goes up from the hammock. A crusted hand grasps at the edge of the oilcloth as it folds around him like the pod of a pea.

'How far up shall we raise him, sir?' she says, panting now. She can feel the heat of the fire on her face. Rivulets of sweat tickle their way down between her shoulder blades and breasts.

A voice wails from inside the hammock, 'Help me! The world spins so. What's happening? Save me. I beg you.'

'A little further, I think,' the doctor says, his breathing laboured. 'The weight of the water will pull the hammock lower. We must counteract that. Oh, I wish he would stop that confounded noise.'

The pulleys squeak and complain, her hands burn with the effort. The doctor wheezes beside her, groaning with each pull on the rope. The voice from inside the oilcloth is now little more than a faint mewling. As the hammock swings before the fire, great shadows dance along the walls, distorting as they run over the rough stonework.

'Is that enough, sir?' she says, her voice straining.

'I think so,' the doctor pants. 'Can you hold it steady while I lash the rope to a beam?'

'I can for a minute, sir. Let me make it fast around my body.' Without releasing her grip, she holds the rope close to her waist. Slowly she turns until it is secured around her middle. 'I have it safe, sir.'

She takes the full weight. She feels the rope bite into her waist, her feet skitter on the floor boards. She watches until the doctor has the rope lashed to an upright and then spins herself free.

'Well done, Miss Griffiths,' the doctor says, bending forward with his hands on his knees to get his breath. 'I must say, you have a most surprising strength.'

The hammock swings gently to and fro before them, the base bowed by the weight of Mordiford. They can hear his mournful whimpers coming from within. The hammock has folded around him like a chrysalis. Elen hauls the bench over, climbs up and prises the edges open. She reaches inside and pulls Mordiford's elbow up and over the lip of the hammock.

'There, my lord,' she says. 'You can see the light again.'

'I am suffocating. The room is pitching. Help me.'

'That will not do, Miss Griffiths,' the doctor says. 'We must have his arms submerged when we fill the hammock.'

'He is afraid, sir. If he cannot see the room around him, he will panic.'

'That cannot be helped.'

'Unless he is calm, he will thrash around.' She looks about for a way to solve the problem. 'Let me brace the head end of the hammock with the bolster,' she says. 'It is packed with straw. It will not fold.' The doctor nods his agreement.

She hops down, fetches the bolster from the bed and, climbing back onto the bench, battles it into position while the doctor reaches in from the other side and supports Mordiford's head. Eventually, she manages to wedge it in place.

'There, my lord,' she says, placing a hand on the swinging hammock to still it. 'You look as comfortable as a cat.'

'Not for long,' the doctor mutters. 'Cats and water seldom make good bedfellows.'

Chapter 18

The doctor goes over to the fire, dips his finger into the warmed saline, tastes it and pulls a face. 'As salty as a cod's kidney, Miss Griffiths. Very well done indeed. Now, let's get this fellow submerged.'

Elen is about to get down from the bench when a hand shoots out with surprising vigour and clutches at her wrist. Mordiford looks up at her. His eyes are like strange jewels, blue sapphires set in lozenges of bright red coral.

'Do not be afraid, sir,' she says. 'You are quite safe. We are going to start filling the hammock with water.'

'No, I beg you,' he says. He grasps the edge of the hammock, trying to raise his head but his ordeal has exhausted him. She presses him back.

A chunk of hair has stuck in the serum on the edge of his lip. He blows at it, pawing his face and grimacing. She reaches inside and eases it free as he winces and groans.

'The water will cure you. We are sure of it,' she says. She may not believe it herself, but she cannot stand the thought of the poor man's final hours being full of fear. 'I will be here, with you, all night. And in the morning, when we bring you down, you will be well again.'

'You promise me? Elen, do you promise me?'

'I promise you,' she says, forgiving herself the lie. In her mind all she has promised is to stay with him through the night. For the rest, she cannot say. She is touched that he used her first name and wonders how he knows it.

When the first bucket of saline goes in, Mordiford begins a strange, high-pitched lament like the haunting cry of a curlew. Elen stops pouring, sees the doctor cocking his head towards the door in case the sound has travelled down the spiral staircase and into the great hall below.

She pours more slowly and Mordiford falls silent. The ropes creak and complain but hold. She hears a steady tap tapping on the floorboards. They have a leak. She climbs down, snatches up a knife and a candle. She dips the knife into the molten wax at the foot of the flame and holds it against the leak. It is surprisingly effective.

'You are an exceptionally resourceful young woman, Miss Griffiths,' the doctor says.

She leans her hand on the purlin and gives him a weary smile, glad of his recognition. By now every part of her body complains – her shoulders from lifting the buckets, her arms from hauling the ropes and her thighs from stepping repeatedly up onto the bench to pour in the brine. The palms of her hands throb, her feet throb. Her back aches. And yet, she must return to the task of filling the hammock, for the doctor tired long ago and has adopted the less strenuous labours of fuelling the fire and checking the water levels.

Eventually, when the water inside the hammock reaches Mordiford's chest, the doctor calls a halt. 'That is enough submersion, Miss Griffiths,' he says wearily. 'The greater part of his flesh is now under the saline.'

From her perch on the bench, she looks down into the hammock. Mordiford lies like a dead man, his head flopped to one side on the straw bolster, now sodden with brine. His naked body floats beneath the water, pale as a corpse, the ghost of the bed shirt shifting and reshaping on the surface of the water like a huge clump of frogspawn.

Elen pushes her hair from her face, her hands gritty with salt. She has a raging thirst from sweating so profusely and ingesting the salt on her lips and on her hands. She climbs down and lets the bucket drop with a rattle at her feet.

'Miss Griffiths,' the doctor hisses. 'Quiet, I beg you. If we are discovered now, we shall be accused of ending this man's life, not saving it.'

Elen takes a step back, looking stricken, but the doctor does not notice. So much for his earlier praise, she thinks. He disappears into the vestibule and comes out with his wig reinstated and his jacket on. He draws his watch from his waistcoat. Then she sees the outdoor cloak draped across his arm.

'Am I to stay with him alone?' she says nervously.

'Of course,' the doctor says, frowning at her. 'There is nothing more for me to do until the morning. It has gone midnight. Take the bed, Miss Griffiths and get some rest.'

'I cannot rest with that poor soul hanging there, sir.'

'You would be advised to try.' The doctor looks at her, his face loose with fatigue, waiting for her to voice a new problem. So many tumble into her head that she cannot speak. The doctor 'harrumphs' as if satisfied she has no further objections and says, 'We must pray with all our might that God sees fit to bring that poor wretch through and deliver him up tomorrow.'

'What time will you return, sir?'

'I shall be here at dawn, do not fear. We will lower him together.'

'And if he should die in the night?'

The doctor gives another puff, almost a laugh. 'Then we shall drain the water and leave him in his shroud. You will not have to do that task without me, I promise you.' He places his hand on her shoulder and gives it a squeeze. 'You have performed admirably tonight, Miss Griffiths. I could not have achieved this without you.'

Elen listens as he descends the spiral stairs. The door at the bottom slams shut. As the echoes fade, other sounds come to her: a crack and rustle from the fire, the somnolent creak of the ropes swinging imperceptibly.

She feels intensely lonely, more so than if she had been alone.

Elen gazes at the hammock, its massive shape unearthly in the guttering light. Steam rises gently from the surface nearest the fire, sweetening the foul air with the scent of linseed oil. It is strange to think her vigil tonight will be like an act of devotion, sitting with a loved one who has already passed from this life to another. She is gripped by a feeling of fear and melancholy that she doesn't altogether understand.

Cautiously she squeezes between the hammock and the hearth to put more wood on the fire. She checks for leaks, pressing her hands carefully on the taut fabric. It feels sweaty and warm, like the flank of a leathery animal. Manoeuvring her way back around the hammock, she climbs up onto the bench. Mordiford's head rests to one side on the bolster but his nostrils are clear of the water. She cannot tell if he is unconscious or asleep but she knows he is alive for his rib cage rises and falls, causing the surface of the brine to ripple.

The salt has crystallised, frosting the scabs and grizzling the hair on his chest. His hands float on the surface of the water as if he is resting them on the arms of a chair. His knees and feet almost break the surface. It is as the doctor described. The salt has made the water so thick it supports his body as if he were a weightless sprite, floating in the air, the pressure on his scabs and pocks relieved.

She climbs down and goes into the vestibule where she pours herself a large glass of water and drains it before rinsing her hands in the ewer. She loosens her bodice and runs a dampened cloth over her skin, leaving the air to dry and cool her. Finally she makes her way over to the chaise longue. Before she lies down she does one other thing the doctor has asked her to do. She kneels and prays.

But she cannot rest. It is impossible to ignore the helpless presence of Mordiford on the other side of the room, floating in the waters of his own personal River Styx, his helplessness as strong as a rock. She finds herself listening to his silences as one would a new-born baby whose rhythmic tides of sleeping and waking measure the night.

Sometimes she imagines she is about to slumber, then a tiny sound propels her back to the surface, sending her wearily to check her sleeping charge. Every time she mounts the bench, she expects to find Mordiford cold and stiff with death. Barely breathing herself, she watches until she sees the water level on his chest ebb as he inhales, inch back up as he exhales.

The heat becomes more and more oppressive, even the water in the pitcher, which she drinks frequently to slake her thirst, is now an unpleasant tepid. When the candles burn low she thinks that dawn cannot be far away. The notion increases her restlessness. She crosses to the window by the bed and peers out. All she can see is blackness, no moon, no stars, no dawn. She wants to go to the storeroom. The windows there look out towards the mountains.

The hammock hangs like a demonic fruit, huge and glistening in the pool of light from the fire, vapour rising up with the smoke from the candles. It emanates a strange, supernatural power, pulling her back, forcing her to look even as she slips behind the tapestry and makes her way to the door of the storeroom.

The long, low room is deliciously cool. She navigates between the ghostly shapes of furniture, her skin tingling as if one of the shapes may at any moment move as she passes. She reaches the window, struggles with the latch, finally freeing it and throwing the casement open.

A light frost pricks out the geometric patterns of the lawns and parterres below. She draws in a deep breath of cold air, and scans the horizon. There is no sign of dawn. Wearily she turns away from the window. Her eyes are well adapted to the low levels of light and she recognises the shape of a deep sofa beneath the dustsheets. She peels back the covering and feels the bounce of the springs with her hands. Overwhelmed with fatigue, she thinks it cannot hurt to sit for a minute in the cool air flowing down from the window and rest her eyes to rejuvenate her spirits for the last few hours of her vigil.

Chapter 19

Elen wakes with a start. She feels chilled and damp, her neck stiff where her head has been bent at an odd angle on the upholstered arm of the sofa. How long has she been asleep? She rises unsteadily to her feet, pulling the laces of her corset tight again, feeling her chemise cold against her skin. As she closes the window she realises the dove-grey light of dawn has reached the gardens below. She runs across to the door, struggles down the narrow passageway between the back of the hanging and the wall and bursts into the vestibule.

She stops. Someone is in the room beyond. The ropes of the hammock are creaking and straining. It is the doctor, she is sure of it, and he is battling to release Mordiford on his own. He has returned early in the morning, as he promised, and yet again he has found her missing.

Suppose Mordiford has died while she slept in the store-room? Suppose he has woken and slipped under the brine, too weak to care if he drowned? She screws her face up, momentarily wondering if there is any way she can flee and avoid the doctor's wrath, but she knows she cannot. She has to face him.

She steps into the room. The doctor is not there. Instead, she sees the hammock swinging and tossing, the ropes groaning under the strain. A great wave of brine sloshes onto the floor as it tips to one side. Another flops out on the other side as it swings, sousing the fire, which spits and roars in protest, sending huge clouds of steam into the room. She dashes over to still the crazy pendulum motion of the canvas, trying to catch it as it comes towards her. It strikes her with its full weight, winding her and pushing her backwards until her heel catches and down she goes. As it swings over her head and away again, the shape of a hand appears, pressed on the oilcloth, and further down, a foot bracing against the fabric. The hammock shudders and jolts. A pair of white legs appear, twisting and kicking to break free of the taut lip of cloth.

She clambers to her feet and, terrified that Mordiford is drowning, pulls down the edge of the canvas, soaking her clothes with another flood of brine. She reaches in and tries to grasp Mordiford's shoulders, but his skin is slippery and she cannot get a purchase. He splashes and struggles in a deadly silence. She presses on the side of the hammock with all her might, desperately trying to empty it, not caring if the water cascades between the floorboards to the rooms below.

But she cannot do it. Every time she presses the edge, the hammock swings away. Her fingernails, softened by the water, bend back on the rough oilcloth. With a cry she nearly snatches her hands away, but Mordiford's struggles are weakening. With a strength born of desperation, she pulls her body up over the lip of the hammock. Her feet leave the ground as the canvas swings towards the fireplace.

Elen grasps Mordiford by the head and, grunting with the effort, pulls and pulls. The swinging giddies her. With fumbling hands, she turns his face to the surface and he coughs and chokes, inhaling a mouthful of brine. He clutches at her hands as if he thinks she means to throttle him but she clings to his neck with all her might.

On the next back-swing of the hammock she grips his head to her breast and holds tight. When her toes touch the ground, she throws herself backwards, plummeting to the floor, bringing him, slithering and twisting, after her. They land in a great tidal wave of water. Her head hits the boards, the crack loud and jarring in her skull. She lies flat on her back, stunned, her arms flung out from the force of the fall. Mordiford lies across her, his head motionless in her sodden lap. The lake of brine flows away from them and across the room, blackening the floor, slinking down between the gaps in the wooden boards.

Elen pushes Mordiford's head up, stares into his face. Does he breathe? She slaps the flat of her hand across his cheek. He gives a great snort and pulls his head free, his eyes still closed and blind, his lashes rimed with salt.

Above the hissing from the drenched embers of the fire she hears voices, a shout from far away, down in the minstrels' gallery. Footsteps pound up the spiral stairs, the door latch releases with a clunk, and the door is flung open with a smash.

–

Cold air washes over her, chilling her wet clothes. The doctor's voice says, 'God's blood, what in the name of all Creation?'

Then Ned's voice and the doctor saying, 'Get back down the stairs, man. You are not safe up here. I will deal with this. Sort it out below as best you can before the earl gets wind of it.'

The doctor's feet pass her, heading for the bed. She pushes herself up onto her elbows as he snatches at the bedding.

'Get up, Miss Griffiths,' he shouts over his shoulder. 'Take this sheeting and catch some of the flood. It pours through the ceiling below.'

The doctor flings the bedding down beside her. He continues to tug a blanket free and tosses it over Mordiford, grasping him by the shoulders and easing him up.

She manages to pull her legs free and get to her feet, lifting her waterlogged dress with her hands. The doctor has Mordiford on all fours, his head hanging down, his coarse hair, spangled white with salt crystals, falling like a curtain over his face. He looks for all the world like Nebuchadnezzar, mad and prowling the wilderness. The doctor wraps the blanket underneath him and sits him back on his heels where he sways, threatening to tumble down again.

'I told you to wait,' the doctor says to her, his mouth tight with fury. 'What on earth put it into your head to do this without me?'

'He woke and was struggling, sir. He was trapped, drowning.'

The doctor surveys the wreckage of the room, shaking his head. She gathers up the sheeting he has thrown down and begins to push it across the wet floor.

'No, leave that,' the doctor says, his voice heavy with resignation. 'The water has drained away through to the gallery below. The damage is done. Help me here. We must get him over to the bed and dried before he chills.'

Elen does as she is asked. Floppy as a rag doll, Mordiford lays his arm across her shoulders. She feels her body compress under his weight. They navigate him across the damp floorboards to the bed.

'There, my lord,' the doctor says. 'A little stronger, I would say.'

'Am I?' he says weakly. 'I was afraid you had drowned me.'

'We did not – but now we must dry you,' the doctor says. 'And see how your pocks have fared.' The doctor patiently slides the blanket off Mordiford's shoulders and presses him back onto the pillows, pulling the cover up to his waist as he does so.

'My legs are all wet,' Mordiford groans.

'Miss Griffiths, I brought a quantity of towels from the private side with me.' The doctor nods over his shoulder towards the door. 'I dropped them in my haste. Be kind enough to fetch them for me, would you?'

Elen gathers up the towels. They are made of the softest linen, thick and the colour of cream, a fabric far too beautiful to use to dry oneself. She holds them to her cheek as she walks over to the bed, smelling lavender on the cloth.

The doctor has his back to her as he works. She feels a sense of abandonment, as if, despite everything she has done for Mordiford, she has been returned to her former station and is no more important than Joan or the pot boy.

'Thank you, Miss Griffiths,' the doctor says, shaking one of the towels out with a flourish. 'Here, take a towel. Dry his hands and arms – but carefully.'

Mordiford tries to shy away from her, giving her a petulant flash of his eyes. She stares back at him and grasps him firmly by the wrist. He pushes his bottom lip out, glaring back at her but she holds her ground until he sniffs and turns away.

In the morning light coming from the little window, she can see that the water has bleached and puckered his skin but as she presses the linen onto him, she notices that the redness around the pocks has gone.

'Well, my lord,' the doctor says as he works. 'Your skin is looking a deal better. How do you feel?'

'Everything feels gritty. I am abominably uncomfortable.'

'That is merely the salt crystallising. Once you are dry, Miss Griffiths can fetch you a fresh bed shirt and change the sheeting. You will be comfortable again.'

'And I am fiendishly thirsty. My throat aches from it.'

'Miss Griffiths, a draught of small beer if you would be so kind.'

Elen goes into the vestibule, returns with the jug. She fills a cup and holds it to Mordiford's lips but he reaches out and takes if from her, gulping at the liquid. He pushes it back at her, saying, 'Give me more.' He drinks again, holds the cup out again. 'More,' he says. 'That hardly touched my thirst.' He goes on gulping until she pours the dregs from the jug.

'That is the last of the beer, sir,' she says.

'Last of the beer?' Mordiford says. 'You mean to madden me.'

'Hurry down to the gallery, Miss Griffiths,' the doctor says. 'Ned and Joan were clearing up the mess. Send one of them quickly to fetch more beer. Viscount Mordiford is parched.'

She finds Joan on her hands and knees in the minstrels' gallery, blotting the floor with a dish clout. Ned is nowhere to be seen.

'Joan,' she says, 'please could you go down to the undercroft and ask the steward to send up some flagons of small beer?' Joan continues blotting the floor. 'Joan, did you hear me?'

Joan throws the clout down with a wet slap and climbs to her feet. The early morning sun falls on her face, throwing her scars into relief. Many have silvered over time, but the skin across her cheeks ripples with pits and troughs, thickening up one side of her nose, pulling her eyebrow down onto the lid below.

Had the maid's smallpox been more severe than Mordiford's? Or had the illness damaged her face so savagely because it struck when her skin was new born? Elen feels a flash of sympathy towards the poor girl and is about to give her a word of kindness when the maid's eye slides up, taking in Elen's soaked and filthy clothes and a contemptuous smile spreads across her face.

'Joan, did you hear me?'

'Yes, miss.'

'I think the doctor needs the beer now, if you would be so kind.'

'Right away, miss,' she says and saunters off, her feet dragging on each step like an insolent child.

When she opens the door at the far end, Elen sees her halt, drop her head bashfully and swing her body back and forth. Ned comes out carrying a bucket and mop. He says something to Joan, which Elen cannot hear, and the maid snorts and laughs, rolling herself round the door and disappearing. Ned looks up and sees Elen.

'Hello there,' he calls, hurrying along the gallery, the bucket clanking in his hand. He cocks his head back towards the service stairs and says, 'That Joan. She's a bit shook on me, poor old thing. Keeps her useful.'

'Useful?'

'You know, fetching and carrying and the like.' He smiles jauntily at her then pops his eyes and says, 'Tell me you don't think I've put those four quarters on the spit, do you?'

'No, Ned. I do not,' she says although she wants to laugh at his cruel metaphor. He drops his bucket and leans the mop against the railings, staring up at the ceiling. 'So, the doctor's scheme was not the sure card he'd been hoping for?'

'We cannot know yet.'

'Is that so? I thought flooding the gallery was a fairly good indication that the dart was a poor one.'

'The scheme with the hammock worked very well but this morning the viscount became so agitated that he brought the whole thing down.'

'I imagine you've had quite a night of it.'

'I have.'

'And your dress.' He reaches out and takes a pinch of fabric. 'You're soaked. Have you nothing to change into?'

'I have a clean chemise but in my haste, this is the only dress I brought.'

'Then I shall send a message to the dairy and ask one of your sisters to bring across another.'

'Thank you, Ned.' She smiles at him. It is so good to see his face after her interminable night. Reluctantly she says, 'I had better get back to the patient or I'll be in a bad loaf with the doctor again.'

'And I had better clear up this mess before the earl thunders up here.'

–

The doctor is busy with Mordiford and does not turn when Elen enters the sickroom. She has a strange feeling of anti-climax, similar to the way she felt at the end of harvest when the trampers and hop pickers moved on and there was little to look forward to until Christmas.

She wonders how long this flatness of spirit will last, if it will lift after she has slept. She presses her hands on the damp fabric of her dress. She will have to make do with it for the present.

With a sigh she kneels down in the grate and begins raking out the soaked ash. She rebuilds the fire and relights it, the crackle and flash of the flames cheering her, warming the damp air.

'Miss Griffiths,' the doctor says, 'I wonder if I could trouble you to fetch that fresh bed shirt?'

She takes one from the linen press and begins the task of taking down the oilcloth. As she works, she smiles to herself. She can hear Mordiford squabbling with the doctor as he tries to get him into the shirt. Eventually the doctor calls out, 'Miss Griffiths, a hand, please. If you could help me move the viscount over to the chaise longue, you can turn the palliasse and put fresh linen on the bed.'

'Leave me where I am,' Mordiford says.

'No, my lord. The bedding is damp and you were complaining earlier that the salt had made the linen gritty.'

'Why have you got to haul me across the room again? Am I not suffering enough?'

'How about the chair, my lord?' Elen says. She feels a strong urge to laugh even though she knows that would appal the doctor and enrage the viscount. She thinks it may be relief that makes her feel so light-hearted. She welcomes Mordiford's return to petulance. It is so much better to have him behaving badly than lifeless and close to death. 'I can bring it over to the bed, then you won't have to walk too far.'

'And have these pocks pressing into the hard wood. Are you quite off your hooks?' She has to turn away for she almost laughs out loud.

'Choose one or the other,' the doctor says irritably. 'Either way, I need you out of that bed. The sooner you do it, the sooner you will be back and able to rest again.'

'Rest? You think I can rest after the torment you have put me through? I fear if I sleep you will souse me in brine again.'

'Viscount Mordiford, I beg you. Find a modicum of pluck,' the doctor says.

'Or perhaps you plan to pickle me in vinegar tonight.'

Elen grips the inside of her cheek between her teeth. She finally gets herself under control for long enough to look at the doctor who catches her eye and raises an eyebrow.

'I am sure you will have a more comfortable sleep tonight,' he says, 'if you allow Miss Griffiths to change your bedding.'

'I need more beer.'

'Not until you have left that bed and allowed Miss Griffiths to do her work.'

Mordiford grudgingly permits Elen to help him over to the chaise longue from where he continues to harangue them while she strips the bed, turns the mattress and covers it with fresh linen.

The industry gives her a moment to compose herself. By the time she has the bed ready, Mordiford has exhausted himself, and sits staring sullenly at the fire. She takes him back to the bed and settles him down on a bank of pillows.

The doctor draws the bed curtain halfway across to screen him from the light and takes Elen by the elbow.

'I am sure he will sleep,' he says. 'He has sloshed enough small beer to render Hercules insensible.'

'He seems a deal livelier. Is the danger passing now, sir?'

'It is hard to tell. His earlier acrimony shows a certain improvement, but we are not out of the woods yet. He may well relapse. The next twenty-four hours will be crucial.'

The doctor leaves, promising to return at dusk. Elen finishes tidying the sickroom. On the other side of the room, Mordiford is quiet behind the bed hangings and soon she hears his breathing deepen as he falls asleep. She gathers up the equipment of the night and takes is through to the storeroom beyond.

She allows herself some time at the window, looking out over the estate. It seems months since she came to the hall, leaving her old life behind. She wonders how the dairy fares. How often in the past she thought her work there a drudge, now it seems a certain kind of freedom.

With a nostalgic longing she thinks of the comfort of resting her head on the flank of a cow as she milks her, and yearns to be able to ramble across the meadows with the herd again in the fresh air. She misses her evenings reading by the fire, Tad slumbering in his chair. She even wonders why she resented sharing a bed with her sisters when the soft smell of their sleeping bodies, lying undisturbed until dawn, would be a luxury.

A shout comes from the sickroom. He is awake. With a sigh, Elen makes her way back and retrieves a fresh flagon of beer. It is bound to be beer he's squawking for.

'I don't feel very well,' he says as she approaches, although he looks quite bright and alert.

'I know, my lord.' He glugs down another measure of beer then lies back, cradling the cup in his hand. 'Has my father sent word from London?'

'He is here, sir.'

'Where?' and he struggles to push himself higher on the pillows, looking around the room.

'No, not up here. But he arrived back at Duntisbourne yesterday.'

'Why was I not told?'

'Dr Argyll did tell you, but you were in a very crushed state indeed. I'm not sure you knew where you were.'

'I think I dreamed...' His voice trails off and he stares into the middle distance. Then he rouses himself and says, 'Does he know how ill I am?'

'You are better today.'

'It does not feel like it.' Mordiford looks at her and says, 'Is he exceedingly irritated that I am not well?'

She knows she should contradict him, but in all honesty, he is correct. Instead she says, 'He told us that Lady Arabella and her mother are deeply concerned about you.'

'Did he, now? Well, I cannot let them see me in this condition.' He flashes his blue eyes at her. 'Can I?'

'I would not recommend it, sir.'

He thumps the cup onto the table beside the bed. A drop of liquid leaps out, splashing the sampler covering it. Elen comes forward to rectify the spill. As she does, she is aware that his eyes are still on her.

'You are like a cat,' he says.

She stands, the spoiled sampler in her hand. 'In what way, sir?'

'In the way you pad around when you think I sleep. In the way you make yourself look comfortable, however unyielding a perch you sit on.'

He has discovered a truth about her. Her mam encouraged her to move as gracefully as possible. It is now second nature, yet he is the only person to remark on it. She feels a warmth towards him, but he swiftly pops her conceit. 'The most feline aspect of you,' he continues, 'is tricking me into thinking you are sweet and mild, then lashing out and scratching me.'

She shakes her head, smiling at her own stupidity for being duped. 'I have no idea what you are talking about, sir.'

'And yet you have done it, just a moment ago. You mean to soothe me by suggesting that the woman I am to marry worries day and night that I suffer. You let that warm glow begin to kindle in my breast, but when I express insecurity that her love for me may be compromised by my appearance, you lash out with a vicious claw and strike me down.'

'I am sorry you feel that way, sir.'

'Ha! But you are not sorry – you are merely sorry for the way I feel, which you imply is my fault. You have not apologised for insulting me at all.'

She sighs. He really is a most irritating man, but she is gratified that his spirits are on the rise.

'However many word games we play,' she says, 'I will not be encouraged to flatter you with half-truths.'

'Oh no. I have little fear of that.'

In the vestibule, she pours some water from the pitcher into the bowl in the washstand and squeezes the sampler in it to dilute the beer before it stains.

'And where did my father receive you?' Mordiford calls out.

'In the private apartments,' she replies, tilting her head over her shoulder as she works so that he can still hear her.

'Which room?' he says.

'The smoking room.'

'Is that so? And what did you make of that?' he says.

'It is an elegant room.'

'Elegant? Pah!'

She continues to squeeze and scrub at the stain. She knows he will not let the matter lie – like father, like son, he means to embarrass her.

'And what did you think of the decor?' he says eventually.

'Fine indeed.'

'Oh, come now, you know exactly to what I refer,' he counters in reply.

She wrings the sampler out and straightens it along the brass rail at the side of the washstand to dry. Wiping her hands on her apron, she comes out of the vestibule and says, 'I assume you want to goad me into an opinion of the tapestry.'

'Of course I do, although it would amuse me more if my father's attempt to discomfort you had gone unnoticed.'

'It did not.'

'Well, what did you make of it?'

'It is an impressive piece,' she says.

'You thought so? Do you know what it depicts?'

'I imagine it is a scene from mythology.'

'It is. Do you know the story?'

'I am not sure that I do, but I have a notion that you have determined to tell me.'

'In that, you are correct,' he says. 'The god Zeus was in love with Leda, the Queen of Sparta. Because she was married to someone else, Zeus came to seduce her in the form of a swan. She bore twin children from the union but she had the foresight to lay with her husband on the same night and bear a further two other children.' He frowns and says, 'I cannot remember the names of all the children. One was Helen. Castor and Pollux come into it somewhere.'

'Gemini,' she says, recognising the names.

Viscount Mordiford stares at her, but it is difficult to tell if he is surprised or affronted.

'Yes,' he says, with a look of suspicion as if she has tricked him in some way. 'I was going to suggest you go down to the library and find a book of myths, but it seems you know the story.'

'I had forgot it.'

'Or chose to forget it. I'll wager your ignorance of high art encouraged you to think the theme somewhat – how shall I put it? Salacious?'

'I'm sure that should I ever have the opportunity to travel to the Continent and see the art that hangs in the great houses of Italy and France, I would find images every bit as unsubtle.'

'Ha! I must agree with you there. My father's tastes can be...' He pauses, narrowing his eyes. A shadow passes across his face, which she cannot read. 'My father's taste could be described as singular.' And as he speaks the word, he raises an eyebrow and falls silent for a moment. Then he says, 'In fact, I am surprised that my father chose the smoking room in which to receive you. It is a place where gentlemen retire after dinner to converse without interruption from the ladies.' He continues to be thoughtful, adding quietly, 'I wonder...'

'Wonder what, sir?'

'Nothing at all. Now I am tired, so if you would be good enough to cease your prattling, I need to rest.'

Chapter 20

Joan comes slouching up the spiral staircase later that afternoon, carrying one of Elen's stuff dresses, along with the message that Elen's father has arrived to see her.

'My father?' Elen says. 'I thought my sister had been sent for to run the errand.'

Joan shrugs and pushes the dress towards her without a word. Elen slips into the vestibule to change, taking off her apron and mobcap. A skein of hair drops over one shoulder and she fights to pin it back in place, piling it up under her outdoor bonnet before picking up her cloak.

When she comes back out Joan has sunk into the shadows in her usual place. Mordiford calls to her, 'Miss Griffiths? Are you leaving me?'

She goes to him and says, 'For an hour, no more. Joan is here.'

Mordiford gives a grunt of resignation.

'You are feeling better, sir?'

He pushes his fists into the mattress, moving himself higher on the pillows. 'I am, as a matter of fact, but deuced bored. I was wondering... we spoke of the library earlier. Would you be good enough, on your way back, to hurry along there and find me something to read?'

'With pleasure, sir. What would you like to read?'

'Nothing too taxing.' He gives her a look she cannot unravel and says, 'Choose something for me.'

'I don't know your tastes, sir.'

'Nor I yours, but I mean to find out.' With that he closes his eyes and lifts a weary hand of dismissal.

When she reaches the undercroft, she sees the large frame of her father silhouetted against the low afternoon light slanting in through the small window in the tradesman's door. He stands half-turned from her, twisting his cap in his hands. He has not heard her approach and he seems more bowed than she remembered.

'Tad?' she says.

He turns. His face is full of worry. He comes forward, hugs her, holds her at arms' length to look at her, hugs her again and then withdraws a large handkerchief from his pocket and blows his nose loudly.

'Good grief,' Ned says, coming round the corner with a bunch of keys. 'You'll have the hounds baying for blood with a blast on the old horn like that.' Ned winks at Elen. 'It is a raw afternoon out there. Are you sure you wouldn't prefer to have a chatter in front of the fire in the steward's pantry?'

'Thank you, Ned,' she says. 'But I miss fresh air almost as much as I miss my father, and I would welcome the opportunity to spend an extra hour outdoors.'

'Very well,' Ned says, making his way up the steps to the door and standing to one side. Just before her father steps out, Ned catches him by the hand and shakes it firmly, saying, 'I will be busy with my duties later, but may I take this opportunity to say what a great pleasure it has been to meet you, sir. I understand now why your daughter is such an exceptional person.'

Knowing Tad to be a plain speaking man, Elen watches his expression to gauge his reaction, but he slaps the valet on the shoulder and beams with pleasure.

'Why, thank you, Ned,' he says. 'It has been a great pleasure to meet you, too.'

Once the path drops down out of sight of the lower windows of the hall, Tad grasps her hand and threads it through the crook of his elbow. There it rests as they walk around the frosted edges of the lake.

'I thought to see Libby this afternoon,' Elen says.

'Libby was sent for, but I came myself. You cannot imagine how worried I have been.'

'I have been well cared for.'

'Yes, oh yes, I can see you have. You look tired – but bonny nonetheless,' Tad says before clearing his throat and drawing himself taller. 'And the viscount?'

'He seemed improved this afternoon.'

'That is a relief. Indeed, it is.' He pats her hand where it lies on his arm. 'He is quite out of danger now?'

'He is not.'

She feels Tad's arm stiffen, his footsteps slow. 'But he will recover?'

'Dr Argyll cannot be certain at present.'

He turns to face her, taking both her hands in his, crushing her fingers in his fists. 'You know, he must live.'

'And I sincerely hope he will, but you of all people know how fickle such an expectation can be.'

'I have been so worried,' he says. 'These past weeks have filled my head with bees. I have no other trade but dairying. I am too old to start again. I think of us turned out of the farm, forced for a life on the road.'

'It is a worry at the front of my mind every day too,' Elen says.

Her father takes a deep breath and says comfortingly, 'I am greatly soothed now to see that you have at least one friend here to look out for you.'

'You mean Ned?'

'I do. He made a particular point of making me feel most welcome and, as he is clearly a great admirer of my daughter, I warmed to the young fellow immediately.'

'He has been most kind to me,' she says.

'And he is a fine-looking fellow.' Elen cannot control her smile any longer and, as it breaks across her face, she pulls Tad closer. 'I suppose he is bound to be connected with an equally pleasant girl,' Tad says. 'Someone who works at the hall perhaps?'

'Not that I have heard.'

'I see.' He gives her an inquisitive look.

'Oh, Tad, stop it now.'

They stroll on a little further before her father adds with sly insistence, 'Valet to the Earl of Duntisbourne would be a fine match indeed for a dairymaid. Oh, the stories I'll tell Libby when I get back home. She will be mad with jealousy and furious that she didn't bring your dress herself and steal a look at your swain.'

'Now, stop your teasing. I'll not have it. Swain indeed.' She shoves him gently with her shoulder and he laughs.

They saunter on in companionable silence. The clock in the hall belfry tolls three o'clock and the dimming light enhances the beauty of the winter landscape. Beyond the walls of the estate, blue smoke from the chimneys in the village climbs vertically into the still air. When they reach the crest of the hill, the lights along the lower windows of the hall are clearly visible, shining out in the gloaming.

'It's quite a place to spend a few weeks,' Tad says.

'It is a bleak place. Not a house to be comfortable in.'

'Not like Maes yr Haf.'

Elen smiles. Maes yr Haf was Mam's dream, a farmhouse on the west of the estate, large enough to be grand, compact enough to be homely. The timber-framed building and barns form a courtyard in a vale with arable fields sweeping down into the valley. Maes yr Haf was aptly named, Mam said, because the farm basked in its own *summer field*.

'Do you ever feel sad,' Elen says, 'that Mam never got her dream? That we never did quite well enough to get the tenancy at Maes yr Haf.'

'No,' Tad says with a chuckle. 'Your mam was a wise woman. She said dreams were free as long as you never fretted about not getting them. We were happy with the dairy. Who knows? If we'd been asked to take on Maes yr Haf, it may have been too much.'

They are nearing the end of their walk. When they reach the archway into the courtyard she stops and says, 'The doctor is a clever man, Tad. Yesterday I did think the viscount might die.' Even in the half-light she sees Tad start. She hurries on, '...and as I nursed him through the night, of course my worries ran the same course as yours.'

'Not without foundation.'

'Oh, I know. Had you come yesterday, I would have said the viscount was dying. Today I believe he will live.'

'And you must be safe, my darling girl.' He comes forward to kiss her but stops and says, 'Oh, I quite forgot. Libby asked me to give this to you.' He pulls a rough little pamphlet out of his pocket. 'It is a silly thing, folk tales she says. She thought it might amuse you.'

'Thank her for me, will you? And give them all my special love.'

—

As Elen walks back through the gloaming, she hears the sound of carriage wheels in the distance. Two, perhaps three vehicles are making their way along the edge of the lake, their torches muted in the failing light. They are on the road always used for visitors because it ensures that their first glimpse of the hall is of the impressive northern facade.

They are some distance away, but all the same, not wanting to be seen out in the courtyard when they arrive, Elen quickens her step. She taps on the door of the tradesman's entrance. Through the small window in the door, she spots Ned making his way along the corridor to let her in. In anticipation of the warmth within, she begins to take off her gloves. As she pulls the left one free, she becomes aware of a dull throbbing at the base of her thumb.

'Thank you, Ned,' she says, descending the steps. 'I saw carriages in the distance, coming this way. They will be here in less than ten minutes.'

'They've been expected for the past three hours,' he says, locking the door behind her. He looks very fine in his livery. 'Have you had an enjoyable afternoon?'

'I have, thank you.'

'What is it on your hand that you study so intently?'

'I don't know. I've hurt it somehow.' Ned holds up his lantern and together they inspect the heel of her palm. 'Now I recall,' she says. 'I drove a splinter in here a few days' past. I had quite forgot it.'

'That does look sore. Come, we must resolve it for you.'

'It's a nothing. You have guests arriving, you'll be needed soon.'

'Nonsense. There's plenty of time and that hand looks as angry as a hot coal. We need to see it in a better light.'

Elen follows him, all the while protesting. The undercroft is a hive of activity, servants she has never seen before hurrying up and down with armfuls of linen, scuttles full of firewood, crates of clanking bottles and trays of crystal glasses and decanters. Weaving his way through the mayhem, Ned escorts her up to the steward's pantry.

In this quiet backwater above the hullabaloo he sits her down beside the fire. He fetches a second lamp and, taking her hand in his, delicately runs his finger across the swelling. 'There,' he says. 'I can feel the end of the splinter. Your body is trying to throw it out.'

'The doctor will be here soon. I can ask him for advice.'

'For a splinter?' he says. 'I am sure there is no need to trouble him.'

Without releasing her hand, Ned hooks his foot around the leg of her chair, slowly drawing her towards him, watching her face all the while as a half-smile fights to conquer all of his face. His hand feels dry and warm.

He lifts her palm towards his mouth. She stares at his coarse hair, raked back and pinioned in the queue. Several robust wisps have broken loose. She wants to lift her other hand and smooth the strands back behind his ear but at that moment she feels the heat of his breath, the wetness of his mouth and the touch of his teeth on either side of the soft rise of flesh at the base of her thumb.

A dull twitch of pain tells her the tip of his tongue has found the splinter. He begins to suck, gently at first but as the pressure increases, his teeth bite into her skin. The pain is almost unbearable. She tries to snatch her hand away but then there is sudden relief.

Ned raises his head and plucks the shard from between his teeth, spitting discreetly into the fire beside them. The clinkers hiss. He holds the trophy up for her to see, the splinter, tar black against the lamplight.

'There,' he says. 'No need for the doctor at all.'

She tries to lift her hand away but he holds it a moment longer, planting a chaste kiss on the wound before releasing her. She looks at her reddened skin. She can still see the half-moon impressions of his teeth, framing the puncture wound and she smiles.

He lays the splinter on the linen napkin covering the table and says, 'That's a hefty mote to carry under your skin for all that time.'

There's a crump from below and the sound of a voice bellowing in the distance.

'I must get back to my patient,' she says.

'You always seem to be running away from me,' he replies, his tone still light and teasing.

'We both have our work to do,' Elen says. 'And I've been away from my patient for most of the afternoon.'

He sits back in his chair. 'I fancy you do not entirely trust yourself, were you to stay with me now.'

His guess is correct. He looks so appealing, the buttons and braids on his livery flashing in the firelight. His eyes burn from beneath his brow, the flames turning the irises to the colour of caramel. The candles gutter on the chimney piece, their wax glutinous in their holders and as he holds her gaze, his pupils seem to swell, wide and black.

The room is hot, very hot. Elen's head fills with the scents of tallow, of resin, of wood smoke and beneath those fragrances her nostrils catch a sigh of musk, heady and feral, pumping fresh from his skin.

As she rises to leave, her foot catches on the edge of her skirt, making her stumble. Ned is breathing heavily, his nostrils flared, as if he has run up a flight of stairs. As he rises to his feet, she moves behind the chair on which she has been sitting, clinging to the back of it to steady herself. He knows, she thinks, he knows exactly what I'm thinking.

Instead she says, 'I think I should go now.'

He comes round to where she stands, his head sinking towards a shoulder as he gazes at her. With a gentle but lithe movement, he slides his hand around her waist, letting it settle in the small of her back. Shame sweeps through her because she longs to bite the generous sculpt of his mouth, to press her teeth close to his blood as he has just done to hers. When the pressure of his hand begins to draw her towards him, she does not resist.

A clatter on the service stairs springs them apart and, covered in confusion, she bumps against the chair, grasping it with her hand.

Mr Antrobus strides into the room and says, 'Ah, you're back, Miss Griffiths. I need Joan as soon as you're ready to relieve her. Send her down promptly.' Mr Antrobus looks from one to the other before adding, 'Make haste. There is much to do before this evening's dinner.'

As Elen begins to ascend the stairs, she steals a glance back towards the steward's pantry. Ned is leaning with his elbow against the edge of the door, his hand resting on the crown of his head, watching her. The air between them pulses with an understanding that an opportunity, although missed this time, needs to be resolved in the not-too-distant future.

Chapter 21

Elen is surprised to find Mordiford no longer in bed, but sitting on the chaise longue with his legs kicked up, idly watching the flames of the fire. He has got himself dressed in his breeches and undershirt, topped with a plain wool waistcoat. Although his face is still badly scabbed and marked, much of the swelling has subsided and he seems greatly improved. Beneath the crusts she can make out the broad forehead and the straight, strong nose she admired in the portrait. On hearing her footsteps he looks up, his face for a moment unguarded. In the permanent twilight of the candlelit room, there is pleasure in his eyes, a smile beginning on his lips.

She returns his look with a gentle smile of her own. It brings him abruptly to his senses. He knits his brow, looks away and scowls.

'You are dressed, sir.'

'It seems I am.'

As soon as Joan has slumped away, Mordiford swing his legs onto the floor and says, 'The chill of the evening air has done you good, Miss Griffiths. You have an exceptionally high colour.'

'You are right, sir. I have enjoyed my walk,' Elen replies, although she doubts her high colour is due to the fresh air.

'And how was your father?'

She frowns at him, unaccustomed to this civility. 'He was well, thank you, sir.'

He looks at the scruffy chapbook that she holds and says, 'And what have you chosen for me to read?'

She has forgotten. The interlude with Ned has quite distracted her. She feels a jolt of frustration that she has lost a chance to please Mordiford.

Unclasping her cloak, she says, 'Oh, not this, sir. This is just a silly thing my sister sent over for me to read. Give me a minute to change from my outdoor things and I will go down to the library directly.'

Mordiford looks exceedingly cross and says, 'You forgot? The minute you left this room, you dismissed me from your mind. Here was I, exhausting myself by struggling into my clothes with no help whatsoever from that useless girl, so that I could sit for an hour in front of the fire and enjoy my book. I may as well have lain moribund in my bed.'

'I did forget,' she says, irritated by his unnecessary drama. 'But as a reward for the effort you have made, I'll go directly and return forthwith.'

Before he has a chance to remonstrate, she drops her cloak and bonnet on the floor where she stands and quits the room.

She hopes to find Ned, but Mr Antrobus is in the steward's pantry, decanting wine over a candle, watching for the moment when the sediment appears illuminated in the neck. She waits until he whips the bottle upright, leaving an inch of dregs at the bottom before asking the way to the library, explaining that she is on an errand for the viscount.

'You'd better go along the staterooms,' he says. 'No one's down yet but be quick and don't go nattering to any of the maids. They've work to do.'

In the staterooms, the footmen are lighting candelabra and the maids are busy with the fires. Despite the fires' merry crackle, the rooms feel clammy and cold. Nevertheless, they look magnificent, the ornate-looking glasses and polished tables reflecting the candlelight, the rich damask draped around the windows, glowing with luscious splendour. The glass drops of the chandeliers flash as they gently twist and turn, throwing light across the high ceilings.

The corridor stretches ahead and as she leaves one stateroom, she is immediately in the next – this one a kingfisher blue with bright ornaments and bronzes, fabulous marble statuettes on the chimneypieces; the next has elaborate tapestries hanging on every wall.

She is now alone and slows her pace, wishing she could spend more time looking at the treasures that cover the tables – the silver boxes and glass vases, the beautiful bowls and jugs. What must it be like to be accustomed to rooms such as this?

She catches sight of herself in a looking glass, her willowy frame, her thick hair escaping from her cap, that little mole at the corner of her mouth that makes her seem as if she's smiling, even when she's trying to frown. She tucks a couple of fallen curls behind her ear and turns sideways to inspect her figure. If only she had Libby's curves. Unexpectedly, she thinks of Lady Arabella. Perhaps she has curves. Perhaps she too has studied herself in this pier glass, knowing that one day all this will belong to her – the vases, the porcelain, the paintings and, yes, Viscount Mordiford. Strangely the thought causes her to sigh, very faintly, before she carries on.

–

The library is not as brightly lit as the staterooms. One or two candelabra burn on low tables, deepening the shadows in the recesses of the long room. Her nostrils catch the scent of tobacco smoke and she peers into the gloom, worried that someone is there. All she can see are walls of books stacked on ornate wooden cases. The furniture scattered down the room appears to be unoccupied. She wishes she had brought her own candle or lantern – the lettering on the spines is hard to read in the low light. The first few shelves contain books in a foreign language, French perhaps, or German. There is another shelf of ecclesiastical tomes, their huge spines ribbed and embossed. The next shelf is filled with books on law, another on natural history.

She lingers on the shelf of travel books: *The Travels of Sir John Chardin in Persia and the East-Indies*; *A Voyage to East-India*; *Coryat's Crudities*, wondering if something here might interest Mordiford. She finds shelves of Shakespeare's plays and although she has read many with her mother, she moves on. She takes down a copy of *Pilgrim's Progress*, but returns it to the shelf thinking that such a journey may depress Mordiford.

Halfway down the room the gloom deepens despite the large fire that is burning in the grate. A large armchair stands before it, with the back towards her. She is on the point of taking down *The Tragedy of the Dutchesse of Malfy*, when she stops. A plume of smoke is rising above the back of the chair. She is not alone.

'Don't stop on my account,' a voice says from the recesses of the chair and a tall figure rises up from it. It is the earl.

He is dressed in a full-length robe of purple velvet, the gold of the heavy brocade glinting in the light of the fire. Instead of the fine wig he wore when last they met, he has an embroidered cap on his head, which has the effect of elongating his face. He places his clay pipe onto a dish on the chimneypiece and comes towards her.

'What, pray, are you doing down here in the library?' he says. 'Are you not meant to be caring for my son?'

'He's asked me to fetch a book, my lord.'

'Has he now? And what book have you been asked to fetch?'

'I am to choose something, my lord.'

'Is that so? Well, you can't see much in this light.' He sets off down the gallery, his robe hissing along the floor.

Taking up a candelabrum, he returns and holds it in front of her. He stands so close she can smell tobacco on his breath, mixed with a tang like over-hung game, the sickly scent of rose water coming from his robes.

Lifting the candelabrum higher he says, 'You're a handsome thing, aren't you? Not to everyone's taste – too thin, too tall. Unusual though. I imagine you might flick up rather well, should you choose.'

She stares back at him with bold insolence, her interest piqued by his eyes. She thought they were pale blue, but the candlelight reveals a milky film partially obscuring their true colour.

Her gaze discomforts him. The vulgar smile on his face fades and he takes a step back. 'Now that's a contemptuous way to stare,' he says. 'You'd better watch your step, miss. Someone might enjoy taking you in hand and taming that spirit of yours. Be thankful my son is not yet full of vigour or you might regret your decision to stay up there unchaperoned.'

'I should return to the sickroom, my lord,' she says, backing away in disgust.

'Not before we have found a book for Crispin,' he says. To her horror, he grabs her by the wrist, forcing her to follow. 'Now, let me see,' he says, moving along the shelves, every now and then rolling a jaundiced eye towards her. His palm is clammy, his hold so tight it pinches. 'Oh, yes, here,' he says. 'This is the one I search for.'

Releasing his hold on her, he draws down a small volume. He studies the spine and licks his lips, an unpleasant smile distorting his mouth. '*The Unfortunate Florinda* by Lady Hester Pulter. I am sure Crispin will enjoy revisiting this little romance,' he says, passing it to her. 'Be sure you read it to him. Run along now.'

He turns away and heads off down the library, the flames of the candles bending towards him.

Her heart bumps in her chest. The earl's attentions repulse her. She even feels angry with Mordiford for sending her on the errand in the first place, although she knows this is a ridiculous fury. If only she'd remembered to come to the library earlier, she would have had the room to herself.

She thunders up the service stairs, taking two steps at a time, but when she reaches the minstrels' gallery, she recoils – she can hear the unmistakeable voice of the earl below. He must have made his way along the statue corridor to the great hall as she was scurrying in the same direction through the staterooms. She approaches the railing with great care and looks down.

The earl is almost directly beneath her and he is in conversation with none other than Ned. She draws closer to the edge, hoping to hear better, but they are too far below her and the echo carries the words away. The earl is clearly giving instructions, but instead of Ned's usual confident swagger and gaze, he seems slumped. He appears to try to reason with the earl who wags a cautionary finger at him before disappearing in the direction of the private apartments. Ned stays where he is, staring down at the floor.

Elen calls him softly. He turns and looks up, his face is a study of misery.

'Ned,' she says, beckoning to him, 'are you in trouble?'

'No,' he calls back, shaking his head and giving a sniff. 'No trouble.'

'Then come up here and tell me why you look so chapfallen.'

'Nothing would give me the keenest pleasure,' he says, briskly resuming to his usual manner. 'But the earl has given me a sheaf of orders and demands for this evening. We have additional guests just arrived. Three carriages. I must take these orders down to the steward or I shall be in trouble.'

'Until tomorrow then?'

'Tomorrow?' he says, his tone cautious again.

'Our walk. Surely you will be free for our walk tomorrow?'

'Oh, yes – tomorrow, in the morning. I was quite at a loss. I have much to think about. Yes, we shall walk tomorrow, of that I am sure. Until then...' He backs away a few steps before turning and disappearing beneath the gallery.

Chapter 22

'Come, Miss Griffiths,' Mordiford says, getting to his feet and momentarily resting a hand on the chimneypiece to keep his balance. 'I am agog to see what volume you have chosen for me.'

She hesitates, looking down at the book in her hand. 'I was not at liberty to make a choice, sir. Your father was in the library.' Does Mordiford take a sharp inward breath? 'He chose this for you,' she says, holding out the book.

He walks over to her, his steps a little slow, but strong and steady. He takes it, returns to the fireplace, and holds it up to the candle to read the title.

'Good God,' he says under his breath. He remains stock still for all of a minute, staring into the fire before turning to her and saying, 'I have been thinking, is it not time you were hastening back to your family? I am so much recovered today except for these wretched scabs. I do not need you loitering around here any further.'

She rolls her eyes, frowning at his rudeness. 'I'll leave when the doctor tells me I can, sir. Clearly you are a deal stronger than you were, but you're infectious until your skin clears. You need someone to tend you.'

'I have Joan to run and fetch for me. I do not need you.'

His manner is so light, his words so blunt, a stubborn irritation wells up inside her. She puts her hands on her hips. 'I suppose that now you're feeling better and bored, you return to your favourite game of baiting me.'

Mordiford throws his head back and laughs. 'You are right, Miss Griffiths. I am damnably bored. Bored with seeing your face day in and day out.'

'You are very rude, sir.'

'Would you like me more if I were polite?'

'Probably not.'

He tosses the book onto the table and, picking up a lamp, heads towards the vestibule. With a sigh, Elen collects a candle and follows. He's been out of bed for less than a day. He could swoon and hurt himself. When he reaches the edge of the wall hanging at the back of the vestibule, she calls after him, 'You're not sufficiently imprudent to fetch that looking glass, are you, sir?'

'What is it to you if I am?'

'The doctor thinks you do yourself a disservice by studying your face before the disease has run its course.'

He stops, leaning back against the wall. 'Is it better that I trace these crusts with my fingers, rendering them larger and more disfiguring than they could ever be in nature? Why, I imagine I have the face of Shakespeare's Caliban, "A freckled whelp, hag-born, not honoured with a human shape."'

'You're certainly freckled, but you are no whelp. I can assure you, sir, the sickness has not robbed you of a human shape.'

'Well, that is a relief,' he says, his voice heavy with sarcasm. He slips around the hanging, which lifts like a wave as he moves along behind it. She's sorely tempted to leave him be, but when she hears the door into the storeroom open, accompanied by a gust of freezing night air, she follows.

The room is clamped with cold. Mordiford weaves between the pieces of furniture, the sleeves of his shirt white as a ghost in the darkness.

'Come back into the warm, sir. It is as cold as the grave in here.'

Mordiford ignores her and moves around the room, lifting one or two of the dustsheets. He slides the drawer of the desk open. Is he going to take out the looking glass? No. He sweeps his hand around inside, shuts the drawer and opens one below. He turns to her and says in a voice of genuine enquiry rather than mockery, 'Someone else has been in here. Have you been asked to move things from this room?'

'No, sir.'

'Then who has?' he says roughly.

'I don't know for certain. I think Joan may have moved some things.'

'Why?'

'I am not sure. She denied it when I asked. I assumed they were needed for the current festivities.'

'Were they, by God?' He goes over to the window where a bloom of frost ferns spreads across the glass, sparkling faintly in the moonlight. After struggling for a moment with the rusted latch, he throws the casement open and takes in a deep breath of the night air. Then he stands on his toes and peers down over the edge.

She comes up behind him in case he tips out, but on hearing her approach, he drops back heavily onto his feet and turning says, 'I see the candles are burning along the west wing. How many people are here tonight?'

'Two gentlemen and a lady arrived yesterday and apparently three carriages this evening. It's very busy. The rooms in the south wing have been made ready for guests and the great hall is being set for a dinner.' He does not respond. 'In fact,' she presses on, 'as you are feeling so much recovered, I wondered if I might not slip down to the gallery later this evening and see the spectacle.'

'You must not.'

Elen is taken aback by his sincerity of feeling. He quickly changes his tone and adds with familiar contempt, 'How like a servant to want to go squinting and spying. You would only embarrass yourself if you were caught trying to watch them at private dinner. No, you must promise me you will have no involvement whatsoever in anything that happens in the hall over the next few days.'

'How can I promise such a thing when I may be asked to help, sir?'

'You must refuse.' He comes forward, and takes her by the wrist. Unlike the iron grip of his father, his touch is firm but not harsh. His expression, however, is one of earnest entreaty. 'Promise me.'

She slips from his grasp and takes a step back. 'I promise I will do nothing to embarrass myself or the family – that is all.'

His body slumps a little and, turning away, he begins to lift the dustsheets until he uncovers a sofa.

'I need to sit,' he says, sinking down and placing the lamp on the floor. 'Will you come and sit with me?' Before she has the opportunity to refuse, he continues, 'It seems I cannot shame you into doing as I ask, so sit with me and I will explain.'

She wonders if, having failed to bully her into submission, he is attempting a more devious approach. She frowns her indecision, but he meets it with a straight and honest look. 'Please,' he says with complete candour.

She throws back the rest of the sheet and takes a seat at the opposite end of the sofa. There is a table underneath the sheet next to her and she sits her candle on it. Mordiford leans forward and rests his elbows on his knees, looking down at the palms of his hands, examining the scabs by the light of the lamp. 'Everything would be so much simpler had I not succumbed to this wretched disease,' he says. 'It has trapped me here and you along with me.'

'Our incarceration is a temporary one.'

'But the timing could not be worse.'

'If you refer to your ambition to join the army, I understand but fail to see why it affects me.'

'Because of them,' Mordiford says, pointing a finger towards the casement windows.

'Your father's guests?'

'Do not make the mistake that because those people hold high office at Court, they are of high moral standing. Nothing could be further from the truth. My father is a weak man and has fallen in with a bad lot. Go down there and you put yourself in danger.'

'Why would I be in danger?' Elen says.

'Ah! Now that I have put my cards on the table, you want to draw a compliment from me. You want me to say you are in danger because you are so pretty. I shall not.'

'I want no such thing,' Elen says, laughing at the absurdity of the conversation.

Mordiford gets to his feet and paces around the room. 'Why do you have to be so contrary? Believe me and stay up here in safety.'

'I do believe you, but I think you are exaggerating the threat. I promise I will not spy on their dinner, but I must be allowed to come and go as I always have.'

He stares down at her for a few moments, then he snatches the lamp from the floor and stalks out of the room.

—

She finds him in the chair by the fire, scowling at the glowing embers. 'Build this fire up. It is nearly burned out and I am cold.' She takes the last two logs from the basket and pushes them into the grate. 'That's not enough to revive it,' he says. 'Put more on.'

'There is no more, sir.'

'God damn it! Why hasn't that wretched girl replenished it?'

'I expect she's busy with the dinner. I am sure she'll be along by and by.'

Elen settles down on her chaise longue. She waits to see if he has more to say but presently takes up the chapbook her father brought for her. She tries to concentrate on her reading, but Mordiford's mood fills the room with tension. Every now and then a particularly loud bellow of distant laughter can be heard in the distance.

The fire blazes merrily for almost an hour but the wood is dry and soon burns down. Mordiford fidgets in his seat, then goes over to the door and opens it. Another gust of laughter booms from below.

'Listen to them guffawing as they stuff their faces,' he says. 'Are the servants not even going to feed me? Am I to stay here, freezing to death and dying of hunger?'

She lays her chapbook aside and says, 'Why do you not let me go down and see what's happening? I can make you ready for bed, where you would be warmer, and I can fetch up a tray.'

'No.'

She returns to her chapbook. Their stand-off continues for another hour.

Eventually, Mordiford goes over to the bed and retrieves a blanket. He returns to the cooling grate and tucks the blanket around his legs with unnecessary drama, grunting with the effort. Elen wonders if his fiancée has seen this side of his character, his petulance, his ill-humour – or does he reserve it exclusively for her?

She continues to read. She hears a clock strike eleven and feels her lids getting heavy. She must have dropped off to sleep because she is woken by Mordiford shaking her shoulder. 'Wake up,' he says. 'It is gone midnight.'

'Would you like me to help you get ready for bed, sir?'

'No. I am cold and hungry, I will not be able to sleep. That blasted girl has not come back.'

'What do you want me to do?'

Mordiford opens his mouth to speak, but closes it again. He paces over to the door and unlatches it, listening at the gap. 'It is quiet out there. You will have to go down and see what you can find. But don't talk to anyone.'

'I thought you did not want me to.'

'For the love of Judas! You have made your point, have you not? Just get downstairs and find me something to eat. Fetch me some liquor too. That will have to suffice to warm me since I do not suppose you can struggle up here with firewood.'

'I could try, sir.'

'Oh, do not put yourself out on my account.'

Chapter 23

All is dark and quiet when Elen steps onto the gallery. A faint glow comes up from below and, concealing herself in the shadows, she peers over the railings into the great hall. The dining table is in disarray, the chairs pushed back as their occupants quit them. Light still comes from the fire, although it has been left to die down. The candles drip and gutter on the branching candelabra.

Bright against this darkened backdrop is a magnificent arrangement in the centre of the table, rising out of a silver basin. At first she imagines it is fashioned from white flowers but when she looks with more concentration, she realises it is constructed from the whitest, largest feathers she has ever seen.

Confident that the diners have quit the hall for the night, she steals along the gallery and makes her way down the service stairs. She finds the scullery empty of people and assumes that the servants have been dismissed until the morning. The table where she takes her breakfast is covered in the detritus of the evening's festivities. To her frustration she can see no unfinished dishes of food. They must have been transported back to the kitchens. She's about to give up her search when she spots a heel of cheese and a chunk of bread on the sideboard by the back door. She smiles as she tucks these into the pocket of her apron. Mordiford will have to chew on the food destined for tomorrow's pig swill.

Unsurprisingly, the alcohol proves a greater challenge because the steward locks it away last thing at night and it is not her place to wake him at this hour. Then a thought strikes her. As the evening has gone on long enough for the staff to be dismissed before the table was cleared, wine may have been left in the great hall.

She creeps up to the steward's pantry, pausing for a moment in the doorway to check that the corridor to left and right is empty. A cool draught moves the air past, scented with tobacco. Perhaps a guest is taking a final pipe before settling down for the night.

Her eyes are well adapted to the half-light now. A fat moon rides high in the sky, bathing the great hall in a cold blue light. Moving along behind the oak pillars, she nears the dining table and is on the point of stepping out onto the tiles when she hears the sound of a door opening on the opposite side of the hall. She slides around the pillar, back into the shadows, her heart knocking on her ribs, mindful of Mordiford's warning.

Voices come across the open space towards her. A group of men file into the hall in twos and threes. She cannot make out their faces. They are swathed in hooded cloaks. Each carries a white napkin in his hand, which they drop onto the table.

They seem to be waiting for someone, because they mill around, making desultory conversation, about what she cannot tell because they talk in hushed voices. Then the confident click of a leather sole across the tiles heralds the arrival of another man who strides towards the group, his cloak eddying around him.

'I have news, gentlemen,' says a voice, unmistakeably the earl's. 'You shall not be disappointed. It has this very minute been confirmed. Our leader will be prepared and waiting for our tableau tomorrow night after dinner.'

The men thump their gloved fists on the table, others clap and a few give muffled guffaws of excitement.

'But which of us has the expressible pleasure of being the first devil to perform?' says a man with a strong French accent.

'We draw lots, my dear Comte.'

'But surely,' another gentleman says, 'this cannot be right. Does only one of us enjoy the pleasure of our leader?'

'Not at all,' says the earl. 'Once the tableau has begun, audience participation is fully encouraged.' The men mutter and shuffle around, one clenching a fist here, another slapping a companion heartily on the shoulder there.

'Now,' the earl says. 'We draw.' From beneath his cloak, he produces a handful of swan's feathers, which he fans apart with the vanes uppermost. Each man comes forward and makes his choice as the others gather around, murmuring commiseration or cheering success as a longer quill than the last is freed. When everyone has chosen, they hold them together in the centre for the earl to judge.

'It is a close run race,' the earl says, 'but the longest feather has been drawn by...' He grasps one of the wrists, holding it and the feather aloft. 'Louis-Antoine de Noailles.' A muffled hoorah, tainted by a modicum of regret, rises up from the remainder of the group.

–

Long after the figures disappear and the footsteps die away, Elen stays in the sanctuary of the shadows where the darkness gathers in drifts. The minutes tick by and still she does not move. A door closes in the distance with a bump, a tinkle of laughter comes from a room far away. Out on the estate an owl hoots.

She told Mordiford his fears were unfounded. Why then is she transfixed to this spot with anxiety? It is probably better to face Mordiford's anger for failing to bring back liquor than to step out into the great hall – he did, after all, beg her to stay away from the earl and his friends.

She must get back to the sanctuary of the sickroom. She prays she doesn't meet one of the guests in the corridor. Earlier, when she made her way here, she was certain the household slept. Now she has no such confidence. And given Mordiford's vehement warnings, she is afraid. Have the revellers gone to their beds? Perhaps, but she cannot be certain. She has an overwhelming desire to use the quickest route up the central staircase.

As she stands in a bind of indecision, the moon passes behind a cloud and the light in the great hall dims. Here is her opportunity. She darts out from between the pillars, moving swiftly and silently across the tiles towards the bottom of the great oak staircase. The shadows of the pillars lie like black rugs across the floor and as she reaches the first step, one of the shadows curdles and moves. She claps her hand to her mouth to muffle a shriek. A figure steps from the gloom.

Chapter 24

Something about the man's gait relaxes Elen's shoulders. She slumps against the bannister as he approaches. 'Ned,' she whispers, 'you gave me such a fright.'

He takes her by the arm and draws her to sit on the step of the staircase, taking his place beside her. 'What on earth are you doing creeping around down here?' he says, his voice quiet but by no means secretive.

She looks over her shoulder, her eyes scanning the blackness. 'We're not safe sitting here, Ned. They may return.'

'They will not, trust me. I know how these evenings run. But I still don't know why you're down here spying instead of taking care of your patient.'

'I was not spying.'

Ned chuckles and pats her hand, but does not reply.

'I had to come down,' she says. 'The viscount's been raving and demanding food and drink. We have been quite forgotten up there this evening. I came down hoping to plunder some leftovers from the banquet, but they all flooded back in here. Ned, what are these men doing? Why were they dressed as they were? I was frightened half to death.'

Ned shakes his head, laughs softly. 'It is just one of their many fantastical and foolish traditions. You know what these old families are like. The knights like to dine in the great hall on their own, then they don their outdoor cloaks, pick up their napkins and trek a good league around the outside of the hall. They come back in through the undercroft and up the stairs in the east wing to take dessert with the ladies who have dined in the lower dining room in the west wing.'

'How extraordinarily complicated.'

'I suppose it is. The Knights of St Sebastian enjoy such distractions.'

'And what about the feathers? Why were they drawing lots with feathers?'

'Some bizarre parlour game, I would imagine,' he says airily. 'It's not our place to ask too much. We are here to stay out of their way, clear up behind them and keep our mouths shut. Now,' he says, getting to his feet and helping her up. 'Let us see if we cannot find you a dram or two of spirit to soothe your difficult patient.'

Making his way over to the table, he takes up a crystal decanter, removes the stopper and sniffs the contents. 'This will do,' he says. 'Fancy a little settler?'

She creeps over to join him as he pours the black liquid into two glasses, holding one out towards her. 'Will we not get into terrible trouble?' she says, her eyes darting around the hall. She feels vulnerable surrounded by so much space, so many shadows.

'Trust me, no one will come back here tonight. They will all be far too distracted with their game. Come, it will do you good. Your face is glowing as white as an apparition.'

She takes the glass and lifts it to her lips. It smells rich and powerful, as if the essence of a plum pudding has been squeezed into the glass. When the sweetness hits her tongue, it tastes as smooth as a mouthful of cream, and as she swallows, the liquor warms her chest and rushes straight into her cheeks and her fingertips and toes.

Ned watches her over the rim of his own glass. He raises it to his lips, narrows his eyes as he takes the first sip, tilting his head back with a little sigh the moment he swallows. 'You must own it,' he says, 'that is the most delicious thing you've ever tasted.'

'It is.' She smiles back at him before taking another sip.

'I cannot let you take the decanter. You may be accused of pilfering and that would never do,' he says. 'Come on, we shall take this back to the pantry and find an appropriate receptacle for you to bring to the viscount. Or perhaps he will have fallen asleep out of boredom and you can finish it yourself.'

'I wouldn't do that.'

'I would.'

He takes the glasses and decanter and sets off towards the servants' quarters, calling softly for her to follow. Her fears are soothed by his confidence. When they reach the steward's pantry he puts his load onto the small table in front of the fire, takes a spill from the chimneypiece and pushes it into the embers of the fire before lighting a candle.

'Sit down. Enjoy your port,' he says and, picking up the candle, he begins to search the cupboards until he finds a pewter flask. He draws a chair up beside her.

'How much do you think the greedy boy would like?' he says, beginning to pour. He stoppers the flask and places it in front of her. Holding the decanter up to the candle he says, 'Hardly any point keeping this last bit. We may as well drink it.' He fills both glasses so full, she fears she may not be able to bring it to her lips without spilling it.

Sitting back in his chair, he gazes at her. He has shed most of his livery except his waistcoat, which is unbuttoned, and he has loosened his neck stock. Catching a glimpse of the olive skin beneath his throat, she looks down to hide her smile.

It is cosy sitting in the candlelight. The wine has rushed to her head, so much so that when he reaches across and takes her hand in his, she feels a tremor run through her body. She looks up at him. His eyes glow in the candlelight with such heat that when he rises to his feet, she follows as if in a trance.

He is going to kiss her. She has wanted him to from the moment she first saw him. His arms fold around her with suppressed strength. The kiss is surprisingly gentle. His lips taste sweet from the port. Her senses fill with the scent of his skin and the vanilla of the wine.

After a time, he draws back, bringing his hand from behind her head and cradling her cheek in his palm. 'Meet me tomorrow night,' he whispers.

'Where?'

'Away from the hall. Every minute I'm here with you, I fear we will be discovered. I want to spend time with you – not a moment snatched here, a kiss there, always looking over my shoulder. I want to savour you, delight in you. Meet me tomorrow night.'

'But where can we meet where we will not be discovered?'

'I've been thinking about that. I think of little else but you. There's an old ice house out on the estate. It's not far from here, but it is quite abandoned. When they dammed the river and filled the valley, the ice cellar flooded, but there's a room in the building above. It's a beautiful place, looking right out across the water. Slip away when Mordiford sleeps and meet me there. I will bring us a picnic, maybe some port. We will have a midnight feast. Say yes, Elen, please, say yes.'

He brushes his lips across hers. When she murmurs her assent, he silences her with another vanilla kiss.

Chapter 25

'Until tomorrow,' Ned whispers in her ear before melting away into the darkness of the minstrels' gallery. Elen makes her way up the spiral stairs, her head light with wine and the passion of his kisses. She screws up her face as she twists the latch. Opening the door, she peers into the room. All is quiet. She slips her shoes off and tiptoes in her stockinged feet.

The hangings around the bed are half-drawn. Mordiford has taken himself to bed, his breeches and waistcoat slung carelessly across the floor. He lies on his back, his hand against his cheek, his face peaceful with sleep.

She puts the port on the table beside him in case he wakes in the night, then moves stealthily back across the room to the chaise longue. Loosening her bodice, she pulls a quilt up over her legs. Tonight, the sound of the wind moaning around the building is like a lullaby. As it plays, she runs through the events of the evening, conjuring up the feelings Ned incited in her. She has known infatuations in the past, even a stolen kiss with a lad who caught her during the midsummer revels, but she has never felt such vivid desire. She knew by the way he trembled as he held her that he was controlling his passion. For the whole of their heated embrace she never once felt alarmed.

Her thoughts begin to fragment, dipping in and out of a dream state. She sleeps soundly for the rest of the night, floating back towards consciousness in a similarly languorous way. In those ethereal moments before fully waking, her mind revels in the dreams that came to her unbidden in the night. The kisses, the trembling embraces, the delight of knowing that someone, somewhere in this vast building cherishes and desires her.

Suddenly she sits up, fully awake, jarred into consciousness. The arms that held her were stronger than Ned's, the chest she rested on, broader. She draws forth the face of the man who has been her dream companion through the night. She remembers his look of desire, the smouldering intimacy of secrets that only they share. The eyes are not a tawny gold like Ned's. They are blue. To her horror she knows that the man who held her in her dreams was not Ned. It was Mordiford.

She flees from the sickroom the moment Joan arrives. When she takes her place at the breakfast table, she catches Ned's eye. He looks troubled and she feels ashamed, as if he has guessed that she has been unwittingly faithless in her dreams. The notion is foolish, but the aura of the dream still has her in its spell. Her subconscious has played a trick on her. It has snatched at the feelings Ned roused in her and given them to another man while she slept.

She glances again at Ned. He smiles at her but his eyes lack intimacy and warmth. He looks regretful, sad even. As breakfast reaches an end, he leans across her on the pretext of collecting her bowl. 'I shall have to forgo our morning constitutional today,' he says quietly. 'I have much to organise in order to leave myself free this evening.'

She nods her understanding, feeling a glow of excitement. How foolish she has been to worry about the dream. Ned's are the only arms she wants around her. What a shame she has to wait until this evening.

On her way back, she passes the looking glass at the foot of the stairs, placed there to facilitate a final check on correctness before serving the family. She marvels at the change in her appearance. A lightness shines from her as if her skin has acquired a deep glow of health and her eyes have the lustre of jet. She fingers the tiny mole at the corner of her mouth — perhaps it really is a beauty spot.

'It was good of you to eventually return last night, Miss Griffiths,' Mordiford says, dressed now and seated by the fire. 'How satisfied you must have been to see that I did not need strong drink to make me sleep after all. To be perfectly frank, the time it took you to collect it would have rendered a dead fish inert.'

'It was no easy undertaking to find liquor after the servants had retired for the night, sir,' she says, busying herself with some pointless task to avoid looking at him, certain that those penetrating eyes of his can guess her dreams, the mood of which still pinches and teases her. 'But by good fortune Ned Harley was abroad and eager to help.'

'I would imagine he was,' Mordiford says, raising a sardonic eyebrow.

He watches her with an uncertain look on his face. She wonders if the change she saw in the looking glass is visible to the entire world.

'You are back up here a deal quicker from breakfast this morning,' he says. 'I thought you were in the habit of taking a constitutional around the lake of a morning.'

'I am, but today has dawned bitterly cold.'

'Do the cows in your father's byre go un-milked when the morning is cold?'

'They do not.'

'Then a sharp frost seems a poor excuse for a dairymaid to miss her morning walk. Has there been a lover's tiff between you and the valet who, I understand, has a habit of accompanying you, much to the consternation of that foul creature who takes your place when you are out and about amusing yourself?'

She pauses momentarily in the folding of a napkin and looks at him. 'You are feeling brighter, sir.'

'I am. And you are feeling cussed, I see.'

'Perhaps I find your censure uncalled for.'

He sits forward in his chair and looks up at her from under his brow.

154

'I feel too well for complete sloth,' he says. 'Yet not fit enough to embrace a more challenging pastime. What you see as censure is in fact nothing more than a forlorn attempt at stimulating a little conversation to fill these idle hours.'

'By vexing me?'

'Come now. If you intend to play the victim, you cannot win. My crusted face and body are powerful reminders that there is only one poor soul in this room who can claim that title.' He makes a small flourish with his hand and dips his head as if taking a bow. 'But as I have failed utterly to animate an interest in a subject that pleases us both, I am content to hand the floor over. What shall we talk about?'

'I am heartened to see that you are feeling a deal recovered for I have seldom known you so loquacious, sir.'

'My, that is a long word for a dairymaid.' She tightens her lip and glares at him. He raises a hand in submission and says, 'I apologise, but I am intrigued. Where did you find your learning?'

'You already know that, sir. From my mother.'

'That does not completely answer my question, but perhaps you have learned "obfuscation" too.'

'If I have, it could only be from you.'

'Ah, Miss Griffiths. How I shall miss these little duels when my skin is clear enough to face the world again. But tell me truthfully, where did you learn to read and write and debate with such skill? I have never met a woman with such quickness of mind.' Not even in your fiancée? she wonders. 'You surely didn't acquire these skills from reading those grubby chapbooks you seem so enthralled with.'

'I've told you, from my mother. She was charity-school educated and sought the post of private tutor to Lady Ludlow's children.'

'Did she indeed? Then she may well have taught my cousin, Arabella.'

155

'I think not, sir.' If she had, Elen thinks, perhaps your fiancée would be equally as entertaining. 'Her time at Ellesmere House was short lived.'

'How so?'

'Because of her association with my father.'

'I see. She sacrificed a life of ease for one of drudgery.'

'I am not sure I would describe the life of a private tutor as easeful, and my mother certainly would not have called her married life a drudge.'

'But a sacrifice, none the less.'

'She did not think so.'

'Was she happy?'

'Exceptionally.'

'Even though she married so much beneath her social status?' Elen stops fussing with the napkin and gives him a withering look.

'Oh dear,' he says merrily. 'I seem to have tainted the conversation again.' He sighs and looks up at the ceiling. 'What shall we talk about now?'

'My appetite for discourse has quite dropped away, sir.'

'Come now, don't be peevish with me. I am content to own that I have not behaved fairly. I offered to throw the floor over to you, but strode in just the same and steered the direction of our exchange. However, let me set that to rights and give you my solemn pledge that you can take the reins and I shall follow.'

He sprawls back in the chair, throwing one arm over the back, and sits with a composed expression on his face. When she does not speak he says, 'Any subject you like – proto-utilitarianism, the orderly cosmos, rational theology. Just name it.'

In order to bring an end to his mockery, she says, 'How about architecture?'

'That is a capital notion. Have you a taste for the Baroque or is your inclination firmly entrenched in the Rustic?'

'I believe there is an ice house on the estate, is there not?'

The ludicrous expression of interest that Mordiford has adopted falls away and he says sharply, 'The ice house? Why do you wish to know about that?'

'I did not query your desire to insult my family a moment ago, therefore I do not think you have the right to question my curiosity.'

'You are absolutely correct. The ice house – what can I tell you about the ice house? It stands on the shore of the lake at the point where the water from the River Lugg is diverted to flow into the valley, the idea being that ice from the river could be stored beneath the ground and used during the hot summer months.'

'I don't need a lecture on the concept.'

'Well, of course you don't, how foolish of me to underestimate your understanding. So, what else can I tell you about it? That a foolish countess, a century ago, had it built with a room above it in which she intended to entertain guests. One can only assume these were guests that decency did not allow her to entertain at the hall.'

'Indeed.'

'When it was complete, she admired the fine view across the lake but refused to use the room. Apparently she took a vehement dislike to the trees on the escarpment pressing down upon it from behind, a geographical feature she had failed to notice earlier, despite the fact that the woods had been there for hundreds of years.'

'It was abandoned?'

'It was. A subsequent incumbent decided to increase the size of the lake by several hectares, and so dammed the river up by the Crud y Gwynt gate, flooding the valley along with the underground ice chamber. And that, Miss Griffiths, is about everything I know of the ice house. Why have you suddenly shown an interest in it?'

'For no reason at all other than to give you some other topic to worry at.'

'You are conscientious to a fault, Miss Griffiths. Everything you do is apparently for the benefit of your patient. How do you manage it?'

'By reminding myself that my patient's enthusiasm for verbal sparring is a confirmation of his improving health and thus an indication that mercifully the end to my duties are in sight.'

'Touché, Miss Griffiths – touché.'

Chapter 26

The moon is riding high, fluttering a ribbon of quicksilver across the surface of the lake. The night is fine and bitterly cold. Elen does not mind. She is wrapped in her thick wool cloak and walking fast, feeling the blood coursing through her body, hot and vital. It is not just the cold that makes her speed along. She needs the vigour of exercise to unravel her conflicting emotions. She knows it is reckless to agree to such a liaison, and yet it is the thought of the danger that spurs her on, just as a high cliff draws one to the edge, an invitation to flirt with catastrophe.

An internal dialogue runs through her head, justifications taking the form of words that she may say to a parent or concerned friend: 'Ned has always looked out for me,' and, 'It is because I trust him that I hurry along to meet him tonight.' Another emotion seethes below these justifications, one that she is not so eager to put into words. She wants Ned to take her just a little bit further than she has ever gone before, his strength and fervour enabling her to abandon the high morals that have been drummed into her from childhood. She does not quite define what she means by this, and feels a niggling sense of wantonness that doesn't sit comfortably with her, and yet she is elated to be free from the sick room, free from Mordiford's piercing scrutiny, free to meet with the one person she has longed to see again all day.

Her soul fills with the beauty of the night. The earth beneath her feet is hard as iron from the frost, except when her steps stray onto the grass, crunching the petrified stalks like straw. The whispers of the countryside are all around, the distant bark of a dog in the village, the chatter of a rill of water running beneath the crusts of ice at the margins of the lake. The air is so still and the water in the centre of the lake so calm, she can even hear the faintest sounds of revelry coming from the hall.

She rounds a curve in the lane and sees a dim light glowing at the foot of the escarpment. Although the forest creates too dense a shadow for her to make out the shape of the building, she knows that the light glows from the windows of the ice house. Ned is there, waiting for her.

The light disappears as an unseen tree or crop of land comes between her and the building. Amplified by the still surface of the lake, the sounds of the revellers seem to increase in volume as if they have flowed out of the building. She imagines them sweeping outside in their capes, their napkins clutched in their hands, as they stumble around the building in search of the ladies already seated for their dessert. As she nears the end of the lake she can just make out the silver glint of the tributary that feeds it. Buried into the triangle of land between the shore and the river, the domed roof of the ice house frames the oak-mullioned window, which glows a welcoming yellow.

She reaches the door and taps gently, the sound loud in the night air. Footsteps cross the wooden floor. A moment later the door opens, golden light flooding out, and Ned's warm dry hand takes hers and leads her into the room.

She steps into a magical space. Every alcove and beam in the long, low room throngs with lighted candles that flicker and dance before stilling as Ned closes the door behind her. There is no fire lit, but the candles are so numerous, the room is heavy with heat. A table is set near a window that occupies most of the east wall of the building, the oak mullions framing a magnificent view across the lake. She can no longer see the moon for it has risen high in the sky, but the silvered path it creates seems to lead directly towards the ice house.

An ornate crystal candelabrum is set on the table, a dozen candles burning on the branched arms. The flames flicker on the bevelled drops of glass hanging from the gilt ware. Next to the candelabrum stands a pot-bellied decanter heavy with rich, red wine, the facets of the glass creating patterns of scarlets, vermilions and blacks in the dancing light. There are silver plates of sweetmeats, bonbons encrusted with sugar, squares of marshmallow, dusty with sweet powder. How has Ned managed to spirit these beautiful things away from the hall?

Apart from the table, there is no other furniture in the room, for the rest of it is taken up by a platform of deep straw, the sweet smell of it filling the room. Layers of damasks and silks have been laid over the straw creating a dipped centre like a huge feather bed, stretching from wall to wall. Bundles of dried reeds and bulrushes stand around it, giving the appearance of a four poster bed.

She cannot believe a man has put so much industry and imagination into creating such a place, and all for one woman – herself.

'Ned,' she gasps, 'however long did it take you to dress this lovely room? And how have you managed to bring all these treasures from the hall?' He silences her with a rough kiss.

'I have longed all day to do that,' he says, releasing the clasp of her cloak, peeling it back from her shoulders and letting it fall to the floor. He lifts her bonnet from her head, tossing it away.

'You have the most beautiful hair,' he says, his hand searching for pins until the thick braid at the back springs free and tumbles down. 'Let me unwind this for you.'

She tries weakly to stop him but feels soothed by his touch, his fingers raking the braid apart, fanning her hair out across her shoulders. He stands for a moment and admires her, then takes a few paces to the back of the room, sitting down on the platform of straw and patting the place at his side as an invitation for her to join him.

For some inexplicable reason, she is seized with awkwardness. Last night she melted into his embrace, but there is something too contrived, too planned about this. It has robbed her of impulse. She is overwhelmed with coyness. She stands on the spot where he left her, twisting her fingers together. Ned tips his head to one side with a perplexed expression, then jumps to his feet and goes to the table.

'Port,' he says, raising the decanter to her. She thinks his glance flashes towards the window as if he is not completely confident they will remain undiscovered. 'Port is what you need. You've had a cold walk and it has quite shut you down.'

He pours them both a glass and hands one to her. 'You enjoyed it so much last night, I managed to acquire another bottle.' He takes a mouthful then bends and places a single kiss on her lips. She tastes the wine on his mouth and as his hand cups her chin, she is relieved to feel the excitement from yesterday returning. She raises her lips to meet his, but instead of kissing her, he lifts the rim of his glass to her mouth.

'Drink, my darling,' he says, 'and let the wine relax you.'

She drinks, but he tips the glass too much, making her gulp. Some of the sweet liquid runs from the corner of her mouth. She feels a flash of anger, but he releases her and runs his finger across her chin, gathering up the rivulet of wine and licking it from his finger. 'I want to drink you up. Not all at once but sip by sip,' he says, taking her by her waist and pressing himself against her.

She lets him kiss her again, before gently freeing herself so that she can take another draught of port from her glass. She has promised herself so much for this evening. She wants to relax, wants to show Ned that she is happy and excited to be here, and that she appreciates all the effort he has gone to. She dashes the rest of the glassful back and puts it on the table.

'Goodness. I cannot keep up with you,' Ned says, refilling her glass. He picks up a sweetmeat and holds it towards her. She smiles at him and opens her mouth. He lets the bonbon hover over her lips before resting it gently on her tongue. As she closes her mouth to eat, he traces her cupid's bow with the tip of his finger, his breath coming in shallow pants of concentration.

When she swallows, he takes hold of her, placing his glass on the table and gently relieving her of her own. She reaches up towards him and puts the flat of her hand on his chest to give herself a little breathing space.

The strength of his embrace and the rush of strong wine have made her giddy. She can hear the revellers in the distance. 'Are we quite safe here?' she says. 'Are you sure we will not be caught?'

'Quite sure,' he says, his voice muffled as he kisses her throat and neck, his tongue sampling the sugar that has spilled from the sweetmeat onto her skin. And yet… something isn't right. Instead of that sweep of helpless delight, she feels the oddest urge to flee.

Chapter 27

Elen no longer feels safe. In the steward's pantry Ned seemed to be in complete concord with her, so much so that she wanted him to take command and release her from the responsibility of censoring her own lust, but now, in this hot, low room by the lake, they seem strangers.

His fingers are tracing the top of her bodice, dipping beneath the neckerchief in an attempt to loosen it. She does not understand herself, but she knows with sudden lucidity that tonight is not the night she wants to be taken any further.

'Ned, wait,' she gasps between kisses. 'Please wait. I feel uncomfortable. I shouldn't be here.'

'Of course you should.' Again, she is certain he looks towards the window. He seems on edge, as if he is not wholly present. Could he be feeling as nervous as her?

'This is the wrong time – for both of us,' she says.

'No, it is not. It cannot be more right,' he says, sweeping her up into his arms and carrying her towards the back of the room. Kneeling with one leg on the straw, he lays her gently on the damask. She struggles lightly to sit up, but he presses her back with the weight of his body, pushing her head against the shoulder of his encompassing arm as he kisses her.

From their elevated position, she catches a glimpse of the lake through the window. As Ned continues to caress her, she is distracted by something glittering out in the darkness. She squirms to get a clearer view. Lanterns are moving between the trees along the margins of the lake.

'Ned... wait. Stop. People are coming.'

He turns a fraction, shakes his head and begins to kiss her again. She insists, pushing him away and sitting up. Sliding off the straw she goes over to the window.

The lights are closer now and she can just make out the shape of figures. In the stillness of the night she can hear chanting. The words make no sense. 'Temptation into not...' the voices chant, before the sound dips out of earshot, only to rise again, enabling her to catch: 'Everyone forgive ourselves...'

She's heard that phrase before: 'Everyone forgive ourselves.'

A noise behind her makes her turn. Ned is at the door. 'I've heard those words before,' she says, 'the words they are chanting.'

'I should think you have.'

There is something odd about his expression, a mixture of excitement and regret.

'I heard Mordiford say them when he was mad with fever.'

'Ah... did you now?' Ned seems momentarily distracted, but then he gives a sly laugh and says, 'You've probably heard the pastor saying them more often – "For we ourselves forgive everyone who is indebted to us. And lead us not into temptation."'

As she stares at him, trying to understand, his hand reaches up and slides the bolt of the door across. She does not know if he is locking someone out or locking her in. 'It is the Lord's Prayer,' he says. 'Only backwards.'

'Whatever can you mean?'

Behind his expression of bravado, a struggle rages. 'I am sorry, Elen,' he says, a crack of regret thick in his throat. 'But what could I do? I thought you safe from him. Willowy is not to his taste. I had you all to myself until you goaded him. You shouldn't have provoked him. I never wanted to acquire you. Not for him.'

'Acquire me?'

'You heard their plans last night. Why didn't you flee? I wouldn't have stopped you. Not then.'

'I heard...' she tries to quell the rising waves of fear, to clear her head and remember exactly what she did overhear last night. 'No, all I heard was that they had found a leader.'

'Yes. That Leda is you. They're coming for you.'

She frowns so hard, her head aches. She cannot understand. Her eyes dart around the room looking for a way to escape. She stares at the platform of straw. With a mounting sense of panic she realises it no longer looks like a bed. It looks like a giant swan's nest amongst the reeds.

–

'If I've been condemned to be Leda in some malign entertainment,' Elen says, her voice wavering as she backs away from Ned, 'who intends to take the role of the swan?'

'Thank God you know the legend. That saves me a job,' Ned says before grinning at her in an apologetic way. 'Truth be told, there is a whole flock of 'em on their way.'

'Ned, for the love of everything decent in this world, let me go.'

Ned shrugs his regret. 'I cannot. The earl would punish me most grievously.'

'How could you lead me on and make me think you cared for me?'

'Oh, I do care for you – just not quite as much as I care for myself.'

She goes to the window, checking over her shoulder to see if Ned will stop her, but he merely watches her struggle with the casement for a few moments before picking up his wine.

'It will not do you any good,' he says. 'It is a nasty drop.' The casement flies open. She gasps as the icy rush of air flows in. The candles jump and sputter, sending jagged shadows dancing across the ceilings and walls. 'Besides,' he adds, taking a gulp of wine, 'they're almost here.'

The words are barely out of his mouth before a chorus of honking starts up from the woods below. Three or four men come into view, staring up at her, their companions hooting as they rush to join them. She can tell by the way they jeer and jostle that they are all very drunk. They tumble into one another, fighting for position at the vanguard as they stumble towards the ice house.

They are hunting in a pack, she thinks, and I am the quarry.

'They mean to kill me,' she says.

'No, no,' Ned says. 'Of course they do not. If you were dead, the sport would be over.' He drains his glass and cocks his ear towards the open window. 'They're nearly here. We had better get you ready.'

'Ned. Stop this madness. I beg you,' she says, pushing as far away from him as the room will allow. He doesn't come towards her. He moves to the door, watching her all the time. The moment he throws the bolt, she races at him. His outstretched hand clutches the top of her arm, the momentum of her dash swinging her round against him, momentarily winding her.

In the confusion, she sees a flash of dirty apron. Someone slips through the gap in the door. He slams it shut and pushes the bolt home.

He shoves Elen back into the centre of the room. As she rights herself, she looks up. Joan is standing beside him, staring at her with an expression on her face of such malice, she doubts her entreaties will help. All the same, she has to try.

'Joan,' she says, her voice tight and shaking with desperation. 'Help me. As one woman to another, do not let this happen to me. I would never let this happen to you.'

Ned throws his head back and roars with laughter. 'Happen to Joan? Of course it would never happen to Joan. Look at her.' Joan gazes lovingly at him, her mouth hanging open.

He chucks her under the chin as you would a child, and says with an infantile murmur, 'But you like to watch, don't you, Joanie? You like to see what posh men and pretty girls do at night in their bedrooms.' Joan snorts and nods her head. 'Go on then, get her onto the straw.'

Joan grasps Elen by the elbows. The maid may be weak in intellect, but she has a powerful grip. Elen struggles against her but Joan presses her fingers into the soft flesh of Elen's arms, forcing her backwards. Joan's face is so close, she can smell the mustiness of her breath, stale and sickly.

Elen braces her feet against the floor to slow the inexorable trajectory towards the bower. Her heels slip on the wood. The back of her legs catch against the edge of the platform. With a sudden surge of power, the maid grabs her by the waist, lifts her, and flings her into the centre of the straw.

'That's my girl, Joanie,' Ned calls across.

Elen struggles to sit up, pushing herself away from the girl. Joan is onto the platform now, scuttling after her on all fours. Elen almost makes it off the dais but Joan grabs her by the wrists, holding Elen's hands together in her large fist. Disregarding Elen's struggles, she snatches at a cord hanging at the back of the platform, and lashes Elen's wrists together.

Elen flings herself about, twisting on the end of the tether. Joan sits back on her haunches, leering down at her captive. The maid is breathing hard, her mobcap tilted at a crazy angle, skeins of greasy hair escaping around it, her eyes filled with a sickening triumph.

She pulls a handful of white feathers from the pocket of her apron. It is the mask that Elen had pressed to her face days ago. Joan clutches the black ribbons in her teeth, pinioning Elen's shoulders down with her knees before pushing the mask up against her face.

Elen tosses her head from left to right, the quills of the feathers scratching her skin. Joan grunts as she tries to get the mask on her. Ned comes forward to help. He does not meet her eyes. Instead he grabs her hair and holds her fast until Joan has the mask in place. He pulls Elen's head up and she feels the knotting of the ribbons yank at the roots of her hair, then they both sit back, panting from their labours.

'In the nick of time,' Ned cries. 'Here they are.' He climbs off the bed, crosses the room and releases the bolt.

Chapter 28

The door flies open. More than a dozen men flood in, their faces red from alcohol, their chests heaving with excitement. They halt and stare. Has the reality of a young woman, bound by her wrists and struggling on a nest of straw, quenched the excitement of their fantasy?

A murmur begins. Someone chuckles, a laugh is shared. The animal within them lies just below the surface. A fire of defiance burns in her chest. The men standing before her are not in the first flush of youth – these are older men, educated men. She despises them not just for the foul act they are about to commit, but for their hypocrisy and abuse of entitlement.

There is a jostling from the back of the group. A man with a heavy, hanging face comes forward, clutching a swan's feather. 'You Englishmen,' he says, his tone jocular, his accent thick, 'you are always so reserved. It is fortunate it is a Frenchman who is first to claim the prize.'

He releases the feather. It flutters to the ground. He starts to remove his cloak.

His boldness animates the others. They begin to bray and jostle, crowding around the Frenchman in a sea of debauched and gloating faces. They pull him free of his jacket and he begins to unbutton his waistcoat.

As Elen writhes and twists, her vision compromised by the mask, she sees a figure standing immobile at the back of the group, the hood of the cloak casting a shadow over his face. For a moment she thinks it is the earl, but then she hears a supercilious bark of laughter.

The earl is right in front of her, howling with merriment as one of the Frenchman's buttons pops off and rattles across the floor. The mob close in around her, a hand clutches her ankle, another pushes her dress up her legs.

As she drives herself further and harder against the wall, struggling in vain against her bonds, the stranger at the back of the group lifts a hand to the rim of his hood.

The hand is crusted with scabs. He throws the hood back. To her utter humiliation and rage, she looks directly into the eyes of Viscount Mordiford.

–

Mordiford steps forward. Elen feels her stomach give a great lurch and heave. Despite the anger and fear she feels, this is the first time since arriving at the ice house that she is truly nauseous. He too is part of this hideous game.

How could her subconscious have brought him into her dreams as a tender lover? He is as base and corrupt as all the other men in this room. Does he intend watching her utter humiliation, only to degrade her further by using her as basely as these other men?

Those words he chanted as he thrashed around with fever were the incantations of devilry, the same incantation chanted just now by this band of beasts. She has already been betrayed by Ned. This second betrayal is an agonising blow.

Mordiford places his hand on the shoulder of the first man at the back of the group. The nobleman is puce with laughter at the spectacle of the Frenchman trying to free his drunken, corpulent body from the confines of his clothing. Still laughing, he turns.

The instant his eyes alight on Mordiford, the muscles of his face seem to melt, distorting into an expression of horror. Elen is used to Mordiford's appearance – the deep, pitted scars on his cheeks, the stubborn crusts still clinging to his forehead. The nobleman is not. He is looking his own death in the face.

He shakes himself free of Mordiford's grip as violently as if the grim reaper had laid a hand upon his shoulder. He staggers back with a strangled cry. Several of the aristocrats turn at the noise. They start at the sight of Mordiford. The debauched gaiety of their expressions snuffs out like candles.

'The pox!' someone yells. Panic breaks out in the room.

'Get away from us, you bloody fool,' the earl bellows.

Through the feather apertures of the mask, Elen watches bodies plunging and pushing at one another, scrambling towards the door. The flames of the candles bounce and judder as the door is flung open. Ned is shoved against the wall as several of the party rush out into the night.

One of them is the earl, his height setting him apart. He pauses momentarily at the doorway, steadying himself on the architrave. He has not seen his son since the illness struck. There is horror in his face. But is it a reflection of his shock at seeing Mordiford's ravaged appearance or his own terror of contracting the pox?

The aristocrats who had positioned themselves down the side of the platform to claw at her dress, and hold her fast, now have their exit route barred by Mordiford. They clutch the hems of their cloaks over their faces, terrified that his diseased miasma will rush into their bodies. The Frenchman, ludicrous in his undergarments, snatches clothing from the ground and crawls along the floor.

Mordiford herds the stragglers together, towering over them. He tears his cloak from his shoulders like a matador, snuffing out candles as he swirls it onto the floor in front of them. He flings open his frock coat, and wrenches his waistcoat and shirt open with a roar.

There they are, the scabs and swellings distorting his body, the open sores awful in the candlelight. The remaining men scream, childish with panic, others whimper. They duck as they pass him, as if he is raining blows down on their heads as they scramble after their companions.

The shouts diminish, and the room falls silent. She is aware of Mordiford's laboured breathing, the ropes at her wrist creaking as she continues to struggle. Joan is wheezing from the shadows somewhere nearby. Mordiford hears it too, strides across and hauls the maid onto her feet.

'You foul creature,' he says, his face so close to hers that she narrows her eyes as spittle hits her face. 'Get out! Out of this room, out of the hall. Be gone by morning. If I ever see you again, I will snap your neck like a rabbit in a snare.' He propels her towards the door, pushing her out. Elen hears the girl's boots clatter as she tumbles down the steps. Then she spots Ned. He hasn't fled.

He raises his chin defiantly, steps towards Mordiford and broadens his chest. 'What?' Mordiford says. 'You think a birth defect can protect you from this? Come on then, wrestle me. We will see how immune you are to the pox when you press yourself against it.'

Ned hesitates. His conviction is weakening, but he stands his ground. Mordiford grabs a knife from the table and brandishes it at him.

'Or do you want me to cut a navel in your stomach and rob you of your protection?'

He makes a mock lunge. Ned hesitates no longer. He turns on his heels and races out of the door.

Mordiford spins round. His eyes flash as blue as lightning as they fall on Elen. His countenance is so livid, his body so charged with violence that for one terrible moment she fears he has hounded the others away to have her for himself.

He stands panting, glaring down at her, but then his shoulders slump and he rests his hand on the table, breathing heavily. The vigour of the past few minutes has taken its toll. Wearily, he shuts the door on the cold night air and comes towards her, his face calm. She is no longer in danger.

She turns away, clutched by a sense of shame that he sees her so compromised. With her hands bound, she is acutely conscious of how wanton she looks, the foolish mask askew on her face, her hair tumbled over her shoulders, her legs bared and vulnerable.

Sitting on the side of the platform Mordiford reaches out, drawing the hem of her dress down before sawing at the cord with the knife until her hands are free. She tugs at the ribbon and frees the mask, flinging it across the floor.

'Thank you,' she says, tears of relief pricking at the backs of her eyes. She is trembling all over.

'You're not safe here,' he says, pulling the edges of his shirt together and buttoning up his waistcoat. 'They will be back. My father cannot let you go now.'

'So they meant to kill me after they had finished using me?'

'No, I think not. Had I not intervened, your shame alone would have ensured your silence.'

She shudders. He is right. She would have slunk back to her father's house. She would never have been able to admit her foolishness. In her desire for excitement and romance, she willingly colluded in a meeting that was at best imprudent. She could not have guessed the full extent of her peril, but she put herself in a vulnerable situation of her own accord.

'You are the last person I expected to come to my aid,' she says. 'I cannot thank you enough.'

He smiles wearily. 'No one else was coming to help you.'

'How did you know what was going to happen?'

He shakes his head, that familiar stubborn expression returning to his face. 'We must make haste,' he says, 'and take you to a place of safety.'

'Tell me how you knew.'

He rolls his eyes towards the ceiling. 'Why can you not for one brief moment do as I tell you without this constant sparring?' She stares back at him, waiting for him to continue. He sighs heavily and says, 'You must understand, I have seldom been at home since my mother's death. I had other pursuits to follow, other interests to detain me...' he hesitates again, as if struggling to find the right words. 'No,' he says. 'This will not do. There is no brief explanation. I must get you away from here. Come, I have a horse and trap waiting. We will talk as we travel.'

She pushes herself to the edge of the platform, gathers up her hair and tries to control her shaking fingers as she starts to plait it.

'Leave your hair,' Mordiford says. 'Hurry.'

'I cannot let my father see me like this.'

'Your father? I am not taking you to your father. It's the first place they'll look.'

'Where are you taking me, then?'

'If you stopped this damned delaying, you would see,' he says, fetching her cloak and holding it out towards her. When she doesn't move he gives it an impatient shake to make her hurry.

Chapter 29

The ice across the ford groans and cracks beneath the wheels of the trap. Fearing the pony may slide, Elen grips the wooden seat with both hands. The fast-moving water has prevented the ford from freezing over, but thick slabs of ice have formed over the shallows, making it hazardous.

They are crossing the River Lugg, leaving the estate far behind them. Mordiford slaps the reins against the pony's rump and the stocky animal drops his head, straining against his harness until he reaches the opposite bank. With a toss of his head, he pounds back onto the track.

'We're south of the river,' she says. 'Where are we headed? Not Presteigne, surely?'

'Why ever not?'

'You are still infectious.'

'No one will be abroad at this hour and besides, the doctor lives on the northern approach. We will not pass through the town.'

'Dr Argyll's house? How long am I to stay there?'

Mordiford shakes his head. 'The doctor is not expecting us, but will be able to offer you a safe haven for tonight. God almighty, this blasted sickness,' he shouts at the night.

Bringing himself under control again he says, 'I cannot deal with my father at the moment. I hate everything he stands for, everything he has done, and yet... No, even I cannot compound the jeopardy I put him in this evening, by seeing him again until Argyll confirms I am no longer infectious. The moment I can walk in society, I will put every pressure on my father to ensure your safety. He must understand the fierceness of my resolve to expose each one of those lascivious brutes, no matter what their position in Court or government, should a hair on your head be damaged.'

The trap rattles on over the rutted highway. She scans Mordiford's profile, trying to understand his motives.

'I see you watching me,' he says without turning.

'I am trying to solve the puzzle of why for weeks every word you spoke to me seemed designed to knock me down. Yet now you seek only to champion me.'

'Guilt. Nothing more than creeping, whispering guilt.'

'For treating me so poorly when I nursed you?'

'Poorly? Ha! You have no idea…'

'Then explain to me.'

In his frustration Mordiford does turn to her, then shakes his head with exasperation. 'I did not want you there.'

'You made that quite obvious.'

'I knew, the moment I saw you, that you would be in mortal, or at least, moral, danger if you were still at the hall when my father returned.'

'And yet you said nothing?'

'I did everything to drive you away but you are a most obstinate girl. It was as if the more disdain I poured over you, the more determined you became to stay by my side.'

'Why did you think me in danger?'

'I have already told you. He has fallen in with a bad lot.'

'A bad lot? Is that not an understatement for what happened tonight?'

'I could have explained more forcefully but a few remnants of my loyalty as a son still remain, despite his association with "Honest Tom" Wharton.'

'Who?'

'The Marquis of Wharton, that's who.'

'If he is honest, why should your father's association with him be of concern?'

Mordiford sighs his irritation. 'Because he is the very opposite. He is a foul debaucher and the very man who pawed at your skirts, while that disgusting Frenchman readied himself to play the Zeus in their hideous tableau.'

'It would help if you didn't speak in riddles,' she says with equal irritation.

Mordiford gives a sardonic laugh. 'You have an incredible ability to make me seem the fool for not explaining properly, when it is you who cannot understand.'

'Oh, this is ridiculous, sir. I implore you to calm yourself and simply tell me.'

They trot on through the shivering landscape in silence until eventually Mordiford begins to speak, his tone subdued and gruff.

'My father was a young man of seventeen when King Charles II was restored to the throne and by the time he wed my mother, he was already part of the king's Merry Gang.'

'You say the word "merry" with a tang, sir. Were they not particularly merry company?'

'They were wits and intellectuals, holding important posts at Court, but they also distinguished themselves by drinking, womanising and gambling.'

'Why did your mother marry him?'

'I know not, for I was not there. All I can say is that my first memories of him are fond and happy. I shared their excitement each time they promised me a brother or a sister. Not a single one breathed for longer than a few hours. Duntisbourne became a sad and gloomy place, my father frequently absent, away with his Merry Gang. I was eighteen when my mother died. It was only then that I truly understood the depth of degradation to which he had sunk. His rakehell life had brought a terrible retribution on the whole family.'

'One of dishonour?'

'Worse. Far worse. On her deathbed my mother acquainted me with the truth about my father. She fervently believed that he had poisoned her with the diseases of the libertine, snuffing out the lives of her children and now taking her to an early grave.'

'Do you believe that to be true?'

'It would explain his increasingly erratic behaviour.'

'Did you ask Dr Argyll for his opinion?'

'And bring further shame on the family? Of course I did not. I left Duntisbourne, determined to buy my commission in a forlorn attempt to return honour to the family. I was pleased when Queen Anne came to the throne and public attitudes changed. Those rakes my father calls friends are now reviled for their reckless, destructive behaviours but instead of repenting, they have turned to secrecy, indulging themselves away from the censure of Court, beyond the borders of England.'

'Here in Wales.'

'You have it. It mattered not to me in my absence. I turned my hearing ears away from gossip and distanced myself from my father and the company he kept. I had a worse tyranny to fight – Louis XIV and France, but God was determined to avenge my father's sins and strike me down when I was on the threshold of redemption. I was too sick to resist when they bore me back to the hall. By the end of that pitiable journey, I came to believe that I deserved to be locked away, a helpless, disfigured wreck of a life.'

–

The pony stumbles. Mordiford snatches at the reins with both hands to pull the pony back on course.

'None of this explains how you knew I was in danger tonight,' she says.

'My worries had been gathering like a storm but the lightning of understanding struck when you returned with that damnable book. I am surprised my father did not pluck *The Rape of Lucrece* from the shelves.' Elen turns and looks at him in horror. He nods his head and adds, 'Yes, the book he picked out for you is a harrowing account of the violation of a young woman by a nobleman.'

Mordiford cracks the reins and shifts uneasily in his seat. Elen hears a fox screaming out in the darkness, its cry eerie in the freezing night. She imagines the dog mounting the vixen and shudders at the brutality of nature, the brutality of man.

'If you knew where I would be,' she says, 'and you guessed what was intended for me, might it not imply that you had been party to these gatherings in the past?'

'It might but it does not.'

'I heard you reciting the Lord's Prayer backwards when you were in the throes of your fever.'

'My father said it was a game to improve mental dexterity. I have heard him practise it with that valet of his, the one you could not stop dropping into the conversation. I assume because you were sweet on him.'

She is glad of the darkness because she feels heat burning her cheeks. 'I thought he was fond of me.'

'He serves my father and his band of hell raisers. I am sure he is paid handsomely for his organisation and discretion. Money is a powerful temptation to a man, more tempting even than you.'

'I beg you, do not be unkind to me on that subject, at least. I need no further punishment for my folly.'

'Folly you call it? How quaint. I call it madness. When you started asking about the ice house, I realised you were planning to meet him. At first, I battled with myself. I wondered if perhaps the green eye had struck me, but then I remembered the paraphernalia that had disappeared from the back room. My mind had been so muddled by the pox that previously I had discounted it, but tonight too many things came together. You had slipped away and that hideous girl had not replaced you. I could hear my father's guests dining below. I knew I had to act.'

Mordiford stands up from the seat and peers into the darkness. Elen can just make out the silhouette of a roof; a long, low building beyond the hedgerow.

'Ah, here we are,' he says. 'My time in this confessional has reached a natural end, thank God.'

He guides the pony into the yard. The building is in darkness but the sound of the approaching trap rouses the inhabitants. A light begins to glow in an upstairs room.

'I will stay away from the house,' Mordiford says. 'You must wake the doctor and ask him to come out and meet with me.'

Chapter 30

Elen taps on the door of the doctor's house. When it opens, Dr Argyll is already dressed in his outdoor cloak with his doctor's portmanteau in his hand.

'Miss Griffiths,' he says with some surprise. 'What on earth are you doing here?' He peers into the darkness. 'I heard a trap. I thought Preece had come to fetch me. His poor wife has been labouring away since yesterday morning. Who is that over there? Is that Ned? Has the viscount taken a turn for the worse?'

'No, he is in the trap, sir.'

'Viscount Mordiford is?' Dr Argyll looks behind him, as if concerned his family have woken and followed him downstairs. 'Have you gone mad, bringing him here?'

'He brought me.'

'Oh, for pity's sake,' he says, pulling the door closed and bustling past her. 'What do you think you are doing, sir?' he calls out as he crosses the yard. 'Do you want to start an epidemic the length and breadth of Radnorshire?' The doctor takes hold of the pony's bridle and heaves an impatient sigh. 'I hope your explanation is good.'

When Mordiford remains silent, the doctor turns to Elen. Not knowing where to begin, she also says nothing.

'I see,' says Dr Argyll. 'Well, it looks as if we need more than a few snatched words out here. There is a stable round the back. You can give me an account in comparative warmth,' he says, leading the pony and trap away.

'There is a lamp hanging on that nail,' the doctor says when they enter the stable. He burrows into his pocket. 'Take my tinder box and get it lit, will you, Miss Griffiths?'

Dr Argyll blunders around in the darkness, manhandling some stooks of straw onto the floor and encouraging Mordiford to sit. Elen manages to light the lamp and carries it over. The doctor arranges the travel rug from the trap around Mordiford's legs.

'Are you cold, my lord?'

'Not in the least.'

'Or feeling weak? Giddy?'

'Weary but as fit as a flea apart from these wretched scabs.'

'And until those have healed, you should not be abroad. You put everyone in danger.'

'I will be locked away in the hall by morning.' Mordiford pauses for a moment, a frown on his face. 'Now I come to think of it, that might not be possible.'

'Why?'

'I am running out of women to look after me.'

'I beg your pardon?'

'I have dismissed Joan and I must ask you to take Miss Griffiths into your care. She cannot return to the hall while my father is in residence.'

'Why ever not?' Dr Argyll says.

Elen moves away from the lamp and into the shadows, knowing her foolishness is about to be exposed, stripping away the doctor's respect for her. She stares at the ground as Mordiford gives an account of the evening's events. She waits for him to use her folly to excuse his father's behaviour, but curiously he does not. He spares no detail, but adds no judgement against her.

In a way, she wishes he would blame her. She wants to reclaim the fury she felt in the ice house. His understanding gives her nothing to fight against except the sour feeling deep inside, which she cannot soothe. Cautiously she raises her eyes and sees that Dr Argyll is utterly shaken by the story. He cannot keep still. He paces around the stables, his head bent, his hands clasped behind his back.

Eventually he says: 'This is terrible, utterly terrible and yet...' He takes his hat from his head and scratches under his wig. 'I cannot say it comes as a complete surprise. Oh, good God, what am I saying?'

He comes across to where Elen stands and grasps her by the elbow. 'This is my fault,' he says. 'Recently I have been so busy, I have as good as abandoned... no, that is not the right word. It is just that...' He looks over his shoulder at Mordiford. 'I knew you were in good hands, Mordiford.'

He turns back to her. 'You have become such a proficient nurse, such a capable young woman. But I should have seen the signs. I was aware the valet was sniffing around you, Miss Griffiths, but I gave the devil the benefit of doubt.'

'As did I, to my shame,' she says.

'There is no shame, none whatsoever. I too misjudged him. I thought him an agreeable young fellow. I did not think there was any harm in his interest. Had I given it more thought, I should have seen it was most inappropriate for you to be at the hall without some sort of chaperone.' He paces away from her again. 'But the earl. What type of madness has gripped him these past few years?'

Mordiford catches Elen's eye but says, 'I shall see Miss Griffiths righted. I give you my word, but until that day, can you give her sanctuary, Argyll?'

'Unequivocally, yes, but unfortunately I cannot for long. I leave within the next few days. There is much to prepare before I depart for Europe.'

'Damn it!' Mordiford says. 'I envy you your freedom. I would be riding east with you to join my regiment, were it not for this wretched pox.'

'Then it seems I must take care of myself as best I can,' Elen says. The beginning of a plan comes to her: she will leave Wales, travel across England to Great Yarmouth and stay with her father's cousin until it is safe for her to return.

'Oh, what a hellish juggle this is,' says the doctor.

'No. Wait. Let me think…' Mordiford says. He hauls himself off the stook and approaches the doctor, taking him by the arm. 'This is surely ideal.'

'It is not ideal. As I have said, I must leave tomorrow or the next day at the latest.'

'Take Miss Griffiths with you.'

'I have relatives in Great Yarmouth, sir,' she says, stepping from the shadows. Mordiford stares at her, frowning and begins to shake his head.

'Great Yarmouth?' he says. 'Do you think you will be safe there? No, you must leave the country. You must sail for The Hague.'

'The Hague?' she says. 'Sir, I cannot. This is madness.'

'You are not safe here, not until I can deal with my father, track down and stifle every one of his cursed band. Something I am not free to do until I am clear of infection. No, the doctor's plans offer the perfect solution to our plight.'

'I could not ask a woman to accompany me to the Continent,' Dr Argyll says.

'Why ever not?' Mordiford says. 'You have just this minute said how capable a nurse she has become.'

'A nurse?' she says, realisation dawning on her. 'You expect me to travel with the army?'

'When the English march,' Mordiford says, 'they take their wives and children with them. You can travel with the doctor as his nurse. You will be safe for the whole campaign season. If you try to hide yourself in England, you will be discovered.' He turns to the doctor. 'Think about it, man. It is perfect.'

'It is not appropriate for an unmarried woman to travel with me. She is not my wife.'

'She is your employee. It is not without precedent. Doctors had nurses helping them at reception stations during the Dutch War, did they not?'

'Gentlemen, I beg you,' Elen says. 'You talk as if I were not here and yet I am the subject of the discussion.' She remembers her initial disgust at nursing Mordiford, how she heaved and retched while carrying out certain tasks, how afraid she was to have another's life dependent on her care. And all this with but one patient. 'If I may speak, sirs,' she says.

'Of course, Miss Griffiths,' Mordiford says. 'Please let us have your thoughts.'

'Caring for soldiers on campaign will be very different from nursing you, sir.'

'I agree,' Dr Argyll interjects. 'The march alone will be arduous and you would be forced to witness unspeakable horrors. The bloody flux is not a pleasant disease to care for...'

'Less pleasant than this?' Mordiford sweeps both hands across his torso. He turns back to Elen and says, 'You have bathed me and administered to me, you never once flinched as my body crusted over.'

'That's not true, sir. You are either being kind, which is not like you, or your sickness has robbed you of your senses.'

'Oh, neither, my dear Miss Griffiths. You shall not provoke me this time. Perhaps you did flinch, and perhaps I have ignored that, but in my eagerness to persuade you, I have no compunction in flattering you. You are the braver woman for so admitting. Even when the work appalled you, still you did not withdraw. You dipped into a well of sympathy that was so deep, I cannot imagine you would shy away from anything you saw on the campaign trail.'

She feels a wave of pride at his endorsement, but the doctor remains unconvinced.

'What about injuries on the battlefield?' he says. 'The consequences of modern warfare are enough to turn any man's bowels to water. It is not something a woman should have to face.'

'The barber surgeons on the battlefield take care of that,' Mordiford says. 'You are a physician, man, you are not involved in that sort of butchery.'

'It is hard to avoid.'

'And besides, Marlborough has been trying to engage the French for two seasons now. Who is to say he will succeed this year? This whole campaign has been one of tactic and bluff.'

'It is a risk I cannot take,' the doctor says.

'It is a risk you are already taking, Argyll. Why do you not ask Miss Griffiths if she is willing to gamble on it with you?'

–

Both men turn to Elen, awaiting her response. The doctor's face expresses anxiety but Mordiford's has a look of desperation to it. 'You would be safer in Europe than you are here,' he reminds her.

A thousand thoughts tumble and stress her. If she stays, she will be a fugitive in her own country. Would she ever feel safe living on the estate after all that has happened, even if she could convince herself that Mordiford had quashed his father's vendetta?

Less than a month ago, she was a milkmaid whose intellectual aspirations were unachievable. Her future was mapped out for her – helping her father until she caught the eye of a country boy. Married, she would exchange the drudgery of the dairy for a lifetime of running a home. She had reached a crossroads. She could follow the path of tradition or she could embrace the opportunity unfolding before her. Mordiford's championship of her surprised and elated her. The thrill of the possible adventure that lay ahead felt seductive.

'It is a big decision to take in so short a time,' she says eventually. Both men nod, waiting for her to continue. 'It would mean abandoning my father and family.'

'Your father has managed perfectly well these past few weeks without you,' Mordiford says.

'I cannot just disappear without a word of farewell.'

'The doctor will bring your father here. You could do that before you leave, could you not, Argyll?'

'Yes, yes, I suppose that would be possible.'

'And we still have to consider what to do with you, sir,' she says. 'You are right to say there will be no one to take care of you at the hall. What do you propose to do?'

Something in Mordiford's smile tells Elen he knows he is winning the argument, with her at least. He turns back to the doctor and says, 'Let me stay here.'

'Oh no, that will not do,' Dr Argyll bursts out. 'I have my family to think of. You are still infectious.'

'I can care for myself, here, in these stables. Ask your wife to leave food outside for me to collect. I promise I will not approach them or your dwelling. I will lie low until I am quite healed. How long do you think that will be?'

'Well…' the doctor puzzles for a few moments, then fetches the lamp from the hook. By its light he studies Mordiford's face, turning his chin with his hand, tugging down the collar to inspect his neck. 'There are very few pustules here. Most have crusted over. How is the rest of your body healing?'

'Exceedingly well. Here, let me show you,' and Mordiford flings aside his cape and begins to undress.

'Stop, sir. You will freeze,' Elen says.

'I care not if I have the opportunity to convince the good doctor here.'

The doctor sighs and lets him continue. When he finishes the inspection he says, 'Dress yourself with all haste, sir. I do not want you contracting pneumonia on top of everything else you have suffered.'

'Well?' Mordiford says, tying up his clothes again.

'You are healing well, I admit, but until every scab has fallen away, you will still be infectious.'

'How long?'

'Medicine is an art not an exact science. I cannot give you an accurate timescale.'

187

'A guess then. Give me a qualified guess.'

'Six days, a week perhaps,' Dr Argyll says reluctantly.

'Hardly any time at all. I will have Miss Griffiths and yourself here for a day or two. That leaves but four days for me to call on the good nature of your wife. I give you my oath that I will not put your family in danger. How could I, when you have agreed to do me this great service?'

'I was not aware I had agreed,' the doctor says.

Part II

The Scarlet Caterpillar

Chapter 1

Elen watches the horizon tilt as another huge swell pushes beneath the vessel. They have been wallowing within sight of The Hague all day, waiting for the tide to be high enough for them to dock.

Dr Argyll is curled up in a ball of misery on the bench beside her. After days of discreet vomiting over the side of the boat throughout the voyage, he is quiet and she is free to let her mind wander. She can hear the boom of the surf against the shore, the cry of the seagulls wheeling overhead before they drop and skim the surface of the grey, heaving water; noises unfamiliar to her barely two months ago. Yet now, as she turns her face towards the stiff breeze laden with the smell of salt and seaweed, they are just another in a battery of new sensations.

She looks out across the vast ocean. In her mind's eye, she retraces her journey back through East Anglia, where she and the doctor spent several weeks organising reception stations for the wounded, and west across the country to the borders of Wales and Duntisbourne.

At this time of day her father will be calling to the cows for the afternoon milking. The countryside will be filled with the blush of early spring, the hawthorn hedges fresh green, the sycamore trees around the dairy still bleak and bony from winter. She longs to be back in the milking sheds, her cheek resting against the warm flank of a cow as the milk hisses into the pail. But her desire to return has a profoundly deeper reason.

As she leaves the leagues behind, she feels as if there is a thread connecting her to Mordiford. At first she feared it would break, now she knows it cannot. It is lashed around her heart, tightening like a poacher's knot as the distance between them increases and the pain of separation becomes unbearable.

Her farewell was hard because behind her father's stalwart words of resignation and encouragement, he struggled to keep his emotions in check. His courage upset her more than if he had wept like a child. If only she could have read the other parting as well.

No amount of distraction or new experiences can override her crushing sense of shame. How could she have been so attracted to Ned? Why did she let his looks and flattery blind her to any traits of character that did not shine a good light on his personality? His casual cruelty to Joan, his swagger and vanity. She shudders at her own gullibility and the feelings he excited in her. What were they? Forerunners of the new emotions that now overwhelm her?

Compared to Ned, she sees Mordiford as the other face of Janus. His sickness robbed him of any physical beauty, leaving him at the mercy of her most penetrating observations. She arrived at the hall prejudiced against him because of the gossip she had heard. In his eagerness to drive her back to the safety of her home, he confirmed all her preconceptions. At the time, she thought it was his helplessness that made her care for him, but throughout their weeks of verbal sparring, a certain honesty struggled up through the guile he affected in order to protect his father. He was at least authentic about his own shortcomings.

As the day of her departure drew near, his frustration of not being able to rejoin his regiment maddened him. However, his frustration seemed to focus more on her leaving than his staying, the irony being that within forty-eight hours of accepting her own feelings for him, she was forced to leave suspecting, but not knowing if he shared similar sympathies for her. Could she be making the same mistake again? Ignoring everything that whispers, 'He cares nothing for you,' and focusing instead on the smallest hint that he feels the same? Surely, her heart says with a lift, he would not have rescued you if he cared nothing for you? But the other voice reminds her that he was righting the wrongs of his father to save the family honour.

'What am I going to do with myself if I haven't got you to take care of?' she risked saying the night before her departure. They were sitting together in the stable, having finished their supper. She was in the habit of taking her meals with her patient, instead of staying in the comfort of the doctor's homely kitchen.

The doctor applauded her dedication. In reality, she did not like the thought of Mordiford eating a lonely meal on his own.

'I am sure you will find more than enough industry during your travels to occupy you,' he replied. He then laid down his spoon and looked at her for a few moments longer than was appropriate and added, 'although I have to tell you, I have enjoyed your company immeasurably.'

'Enjoyed it?' she said with a laugh. 'Most of the time you were hell bent on baiting me, sir.'

The ardour in his eyes subtly changed to amusement and he replied, 'What greater joy can there be in life for a man such as me?'

When the time came for her and the doctor to depart, Mrs Argyll and three of the children gathered on the threshold of the cottage to wave farewell to their father.

On the other side of the yard, Mordiford came out of the barn, lingering in the doorway so as not to pose a threat to the family. He had wrapped the carriage blanket around his shoulders and when Elen turned to wave her own farewell to him, he lifted a weary arm in response before leaning his head against the doorway.

As the trap set off, she longed to turn to see if Mordiford was watching until she was out of sight. 'If he is still there,' she said to herself, 'I will know he cares for me.'

The pony trotted towards the crest of the hill. When they were on the point of disappearing from view, she could resist the urge no longer. She spun round in her seat.

He was there. When he saw her turn, he stepped out into the yard and placed his finger to his lips and his other hand on his heart. Then the trap dropped down the other side of the incline and his figure was lost from view.

'Miss Griffiths,' a voice says. Turning, she sees one of the other passengers by her side, a pleasant-faced merchant who is travelling with his wife. 'The captain has asked if we wish to disembark on a beach a few leagues up the coast. He is not confident that the tide will be high enough this afternoon to make it into port.'

'Oh, that is unfortunate,' she says, glancing across at the crumpled figure of the doctor. 'When is the next high tide?'

'Not until the small hours of tomorrow morning. But the captain says he has contacts with local boatmen who will transport us and our luggage to shore by row boat, should we wish.'

'That is kind of him.'

'I am afraid no kindness is involved,' the merchant says. 'It appears the charge for this service is more than the crossing itself.'

'Oh, dear. I think I must wake the doctor and ask him for a decision.'

She rocks Dr Argyll gently by the shoulder. He stirs with a groan and mutters, 'Are we in port?'

'No, sir. We have an offer to leave the ship by row boat but it is very costly.'

The doctor struggles up until he is in a sitting position, his shoulders hunched with misery. 'I will pay whatever they want, just get me off this infernal, heaving ocean.'

He turns, clutches the gunwale, his knuckles whitening as he grips. He swallows rapidly several times before standing and leaning out over the water.

Elen and her fellow passenger turn away, but the poor doctor has nothing left to bring up. After a few minutes of retching, he sinks back on the bench, grey and exhausted, his wig crooked on his head. He pushes one of his bags towards her.

'My money is inside there, Miss Griffiths. Take whatever you need, but please, I beg you, let me die in peace.' He topples sideways again across the rest of the luggage.

–

Elen follows the handcart as it rattles across the cobbles. The doctor left her as soon as they crossed the city moat, determined to find the quartermaster despite his fatigue and sickness. She has been sent with a porter to take their luggage and secure lodgings for the night. They left the broad sweep of the canal some time ago and now the porter fights his way through the market crowd. She sees paintings stacked on the ground, baskets of fruit and bread and live chickens and linen and furniture and a hundred other familiar and unfamiliar things.

Dogs bark and sniff, children run and tumble and cry. A fish runner sashays around her, glistening bodies stacked in the basket on her head. The porter plunges into a street off the square, a narrow artery of the city clogged with people and foul smells.

The steep red roofs tower above her, blocking out the sky. She passes bone boilers and glue makers, blacksmiths and dye works. She pushes the edge of her cape up against her nose to block out the stink. Between a gap in the houses she sees a putrid canal blocked with the sweepings from the butcher's stalls – guts and dung, blood and stinking sprats all drenched with mud.

The porter stops. He heaves the trunks off the cart, tips his hat and disappears into the crowd. She stares up at the building, at the sign swinging like a gibbet from the jetted floor above. She dare not leave the trunks outside but she cannot drag them in herself. Passers-by stare. A group of men sitting round a table, pressed up against the wall of the hostelry, call out to her. She cannot understand the words but she understands the invitation and looks away.

Then she hears an English voice, a woman shouting somewhere out in the crowd, 'Out of the way, you fiends.' A large woman, red hair tumbling out from beneath her bonnet, splits the crowd apart and strides towards the door.

As she passes, Elen reaches out, clutches at her wrist. She turns, her face full of effrontery but when she sees it is a girl who grasps her, her expression softens.

'You speak English,' Elen says.

'And so do you. What a clever couple of cats we are.'

'Would you mind standing with these trunks while I try to secure a couple of rooms inside?'

'Well, you don't hang about,' the woman says, popping her eyes at her. She peels Elen's hand from her wrist, grasps it firmly and shakes it up and down. 'How d'you do. Mrs Sarah Barker, at your service.'

'I am sorry,' Elen says. 'I think I have been rude. My name is Elen Griffiths and I didn't mean to ambush you. It was such a relief to hear words I could understand.'

'Oh, don't you worry.' She peers round Elen at the pile of luggage and shouts in English to the men at the table.

'Hey, you... and you. Off your feet, help us here.'

The men shrug, look at one another, determined to misunderstand. Mrs Barker shoves one of them by the shoulder, points at the luggage, miming at them to lift them from the ground.

She claps her hands and they rise, grinning sheepishly, lifting the trunks and following her through the door of the hostelry.

Mrs Barker substitutes volume for Dutch, secures rooms for Elen and orders the tavern keeper to have the luggage taken upstairs.

'And now,' she says, turning, 'let's find ourselves a bit of bait.'

She pushes her way through the press of soldiers crowding into the tavern. Elen shuffles along behind her tall companion, turning sideways to force her way through as they fight towards a table at the back of the room. The noise is deafening, every man and woman within, bellowing conversations at one another. Dogs scavenge under the tables for food, cowering if a hand is raised above them, snarling should another dog approach.

'Finally,' Mrs Barker says, sinking onto the bench with a gasp and loosening the kerchief at her throat. 'Come on my dear, sit beside me where I can give the devil's eye to any man glimming you. We'll organise something to eat the moment your father gets here.'

'I am not travelling with my father.'

'Ha! Trust me to let my tongue rattle on,' says Mrs Barker, with a roll of her eyes.

'I assure you, you do not. I am here to assist Dr Argyll.'

'Oh, I see. And should I wish to jibe you a little more, I could ask, assist him with what?' and her new companion throws her head back and laughs loudly.

Elen guesses that Sarah Barker is probably no more than ten years her senior but her confidence of manner and ample bosom give her the authority of an older woman. She towers above most of the men in the tavern, which makes Elen feel almost delicate and feminine in comparison.

Her new companion's red hair is not so much greying as fading but still it crowns her head with the thickness of youth, great snakes of braid pinned up into her cap. She has clever eyes and a wide, open face. She tends to lean a little too near when speaking, grasping Elen by the arm to pull her closer. Her harsh accent suggests she has lived her life in the rougher environment of a city; another reason Elen is glad of her patronage, confident that Sarah Barker can keep her safe from this hoard of rough soldiers.

'Left someone at home, I imagine?' Mrs Barker says.

'No. I have not,' Elen says, feeling a blush rising to her cheeks. Mrs Barker does not notice for her eyes have returned to scanning the faces around them.

'So why are you travelling with this Dr Argyll?' she asks presently.

'I am a nurse,' Elen says with a confidence she still doesn't wholly own.

'I knew the moment I clapped my eyes on you that we were sisters under the skin. I'm nurse and assistant to my dear husband. Mr Barker's a medical man too.'

'Is he?'

'Barber surgeon – and here's the darling man himself.'

Elen's new friend jumps to her feet and bawls a salutation across the crowded tavern. A hat is raised above the crowd and as they part with resentful glances, the owner of the hat pushes his way into view.

He is a good foot shorter than his wife but stockily built. He greets Mrs Barker with a hearty kiss full on the lips before taking his place on the opposite side of the table, pulling his club wig off his head and giving his scalp a good scratch. He is a pugnacious-looking fellow, a deep scar across his chin, dark eyebrows sprouting long white bristles and eyes bright with good-natured amusement.

'I am quite unable, Mrs Barker, to leave you alone for more than half an hour if you haven't gone and found yourself a new friend.'

He smiles benignly at them both then stands to reach across the table, grasping Elen's hand in his bear-like paw and pumping her arm up and down. She is disconcerted to see that he has several drops of dried blood spattered across his forehead. 'And who might you be, my dear?'

'This is Miss Griffiths, travelling with Dr Argyll who is not her father but...' Mrs Barker raises a warning finger towards her husband. '...nor is he anything other than her employer, it would seem.'

'Indeed,' Mr Barker says, reseating himself. 'A physician, I assume, not a man of letters.'

'Maybe both, Mr Barker, maybe both.'

'Dr Argyll is very well read,' Elen says. 'But he is here in the capacity of physician, and I am here to help him.'

Mr Barker pulls a disbelieving face. 'I hope the good doctor knows what is expected of you. I wouldn't ask a slip of a thing like you to help me.'

'Of course you wouldn't, Mr Barker,' his wife says. 'But your craft is altogether different. You're not concerned with a peck of this or a prick of that. No, yours is a blood sport and damned good you are at it too.'

'Why, thank you, Mrs Barker,' her husband says, sitting tall and widening his chest like a bantam cock. 'Still, I should imagine Miss Griffiths here will have to deal with her fair share of the bloody flux and that is a very unpleasant sickness.'

'As is the pox,' Elen says. 'I have recently and successfully nursed a patient through that.'

'Have you now?' Mr Barker says with a change of attitude in his voice. 'That is a singularly horrible distemper.'

'As I've said a hundred times before, Mr Barker, you cannot judge a wine by its barrel,' his wife says.

'You certainly cannot.' He reaches out and grasps his wife by both hands. 'See these wrists, Miss Griffiths? You may not think it, but there is power in these wrists.' He shakes them gently and beams at his wife. 'Power and confidence. I could have done with both this afternoon, my sweet. I was swinging on that man's molar for a good half hour before a foot to his chest gave me enough purchase to get the devil free.'

'You always win a fight with a molar, Mr Barker.'

'I haven't met one that's beaten me yet.'

Elen spots Dr Argyll fighting his way through the crowd but unlike Mr Barker, he stops so often to tap a shoulder and raise a hand of apology, that he makes very slow progress indeed.

He sees Elen and smiles but when he spots her companions, a frown forms on his forehead. 'Good evening, Miss Griffiths,' he says. 'I am sorry I have taken so long. Did you manage to secure some rooms?'

'I have, sir, thanks to Mrs Barker here.'

'We've become such friends already,' Mrs Barker says, 'we're almost on first name terms. Pleased to make your acquaintance, Dr Argyll.' She lifts one of her powerful wrists from the table and shakes the doctor's hand. 'This is my husband, another medical man.'

'Indeed,' says Dr Argyll, looking down on the grinning face of the surgeon.

'Mr Barker, barber surgeon,' he says, half rising in his seat.

'I see.'

'We were waiting for your arrival before we asked for food,' Mrs Barker says. 'Will you be joining us?' The doctor clears his throat and looks around the room as if hoping for an alternative place to sit. 'Or perhaps you've eaten already?' she adds.

Apparently unable to spot a means of escape, the doctor loosens his cape and says with reservation, 'No, no I haven't,' before perching on the end of the bench beside the surgeon. Elen is sure his hesitancy has not gone unnoticed because an awkward silence descends on the table.

'Well, Mrs Barker,' the surgeon says presently. 'I suspect that if we sit here waiting to be served, our stomachs will think our throats have been cut. Beat a path through this crowd for me, Mrs Barker, and the pair of us will fetch ourselves and our new friends some supper and some wine.' The husband and wife set off into the throng.

The doctor removes his riding coat, rolls it into a ball and places it in the centre of the bench, his hat on top. He is building himself a barrier, Elen thinks, and looks down to hide a smile.

Dr Argyll twists round in his seat and looks out across the room. When he apparently tires of watching the crowd, he turns back to her and says, 'I reproach myself for bringing you into such a rough environment. This is no place for a young and impressionable woman such as you.'

'I am safer here than I am in England, sir.'

'So I believe, so I believe.'

'Mrs Barker has been very kind to me. If she hadn't helped me, I would have been most alarmed and anxious but she is very capable.'

'I should have settled things myself. It was thoughtless of me.' The doctor traces his finger through a pool of spilt ale from an earlier diner.

Elen can stand the atmosphere no longer. 'Why did you take such a swift dislike to the surgeon and his wife, sir?' she says.

Her abruptness makes Dr Argyll look up. He opens his mouth to speak, closes it again, sighs irritably and says, 'The man calls himself a barber surgeon but let me tell you, people like that are little more than butchers. How dare that woman describe him as a medical man. He is nothing of the sort. He is just the type to revert to quackery to cover up his ignorance of medicine and anatomy. When he is not pulling teeth and lancing quinsies, he'll be sawing away at cadavers. It is a barbaric profession and I am expected to sit at table and break bread with the man. Heavens above, the blood of his last victim still clings to his forehead.'

'He had to perform an extraction before he arrived.'

'Did he now? Well, it looks as if he did it with a quantity of blood-letting and very little skill.'

Elen can still remember a time when she imagined her seniors were, without exception, wiser and more knowledge-able than she; watching the doctor playing with the pool of ale, she knows he is being unreasonable.

'I am sorry you feel that way, sir. I find their company cheerful. They have both shown me nothing but kindness. I suspect, if the Duke of Marlborough does engage the French, Mr Barker's skills will be in great demand.'

'And mine will not?'

She is excused a reply by the return of the Barkers. The surgeon brings wine and cups, his wife carries a large tureen of beef and potatoes, the dinner plates stacked on top to keep them hot. Elen thanks them heartily. The doctor eats his food in sullen silence.

Later that night Elen climbs into the narrow plank of a bed, well fed and bone tired. She lies in the darkness listening to the laughter and singing rising from below and the heavy clop of wooden sabots on the floor above her head.

She smiles to herself because, instead of irritating her, the doctor's poor behaviour has brought someone else to mind, someone she cares for, someone who could also sulk like a child if he did not get his own way. He will be well and must have joined his regiment by now. He may even be here on the Continent. She imagines looking into the crowd of a tavern and seeing his eyes burning across the room at her. She turns in her bed, gathers the bolster against her body and slips off to sleep as if she lies next to him.

Chapter 2

July 1704
Bavaria

There is a hole in the canvas a few inches from Elen's face. She can see the grey light of dawn through it. She sighs. It is a relief not to wake to the steady patter of rain, which has greeted her every morning for the past few months.

She lies quite still under the blankets, listening to the familiar noises of a camp readying itself to leave. The scarlet caterpillar is usually on the move before dawn but she has not heard the drum signal yet. Surely she can lie here for a few more minutes before she has to drag herself off her bed and help to pack up their part of the camp.

She feels deeply weary. Ever since the storming of the heights of Schellenberg, everyone has known a big battle is coming. A few months ago, the thought would have terrified her but she has seen enough, done enough, on the long march to the Danube to wish it would come and put an end to these months of mud and drudge and boredom.

At first, she travelled with a glad heart, certain that Mordiford would find her. As the weeks passed and more and more troops joined the march, that hope guttered and died. Now she tortures herself by imagining he succumbed to a new sickness and was unable to rejoin his regiment. Worse still she fears he may have found comfort in the arms of Lady Arabella, consigning his dalliance with the dairymaid to memory.

The distant drum signal nears. Wearily she swings her legs out from under the blankets and pulls her dress on over her chemise. Her skin feels tight but she cannot face a small beer first thing in the morning and dares not drink the water.

She looks down at her hands, at the nails, broken and dirty. With a sigh, she gathers up her plait to pin it in place and studies the brittle ends of her hair, dry from months of salt beef and bread. She longs to be in her father's garden, eating fresh green gooseberries off the bushes or pulling carrots straight out of the ground to eat raw. She wonders how Libby is and if Rhodri is as tall as her now – he only had an inch to go before his mark on the doorjamb reached hers. And Marc at thirteen was growing at a terrific pace when last she saw him, his movements clumsy, his stride ungainly as if he hadn't quite come to terms with the long limbs of adulthood. And Judy, would little Judy remember her? Or has she become a story, told at night by the fireside, the brave big sister who went to fight the French? Perhaps in a child's mind she has ceased to be a real person altogether.

Coming back from the latrines, she looks out across the countryside. There is so much space on the Continent, vast flat land stretching off into the distance. How she misses the valleys and foothills of Wales.

She finds Sarah Barker seated on a barrel beside the ox cart. Her friend looks up and greets her with a smile, but Elen thinks she is also showing signs of fatigue. The surgeon and his wife worked with the casualties from Schellenberg, but Dr Argyll kept her in Schwabach with his dysentery patients.

'Come and sit with me for a minute,' Sarah says, for they are firmly on first name terms. 'I've a little piece of gossip for you.'

'Have you?'

'Indeed I have. When I was over at Hellenstein yesterday evening, a rather nice young fellow was asking after your Dr Argyll. I had a feeling he was really asking about you.'

Elen feels a clutch of excitement in the pit of her stomach. It must be Mordiford. 'What was his name?'

'Oh, my dear, I had no time at all to ask. The state of the place. There were wounded soldiers lying inside and out, drinking, smoking or just rolling around either half drunk or mad drunk.'

'But he must have given his name. He was an officer, surely?'

'You may imagine hospitals are safer places to recover than the field stations, but they are not. They're hellish places. There are so many stretched out, it's hard to work out who's drunk and who's dead.'

'Tell me exactly what he said.'

'And the women. Most of them have quite forgot they came in the hope of finding their husbands. The grog has turned them from angels of mercy into fiends.'

'Sarah! The officer, the one who asked after the doctor? How did you come across him in this hell?'

'Oh, I'm not sure he was an officer. He was a pleasant buck, wearing just breeches and a shirt. I spots him standing near, giving the impression he has a question for me. Am I travelling with a Dr Argyll, he says? I am, I says. And a young woman, he says, tall, unusual-looking girl? She with him too? he says. Yes, I says.'

'And what did he say?'

Sarah shrugs. 'Just then, right beside me, some girl sets up a wailing that's enough to curdle your blood. She's got the head of her husband crunched into her bosom, strong enough to kill him if he weren't dead already. A foot soldier tries to wrestle her away and she clings to that cooling body, screaming so loud that Mr Barker bellows across to stop the racket and that was that. By the time I'd slapped the widow around the face a few times to stop her keening, the fellow was gone.'

'What did he look like?'

'I've said, haven't I? He was a pleasant sort of fellow but I really didn't get much of a look at him.'

'His face. Was it scarred? Had he had the pox?' Elen says.

'I don't know, I was helping calm that poor girl. She was mad with grief. Her husband was quite dead.'

'Where did he go?'

'Her husband? I'm no priest, how should I know?'

'Not the woman's husband. The officer.'

'He could have gone anywhere in that hell. I wasn't watching. Mr Barker needed my help straight away with another soldier who was putting up a ferocious struggle. In fact, I think I pulled something in my innards holding him still.' Sarah presses her hand into her midriff and winces. 'Either that or I've caught myself a touch of campaign fever.'

'Sarah, I implore you. You must remember.'

'Such alarm, Elen. I wish I'd kept the story to myself.'

'No, no. You must never do that. Promise me you will never do that. I am sorry to press you so but I have a friend from home who means to follow.'

'A friend?' Sarah's clever eyes narrow and a frown puckers her forehead. 'Don't you go running over to that hospital at Hellenstein to find your "friend". The doctor has kept you from a deal of unpleasantness but there are sights there...'

'I would not call nursing the bloody flux pleasant.'

'No, it's not, but I tell you, worse things drop out of a man's body once musket and canon ball start flying.'

'Why does everyone treat me as if I tottered out of the cowsheds yesterday? Have I not spent months boiling water and feeding it into the mouths of men with faces shrunken to skulls from the flux? And let them clutch at my hands as their bellies knot in agony?'

'Elen, Elen. What's got into you this morning? I thought this news would chirp you up. I didn't mean to upset you so. We all of us have many beastly things to do and you know how much the doctor values you. But those hospitals are terrible places, truly terrible. Stay away for as long as you're able. Whoever this fellow was, he'll find you if it's important. If he doesn't, it's but a nothing.'

Elen wants to tell her, longs to tell her, but she hesitates. Her affections are so extreme for Mordiford but her sense of future happiness is fragile, based on dreams and imaginings. She does not want her friend to turn her penetrating reason onto her fantasies.

Chapter 3

Ignoring Sarah's advice, Elen goes to see if she can persuade Dr Argyll to take her over to Hellenstein. She finds the doctor arguing with a sergeant outside the barn where many of the dysentery patients lie.

'New latrines must be dug daily,' the doctor is saying. 'As far away from where the soldiers are bivouacked as possible.'

'It is not possible, sir. This rain has turned the earth to clay and mud and so many of my men are sick, we cannot dig new latrines every single day.'

'Then sickness will destroy the English army before we ever draw the French out.' The sergeant stares at the doctor with a cussed expression on his face but does not reply. 'Oh, do the best you can,' the doctor says wearily.

'At least the rain has stopped today,' Elen says when the sergeant has gone.

'Yes, that is a blessing,' the doctor says. He sinks down onto a bench and beckons her to join him. 'We seem to have reached a kind of curious, dragging anticlimax since the skirmish at Schellenberg. It looks as if that infernal marching has ceased for a time. They say the duke is busy destroying the countryside across Bavaria at the moment...' he shakes his head. 'So much devastation and still he longs for more.'

'Perhaps we are over the worst, sir,' she says.

The doctor gives her a mournful look.

'The duke will draw the French out, you can be sure. Schellenberg will seem like a scuffle compared to what is to come.'

'How do you know?'

'From Mr Barker. The officers waiting their turn to have a limb hefted off over in Hellenstein know what is to come. He says most are glad to be on their way back to England before it begins.'

'Officers? I did not know Schellenberg was a battle.'

'It was not. They merely stormed a town but there were terrible losses. The fort is in the hands of the English now but you can be sure there is far worse to come.'

'Perhaps the French will rethink their tactics after that defeat.'

'They will not. Tens of thousands of them are closing in. Tallard marches through the Black Forest and if the duke cannot force the Bavarians to engage before the French army arrives in force, we are merely in the eye of the storm. Mark my words, the next engagement will be more deadly than the last. In fact, I have been wondering for some time now if the moment has come for you to return to England.'

Had the doctor said these words when they left The Hague, she would have sprung back to Radnorshire like a bowstring, but now Sarah has seeded the suspicion in her mind that Mordiford may be in Franconia, she cannot go. If the doctor is correct and a great battle lies ahead, she must find Mordiford. She must stay in case, once again, he needs her at his side.

'You know, sir, that I cannot return to England,' she says.

'It is midsummer. Whatever Mordiford planned to do to ensure your safety is surely done by now.'

A sudden thought strikes her. Perhaps the doctor himself has come across Mordiford. 'Do you know this?' she says.

The doctor looks at her with a frown.

'Of course I do not know, but I am sure it is true. You can return to your father who will be heartily glad to see you.' The doctor sighs and his expression softens. 'I do not have the constitution of Mr Barker who can munch toasted almonds from his waistcoat pocket while he saws off a man's leg. I cannot look at those poor men with terrible injuries and not suffer with them. You have been saved it thus far. If the duke engages the

French army, you will be forced to see men in a hideous and parlous state.'

'You told me once that I would not fear death and suffering if I understood it. You have taught me to do that. It exhausts and drains me but I do not fear it.'

The doctor makes a small nod of his head. 'I own that you do your duties with calmness and courage, but you are also a young woman with the whole of your life ahead of you. I do not want that kind heart stunted by the horrors of war. I want you to fill it first with beauty and wonder.'

'Why doctor, you must be tired to wax so lyrical this early in the day.'

Dr Argyll smiles at her and says, 'Mr Barker is a fine surgeon, I admit that now. I saw him in action last week. His skill is speed, his technique is almost balletic in execution. Once the gag was between the man's teeth, he wrapped his arm around the limb and with a swift *coup de grâce*, was through the flesh and onto the saw almost before the screams had time to begin.'

She winces at the thought of metal through flesh and a saw against bone.

'There now,' the doctor says, 'that's your empathy making you gasp. I could not stand to see you become as inured as Mr Barker to the suffering of others. It greatly concerns me that, should you stay, dispassion would replace the very qualities that have earned you the name of angel.'

She shakes her head. 'That is just something the soldiers say about the women who tend them.'

'Ha! You think so? Can you imagine any poor soul referring to the good Mrs Barker as an "angel" when she pinions him down, telling him to stop his screaming in case the French hear and think the English soft?'

Elen laughs. 'Perhaps not,' she says. 'But, I must stay. Take me over to the hospital. Let me see these horrors so that I can be of some use to you when the real battle begins.'

'I am not so sure.'

'I am. Let us find ourselves some transport. Take me over to Hellenstein, sir.'

The doctor holds her gaze for a few seconds more and gives her a weary smile of reconciliation. 'Perhaps I should. I can think of nothing more sure to send you back home than the sight of that hell hole.'

He gets wearily to his feet and picks up his hat, plucking at a patch of mud on the rim before placing it on his head and giving the peak a little tug. 'You can go and enquire,' he says. 'I will accompany you if you are determined.'

—

By the time she returns, the doctor's mood has turned from gloom and anxiety to suppressed excitement. 'Forget our trip to Hellenstein,' he says.

'Please, sir. I have organised a trap.'

'Did you not see the hussar ride in?'

'A hussar? No, I did not.'

'He came post haste to find me. You will not believe the thing that has happened. The surprise, the honour...' The doctor becomes speechless for a moment but calms himself, digs into the pocket of his coat and, pulling a handwritten letter from it, he brandishes it in the air and says, 'I have been summoned to Friedberg.' He nods at her, his eyes eager with excitement.

She stares back at him, smiling at his pleasure but frowning at the same time. 'Friedberg?' she says. 'And what is at Friedberg?'

'The Duke of Marlborough is at Friedberg – that is what. I have been summoned to administer to the Commander-in-Chief of the allied armies, John Churchill himself.'

'He has been wounded?'

'No, no, no,' the doctor says with good-natured irritation. 'For the past two days, his blood has been so heated that he has been quite prostrate with the most violent of headaches. Apparently – and this is the most extraordinary piece of good fortune – there is a man in his company who knows of me and has extolled my experimental treatments of a whole range of conditions. When asked if I had ever dealt with hemicranial afflictions, this good fellow apparently could not say enough in praise of my liberal and alternative ideas.'

'Who is your champion?'

'Well...' the doctor stops short. Perhaps he had not considered the question. 'The hussar did not say.'

'It must be Viscount Mordiford, must it not?'

'The viscount? Is he here?'

'I do not know, but Sarah said this morning that someone was enquiring about you, asking if you and I were stationed near here.'

'Ah, well, that is the answer then. I cannot think of another person who could recommend me by name. He would have told the duke from first-hand experience that I am not a great believer in purging and bleeding my patients. Of course, it must be Viscount Mordiford. Yes, yes, how capital. Oh, I am so delighted that he is fully recovered and will be part of a most glorious victory.'

Elen is equally as delighted but to cover her excitement she says, 'I haven't yet heard anyone describe Schellenberg as a glorious victory.'

'No child. I have told you, Schellenberg was a forerunner. The great victory is yet to come and we have been given the opportunity to play our own small part in it.'

'I am to accompany you, sir?'

'Of course. I have no intention of treating the greatest general our country will ever know without my angel beside me.'

Chapter 4

By the time they arrive in Friedberg, dusk is falling behind the tall, sloping roofs, turning the terracotta tiles a soft pink. They are escorted through the streets and on to the duke's camp, which lies just outside the town's boundaries. Towards the eastern end of the camp, where meadows deep with ripe corn sweep down to the River Lech, Elen and the doctor are escorted to a much larger tent, standing among the smaller bivouacs like the queen bee at the centre of a hive.

Elen follows the doctor in. A curtain, heavy with crewel work, flops down behind them and to her astonishment, she finds herself standing in a large room. As they move forward, she sees that this is the first of several connected chambers. Elaborate oil lamps glow on tables, candles flicker in stands. Rugs and carpets dip and rise over the uneven field beneath and campaign furniture of the finest quality is arranged within this first ante-chamber. There is a large desk against one of the canvas walls, spread with rolls of parchment, the seals broken.

Two subalterns stand to attention as the footmen used to at Duntisbourne and at the back of the room, two men sit opposite one another, deep in conversation. She steps behind the doctor who inches his way forwards, fidgeting with his hat. The duke has his back to them. He is dressed in fine clothes and wears a fantastic wig, white with powder, curled and silky like the ears of a spaniel.

The doctor clears his throat and she looks meekly down at the ground. Surely it is impertinent to interrupt the duke. He pauses and turns towards them. She lifts her eyes, eager to see if everything they say about John Churchill is true.

She is disappointed. Beneath his finery, he has a rather long, thin face, his eyes spaced wide in the skull at the top of a bony nose. She had always heard it said that the Duke of Marlborough was an extremely good-looking man, even now, in his later years, but he reminds her powerfully of a sheep.

He waves them away with an irritable flap of his hand and resumes his conversation. How like a member of the aristocracy, she thinks, to demand that she and the doctor travel all day because he suffers, yet here he is, up and about, arguing in French with the vigour of a man in full health.

The officer he addresses has large features but his face is not displeasing. There is something about the upturn of the mouth and eyes that indicates this fellow has a humorous attitude to life. He wears his own hair, greying at the temples and drawn back into a simple braided queue. His scarlet coat is lined with the blue of the ordnance.

The discussion is heated and although he clearly understands the French that is being spoken to him, he makes all his replies in English.

'We cannot possibly attack Augsburg without increasing our number of siege guns. You sir, promised to supply them but now it is down to the English.' No, she thinks, the man with the face like a sheep is not the Duke of Marlborough. 'You have wasted our time with your hollow promises and we are in danger of having all our communication to the north cut off by Tallard.'

The gentleman in the wig snaps something back in French.

The ordnance officer flings his hands up in exasperation. 'There is little point cutting off Max Emanuel and Marsin from Bavaria now that they have accumulated enough resources in Augsburg to sit and wait for Tallard's arrival.'

The other gentleman gets abruptly to his feet. He stares down at the ordnance officer for a few moments, his eyes following him as he slowly stands, returning his glare with a mocking smile.

The gentleman in the wig is the first to break, sweeping towards the exit of the tent with such fury that Elen, certain he will stop for no one, jumps aside to let him through. The ordnance officer catches her eye and shakes his head. At that moment, a weak voice calls from the other side of a thick, embroidered curtain, which partitions off another section of the tent.

'Blood,' the man's voice says, 'a moment of your time.'

'Your Grace,' Colonel Blood says, going across to lift the curtain.

'Come through, I beg you,' the voice says. 'I cannot stand the light.'

Elen creeps forward behind the doctor and as Colonel Blood steps through the curtain, they slip around it before it drops.

In the scant light that penetrates around the partition, she can make out a man lying on a bed, propped up on pillows covered in fine linen. The hair of his scalp is grey, close cropped and although his skin is pallid, she knows immediately that she is in the presence of John Churchill, the Duke of Marlborough. The duke turns his head and looks directly at her before his eyes sweep across to the doctor. 'Who is this with you, Blood?' he says.

'I have no idea, Your Grace,' says Colonel Blood with some surprise to find he is not the only one to enter the chamber.

'It is I, Dr Argyll and my assistant, Miss Griffiths.'

'Thank God you have come.' The duke struggles to swing his legs over the side of the bed. Although the light is low, Elen can see the stories are true. Even without the trappings of a wig and uniform, the duke is a fine-looking man, his eyes liquid black, his lips full and well defined.

'I have been assured you can help me,' he says to the doctor, before giving her an acknowledgement with a slight bow of his head. 'But if you will excuse me for a moment, I need a word with the colonel.'

He is clearly in great pain. He presses his fingers deep into the temple on the left side of his head, then runs his hand over his scalp and grasps the muscles at the back of his neck, straining his head up. 'Blood, I have another job for that good friend of yours, Louis of Baden,' he says.

'Good friend? Pah! That man,' Colonel Blood says, stabbing a finger in the direction of the exit. 'He is a hot-head and a liability.'

'He surely is,' the duke agrees wearily. 'I too am done soothing and parrying his short temper and Prince Eugene is suspicious of his close friendship with the Elector.'

'There is little to be done about it.'

'That is not the case. I have a plan for our friend. I am sending him sixty leagues further down the Danube to take Ingolstadt. He can secure another crossing for us in case we lose Donauwörth.'

A canny smile lightens Colonel Blood's expression. 'The promise of a skirmish at Ingolstadt may tempt him. It would certainly remove a source of irritation from your camp.'

'Then hold your patience a while longer, Blood. But go now. I must put myself into the hands of this good physician.'

–

When Colonel Blood leaves, the duke struggles to lie back down. Elen would help any other man but she hesitates, wondering if she should touch a man so famous, of such high birth. He groans and she dismisses the notion immediately, guiding the duke back into the bank of pillows. She steps aside to let Dr Argyll come forward to hear his symptoms.

'The pain in my head is almost unbearable,' he says. 'It throbs and pounds as if it will split my skull asunder. I cannot stand the light and the noise of those two arguing was intolerable.'

'And have you experienced any nausea, Your Grace?' Dr Argyll says.

'I spent most of the previous day vomiting. Each time the pain was momentarily relieved but it returns with a vengeance. I have been a martyr to these abominable heads since childhood, but now is not the time for me to be prostrate and exhausted. All my limbs are heavy with fatigue.'

Disease is such a leveller, she thinks. Here this man lies, surrounded by beautiful furniture, carried across the Continent for his comfort and yet he suffers just the same as a hop traveller, lying in a barn after too much cider.

'That is not unusual, Your Grace,' Dr Argyll says.

'I am much afeared that when the French attack, I will not be fit enough to lead the armies.'

'You will, Your Grace.'

'You have a cure?'

'I do indeed. However, even without one, I have noticed through my observations of this condition that, perversely, it is most likely to strike when the pressures on a man's life lessen rather than the opposite.'

The duke furrows his brow then says, 'You are right. They seem to come just at the moment I have resolved a stressful situation and indulge in a little relaxation.'

'Then you can be sure, whether my cure works or not, an engagement with the French will drive the wretched thing away.'

The duke smiles weakly at the thought. 'Then I have yet another good reason to draw them into battle. But the cure,' he says, 'tell me about the cure. Please let it not be leeches or the letting of my veins. I feel I need all my reserves of strength in the coming days.'

'It is not, Your Grace.'

Dr Argyll turns to Elen and says, 'Miss Griffiths, my apothecary box is in the other room. You will need to open the compartment at the back. You remember how?' He gives her a look of profound gravity.

He means the poison compartment, released by a clasp in the hinge at the front. 'You will find the jar of red powder. Would you please be so good as to mix a scant half spoonful, no more, into a small measure of wine and bring it back in here?'

'I will, sir,' she says.

'Wait,' the duke says. 'I must understand what it is you are giving me. Why do my physicians not know about this powder?'

Elen thinks the doctor shifts his weight a little uneasily. He has not discussed the treatment with her, but she needs to know how he intends to use the poison.

'It has a somewhat surprising origin, Your Grace.'

'Oh, God. Tell me it is not extracted from some foul organ of an animal.'

'Not at all. It is a powder that grows from rye in the north of the Continent, when the harvest is late and the summer has been cool and wet. Too much of it acts like a poison, as do so many of our natural remedies. I have studied its use carefully and have noted that by chance it has a profound effect on hemicranial headaches such as you describe as well as…' Here the doctor pauses.

'As well as what?'

The doctor leans nearer to the bed and in a dropped tone says, 'As well as helping to bring on labour in women, Your Grace.'

Elen draws the corner of her mouth between her teeth to stop herself from smiling.

The duke rolls his head slowly on the pillows to look at Argyll then gives a weak laugh. 'Good God, man. This had better work. But whether it does or not, let no one know you are treating me as a woman in her confinement.'

'I assure you I will not. It will remain a secret, known only to you, myself and my assistant, Miss Griffiths, here.'

The duke turns his gaze onto Elen. 'I have your solemn oath?' he says.

'You do, Your Grace.'

'Then fetch me the draught and we will see if the good doctor here is as brilliant as his reputation.'

Chapter 5

'Can I fetch you anything, Miss Griffiths?' Sergeant Hacker says in a quiet voice so as not to disturb the duke in the chamber beyond. Elen has settled down for her nightly vigil now that the doctor has retired for the night.

'I am quite content, thank you, sir.'

The sergeant gives her a good-natured smile. He is a man in his fifties, solidly built with the weather-beaten face of someone who has spent most of his days outdoors. 'I see you are a scholar,' he says, pointing to the book open on her lap.

'Not at all, but my mother believed we should all know how to read. I am glad of it. It helps to pass the night when I am sitting with a patient.'

'What is it that you read?'

She makes a face of apology. 'I am afraid it is a rather shocking account of a woman's captivity by native Americans out in the colonies. One of my fellow travellers thought such a story of hardship and survival would fortify me.'

'And has it?'

'In many ways, yes, although I cannot pretend to suffer as this poor woman did.'

'Each of us has our own cross to bear.'

'Indeed.'

'It is a relief that His Grace sleeps now,' the sergeant says, plumping and rearranging the cushions on a sofa. 'He has rested little the past two nights, the sickness has been so severe.'

'It is a horrible condition.'

She returns to Mary Rowlandson's narrative but within a few minutes, her concentration is disrupted again by Sergeant Hacker who picks up a camp stool and, carrying it over, seats himself down in front of her. He continues in a hushed tone, 'I have seen him suffer this horrible affliction often but this time… why, for a while I feared it was apoplexy and we were to lose him on the eve of a great victory.'

She closes her book. The duke's orderly is in the mood for conversation. 'It is not apoplexy,' she says. 'The doctor is quite certain of that.'

'I know. He explained everything to me, although I cannot pretend I follow all that he says.' The sergeant reaches down, grasping one of the legs of the stool to move himself closer. 'He is certainly a man of courage, your Dr Argyll. There cannot be many country doctors who would feed an unknown medicine to the Commander-in-Chief of the allied forces when the French stand at our door. How did the doctor acquire so much knowledge?'

'Well…' she thinks for a moment. 'Dr Argyll is a highly educated man who reads much and follows the writings of medical pioneers. I understand that he travelled extensively during his youth and took a great interest in the way other cultures comprehend and treat disease. He showed a great interest in the folk remedies used by my neighbours, for example. I am sure it is this that has made him so knowledge-able.'

'It was fortuitous that one of your neighbours was on this campaign or the doctor would not have come to the duke's attention.'

She smiles at the sergeant. 'You mean Viscount Mordiford?'

'Who?'

'He may use the family name of Sildenstein,' she volunteers with less confidence.

Still the sergeant furrows his brow and shakes his head. 'Which company is he with?'

'I do not know for certain but I would imagine the horse.'

'Ah, perhaps that explains it. The cavalry has been involved in the spoliation of Bavaria over the past few weeks.' The sergeant pauses, frowning again. 'No... but wait a minute. The intelligence about the doctor's skills came to me the day before yesterday and the cavalry is yet to return. Your friend cannot possibly be with the horse.'

'Oh, I see.' She is thoughtful for a few moments but then an idea strikes her. 'How did this soldier know that the duke was ill?'

'Gossip in camp is always rife and what with the duke taking to his chamber for days on end, there has been much speculation and concern about his health, as you can imagine. It was Corporal Mist who told me about the doctor and he'd heard it from one of the soldiers.'

'A soldier, not an officer?'

'Yes, I think so.'

'How curious.' The scandal he left behind in England must have made Mordiford determined to keep his anonymity.

'I will hunt the corporal out in the morning and make some enquiries,' says Sergeant Hacker. He looks at her with an amused and lively interest. 'And this neighbour of yours? Was he a sweetheart?'

'No, not at all.' However, she can feel herself beginning to blush.

Seeing this, the sergeant chuckles and gets to his feet. 'Well, I suppose I shouldn't spend the evening chattering. I will leave you to your book and see you first thing tomorrow morning. Unless of course His Grace requires anything during the night. The guards know where to find me. Goodnight, Miss Griffiths.'

'Good night, Sergeant.'

She returns to her book, but despite the horrors recounted in the pages, she finds she cannot concentrate. If Mordiford, under whichever pseudonym he had chosen to conduct his army life, listened to sufficient gossip to know that the duke was ill and could be helped by Dr Argyll, he must also now know that she has arrived at the duke's camp. Knowing the doctor's methods, Mordiford must realise that she will be conducting the same nightly vigil she undertook during his own illness.

Instead of reading, Elen sits listening to the noises of the evening: snatches of conversation and laughter coming from the thousands of soldiers moving around the camp; the whinny of a horse in the distance; and the steady breathing from behind the curtain at her back that tells her the duke is in a deep and healing sleep.

How she wishes Mordiford slept in the bed behind the curtain, that it is he who will call her to his side when he wakes. She closes her eyes and conjures up the image of his face, turning on his pillow to gaze at her. In her waking dream she moves towards him. When their fingers touch, his hand is warm and dry as he draws her close.

Just then, she hears a murmur of voices outside the duke's tent. Someone is talking to the guards. Her heart leaps. Mordiford has waited until the camp is almost asleep before seeking her out and at last he has come.

Laying her book aside, she creeps towards the deep shadow at the entrance of the tent. Someone is pleading with the guards. There is a cautious agreement before a figure stoops and dips into the darkness. She steps towards him, longing for him to take her in his arms, determined that this time her response will leave him in no doubt as to her feelings for him, or his for her. His strong arm encircles her waist and draws her in.

Her body submits but his passion is so urgent that, as the restraint around her increases, she has to tense her muscles to protect herself. She takes a quick breath and along with the scents in the tent, the crushed grass, the tarred rope, she catches an unmistakeable tang of cloves.

She pulls back. The face of her captor catches a shaft of light from the lamp. It is Ned Harley.

Chapter 6

'Elen,' Ned says. His grip is so tight she feels a desperate rising panic and pushes her hands against his chest, straining to break the embrace. As she turns her head to one side, his breath booms on her eardrum. 'How eagerly you rush into my arms. I am quite taken aback.' She writhes and struggles, she must free herself. 'Oh... you fight to repel me? Why is that, when you were so eager a second ago?'

'Let me go, Harley.' She presses down on his arms, pushing herself above the band of pressure that threatens to crush her ribs.

'Harley now, is it? When I was always Ned to you.'

'I will never call you that again.' She wrenches herself free, stumbling back, deeper into the vast tent. 'Leave now,' she says, her voice low and threatening. 'Or I shall call out for the guards.'

He takes a stealthy step forward, puts his finger to his mouth. 'You must not,' he says quietly, glancing towards the heavy curtain, which hangs across the duke's chamber. 'We must not wake the Duke of Marlborough. All I want to do is speak to you, make amends for those terrible things that happened in the winter.'

'You can't.' She has moved back into the huge ante-chamber in the centre of the tent now. She knocks against one of the ornate candle stands and snatches at it to steady it. It rocks precariously, a patter of molten wax falling onto maps and parchments spread across the campaign desk beside it. 'Go, I beg you.'

'I will, I promise. But let me speak to you. Oh, please, Elen. Don't keep skittering off like that.'

She slips around the desk, putting it between them. The camp is just beyond the hangings on the walls. She is feet away from salvation if only she could dart behind one of them, slip under the covering skin of canvas to freedom.

'You were pleased to see me just now,' he says. 'You were, I know it.'

'I thought...' but she will not share her hopes with him. He looks at her, his expression dropping, his lower lip loose with fake disappointment.

'Oh,' he says, 'you thought I was someone else.' He gazes around at the chamber and sighs. 'Have you been waiting for Viscount Mordiford?' She shakes her head. She cannot trust him, but her need for information is too strong.

'He is here?' she says.

His face brightens and he comes towards her. She steps back, feels her calves bump against a leather chair. He raises his hand as if he's calming a nervous animal and stops on the opposite side of the desk.

He nods his head at her and says, 'He's here all right. Well, not here precisely, of course. I think he rides with the horse and they're busy plundering the countryside around Munich at the moment.'

She remains utterly still, her desire to flee overwhelmed by her need to know about Mordiford. Ned lets his hand drop, hitches a hip onto the edge of the desk, his leg swinging beneath.

His manner is so opposite to the feelings rising up inside her that she feels confused, dizzy. He leans forward, speaking in a conspiratorial tone, 'He rides with Wood's Regiment of Horse so that he could lead hundreds of hapless soldiers, with no combat experience whatsoever, to their deaths.' And he gives a chuckle as if they are sharing a joke together. She wonders if he has gone mad.

'You have seen him?'

'No, and I am heartily glad of it. If he knew I marched with the army, I'd have been recommended for the forlorn hope at Schellenberg. I'm sure he would have loved to push me out of the ruins of Berg to send me up those charnel slopes.'

'Can you blame him?'

Ned screws his face up and shrugs. 'Maybe not,' he says. 'Mind you, if he knew how much I'd suffered, he couldn't possibly wish any further misfortune on my head.'

Can she make a dash around the desk, across the tent and through the exit where the guards stand?

'You see, thanks to you and Mordiford, I am destitute.' Ned says, intermittently swinging his leg to block her way. 'How many options do you imagine are open to a young man who's been run off an estate where he lived and worked since birth?'

'I neither know nor care. I am sure your animal cunning came up with something.'

The route around the other side of the desk is too cluttered with furniture and trunks for her to run through, but run she must. Despite his appeasing tone, she knows she is in danger.

'So cutting,' he says. 'I am quite hurt. No, for a while my animal cunning deserted me. I could not stay in Radnorshire after Mordiford razed the estate with his cleansing fire. I took myself off to London to try my luck at Court. After all, I didn't lack for contacts after everything I had done over the years to entertain those rich and powerful men. But do you know what? They wanted nothing to do with me.'

She wonders if perhaps this is all he wants, to show her that he has been punished. He pauses. Does he expect her to answer?

'You were the fool,' she says, 'for imagining such men would behave honourably.'

'Hmm. Maybe. But their rejection was so complete. They shook me off as if I were a piece of muck they'd found sticking to the sole of a boot. As far as London society is concerned, without money or an introduction, no one is interested in a fellow. It is very hard to keep one's dignity when one's belly and purse is empty. I tried to fall on the mercy of charity but with no settlement rights they threatened to pass me on to my home parish and I could not return there.'

'I am sure you got what you deserve,' she says. 'You showed me little mercy.'

'That is unkind but I will not let you irk me. I will finish my story. I tried begging, but found it a very dangerous activity, as I risked daily whipping or imprisonment.'

'You have the army now.'

'I do – but not from choice. In the end, my vagrancy got me conscripted and the army is rather worse than trawling the Strand with the other street walkers, especially when one is fighting hand-to-hand with a Bavarian grenadier who wants to tear one's eyes out with his fingernails. I often think fondly of my days in London with that ragged bunch of crippled drunks.'

His tale is getting dreary and his suffering is small consolation for the shame that sours her stomach when she thinks of her former feelings for him. How could she ever have run so trustingly into his arms last winter and not seen the cruelty in his eyes?

'Why do you not go back there, then?' she says, certain that her safest option is to keep him talking. Something in his manner stops her from angering him.

'You mean desert and risk branding or death? It is a choice I am no longer free to make, thanks to you.'

'If you cannot help yourself, there is little I can do for you – even if I wanted to.'

'Oh, there is plenty you can do for me.'

He reaches out. She flinches. He lifts a heavy seal from the desk, studies the base of it for a few moments, then sets it down again. 'You see, both of us have been carrying a little fantasy. Shall I tell you what mine is?'

'I wish you would not.'

'Very well, I will tell you yours. You think Mordiford has feelings for you.' He waits for her confirmation but she remains silent. 'If that's so, why has he not sought you out?'

'He does not know I am here.'

'You think not? I heard that you and the doctor were travelling with the army weeks ago, which is why, in my roundabout way, I recommended Dr Argyll to the duke.'

'You?' She frowns. She is conscious of a sucking void opening inside her. She looks down at the ground, forcing herself to reshape her beliefs. With a dropping sense of horror, she knows the dream she has carried since Hellenstein has been based on a disastrous misunderstanding.

'Oh yes. I was so keen to see you that when word got out that the duke was suffering, I made sure that Dr Argyll was recommended to him with all enthusiasm, knowing he would hasten over with you at his side.'

She shakes her head. She wants to clap her hands to her ears, shut him out. Ned laughs softly, slips off the desk and slinks towards her. She moves further back, deeper into the tent. Her leg bumps up against something and she turns.

She has reached the back of the chamber. Behind her stands a sofa. He is right in front of her, very close. His voice purrs on, 'Through all these months of hardship and misery, marching mile upon mile through mud, fighting while musket shot and grenade shower down around me, splattering me with the blood and brains of my comrades, I dreamed of you.'

'I don't believe you.'

'It's true. You have never been out of my thoughts. Of course, my dreams have not been free from regret. I realise now I could have saved you myself that night.'

'You tricked and imprisoned me. How can you talk of saving me?'

His arm shoots out. She tries to swerve away but she is trapped against the sofa. He grips her by the waist, pulling her towards him.

He whispers, 'I should have taken you myself, in that bower. I could have been Zeus to your Leda.'

The words trigger a vile emotion in her and her body stiffens.

'How often I have dwelt on the sight of you tethered there,' he says. 'Writhing against your bonds, your petticoats sliding up your legs, soft and white in the candlelight. Why, an inch or two higher and your sweet commodity would have broken cover. Oh, thoughts of coursing after that little black hare have brought me temporary relief many a night.'

Her shame washes over her, as fresh and bitter as the night it happened. She writhes against his grip and hisses, 'Stop it. Let me go.'

He grasps the back of her neck, his fingers knitting into her hair and turning her head. He brings his lips towards her mouth but she twists; sharp white pain at the roots of her hair and the wet kiss clamps onto her cheek, disgusting her.

Abruptly he plucks her away, holding her at arms' length. 'Why so cold?' he says, tipping his head to one side in mock enquiry. 'I recall the last time I pressed my lips to yours, you seemed to desire your ruin more than study to avoid it.'

She bucks and squirms. She wants to wipe away the spittle of his kiss. She squints down at the hand on her shoulder, wonders if she can reach his fingers with her teeth, snap at his knuckle, feel the skin crunch against the bone.

He smiles. It is not a smile, it is the snarl of a dog before it takes a bite to the face.

'None of those fine men would have enjoyed the conquest of a maid once she had been covered by a servant. The same still holds true. I will have you now, then you will know how it feels to fall from grace, to have all your prospects of a productive life and future snatched away from you. While Mordiford rides with the horse to burn Munich, I am here and I intend a glorious spoliation of you.'

A great rage builds inside her but she cannot break away from him. He pushes her back and her legs fold, dropping her onto the sofa, his body falling with her, pinioning her beneath him.

'I will yell for the guards no matter if it should wake the duke,' she says, pitching beneath him.

'And I shall say you sent for me to come to you this very evening. I will have my revenge. You will be shamed one way or another.'

Chapter 7

'Harley!' It is the doctor's voice. 'What the deuce are you doing here?'

Ned springs off her. Elen struggles to sit, pulling her skirts down, and straightening her cap. The doctor stands by the desk, a lantern in his hand, staring. She can see his brow furrowing. Surely he cannot believe she was willingly tumbling around on the sofa with Ned Harley? Ned strides up to the doctor, pushing a shock of hair back from his face.

'Why, doctor,' he says. 'How delightful to see you again.' The light from the doctor's lantern illuminates Ned's face. He is thinner, greyer. 'I came by to offer you my congratulations,' Ned hurries on, backing towards the exit as he speaks. 'I understand the duke acted on my recommendation and you have been elevated to chief physician to His Grace.'

The doctor is confused, angry, his lips compressed to a thin line. 'Stay where you are,' he says, glaring at Ned.

Ned gives a light laugh of surprise. 'Your manner has certainly changed somewhat since last we spoke, doctor.' The doctor moves towards him, keeping his voice low.

'That is because I know about your despicable conduct,' he says. Elen feels a wave of relief that his faith in her has not been shaken. She shadows the doctor as he closes in on Ned.

'Do you, indeed?' Ned looks at Elen. She stares back at him, a trace of victory narrowing her eyes. 'How very indiscreet of you, Miss Griffiths. You astonish me. I would have thought your modesty alone would have prevented you recounting details of that night to the good doctor here.'

Oh, he is too clever, she thinks, he is going to make fools of both of us. She bitterly regrets her look of triumph.

'Keep your voice down, man,' Dr Argyll says. 'You will wake the duke.' The doctor flicks a hand towards Elen to bring her to his side.

'Did she also tell you, how eagerly she rushed unchaperoned to the ice house for our rendezvous?' Ned says to the doctor. 'Or the delight in her eyes when she saw the pretty bed I had created for our liaison?'

Elen cannot defend herself against this accusation without a lie. Is there doubt in the doctor's eyes beneath that frown? She wants to cry out: 'I did not know what type of man he was. Does my naivety lessen his crime?'

The doctor sniffs angrily and pushes Ned towards the exit. He calls through the canvas in a quiet, insistent voice, 'Guard. I need you in here. Now.'

One of the privates dips under the flap, his hang-sword ringing on his musket. He looks at each of them in turn, his eyes finally falling on Elen and sliding down to where her chest rises and falls.

'Place this man under arrest,' Dr Argyll says.

'Now, doctor. Whatever can you mean?' Ned says, but the guard has taken a step towards him, his musket raised.

She feels a momentary flash of satisfaction but Ned rests his hand on the mouth of the musket, guiding it away from his face. 'A moment, Private,' he says. 'There has been a misunderstanding here. The doctor is not an officer. He has no right to give you an order.'

'Then I make a request,' Dr Argyll says, his voice clipped and sarcastic. 'Send the other guard to fetch the sergeant and let him give you the order.'

The soldier looks from one man to the other, his youthful face slack with indecision.

'Come now, Private,' Ned says in a jocular tone. 'The good doctor here has misread the situation – not surprisingly, he is a civilian after all.' Ned gives the private a conspiratorial smile.

There is a bond between the two soldiers. In an instant, Elen knows which man the private is going to trust.

'I believe for a moment he mistook me for a French spy,' Ned says. The guard's expression softens, there is amusement in his face and he lets the muzzle of the musket sink.

Ned's animal cunning has not deserted him. He has honed his skills with his misfortunes. He pats the soldier on the arm, steps forward, moving the friendly hand onto the boy's shoulder.

'The fact is,' he goes on, 'I know both these good people from years ago. We are all from the same village back home, are we not, doctor?'

The doctor purses his lips. His mute agreement scoops another handful of sand from beneath her feet. Ned leans in towards the soldier and says, affecting a loud whisper for all to hear, 'I came by to speak to Miss Griffiths – and who can blame me?'

The young man sniggers and nods. She wants to speak, she wants to defend herself, but Ned is too plausible. A vehement denial will make her seem guiltier.

'Do not listen to him, soldier,' Dr Argyll says. 'I have every reason to believe this man is a scoundrel.' But the doctor has already lost too much ground with the guard. Although Ned has never met the soldier before this evening, they share a bond that over-rules any seniority the doctor may have.

'It matters not what you believe,' Ned says. 'I will trouble you no longer. I was about to leave anyway.'

Releasing his comradely hold on his fellow soldier, he bows, with great insincerity and charm, to Elen and the doctor. He then turns to the soldier and says, 'Best of luck to you when we meet the French.'

'And to you, sir.' Then Ned is gone.

'You fool,' the doctor says to the private, but compared to Ned's measured certainty, he sounds agitated and weak.

The soldier runs his eyes down Elen's body then turns to the doctor and raises a sullen eyebrow. 'Tell the sergeant about it in the morning, if you want,' he says and with that, he leaves the tent.

Outside he says something to the other guard and the two of them cackle. What horrid stories are they weaving? Elen is certain it is her they mock, but the doctor, who has stalked off towards the back of the tent, turns sharply at the sound.

'That man should be disciplined also,' he says, wagging his finger towards the entrance. He takes a few more paces up and down, tapping his hands, one upon the other, behind his back, before making a detour round to the crewel-work hanging, lifting it and peering into the duke's chamber. Then he makes another circuit of the tent. 'Yes,' he mutters, 'a most unpleasant incident.'

Elen does not doubt he refers to his own humiliation. As an afterthought he swings back in her direction, approaching her almost crabwise, and drops his voice. 'Thank goodness you are all right too, Miss Griffiths.'

'I would not claim to be all right.'

He looks at her with an expression more of irritation than sympathy. 'Did he hurt you?'

'He did not but I am sure I was only saved by your timely intervention.' The doctor resumes his pacing. 'I am not safe here, sir,' she says in a stage whisper. The doctor sighs and comes back to her again.

'I am afraid that puts us in a bit of a bind. We cannot possibly leave until the duke is back to full health. Even then, I cannot expect to be released from his service. To be honest, I hope I am not.'

'If that is the way you feel, sir, I can no longer stay as your aide.' The doctor glares at her. 'I must return to Hellenstein where I can seek the protection of Mr Barker and his wife.'

'Oh, come now, Miss Griffiths. Are you not overstating the situation? You cannot abandon me now. Look at how far you have come. You, a dairymaid who until a year ago had nursed only your siblings. Yet here you are, tending the Commander-in-Chief of the allied armies. The victory of England could be in your very hands.'

'That is little comfort to me,' she says. 'I am in constant danger as long as Ned Harley is in this camp.'

Dr Argyll ponders the problem for a few moments then says, 'I will keep watch with you for the rest of the night and speak to the sergeant in the morning. I am sure Harley will be disciplined.'

'He will not. He is too cunning. You saw what happened with the guard.'

'I know, that was unfortunate. I was wrong-footed, momentarily distracted. I will solve everything in the morning, I assure you. You can count on me.'

The doctor finds himself a comfortable couch at the back of the tent. Elen returns to her chair near the duke's chamber.

Ned's appearance has stirred up a silt of anxiety, muddying the purity of hope that had sustained her since she left England. On the long march south, she felt Mordiford with her, in her. When she looked at the sky she imagined Mordiford watching the same clouds passing overhead. When the days lengthened and the moon rose, she felt certain that Mordiford gazed up at it too.

As more and more soldiers joined the march, she was convinced that his eyes were searching the crowds of camp followers, as she searched for his face amongst the English officers gathered outside a tavern or resting in their encampments at the end of the day. Ned's taunts have spoiled her dreams. Mordiford has been on the Continent for months, but he did not search for her. And why should he? The doctor was so easily convinced that she was not wholly innocent. Mordiford knows she is not. She thought his lack of censure was proof of his affection. Now it seems more likely it was proof of his disinterest. She grieves the loss of hope and reflects that those past months, filled with longing, were the best and only part of her imagined understanding with Mordiford.

-

At dawn, the duke emerges from sleep refreshed and amazed, resplendent in his wig, his uniform immaculate on his tall, handsome frame. Elen watches from the shadows as he proclaims himself miraculously cured.

'I have to tell you, Argyll, that my relief is so great, I am almost moved to welcome my suffering of the past few days as it shines such a brilliant light on my return to health. I simply cannot believe it. If we lived in a less enlightened age, I would suspect you of alchemy and witchcraft. You are indeed a magician.'

Elen listens to the doctor batting aside the praise with false modesty and busies herself packing the apothecary box. As she works, Prince Eugene of Savoy-Carignano is announced. The contrast of this short, ugly man in his plain clothes next to the duke, flashing bright in scarlet and gold, is striking, and yet the two commanders greet one another with genuine affection.

She supposes her presence here will one day set her apart. People will ask, what is the Duke of Marlborough really like? Will she say he is a great leader, or that he is a man like any other, brought low by headaches? She closes the doors of the box and locks it, eager to quit the duke's tent and insist the doctor speaks to the sergeant; however, before they are dismissed, the duke makes a particular point of including her in his entreaty to stay close by. In the future she will perhaps say that the duke had great charm despite his high station.

-

Sergeant Hacker listens sympathetically to Dr Argyll's request to have Ned Harley disciplined, but says, 'The duke is famously soft. He is too kind-hearted to chide a servant let alone mete out justice on a fellow who has apparently shown little more than zeal in the pursuit of love.'

The doctor nods his understanding and looks at Elen with resignation, which infuriates her. 'That is not the case, sir,' she says to the sergeant, but she can tell he has reached his own conclusions.

'It hardly matters,' Sergeant Hacker says. 'We are breaking camp later today. It seems the French are on the move. Private Harley's unit has been despatched to hold the pontoon bridges over the Danube. So, you see, you cannot be troubled by him again.' The doctor begins to walk away, but she will not let the matter drop.

'If we travel with the duke, we will catch them up,' she says to the sergeant.

'The duke intends marching to Donauwörth. You will be thirty leagues away from Private Harley. You should be able to sleep easy in your bed.' The sergeant smiles benignly. 'Now, you need to break camp. We must be on the road before midday.'

'There, Miss Griffiths,' says Dr Argyll, 'you have nothing to worry about.'

But she does not, cannot, agree. Ned's appearance has so alarmed her, his presence so shamed her, she is gripped with foreboding.

'He will find me again,' she says. 'As long as he is at liberty, I am in danger.'

'He is one man in tens of thousands, Miss Griffiths,' the doctor says, his patience clearly waning. 'Far greater events are unfolding around us. Make haste now. We must march north with the duke.'

All around them the soldiers are dismantling their bivouacs, the cooks are loading up the ox carts and the foragers are organising the provisions they have plundered.

'Do you not feel excitement in the air?' the doctor says. 'The Duke of Marlborough and Prince Eugene are close to achieving the battle they both desire.' He clasps her heartily by the shoulders and gives her a little shake. 'England is about to turn the tide of fortune against the armies of Louis XIV and we are to be a part of it.'

Chapter 8

August 1704
Blindheim, Bavaria

'Elen. Wake up! Marlborough's army is on the move. Get your things and hurry.'

Elen rolls onto her back. Sarah looms over her. In the darkness of the tent, her face glows as white as the moon.

'I didn't hear the drum,' Elen says. She feels disorientated, reprimanded. She struggles to sit up, rubs her fists into her eyes.

'No drum this morning.'

No, there is no reprimand in Sarah's voice, just urgency and maybe a touch of excitement.

'What time is it?' Elen asks.

'Early. The sun is not yet up. Mr Barker is outside with a tumbrel to load our things on to. The doctor has already gone ahead with the duke's party. We'll wait for you outside.'

The air in the tent is oppressive, some of yesterday's heat still lingering underneath the canvas. Elen pulls her dress over her chemise and pins her hair up underneath her cap. Her fingers tremble. There is a pressure pushing up inside her; the echo of a memory back in her childhood, whispers in the dark morning and torches flaring. She could taste fear, but it wasn't her own. The screams of the cottage pig brought her to the window once, only once. Never again did she want to see the mud black with blood, her father slashing and cutting at the animal like a man possessed. So when the weather cooled the following year, and she heard the whispers again filling the morning air, she held

237

her sisters tightly, and pressed the bedding to her ears. Today, she cannot turn away from the window, and hide her eyes or block her ears. Today the fear is her own.

She steps out into the field where they are bivouacked. A mist has risen during the night from the marshy land around them. Above it, the spectral shapes of soldiers flow like a great river, pouring west across the countryside. She can taste their fear, rising like sweat into the air. Few speak, but now and then she hears whispers, the sound of an officer nearby giving an order in a hushed voice. The soldiers' kits clink as they march, the noise layering away into the distance until it sounds like the babble of water over rocks. She scans the landscape from horizon to horizon and sees nothing but columns of men misted in early morning twilight, thousands and thousands of them, pouring across the fields of Bavaria.

Mr Barker sits on top of a cart piled high with stretchers and poles thick with bandages, their harlequin patterns of red, brown and dirty white visible in the half-light. He too seems hypnotised by the sight of hordes of men, moving silently towards the French.

'Mr Barker,' his wife says in a church whisper. 'Stop your gawping and give me a hand up.' The surgeon comes to his senses and hauls his wife onto the makeshift seat of canvas bags. 'Come on, Elen, there's room for a skinny one.'

Elen clambers up, grabbing hold of the edge of the cart. Once she is secure, Mr Barker clicks his tongue at the ponies and they move off, joining the columns of silent men trudging along the dark paths.

Elen does not speak, and unusually, the Barkers are also silent. The surgeon stares ahead, deep in thought and Sarah, her arm linked through her husband's, watches the soldiers as one by one the cart overtakes them. Elen wonders if, like her, Sarah is thinking how many of them will live to see another dawn.

The Barkers joined Elen and the doctor a few days earlier when it became clear a decisive battle with the French was imminent. Mr Barker looked exhausted when he arrived. Sarah told Elen he had done all he could with last month's casualties. The lucky ones were heading back through Franconia and home, on to England. The cadaver pits at Hellenstein had been limed and covered over. The uniforms of the dead that escaped the scavengers, had been handed to new recruits. She wonders how it feels to pull on a scarlet justacorps stiff with another man's blood. Does it fill you with rage and determination to destroy your enemy, or does it remind you of your own mortality? She nursed a young lad through dysentery a few weeks ago. He had been so proud to wear the scarlet. She hopes he is wearing it still. She wants to think about Mordiford, but she dare not. Instead she thinks of Ned and she is afraid.

As the allied armies converge on the marshy plains around the River Danube, she can no longer depend on distance to separate her from her nemesis. Any one of these pale, determined faces, looking up at the cart as they pass, could be his. She dreads seeing him, but a worse fear troubles her. The chances of Ned dying during the battle are high. It is common knowledge that the Franco–Bavarian army far outnumber Marlborough's allies. Will God punish her for failing to find forgiveness in her heart and wishing her nemesis meets his end today?

The route leads them through a forest, the smell of pine resin is strong under the canopy of branches, but corrupted by the tang of sulphur from the gunpowder carried by the fusiliers. Thoughts of Mordiford push into her mind and the old habit of hope rises before she catches it, before she can remind herself that whatever passed between them was nothing more than a temporary closeness triggered by circumstance. He has probably made his fiancée his wife by now. Yes, he would marry before leaving to fight. But, oh, the thought scrapes such a hollow in her.

The cart leaves the shelter of the trees just as the sun breaks the horizon. She gasps at the immensity of the view. The early morning shadows spread over the gentle slopes of farmland that dip down towards a shallow valley.

The valley heaves with a multitude of soldiers as if a legion of poppies has sprung up to fill the fields, the sun flashing on swords and bayonets. As the cart nears the melee, she sees a chaplain beside a makeshift altar built from a pile of drums. Hundreds of soldiers stand before him, their heads bent, their hats in their hands. She imagines the French also praying for victory and wonders how God will decide.

Chapter 9

'There are barns along the Donauwörth road,' Mr Barker says. 'We'll set up there for the time being.' Some obscure hesitation, a momentary concern perhaps, makes the surgeon frown. He looks across at Elen in a more personal manner, giving her a thin smile. Has he sensed her anxiety or is he covering his own?

They leave the plains behind. After ten minutes Elen sees a road ahead, full of soldiers marching towards the gathering army.

'Hey, you there – Captain,' Mr Barker calls out to one of the officers. 'Lend me a handful of your men to get me unloaded.'

'And let them pray they do not set eyes on my darling Mr Barker for the rest of the day,' Sarah says under her breath to Elen.

Mr Barker steers the ponies along the wall of a large barn and into a rough courtyard surrounded by farm buildings. There is a small farmhouse on the opposite side, its door open, the blank windows staring blindly ahead. The family must have fled, taking their animals with them to safety. The cart stops outside the wide entrance to the barn.

'Shimmy along to the back and start handing down,' Sarah says, lowering herself to the ground, sending up an eddy of dust. Elen struggles over the luggage to the back of the cart. The soldiers lean their muskets up against the wall and stand, waiting for her to tell them what to do. There is no teasing or banter, just a strange, brooding tension as they ferry the supplies and bags into the barn.

When everything is unloaded, Elen follows them into the building. Among the rakes, besom brooms and baskets scattered near the entrance, she sees a doll, whittled from a piece of wood, dressed in rough calico, lying face down in the dust. She stoops to pick it up, turning it in her hands. The eyes stare back at her. It's an unworldly thing, like a mandrake root. She shivers but cannot drop it back into the dirt. Instead she sits it on a beam, turning its face to the wall.

Mr Barker is giving instructions. The soldiers are carrying hurdles and planks. He tells her to find the well and take some men, fill as many buckets and tubs as they can with water and bring them back to the barn.

When she returns, he has set up tables, row upon row of them. A message has been sent. The orderly sergeant will be here soon and they are expecting Prussian surgeons to arrive shortly. Mr Barker tells her to scrub the boards down, clear them of dirt and bird droppings. Elen breaks open the bales, scatters the hay thick on the floor underneath the tables. 'A slippery lake of blood on these stone slabs will be perilous,' Mr Barker says cheerfully as she works. Activity has renewed the surgeon's good humour.

'Leave some pails empty, soldier,' he calls out. 'We shall have need of them when limbs begin to fly. Private, go and ask the captain if I can send you with a message to Dr Argyll so that he knows where we are when the battle begins. I will need him here. And any of you with nothing to do, start digging. I need a pit to rival that of Hellenstein. Dig deep to make sure those ruddy Bavarians take nothing from you should you meet your maker today. Miss Griffiths, take one of the bandage poles outside and find a place where it can be displayed. The wounded will need to know we are here.'

–

Elen is battling to free the largest pole from the heap of luggage when the orderly sergeant arrives with his unit. He's a startling-looking man with a long and curled moustache. A veteran she imagines for she has never seen such a fine set of whiskers on a fellow's face. She takes him to the entrance of the barn and points out Mr Barker.

The great space is peaceful, a small crew of soldiers fiddling with things here and there, spinning out their time in this oasis of calm before rejoining their marching comrades. Dust motes rise towards the ceiling in the shafts of early sunlight, scything down from gaps in the walls. It reminds her of the lofty nave of a church, the tables set out row upon row like pews, waiting.

She drags a barrel across the courtyard and onto the road, propping the bandage pole inside it at an angle. It is strangely quiet now that the infantry has passed. The early morning air is still fresh, but looking up at the pale blue sky, she knows the day will swelter once the sun is high.

Most of the mist has burned away. Up the road, a cloud of dust is rising, a dark haze where before there were thin wraiths of fog. The sound of drumming reaches her ears. Over the horizon come the bobbing tricorn hats of a regiment of dragoon guards. She steps further back onto the verge to let them pass. The horses are fresh, the colour of the men's uniforms rich despite the dust, their hang-swords jingling in tune with the snaffles in the horses' mouths, and the steady drum of hooves. The ground beneath her feet vibrates as they pass, the sensation rising and filling her chest with a sizzling exhilaration; an expectation, a joy. She feels her eyes fill with tears. The horses toss their heads. They nicker and whinny, eager for a gallop, hungry for the charge. The excitement over-whelms her. If one dragoon says, take my place, ride with the cavalry into battle, she will spring into the saddle and thunder down towards the French.

The passing soldiers catch her mood and tip their hats as they pass. She feels a swell of passion and comradeship. One of the riders abruptly opens his rein, turning his horse so sharply towards the verge that the animal behind is forced to veer.

Someone shouts in protest. The dragoon has slipped down from his horse, the body of the animal screening him.

A gloved hand soothes the horse's nose, a voice talks to the animal. She cannot catch the words. The reins drop and the horse ambles over to the wall where the grass grows long and lush. Only then does the rider step around the back of his mount and into view, pulling his hat from his head and clasping it to his chest.

Her eyes travel up the tall frame, across the broad chest and scarlet justacorps. She sees the deep cuff of his sleeve, green against the red. The level light of the rising sun streams across his cheeks, rough and pitted with white scars. It touches the tips of his eyelashes. His eyes blind her with the purest blue.

Mordiford stands before her.

Chapter 10

The weapons hanging around Mordiford's body give him a noble and savage look, yet his expression is so pleading, so tender, she wants to comfort him as she did when he lay racked with pox.

As she moves towards him, a whoop goes up from the passing dragoons. He does not heed them. He grasps her by the hand, wordlessly leads her into the yard, away from the eyes of his comrades and into the shadow of the wall.

His hat falls from his hand. He strips his gauntlets off with his teeth and drops them to the ground. He takes her other hand, drawing her closer. His palms are warm and roughened. As he raises her hand, she smells leather. He dips his head, his eyes holding hers all the while, and presses her fingers to his lips.

Recovering some of his equilibrium, he takes a step back. 'Miss Griffiths,' he says, his voice full of wonder.

Elen cannot find her voice, cannot speak. He gazes at her. His fellow dragoons clatter past in the lane. His eye momentarily flicks towards them but he does not move. He cannot release his hold of her. His face shows an agony of indecision.

'Is the good doctor here with you?' he says finally.

She's breathing too hard to speak, her heart crashing in her chest. She finds her voice. 'He's with the duke at present,' she says. 'We've sent word for him to join us before the battle begins.'

Mordiford looks towards his men, his weight already shifting to join them. 'When did you arrive?'

'I have marched with the army from The Hague.'

'The Hague? I joined the march at Ladenburg.'

'I never saw you.'

'I arrived along with thousands of Danes and Prussians. Were you there also?'

'Yes, we were…'

'Well, I'll be damned.'

'Did you fight at Schellenberg?' she says.

'Yes. I rode in Wood's Brigade. You were there?'

'No. I was at Schwabach, nursing camp fever.'

He gazes at her, his lips move as if about to speak. He looks away in frustration, 'God's teeth!' he says. 'This is an intolerable moment to find you. I cannot believe the injustice.'

Guns boom out across the plains, so loud she darts towards his protection. He envelops her with an arm.

'The French have finally woken,' he says. 'They are firing salvoes to recall their foragers. Now the mist has risen, the duke's trick is discovered. I must get to my position.'

'Must you ride today?' As the words spring from her lips, she instantly regrets them.

'Yes, dear Miss Griffiths. Of course I must ride today.' His eyes scan her face. She does not need to tell him her fears. 'The duke is a great general,' he says. 'He will lead us to victory before the day is through. Our luck will hold.'

She cannot let him tempt fate, she opens her mouth to contradict him but he rushes on, 'See how today has begun. In this great teeming mass of soldiers, I ride down the very road where you stand. Fortune smiles on us, I know it. We will beat the French today and I will come back for you.'

But if you don't, she wants to cry. If you don't I cannot live.

'Take your hands off that girl,' a voice bellows.

Sarah is thundering across the yard towards them, brandishing a hand scythe. In some surprise, Mordiford swings round and Elen rushes forward to intercept her. 'No,' she shouts. 'Stop, Sarah. This is not the man.'

Sarah slows as she approaches but the look on her face is savage with suspicion. 'Not the man? Does every soldier in the English army have designs on you?'

'No, of course they do not. This is Viscount Mordiford. If the doctor were here, he would reassure you that I am in no danger. In fact, he helped me to escape from Harley when first he attacked me in Wales.'

'Ned Harley?' Mordiford says. 'Is that fiend here?'

Another thunderous salvo fires in the distance. As the rumbles die away, the trumpets and drums of both armies start up.

'Ha!' Mordiford says, 'The armies have begun to challenge one another.'

'The battle has begun?'

'No. Just the drummers and the pipers. But quickly – Harley, tell me about Harley.'

'He is here, somewhere,' she says desperately. 'He was pressed into service for vagrancy, but the story of his reappearance is long. There's no time to tell it now.'

She knows that their exchange is beginning to convince Sarah when, by way of an apology for her hasty intervention, she says to Elen, 'The doctor told me to watch out for you, to keep you safe.'

'I know,' Elen says, reaching out and grasping her friend by the arm. 'I am grateful, truly grateful for your protection.'

Elen nods at Mordiford. He comes forward and offers Sarah his hand.

'Captain Mordiford, at your service, madam,' he says with a respectful bow of his head.

'Mrs Barker,' she replies, giving him a haughty look, but allowing the scythe to settle at her side.

'I am honoured to make the acquaintance of any friend and champion of Miss Griffiths,' he says. 'Many months ago, she nursed me through a ferocious attack of the pox and I am much indebted to her. Without her, I doubt I would have survived to fight this day.'

'Then I pray you survive today also, although I cannot say the same for Private Harley.'

'Indeed,' Mordiford says, 'perhaps that is the justice that awaits him… but so does my unit. I must say fare you well for the moment and hasten to rejoin them. When the victory is won, I will return and perhaps break bread with you, Mrs Barker, if you would permit me.'

Sarah lingers. Elen widens her eyes at her, beseeching her to walk away. The surgeon's wife nods and turns. Mordiford snatches his hat and gloves from the ground.

His eyes search Elen's face as if he wants to imprint her image deep in his mind. With a look of utter despair, he takes a step towards the road, his eyes never once leaving her. Five minutes, no more, is all she has had of him. He has been in her imaginings so often that his physicality is breathtaking. Within moments he will be swept away from her, gathered up into that vast river of jangling kit and scarlet coats, but in this moment she can still wonder at a single dark hair caught in the rough wool of his justacorps, the sweet run of skin at his throat, the warmth of his gaze. With one final look of desperation, he mounts his horse and spins the gelding round.

'Until this evening,' he says, cramming his tricorn onto his head and squeezing his legs against the animal's flanks. He canters off down the verge that breasts the road, his head and shoulders slumped as if the effort of tearing himself away has drained him entirely.

Chapter 11

Elen watches until Mordiford disappears. As she makes her way back through the yard, her legs feel weak and her head begins to swim.

'Elen,' Sarah calls, coming back across the yard. 'Whatever's the matter now? You're as white as sun-bleached bone.'

'I'm feeling a little faint,' she says, grasping onto Sarah's arm for she has lost confidence in her own legs.

'Come and sit you down for a minute.' Sarah says, bustling around and moving a bench into the shade. 'There you are,' she says, rummaging through her pockets. She holds a bottle of smelling salts under Elen's nose and, as the ammonia catches her, Elen snatches a breath and pushes the bottle away. The dizziness passes.

Sarah peers into her face, her expression inquisitive. 'Am I to understand that you had a previous understanding with that soldier?' she says.

'I wasn't sure of it until this moment.'

'Not sure? I would hazard a guess that you've been sure of it for many months.'

'Perhaps.' She feels her lids begin to sting. 'It appears we have wandered across the Continent this way and that, just missing each other.'

'And now you have come together, you feel a great rush.'

'Why would God bring him down this road if He didn't mean us to be together?'

'Ah, together, you say. Did you not tell me he was a viscount? Perhaps it was the Devil who sent him this way.' Elen gives her

249

friend a sharp look of warning. 'The meeting of two forces of nature is not always a good thing,' Sarah says, softening her tone.

'It is.'

'It certainly will not be today.'

'The allies will win.'

'There will be a victory, but no one will win.'

'And you mean to warn me?'

'Have a care, Elen.'

Elen tries to stop her tears but they spring from her eyes and pour down her cheeks in a hot stream. 'Oh, Sarah. What if he should die the very day I discover he returns my affections?'

'You poor little pigsney,' Sarah says, pulling her into a hug. It is not the soft embrace of her mother. Sarah is too robust, the smell of her sweat too lusty to comfort in that way, but Elen rests her head on her friend's shoulder and sobs until her temples ache.

When her tears subside and she draws away, she sees that Sarah is weeping too. Sarah dashes the tears away with a laugh and says, 'I should have warned you, I cannot let a person weep without coming along for the keening.'

Sarah pulls out a large napkin and blows her nose noisily before offering the damp, warm rag to Elen. 'There now, there is nothing like an acute lament to set the world to rights again.'

'It is not right though, is it? So many of these men will die today.'

'Of course men will die, but many will survive. I have upset you needlessly by being contrary. Perhaps you're right, we do have God on our side. If you truly believe He brought your captain down this road, why would he want to snabble him today?'

'Our pastor at home is fond of telling me that His *sovereign will* is difficult for common mortals such as us to understand.'

'Enough of that talk. I should not have encouraged it. You have as much, if not more courage than half the men out there on the plains. No man must see your tears or they will think you weak and I know you are not.' Sarah gets to her feet and gestures to her to follow. 'Stiffen up those shoulders, my little sparling. There, that's better now.'

—

By the time Dr Argyll arrives, Elen has banished all signs of her earlier distress, although she still feels that the tears lie just below the surface. However, the doctor is in such high spirits, she thinks it unlikely that he would notice any change in her at all. When she gives her account of the appearance of Mordiford, he says, 'That is capital news. What a shame that I was not here to greet him myself, but I have had a most invigorating morning. In fact, I took communion with the duke himself this very day. His Grace woke quite free from headaches and ready for today's battle. His faith in me was amply demonstrated by the freedom with which his subordinates answered my questions about strategy. And His Grace has released me from attending him for the day, so I am here to assist Mr Barker. But first, before the battle begins, all of you must come to the top of the defile and look down on the spectacle that fills the plains.'

'There is no need,' Elen says. 'We were up before dawn to see them marching.'

'If that impressed you, wait until you look down on the plains of Höchstadt now. You are unlikely to see such a sight again in all your lives.'

And so, as the first abrupt slams from the artillery are heard, Elen finds herself on top of another tumbrel, riding out to view the battle.

—

As the cart reaches the top of the rise, the doctor pulls on the reins to bring the horses to a halt. The sun is warm on Elen's back, casting slender shadows across the grass of late summer, still beaded with morning dew.

There's a creak as Mr Barker gets slowly to his feet on the cart's platform behind her and says in a solemn voice, 'May God help us all.' Sarah leans against her husband's leg, wrapping her arm around his thigh. She looks up at him and nods, an expression of resignation on her face.

Elen, seated beside the doctor, turns back to look down on the sunlit plain below. It is alive with colour and flashing with small reflections of light. At the centre of the plain, the vegetation is lush and green. Marshland, she thinks, for she can see the occasional glint of water and wet soil.

'See the pioneers,' the doctor says, pointing to a group of figures in the distance, as small and numerous as worker ants. 'They are improving the crossings, filling them with fascines of brushwood and moving pontoons into position.'

'Is that the Danube?' she says.

'No, my dear, that is the Nebel, little more than a robust tributary,' he says. 'The Danube is over there to the left of Blindheim, behind those trees. It's a huge, fast flowing body of water, even at this time of year. Marlborough would never be able to cross his troops through the Danube, but the Nebel – he plans to attack across the Nebel.'

'Where the French hold the strongest position?' Mr Barker says. 'He must be mad.'

'Time will tell,' the doctor says, turning in his seat to face Mr Barker. 'I have been privy to much of his planning,' he adds, drawing himself up a little and broadening his chest.

The surgeon splutters. 'The Duke of Marlborough discussed battle tactics with a country doctor?' he says, more with surprise than condescension.

'No, no. Not at all. But I was able to glean a deal of information from his subordinates.'

'And they did not think you a French spy?'

'Hardly.'

'I do believe you have been eavesdropping, doctor,' Sarah says. There's an edge of ribbing in her tone and Elen begins to smile.

'That may be so,' the doctor says, 'but who would not show an interest in all the discussions on a day such as this? The duke is a man of uncommon penetration and presence of mind. His foe is the mighty Marshal of France. I believe today we will see history unfolding around us.'

The surgeon and his wife fall silent. Perhaps, Elen thinks, having witnessed the horrors of Schellenberg, they do not agree with the doctor's vision of victory when so many men must die today.

She looks out across the valley. A small village is burning in the centre of the plain, the smoke rising up into the still air. Then she notices a row of red coats lying on the ground near the village, then another, and another, their white splatter dashes brilliant in the long grass beneath the morning sun.

She clutches at the doctor's arm. 'Those soldiers,' she says, 'down there, by the burning village. Are they all dead?'

'No, my dear. I do not believe the battle has yet begun. I think that is the village of Untergläu. Apparently, the French set fire to it.' The doctor begins to chuckle. 'The first thing the French saw on waking this morning was the plain full of enemy. What a shock! I imagine they thought the fires would hamper our advance. Little wonder the French are so reviled by the locals. Those villagers gave them food and shelter last night and the French repaid them by setting fire to their village.' Dr Argyll turns to the others, laughing at his wry observations, but his amusement cannot lift the air of gloom that grips his companions.

He clears his throat with a slight cough. He's feeling peevish, Elen thinks. He continues speaking pointedly to her, ignoring the Barkers. 'The soldiers you see upon the ground have probably been told to lie down to keep them out of danger from the French guns. I expect the duke is still getting his men into position. See there, the cavalry seem to be forming behind the infantry.'

She lifts herself in the seat to see where he points. By the cavalry she knows he means the dragoons.

'I expect they too will be instructed to lie down with their mounts,' the doctor says.

Mordiford is out there, she thinks. Perhaps he's by that burning village, lying against the flank of his horse in that damp shelter of marshy ground, waiting for the order to ride into battle. To distract herself from the swooping weakness the thought produces, she says, 'Where will the duke be?'

'Today?' the doctor says proudly. 'He will be everywhere. Before he rode out this morning, after receiving the Holy Sacrament, he mounted his horse and said, "This day I conquer or die." He was the epitome of Christian and hero on his white mount, wearing his scarlet coat and blue ribbon of the Garter. He will be visible to all, especially the French gunners.'

'Complete insanity,' Mr Barker mutters from behind.

'It is his courage that will win the battle.'

'If the battle is to be won by anyone,' the surgeon says, 'it is the cannon fodder he sends into the teeth of the French muskets that will do it. What's left of them will be returned to me to make of what I can.'

Mordiford must ride towards those muskets, she thinks. How can he live, how can any man survive such weapons?

'Come now, Mr Barker,' his wife says softly. 'Let us not have talk like that so early in the day.'

Ignoring the surgeon's outburst, the doctor continues as if he were conducting a tour of an ancient monument. 'Right over there, Miss Griffiths,' he says. 'You can just make out the village of Blindheim, or Blenheim, as the soldiers insist on calling it. Over there, is the body of the Franco–Bavarian army.' He points into the distance. 'This is ideal cavalry country. The French will try to keep control of the three villages, but the feeling this morning among the commanders was that they have spread themselves too wide.'

Elen winces as the batteries begin to hammer away to their right.

'That is the French,' the doctor cries over the noise.

She hears a thunder of answering fire to the left.

'English cannons!' the doctor shouts, pointing to the fresh gouts of smoke rising up from the plains. 'That'll be Colonel Blood.'

'Enough, Argyll,' the surgeon bellows. 'It is time we made our way back to our posts.'

At that moment, Elen sees a horseman galloping hard along the top of the plain. Within minutes the soldiers rise from the shelter of the corn and start to advance.

'The battle has begun,' Dr Argyll cries. 'They head for Blenheim.' He points towards the town in the distance.

Elen holds her breath. The soldiers cross the stream. Still the enemy does not fire. With an awful concentration, she cannot turn away. The sheer number of soldiers make her forget momentarily that each moving splash of red and white is an individual human being; a man as real as herself, whose life is as precious to someone as Captain Mordiford's is to her. The red coats are nearing the mass of cut trees and overturned wagons packed around the perimeter wall of the village.

'They are approaching the fortifications,' the doctor says.

Thick smoke pours across the advancing infantry. Moments later the thump and rip of the French cannons reaches her ears. Before the smoke of the gunfire veils the soldiers completely, she sees men sink to the ground, some spinning before they fall, others twitching and beating themselves in a macabre dumb show, the sounds of their distress muted by the roar of the cannons. She is overwhelmed by helplessness and dread.

'That is canister shot,' the surgeon announces gravely. 'By our Lady, Argyll, take us back to the transit station. This is not a spectator sport. Men are being cannoned out there.'

Elen ducks. Musket fire clatters from deep within the pall of smoke. Even at this distance, the sound is so loud it drowns Mr Barker's words. As the echo of the next salvo of guns fades, the surgeon raises his voice and says, 'They are firing from inside the town now. The losses will be monstrous.'

'Take us back, Dr Argyll,' Elen says. 'I beg you.'

'If any soldier has survived that terrible onslaught, I want to be waiting and ready to deal with his wounds,' Mr Barker shouts from behind.

The smell of sulphur and cordite is in the air, making the horses, already alarmed by the ferocious noise of the guns, skitter and plunge. She holds tight to the edge of her seat. Mr Barker sits down and shoves Dr Argyll on the shoulder to spring him into action. The doctor, muttering to himself, pulls on the reins, taking the cart over the edge of the rise and back in the direction of the road.

The sound of the battle dims and swells as a hot wind blows along with the cart, a breeze really, she thinks, but animal, a whispering dragon of a wind. She hears the pop of musketry in the distance; a salvo closer to hand rasps like rending calico.

'It is a great shame that we could not stay to see the cavalry charge,' Dr Argyll shouts over his shoulder to his passengers.

Elen looks behind and sees the surgeon roll his eyes. 'You will be seeing our brave dragoons quite soon enough, I fear,' he replies. Between the gunfire Elen catches the skirl of bagpipes, the sound blown on the warm wind across the plains.

'Those must be Orkney's battalions,' Dr Argyll says, slowing the horses and cocking his head to listen. 'Can you hear the pipes?'

But Elen hears something else. She hears screams. Terrible, ghastly screams. She looks from left to right but cannot see where they are coming from.

'Hurry!' she says.

The doctor slaps the horses with the reins. The cart rattles and jumps over the parched ruts in the path. The barns at the foot of the slope loom up in front of them.

Now she sees where the noise comes from. The road is filled with running men, and as they run, they scream. Wherever she looks she sees horror; one man is missing an arm, another a cheek. One is almost naked, his body burned where his clothing has been ripped away. Another is trailing rags, peppered with canister shot and blooming red.

The cart rattles into the courtyard and the noise – it is the noise of her childhood – but this is worse. This is the sound of a hundred cottage pigs, panicking and squealing and shrieking at the same time.

Mr Barker leaps down from the back of the cart and runs forward, holding the horse by the bridle as it jerks its head up, rolling its eyes. 'Get this cart back on the road, Argyll,' he shouts. 'Start picking them up. You girl, go with him.' Elen stares at the horror, unable to move, no idea where to begin. 'Get down then. Off!' the surgeon shouts at her.

Does he think her afraid? She is not. She is dumbfounded. She clambers off the cart and drops into the sea of injured. She is trembling. She thinks she is going to be sick. She looks for Sarah, her ally, her friend, but Sarah has gone. Elen stands immobile in the centre of the courtyard. Mr Barker stalks away from her, tearing his coat off, flinging it down onto a barrel at the entrance of the barn and disappears inside. A soldier is dragging himself through the dust towards her. He reaches his hand up and grasps at her apron. She tugs it from him. He leaves a great welt of blood and dirt and straw across the fabric.

She stares down at him. He has no foot. Sarah is at the doorway of the barn and rushes out. The noise coming from the barn is louder, the panic keener in an enclosed space. Sarah shouts orders. 'That man. That man there.' An officer is limping away from the barn, his leg is trailing uselessly behind him. 'Elen, bring him in. Now!'

Elen does not move, she cannot move. Sarah grabs her by the shoulders, spins her round and pushes her towards the officer. Something springs open in Elen's chest, as if iced water has poured over her, woken her. She rushes forward and grabs at him. 'Here, sir,' she says. 'You must come with me.'

He puts his hand on her shoulder. His fingers are missing. 'Leave me,' he says. 'Let me be. I will not go in. I will not lose my leg.'

A terrible scream from inside the barn rises up, louder than all the rest. The whites of the officer's eyes flash as he strains his head towards the noise.

'Take me away,' he says. 'Help me. Get my boot off. I can still move my toes. Let the surgeon know I can still move my toes.'

She nods her agreement. If she can help one soldier, she can begin to be of some use in this inferno of suffering. He leans heavily on her, hobbling along the wall of the barn until they are away from the crush. She helps him to the ground. He leans his back against the wall.

'The cavalry,' she says. 'Have the cavalry charged yet?'

He frowns at her and shrugs, looking down at the bloody pulp of his hand. 'A cannon ball glanced off my leg. It is fine. Fine. It got my sword. Damned thing shivered to pieces from the blow, cut off my fingers.' From the mash of skin and blood he raises an index finger, then his thumb. 'Oh, look,' he says. 'Only three gone.' He rests his head back against the wall and repeats wearily, 'Only three.'

Elen races back to the barn, unwinds some linen for his hand. Sarah shouts, 'Here, Elen. Help us.' She drops the bandaging into the dirt.

Mr Barker is standing between two tables. A hole has been smashed in the side of the barn wall to let in more light. He is stripped down to his shirt, his waistcoat and wig hanging on a beam beside him, like a coat on a chapel hat peg. He has tied a piece of sacking around his waist. It is splashed with blood. He looks like a small mastiff, his pink tongue working along his lips as he concentrates. He snarls each time the knife snags.

He's working on a mountain of a man – three orderlies hold down his shoulders, two his pelvis. Sarah battles with the thigh. She looks up at Elen, her eyes entreating her to help. Elen comes forward, pushing between the orderlies like cows in a double byre and grasps the ankle.

Mr Barker is already through the flesh. Elen cannot see the soldier's face because of the press of bodies holding him down.

He doesn't scream. He growls savagely as Mr Barker sets to with the saw. The man's body rises, bucking and trembling. She pinions him harder. If the leg rocks the saw will take longer. She has taken a giant step back inside herself. She watches the leg thrash and quiver but the strength with which she holds it is not her own.

The ankle is still. The leg is severed. An orderly lifts her hands free of the limb and drops it with a sodden clatter into the pail on the floor. Mr Barker pushes forward, catches her eye, and nods.

Elen takes hold of the living knee, her hand slippery with blood. Mr Barker lashes the arteries. He wipes his hands down the sacking apron, turns to the peg where his waistcoat hangs and pushes his fingers into the pocket. He pulls out a handful of almonds and holds them out to her. She shakes her head. He shrugs, tosses them into his mouth and begins work on the patient behind.

Sarah grabs Elen's hand, pushes it into a tub of paste. It is dirty yellow and smells of turpentine. 'Push it onto the wound,' she says. 'Press it in hard.'

She turns to the soldier and says, 'Oh, stop your thrashing man. If you want it sealed with hot oil, I'll call one of those Prussian butchers over to you. They'll be happy to oblige.'

Chapter 12

The wounded continue to arrive in wagonloads. All of them bleed. All of them stink. There is blood and dust and flies and muck. The suffering squeezes every other thought from Elen's mind, except her fear for Mordiford. She wants Mordiford. She wants him here. She wants him safe.

She stays close to Sarah. She follows what she does. There's no time for sympathy, there are too many. She cannot listen to their entreaties. They beg her, plead with her: *save me, save me from the knife, I have suffered enough.*

In the violence of the barn, where Mr Barker spins and slashes, the pail between his tables fills at twice the speed of any other surgeon. He's so swift with his knife, she has to watch her fingers. He wraps his arm right round the limb and says, 'Bite down.' With barely a flick, he's through the muscle and onto the bone. She cannot feel compassion or she will stop, and if she stops, someone else will take her place and pin the soldier down.

Every fusilier has fouled himself. 'It is the gunpowder,' Sarah says. They swallow it each time they tear the paper cartridge with their teeth. It opens the bowels. That and the fear. When she pulls away the breeches, some don't care. She breathes through her mouth and flings their stinking clothes to the ground. Others try to hide their humiliation, grabbing at their belts as she struggles to free the leg for the surgeons. They are stupid with pain and fear. They cannot hear her, deaf from the musket fire.

The sun rises high in the sky and the heat beats down on the barns and still the wounded come. Her apron is stiff with blood and mud, her nostrils thick with the smell of death. She works like an automaton.

The men whom the surgeons cannot save are laid out in the meadow in the shimmering heat. Some writhe and yell. They cry out for their mothers. Some lie mute and trembling. Elen tries to scan every face. She knows his uniform by heart, the deep cuff of green against the scarlet. She dreads recognising the dragoons' justacorps, but she longs to see it. And then, as the sun drops lower in the sky, she sees the cuff. It is green. The green of the Wood's Regiment of Horse.

She is up on the wagon in an instant, pushing her way through the wounded. She is on him. The man looks up at her in wonder. But it is not Mordiford. This man has red hair and freckles. This man is a lieutenant.

Elen feels suddenly weary. The soldier shuffles a few inches to the edge of the wagon, his knee swollen to the size of a man's head. An orderly comes to help, and Elen thinks, this soldier will know if Mordiford lives. She pushes the orderly away and helps the lieutenant down, taking him away from the barn even though his leg must come off. She must question him before losing sight of him. She takes her knife and snicks the buttons from his boot.

'You ride with Wood's Regiment,' she says, breathing hard as she works.

'I do.'

'You know a man called Mordiford?'

'Captain Mordiford? He led the charge.'

She sits back on her heels. A tremor passes through her body. She hears Sarah shouting for her, but she must know if Mordiford rides still. The guns are ripping and rattling and booming. She must ask, does he live? Why can she not ask it?

She shrinks from the words, too afraid of the damage they will wreak. She hears Sarah shout again, closer this time. She peels the boot away. The shot is lodged against the linen of the stocking.

'Elen. Leave that man. His boot has saved him. There's no wound there. Leave him.'

'Let me soak his cravat and cool the bruising.'

'Leave him.' Sarah has her by the elbow, pulling her up and dragging her away.

'I will come and find you,' Elen calls back to him. She still has the shot in her hand. She breaks away from Sarah and shouts to the lieutenant, 'Mordiford rides still?'

'Yes,' he calls back. 'When I left the field, he rode still.'

–

The sun sinks lower. Elen's neck is slicked with sweat. It trickles down her back, between her breasts. Her cheeks burn with heat. The din from the battlefield thunders and roars. The flies follow the wounded to the field hospital, droning in swarms over the dead and dying. The flies are winning, she thinks. They are growing fat on flesh.

She cannot find the lieutenant again. She finds others. She says, are the cavalry defeated? She hears that Prince Eugene is foundering on the allied right flank.

The cannons boom, shaking the earth at her feet.

She says, do you know a Captain Mordiford? She hears that the Duke of Marlborough is pinning down the French.

A ferocious salvo rattles and pocks.

She says, he rides with Wood's Regiment. She hears the French are trapped in the town.

Horrible wounds start to arrive, different wounds. Men torn open by bayonets. They are fighting hand-to-hand now. How can he survive? He must be dead. He can't be dead. She would know. She feels him. Every wound she sees, she sees on his body and yet he lives in her thoughts.

The sun is low in the sky. Surely night will fall before either side gives in, but as darkness comes, the guns stop and the screams of the wounded fill the vacuum. Just then, Sarah finds her. A loan rider has arrived with news.

Elen's heart leaps. 'He has news of Captain Mordiford?'

'No, my dear. Not that. The French have laid down their arms. The French are defeated.'

Defeated. But where is Mordiford? She hears shouts go up. Someone close by, fires a musket into the air. The sound is so loud, she winces, claps her hands to her ears. Victory, and yet she is utterly defeated. She wants to crawl out of her skin. She cannot wait for news any longer.

'Take some rest,' Sarah is saying. 'The worst casualties are on their way to Nördlingen. The fellows arriving here can wait a few more hours. Mr Barker is dead on his feet. He is snatching a few moments' sleep himself. He will start again at dawn.'

The night is full of voices. Men bellow and bawl, their shouts loud now that the guns have stopped. 'I cannot rest until I know that Captain Mordiford is safe,' she says.

Sarah takes Elen's arm and draws her over towards the farmhouse, away from the groans and the yells in the barn, away from the shouts of triumph and singing in the yard. She pulls her down onto a bench and gives her arm a squeeze. 'You must be ready, my dear, for the worst. The Duke of Marlborough has had a glorious victory today, but they say the last few hours of fighting were especially hard.'

'What have you heard?'

'I think the cavalry were at the heart of the most savage fighting by all accounts.'

Elen stares up at the sky, at the waning moon rising above the buildings. She wonders if the halo around it is mist or smoke. She sees Mordiford in a sea of blue, a horde of French. He is slashing and cutting, scattering the enemy. Suddenly she remembers the tapestry at the back of the vestibule at Duntisbourne, the tapestry she hated, even then – a white hart surrounded by dogs, snapping and snarling, leaping up. She sees the stag, the strong neck, the fine head, the crown of antlers.

She remembers the hounds tearing at the flanks, pulling the mighty beast down into the pack. She thinks, not that. Please not that.

'I would know if he were dead.'

Sarah pats her hand. 'Let us believe for the time being that your Viscount Mordiford is alive.'

Yes, that's what Elen believes. Not for the time being, but for ever. He lives for ever.

'You must ask yourself, what awaits you now?' Sarah says.

No, Elen thinks, I see no further than this moment. I cannot get past the fever of not knowing.

'Campaign romances cannot survive ordinary life,' Sarah is saying.

'I do not care what lies ahead,' Elen says. 'As long as he lives, I can be happy.'

'Are you sure of that?'

Oh, Sarah. What are you doing? Let us talk about him then. He is my dearest subject. You would not give me this advice and counsel if we knew he was dead, so let us continue to pretend he lives.

'If you mean to remind me that one day he will be earl...' Elen says. 'I have not forgotten. You think that a dairymaid should not harbour such an affection?'

'We are all free to love whomever we choose.'

'And free to long for a soldier's return.'

Sarah nods, pats her hand. Presently she says, 'Does your happiness depend simply on his survival?'

'I know I cannot hope for more.'

'I think you can, judging by his obvious passion.'

Her words drop into Elen's ears like honey. His obvious passion, witnessed by another, believed absolutely. How beautiful a thought. Crystal clear, like water rising clean and bright between the pebbles.

'You do?' Elen says.

'Of course. His passion, at present, runs high because danger is at his shoulder. But I worry for you. Do you want to be a mistress? There is precious little other choice.'

Elen feels herself beginning to blush with a smile she must hide, for the word alone makes her heart accelerate.

'A high-born man is seldom free,' Sarah says. 'He'll have a bride already chosen.'

And there it is, the jolt, the crunch.

'He has,' Elen says, as if it is a nothing. 'Her name is Lady Arabella, but he has been away from home for so long, I have no idea if they are still betrothed.'

Sarah gives her a look, sympathetic, understanding, but there is something else. Is it pity she sees in her friend's eye?

'Be careful is all I say to you, Elen. The brightest flames burn out the quickest.'

Sarah gets to her feet with a stretch and a mighty yawn. 'That is enough advice for one night. We have done well today. You get along and rest. I will be here for the late arrivals. Find a bed in the house. No one will disturb you there.'

Elen takes a lantern but before she reaches the farmhouse, she knows it is pointless. She aches with tiredness but she will not sleep. Even if she could, it seems a betrayal. She must keep a vigil tonight.

She sets the lantern down and goes out onto the road. Wearily, she begins to climb the hill, thinking that perhaps she can walk far enough to look down on the plains. Although the night is warm and the moon high, she knows that the pale wraiths of mist that curve around her ankles will eventually wind slowly down into the darkness on the other side of the hill and curl around the twisted corpses lying on the plains.

A damp coolness rises up from the grass. She catches the sweet smell of countryside that has lain panting through a hot summer's day and is now cooling; a perfume of hay, warm from the sun, blown on a lazy wind, but now tainted with the smell of smoke and sulphur drifting up from the battlefield half a league away.

Death is so close at hand and yet she feels an aching nostalgia for home, for those nights when she lay in the meadow behind the house, staring up at the sky, wishing for something to shake up her life. Back then she didn't mind if it was a good something or a bad something. Either would have done, as long as it promised adventure. How she wonders at her innocence. Would she have wished so ardently for change if she knew that adventure came at such a cost?

She is only a few yards from the barns when she stops and stiffens. She turns. She knows something awful is about to happen. She hears the wheels of a cart on the road below. It stops outside the barns, the moonlight strong enough to see the orderlies gathering to carry the stretchers through.

She recognises Sarah's silhouette, standing at the back of the cart. She sees her place a hand on the shoulder of one of the orderlies, then bend and peer at the soldier on the stretcher.

Elen stares down at the scene. She prays for Sarah to rise again and follow the stretcher bearers. She knows she will not. Her friend directs the orderlies to carry the soldier through. She walks to the foot of the hill. She calls softly to Elen to come with all haste. Elen starts to run.

Chapter 13

Elen lifts her skirts free of her feet and runs. She travels so fast down the hill that she nearly loses her balance, and lets go of her dress. Her strides are huge; she almost falls. She lands jarringly on the road and sprints across it. Sarah is heading towards the stables that run along the east side of the courtyard, the orderlies ahead of her, carrying the stretcher.

Elen thunders after them and bursts into the building. She sees a row of wide mangers at the back of the stalls, a few feet off the ground. Sarah turns, standing across the entrance to one of the stalls. She catches Elen by the shoulders as she tries to push past her.

'Is he dead?' Elen cries.

'No, not dead.'

'Badly wounded?'

'There is a deal of blood.' Elen feels her heart seize. Sarah says, 'It's not possible to tell how bad his injuries are until we have more light and can clean away some of the gore. Go now. Fetch me water from the well. Hunt for a lantern that still has oil in it.'

Elen hears a rustle of straw as they lift the stretcher up onto the manger and a sound that could be a word but may simply be a moan. He is conscious. She makes another lunge to get round her friend, straining against her, but Sarah resolutely blocks her way. 'Go!' she says.

Elen stumbles into the courtyard, snatching up a pail and going to the well. She hauls the heavy bucket up from the depth, grazing her knuckles on the rough stone of the parapet.

He lives, she thinks. He moves. He moans.

She is almost back at the stables, the pail rapping against her shin, the water spilling down her dress, when she remembers the lantern. She stops, barely able to control her feet. She drops the pail and rushes to fetch the lamp she left by the gate.

She gets to the stables as the orderlies are leaving. She clatters into the stall. The stretcher is on top of a wide manger the height of a table. Sarah is removing Mordiford's scarlet topcoat. Elen drops the bucket, rushing forward with the lamp.

'Here,' Sarah says over her shoulder as she struggles to raise him and pull the coat free. 'Hang the lantern up, quick as you can. Come and help me. Go carefully. He swooned again when I removed his boots.'

With shaking hands, Elen grasps the chain hanging above the manger, struggling to hook the lantern on. Her fingers will not obey. Finally the lamp drops onto the hook and she lets go. It swings away from her, like a pendulum above them, throwing fantastic shadows and shapes around the walls. She cannot catch it, cannot still it.

Sarah looks up and frowns. 'Leave it,' she says, 'it'll settle. Climb up and take the weight of his head while I slide out the coat.'

Elen clambers onto the manger. She has him. Finally, she has him. She slides her hand underneath his neck, feels the heat of him pressing into her, the dead weight of his head, his shoulders, as Sarah pulls at the coat.

With each swing of the lantern, Elen searches his face. His hair is filthy with dirt and blood, his skin glazed a horrible copper colour. Is it his blood or someone else's? Black powder burns speckle his face and, as the light gleams and dims, she walks her fingers across his skin, searching for signs of shot. She finds none.

She clambers down, snatches up a cloth and soaks it in the pail of water. She climbs back up, starts to wipe away the blood and muck. Slowly the face she loves begins to emerge, the broad brow, the straight nose, the lips etched with pits along the margin. Once she thought him an ordinary-looking man. Now she thinks he has the most unique face she's ever seen. Of course, the pox has roughened and dulled his skin, but it cannot spoil his looks.

As she gently wipes his face clean, she feels a great calmness wrap around her, bathing her, as she bathes him. When the blood is cleaned away she starts moving her fingers into his hair line. His scalp is hot, his hair catches underneath her fingernails. Beneath a wet rag of hair she finds a hard lump the size of a goose's egg, the hair around it sticky with blood.

'He's had a blow to the skull,' Elen says, 'but I cannot find any shot to his face or head.'

'Thank the Lord for that.'

Elen looks down on Mordiford. His eyes are closed, but the face she has longed to see throughout this endless and terrible day is here before her. The love she feels for him thrills her with a power that frightens her.

Sarah is busy unbuttoning his vest and confident she is unobserved, Elen lets her hand caress Mordiford's forehead, her palm cupping his cheek with a loving tenderness. He moves his head. The lids flutter and slowly he opens his eyes, watching the steady swing of the lantern before coming to rest on her.

His voice is so deep in his throat she can barely make out what he is saying. 'Am I quite dead?' he murmurs.

'No. Not dead,' she says.

'But I was in Purgatory and now a cool hand draws me through to Paradise.'

Sarah pauses between undoing vest buttons. 'And who do you think I am?' she says. 'The ruddy ferryman?'

His eyes swing away from Elen and he lifts his head then struggles to sit up.

'Oh,' he says. 'Mrs Barker.'

'The very one, at your service.'

Elen slips down onto the floor and gently lays her hand on his shoulder, guiding him back. 'Lie still,' she says. 'We must see where you are hurt.'

'I hurt all over,' he says, submitting to the pressure of her hands. 'I have lain, God knows how many hours, underneath my poor Bucephalus.'

'Aha,' Sarah says, 'and Miss Griffiths here thought you only had eyes for her.'

'Do not joke, Mrs Barker,' he says, lying back. 'That magnificent horse was felled most dishonourably...' His sentence is cut short by an involuntary but piteous cry that lances through Elen. 'God's teeth, woman! What are you doing to me?'

Sarah's fingers are on his rib cage. Elen tries to push her away, but Sarah turns her back to block her.

'What have we here?' the surgeon's wife says.

Before Elen can stop her, Sarah grasps the placket of Mordiford's shirt, bending her head and bringing her teeth down on the opening. She spits out a thread and rents the shirt open with a mighty tug.

'Stop!' Elen says.

Sarah frowns at her in confusion. 'You've held men down as their limbs fly, Elen. Don't lose your nerve over a bit of bruising.' Sarah probes and pushes. Elen feels Mordiford tensing and pleating, his breaths creaking as he tries not to shout out.

'Your rib cage is mushy,' Sarah says. 'You have certainly fractured a number of ribs. Come, Elen, we need to make sure there are no more hidden wounds.'

Elen has examined the bodies of many soldiers, hunting for injuries lurking under the screen of skin and muscle, but now she hesitates. She's dreamed so many times of running her hands across his body, of digging her fingers into the hardening muscles of his back; however, she fears her touch will reveal a wantonness.

Mordiford rolls his head to look at her, his eyes brittle in the half-light. Slowly she works his cravat free and slides it off as she has so often done in her dreams.

The skin of his neck is curiously pale in the lamplight, protected from the filth of the battlefield. Her fingers move around his throat. She feels the bounce of his pulse in his neck. It is fast. Leaning closer to him, her hands move onto the firm muscles at the back of his neck. It is almost an embrace.

She is so close to his face, she could lift his head just a little and press her lips to his. She tries so hard not to look down into his eyes, but she knows he watches her. His body is still tensing, bracing himself for the next injury that Sarah's practised fingers discover. Elen moves her hands to his throat, feels along the ridge of his collarbone, walking her fingers onto his chest. She cannot keep her eyes away from him for any longer. She flashes a glance at him. He gives her a rueful smile.

Sarah reaches his leg. Elen leaps back as he gives an animal roar, his shoulders rising off the stretcher. He twists, trying to dash Sarah's hands away, sweat springing from his forehead. Elen grasps him by the arms, feels the muscles fluttering and cramping as he fights the pain. Sarah joins her, pressing Mordiford back down, her teasing ended for the night.

'Your leg is fractured, sir,' Sarah says.

Dear God, Elen prays, *stop now. How bad a sinner could this man have been for You to punish him so? I beg You, stop testing him. Stop testing me.*

'It is a bad break,' Sarah is saying. 'Even under this poor light it is plain that the bone has broken the skin.'

'It will heal,' he says, panting with pain. His hope compresses Elen's heart. She grasps his hand in both of hers and holds it against her. He does not notice. He is overwhelmed.

Sarah shakes her head and says, 'You have lain in mud and dirt with an open wound for many hours. It will be quite corrupt by now. Elen will fetch you some brandy. Lie still for the next few hours. The surgeon will deal with it in the morning.'

'He shall not have my leg,' he says through gritted teeth.

'There is no other choice,' Sarah says. 'Elen, get that brandy.'

'Wait,' and Elen squeezes his hand, rocks his arm to make him look at her. 'I will be with you. All night. We have faced worse nights together, worse horrors.' He opens his mouth to protest, but she hurries on, 'In this heat, it will not be many days before the wound begins to sluff. At present, you will lose the leg below the knee, nothing more.'

'Leave it and you will lose it all,' Sarah says, 'including your life.'

He turns his face to the wall. Elen thinks, he is trying imagine it. He cannot.

'We can't leave you perched up there all night,' Sarah says. 'Think you can get down if we help?'

Mordiford looks at Elen and nods. He lets go of her hand, struggles onto his elbows, the movement making him draw down his chin and snarl with pain.

They help him off the manger. Sarah bustles and bosses around them, but Elen listens to Mordiford's breathing, hears the strain in his chest and steadies him, whispers to him. The words do not matter. We are all animals, she thinks. I can calm a horse, a cow, a dog in pain. These whispers are the same – you are not alone. I am here.

She makes a bed of hay for him in the stall, piles stooks against the wall as a pillow, lowers him down, props him up and tells him she is going to fetch brandy and will be back soon for the rest of the night.

'You should sleep too,' Sarah says to Elen as she walks with her to the door of the stable.

'I could not even if I tried. I have sat with him through far worse.'

Sarah takes a steadying breath and looks out across the yard. 'This is not real life, Elen, and this is not real love.'

Elen is too drained to argue. 'To sit with him is enough.'

Sarah raises a disbelieving eyebrow, but then she grasps her by the shoulders and gives her a quick peck on the cheek. 'Goodnight, my dear,' she says.

When Elen returns with the brandy Mordiford is staring morosely at the ceiling. His face is very white in the lamplight. He hears her and smiles wearily at her. She pours a large measure of brandy into a cup and kneels beside him.

'Oh, Miss Griffiths,' he says with a sigh, 'how dearly I wish you had known me when I was a fine figure of a man instead of a scarred and useless cripple.'

'I did know you then and I did not like you.'

'You do say the most extraordinary things. Whatever can you mean? I was an Adonis. I needed neither wit nor conversation for women to swoon in my company.' He knocks the brandy back in several large gulps and holds the cup out to be refilled. 'Alcohol is a truly wonderful medicine. How I used to love to drink it.'

'Are you in much pain?' she says, sitting on the hay beside him.

'It hurts damnably to tell you the truth.' He takes several more gulps of brandy. 'But trauma is a simple pain to endure. There is another, far more agonising.'

'You mean the pain you must face tomorrow.'

'No, not that.'

'What then?'

He does not reply, but raises the cup to his lips, watching her, his eyes as black as plums in the lamplight.

–

'The day was ours,' Mordiford says, 'but it was won at a terrible cost.'

Elen sits next to him, leaning back on the stooks piled against the wall of the stable, the captain's coat covering the hay to stop thistle spines pushing through the muslin of her dress. The lamp has long since burned its last drop of oil, but the doors to the stables stand open, letting in the air of the summer night.

Mordiford's voice is husked with tiredness and alcohol. Elen knows she should let him sleep, that it is selfish keeping him

273

awake, but she cannot bear to lose him for a moment, not even to his dreams.

'Tell me about the battle,' she says. She thirsts for every detail. She wants to live through it with him, imagine everything he saw, experience everything he felt. He pushes himself a little higher in the hay. His profile is silhouetted against the lamplight, so close that she could reach out, trace each feature with her fingertips.

'It was not until late in the afternoon, that we began to take the upper hand,' he says. 'The French command weakened and their horses tired. The duke sent fresh cavalry streaming in, and suddenly all was confusion, French troopers breaking rank, fleeing in panic. We could hardly move. The tracks were clogged with the enemy, desperate to escape the fighting. Some even tried to swim their horses across the Danube. A few may have made it, but many would have drowned.' Mordiford takes more brandy. He rests his head back and she fears he may fall asleep.

'What cowards these French are,' she says. He scoffs softly.

'Not all of them. I saw such a pitiful sight as I hacked and fought my way through them. As thousands fled, a small group were left out on the plain completely unsupported. I could see they were no more than youngsters. They were either too brave to run away or too foolish to know when to surrender. They faced a storm of canister fire and died where they stood, cut to pieces in rank and file.'

'How old were these boys?'

'I do not imagine any of them had seen their twentieth birthday.'

'And it was all for naught?'

'Alas, yes because with darkness almost upon us, the French in Blenheim laid down their arms. I was inside the walls by then, the crush so great I thought Bucephalus would be lifted from his hooves and carried along by the mob. The French burned their colours rather than let them fall into our hands.'

'What a shameful thing to do.'

'It was. I saw French officers weeping tears of despair and humiliation.'

'And you came through all this uninjured?'

'I did by some miracle, but I was soaked in the blood of my fellow dragoons who died beside me.'

He falls quiet again, lost in thought.

'With the battle over,' she says presently, 'how did you manage to injure yourself so comprehensively?' He laughs quietly and reaches across to where her hand lies on the hay beside him. He lifts her fingers to his mouth and brushes them with his lips.

'I am tired. And so must you be. Look, I think I can see the dawn. We have talked all night.' There is something else in his tone, his manner perhaps, which warns her this is not the reason.

'Why do you hesitate?' she says, an anxious worm of an idea forming in her head that war makes animals of men. Does he hesitate because killing has revealed a part of his nature he would prefer to forget?

'I suppose because today has made me regret that I did not act honourably in the winter.'

'You did act honourably. You saved me from your father.'

'Eventually.' He turns his head away.

'You were too sick to act earlier.'

'Was I? If I had been the man I am now, I would have spoken out, warned Argyll and forced you back home.'

'That may have done me a greater disservice. The doctor made it quite clear that if I refused to come, the earl would punish my whole family. My father would have lost the tenancy of the dairy. We would have been destitute, forced to wander the countryside in search of work, impossible to find in the middle of winter. No, I had to stay. The stakes were too high.'

'Why was I cursed with such a pitiless wretch of a father?'

She sits forward, holds his hands to her and forces him to look at her. 'Has the battle brought up these reflections?'

'Perhaps,' he sighs. 'I hesitate to tell you...' he presses her hands to his forehead as if trying to force the words from his head. 'I am at a loss. I do not want to shock and frighten you.'

'What?' she says, alarm building inside her.

'The man who brought down Bucephalus and left me on the plains to die was Ned Harley.'

Ned Harley. The man had not entered her thoughts for the whole of the day and now her heart bangs erratically in her chest, a terrible certainty that his revenge will never end. She lets Mordiford's hands drop from her clasp. He reaches up to stroke her cheek.

'You understand my remorse now?' he says.

'No, not entirely. You must tell me everything that happened between the two of you.'

'And increase your anxiety about that diabolist?'

'I am no longer that delicate girl who turned her eyes away from a bowl of spittle. You say you have changed. So have I. You regret that you did not tell me the whole truth in the winter and I agree with you – you were wrong.' He bows his head, picks at a piece of hay and begins stripping the outer sheath. 'Do not make the same mistake again. Save no detail from me, I must know everything that occurred and deal with the anxiety myself.'

'It is an ugly story.'

'Then start now before we have uglier things to contend with.'

'By nightfall, the plains were seething with French prisoners under the guard of our soldiers. Everyone was tired and battle-weary. I was moving among the infantry and looked out at that sad corner of the plains where those youngsters had died. It was such a mournful sight to see them lying in their ranks as if they were on parade. But then, to my horror, I saw movement among them, a looter.'

'Ned Harley.'

'I was not to know that then. All I could see was a man stripping the boys of their personal effects, stuffing his spoils into a haversack. Despite my exhaustion, I felt my fury rise. I mounted Bucephalus and cantered out to stop this cowardly desecration. I meant to chase the fellow away and as I spurred my horse to a gallop, he did indeed begin to run.'

'You still had not recognised Ned Harley?'

'No, not at all. It never crossed my mind it was anyone other than a Frenchman. The darkness had robbed the field of colour. As I neared I shouted out to him, "I am Captain Mordiford of Wood's Regiment of Horse and I order you to stand fast." On hearing my shout, he stopped, but as I bore down on him he snatched a musket from the ground and drove the bayonet into the throat of Bucephalus.'

Elen sits bolt upright and presses her fingers against her mouth. To thrust a bayonet into a man bent on slaughtering you in the heat of battle is one thing. To fell a magnificent animal when the battle is done is heinous.

'I cannot believe it.'

'Oh, Miss Griffiths. I cannot describe to you the extent of my anguish and that of my poor animal. He would never have thrown me had he not been mad with pain and terror. I tried desperately to calm him, but down we both went. I took his full weight across my leg before he rolled, trapping me beneath him before he died.'

'And still you did not recognise Ned.'

'It sounds impossible I know, but as he came close, to my amazement I saw he wore the English scarlet. I imagined he had mistaken me for the enemy and was now coming to my aid, but instead he swung the butt of the musket and struck me a heavy blow to my head. It was when he raised the butt to take a second strike, the terrible vision fused before me...' Mordiford pauses, staring ahead, his face tight with incredulity. 'A split second before the final crack, I knew that I looked into the face of the man who served you so despicably last winter.'

'As he did again, here in Franconia, but a few weeks' passed.'

He stares at her confused, his brows pulling his forehead into soft folds, then he says, 'Is that why your friend and champion rushed out to defend you?'

'Yes. She assumed you were he.'

'How did he find you?'

'He engineered circumstances to bring Dr Argyll and myself to Friedberg, where he apprehended me and made a second attempt on my honour.'

At this, Mordiford moves so violently that his leg rolls on the hay and he falls back with a cry.

'My cursed leg,' he bellows. Elen takes his hand, holding it to her as his fingers pulse. When the acute torture abates, he turns to her, running his tongue across his parched lips. 'Why did that brute follow us here?'

'He is in a most bitter and disturbed state of mind. His dismissal threw him into poverty and degradation. He takes no responsibility for this. He lays the blame for his misfortunes squarely at my feet and is determined to have his revenge.'

'Now I understand why Mrs Barker saw fit to arm herself with a sickle. How I wish I had her rushing to my aid on that battlefield.'

Mordiford turns her hand and places a lingering kiss in the palm. She feels the roughness of his stubble and the moisture of his mouth on her skin.

'You are not the only person in danger from that fiend,' he says. 'The locus of his revenge no longer lies solely with you. He was set to flee before I shouted my name. He meant to kill me. Indeed, he believes that he already has.'

She hardly hears his words, the sensation of his lips on her palm has quite distracted her. Sensing her stillness, he gazes at her, his eyes shining vividly in the dawn twilight that has crept into the stable.

'When I awoke, out there on the plains,' he says, his voice barely a whisper, 'it was surprisingly cold. The sky above my head glittered with stars. My heart was aching for my poor horse. The pain in my leg was so excruciating I cursed God for creating a body that could feel such agony and yet not die. I feared I would not live to see another dawn. In the winter I would have welcomed it, but I knew that if I died I would never set eyes on you again. That notion caused me far greater pain than my shattered bones.'

She placed a kiss on each of his fingers in turn. 'You would have seen me again,' she says. 'If not in this world, then in the next.'

'Ha! You think that? I do not share your confidence. You had a poor opinion of me before I fell ill.'

'I did not know all then. Let me judge you as I see you now, not as the man you might have been, but as the man you have become.'

'Not as good a man as you may think.'

'Whatever do you mean by that?'

'Oh...' But instead of answering, he yawns and slides a little further down in the hay, all the while holding onto her hand. 'I feel so tired now. If I was not so cold, I fancy I would sleep.'

'Let me lay your coat over you.'

'No. I do not want my coat. Lean against me and let me feel the heat of you beside me.' She pushes herself closer on the hay and lays her head on his shoulder. Languorously, he releases her hand, lifting his arm to encircle her shoulders, drawing her body close to his. 'When you are next to me, I can feel your goodness flowing into me.' He murmurs into her hair. 'It is a salve to my soul.'

'It is just my warmth.'

'Perhaps.'

He is silent for a few minutes although she can tell by the pattern of his breathing that he does not sleep.

'Miss Griffiths,' he says presently, his voice thick with tiredness. She rests her hand against his chest, raising herself up to look at him. 'Did you not say that Dr Argyll travels with you still?'

'I did.'

'Find him for me when we have rested a while. This poor old body of mine has taken such a pounding of late. I cannot lose a leg as well as everything else.'

'But you must, sir. You heard the surgeon's wife. There is no other choice.'

'Argyll brought me through the pox without shedding a drop of my blood or submitting me to the indignities of purging. Let me at least speak to him before I hand myself over to that good woman's husband.'

Chapter 14

Elen does not need to seek the doctor. Dr Argyll's voice rouses her from a fitful sleep.

'Captain Mordiford,' she hears him call from the yard. 'Where are you, my lord?'

She springs up from where she has lain for the last few hours and crams her cap back on her head. She is still smoothing her clothes when Dr Argyll's genial face appears around the stall.

'Miss Griffiths. Good morning. This is quite like old times, is it not?'

The doctor strides past her to where Mordiford is stirring and says, 'I am pleased to see you, my lord although I am sorry to find you in this parlous state.'

As Mordiford struggles to sit up, she slips past the doctor and kneels down, offering him her forearm to pull on. The doctor encourages them both with sympathetic comments until she manages to manoeuvre Mordiford into a reasonably comfortable sitting position.

'You are the very man I wanted to see, Argyll,' he says. She knows from his laboured breathing that the movement has fired up the pain in his leg.

'Am I indeed?'

'I want to know your opinion of my injury before I hand myself over to the barber surgeons.'

The doctor frowns. He is wondering what sort of opinion he can give, she thinks, when amputation is the only option left. 'I heard your leg was broken, my lord,' the doctor says. 'There is only one treatment for that.'

'Look at it for me, I beg you.'

'I cannot imagine it will alter anything…' The doctor gives a great sigh. Elen knows nothing will change his opinion, but then she sees resignation soften his brow and feels a flutter of hope in her chest.

'Shall I lift the muslin that covers the wound, sir?' she says before he changes his mind.

'Yes, Miss Griffiths, would you be so kind.'

Mordiford narrows his eyes as she reaches over him. 'I will be as careful as I can,' she says. The gauze, which was laid across the lower part of Mordiford's leg the night before, lifts with comparative ease. He exhales with relief. The doctor removes his hat and kneels beside Elen, a frown of concentration on his face.

'It is quite a mess, is it not?' Dr Argyll says. 'And difficult to make out exactly. Miss Griffiths, I wonder if you would be kind enough to peel back some of this fabric here.'

She can see that the ripped edge of the stocking is stuck fast in the dried blood around the wound. Mordiford tenses as, with the greatest care, she starts to peel back the fabric, supporting his leg firmly by the ankle with her other hand. She can feel herself drifting away from the man she has lain next to all night, stepping back inside herself again. She knows she hurts him, but if he is to be convinced that amputation is imperative, the doctor must see the full extent of the damage.

She has to ignore his trembling, but it is difficult not to feel despair as she uncovers the crater in his leg. There is a deep gouge all the way down his shin, packed with mud and grass from the field. As she works she sees the jagged end of a small bone slicing up through the skin. The brandy would have helped but even so, she cannot imagine how he talked all night with such a wound as this.

Mordiford never once tries to dash her hand away or beg her to pause to let him catch his breath. Several times she stops to check he is coping. He gives her a stiff nod to continue.

Throughout the process the doctor peers at the wound, tilting and cocking his head to get a better view. Finally, he raises his hand and gets stiffly to his feet, knocking the dirt from his knees with his hat. 'That is enough, Miss Griffiths,' he says. 'I can see the extent of the injury without you having to expose it any further.'

The doctor makes himself comfortable on a bale of hay. She can see by his expression that the verdict is the same as everyone else's. 'I cannot begin to tell you my sadness, on hearing that you had been injured on the battlefield,' Dr Argyll says. 'I wish that I could bring you some comfort and give you the answer you want, but I cannot. In my opinion, you would risk everything if you did not submit yourself to the care of Mr Barker.'

Mordiford groans, rolling his eyes away. Dr Argyll begins to tap the brim of his tricorn onto the toe of his boot. After a few minutes he continues, 'When Miss Griffiths and I first arrived in The Hague, I was reluctant to make Mr Barker's acquaintance. Was I not, Miss Griffiths?'

She smiles; that is an understatement, she thinks. 'Indeed you were, sir,' she says.

'I thought these surgeons were little more than butchers, but Miss Griffiths – who, I have to tell you, has shown me up somewhat by her openness of mind – championed concord between us, a necessary discipline as we were travelling companions for many months.'

'And you have become firm friends, have you not, sir?' she says.

'Yes, I think I would almost go as far as to say that.'

She is not going to allow the doctor to undermine Mordiford's faith in the surgeon. 'Did I not hear you saying only the other day, sir, that Mr Barker was a thoroughly sound fellow?'

'Did I go that far? Well, perhaps I did.'

Oh, for pity's sake, Elen thinks, will you set your squabbles aside and put this soldier's mind at rest. 'And you have revised your reservations about his profession?' she says, drilling him with a look.

'Oh, I am sure there are as many quacks and charlatans among the barber surgeons as among my own branch of the profession...'

'But that is not really the point, is it Dr Argyll?' she says.

Elen gives him such a glare that the doctor clears his throat and says, 'No. Mr Barker is not one of them.'

'He is extremely skilled,' she says to Mordiford. 'I worked next to him, all through yesterday. His speed and precision is breathtaking.'

'I must agree with Miss Griffiths,' the doctor says. 'I have also seen him in action. His attack with the saw is formidable...' Elen winces. This was not the line she had hoped he would take. '...and he cuts so clean and quick, that soldiers relieved of a limb by him, have a far greater chance of making it home than a soldier who has been operated on by one of those Prussians. If I had to lose a leg to anyone's knife, it would be to his.'

It is hard to read Mordiford's thoughts. If he does not have the leg removed, he will die, but who would not flinch from the agony to come?

'As for the pain...' the doctor continues, having received no reply.

'It is nothing to do with the pain,' Mordiford replies, somewhat abruptly.

'...but if it were...' Dr Argyll persists. 'Let me assure you, with Mr Barker, it is over in under a minute.'

'I said it is not the pain.'

'Then my advice to you is to have the damned thing off,' Dr Argyll says. 'The sooner the better and that is an end to it.'

'And an end to my life as a dragoon.'

'Ah, I see. Well, yes, that would be true but...' The doctor hesitates, then casts a look at Elen. Clearly he is struggling to understand. 'Surely, my lord, this dalliance with the army is a temporary thing.'

In an instant, Elen knows the doctor has made a mistake.

'I did not see the purchase of my commission as a dalliance,' Mordiford says. 'And for the love of God, stop calling me Lord.'

'No, quite,' the doctor blusters. 'I have probably clutched at quite the wrong word in my puzzlement, but I had assumed that at some time in the not-too-distant future you would return to Wales and take up your role as master of the Duntisbourne estates.'

'I have no desire to return while my father lives.'

'No, indeed.'

An awkward silence descends on the group, which the doctor eventually breaks. 'I must say, it is most encouraging to see how well your skin has healed from the pox since I saw you last.'

Mordiford looks up sharply. Elen expects his face to show contempt, as it would have in the past, for Dr Argyll's clumsy attempt to move the conversation onto a more encouraging footing. Instead he smiles weakly at the doctor and replies, 'I barely think of it now.'

Dr Argyll chuckles, probably from a sense of relief as much as anything else.

Mordiford leans forward in the hay and says in an urgent tone, 'I cannot lose my leg. Let a few hours pass so that your creativity can begin to burn again.'

'I cannot imagine what you mean,' Dr Argyll says. She knows well from his tone that he is not immune to flattery. Mordiford catches her eye and she feels such a closeness to him that hope rises in her chest.

She goes over to the bale and sits down beside the doctor. 'You have read much, sir,' she says. 'You have travelled and seen how other cultures treat their sick.'

'Indeed I have,' the doctor says.

'Do you think, that the captain would have survived smallpox had a London physician been brought down to bleed him, purge him, and bleed him again? Somehow, I imagine he would not.'

'We will never know,' Dr Argyll says. Mordiford's eyes are glowing with keen interest and gratitude that she is championing his cause.

'But see,' she says, warming to her theme. 'The scars the captain carries now are mere ghosts of the boils that covered him. No other infection hurried in.'

'Thanks in its entirety to the care you, and of course, Miss Griffiths, under your instruction, gave to me.'

'None of your treatments are currently practised or recommended,' Elen says. 'Not even at Court – and yet, the captain lives.'

'Well, it is most gratifying to hear you both speak so enthusiastically of my work,' Dr Argyll replies. 'But wounds inflicted on the battlefield are not my area of study.' Mordiford looks away, sinking back again. She can sense his despair. 'However...' the doctor says slowly.

'Yes?' Elen says with an intense urgency.

The doctor gets to his feet and begins pacing around the stall. After a minute or so he turns to his expectant audience and says, 'A moment. I need the advice of the barber surgeon.' He hurries out of the stable. She hears him calling Mr Barker's name.

'He will not be persuaded,' Mordiford says.

'I am not so sure,' she says.

–

Within minutes, the doctor and surgeon can be heard in lively discussion approaching the door of the stable. Mr Barker has clearly been pulled away from his breakfast, for he still clutches a hunk of bread in his hand, which he passes to Elen for safekeeping as he approaches the patient with Dr Argyll at his shoulder.

He looks down at the wound and says, 'I cannot see enough to advise you.'

'But in theory, Paré's principle could apply?' Dr Argyll says. 'In theory.'

Elen looks from doctor to surgeon as if watching a game of catch. Eventually she says, 'I beg you, gentlemen, do not keep

286

my patient in suspense longer than is absolutely necessary. Will one of you please tell us what you are planning?'

'Nothing at the moment,' Dr Argyll says. 'I do not want to raise the viscount's hopes.'

'For the love of God, man,' Mordiford says. 'This is more agonising than my wound.'

'Very well,' Dr Argyll says. 'I read a translation a number of years ago written by a man who had studied survival rates among soldiers wounded during the campaign of Francis I.'

'The man was French and a barber surgeon,' Mr Barker says, his eyes alive with merriment.

'So a rascal on both accounts?' Elen says.

Dr Argyll makes a tutting noise and narrows his eyes at her. 'This is no time for mockery,' he says a little testily.

'I think it an excellent time,' Mr Barker parries, giving Elen a broad wink.

'Come along, gentlemen,' she says. 'Only minutes ago we were regaling Captain Mordiford with stories of your developing camaraderie.'

'Which is still there, is it not, doctor?' Mr Barker claps Dr Argyll heartily on the back. 'I have never been known to tease a fellow I do not like.'

'You are teasing us all, Mr Barker,' Elen says, 'if you do not tell us about this surgical pioneer.'

'Ah, yes, Ambroise Paré. He has been a great inspiration to me especially as the phenomena he observed were contrary to expectations. During the Italian campaigns he noticed that a soldier who lay neglected on the battlefield for long enough for maggots to infest the wound, made a swifter and surer recovery than one whose wound remained clear.'

Elen shudders. She cannot abide maggots. One hot and humid summer a neighbour lost his flock and livelihood to fly-strike, but before he accepted their inevitable demise, she saw the wretched sheep agitated, and mad with pain, as they gnawed at their rotting flesh. Surely amputation was preferable to that.

'Oh, hell's teeth. Where is this going?' the captain murmurs. Mr Barker shrugs and looks at Elen.

'It is worth some consideration,' Dr Argyll says.

'Surely not,' Elen says. 'Once a patient recovers from the shock of an amputation, our single aim is to keep the wound free from sluff and corruption.'

'It seems,' Mr Barker says, 'the maggots' sole interest is to feed on that very sluff and leave the living flesh alone.'

'That is not how the maggot feeds on the breech of a sheep,' she says. 'I have seen them quite eat the back of an animal away.'

'It is the fleece that encourages that, I expect,' Dr Argyll says. Although Elen is not certain he is convinced by his own argument. 'Provided the wound is open to the air, the maggots sate themselves solely on the dead flesh.'

'Let me add a caveat to that,' Mr Barker says. 'I am referring to wounds open to the air without any complicated injury beneath. Until I can investigate the wound, I cannot recommend such a course of action. I understand the inestimable Mrs Barker has already acquainted you with the consequences of failure.'

'She has,' the captain says.

'In that case, if you are willing to take the risk, you must let me probe the wound.'

'Mr Barker, I beg you,' Elen says. 'The captain is already in extreme discomfort.' Mordiford holds a hand up to her to cut her short.

'Am I allowed to ask why you need to probe?' he says.

'Of course. After all, it is your wound.' Mr Barker wipes his hands down the front of his waistcoat. 'Miss Griffiths, I think I shall finish my breakfast, if you would be so kind.' She passes him the hunk of bread and he drops to the ground, settling himself on the floor next to the viscount. 'I have studied anatomy...'

'On cadavers,' interjects Dr Argyll.

'Cadavers have the same bones as the living,' Elen says quietly.

Mr Barker smiles broadly up at her and takes another bite out of his bread, chewing it with relish. 'The lower leg is made of two bones – one large, one small. I cannot be sure, but it appears in your case that it is the smaller bone that has broken through the flesh. If the larger one remains intact, it could act as a splint for the other.'

'And if it isn't?' Elen says.

'Then there is no way on God's earth that I could realign the bone in such a fashion as it would heal, maggots or no maggots. You would have to allow me to amputate.'

'And this probing – painful?' the captain says.

'Exquisitely.'

The captain looks at Elen who shakes her head, her heart begging him not to embark on this risky and agonising course. After some consideration, the captain says, 'I am willing to let you probe, Mr Barker, but on one condition.'

'And that is?'

'Miss Griffiths does not witness the procedure.'

'Sir,' she interjects, 'I have seen much worse during this campaign. You, of all people, should know I am not the same as a woman of your class who might swoon at the sight of blood or distress.'

'I do know, Miss Griffiths. But if I am to allow Mr Barker a free hand with his knife, I intend to scream like Polyphemus and curse this good gentleman to Hades and back before he's done. Should you hear such a thing from my lips, that fragile good opinion you have of me would be destroyed for ever.'

Part III

The Summer Fields

Chapter 1

August 1704

Donauwörth, Bavaria

'We should start back,' Elen says. Sarah is leading her through the meadows to one of the many lakes that crowd along the banks of the Danube.

'There's no hurry,' Sarah says. 'Whatever will be, will be. Getting back to the barns will not change that. We have many days ahead of us filled with the smell of death and decay. Let's enjoy tranquillity for a while longer.'

When they reach the water's edge, the lake is spangled with the floating cotton of the willow herb. Iridescent damsel flies flare blue as they flick over the surface. The hollow call of a moorhen comes from somewhere in the reeds, followed by the slap of a wing on water. It's hard to believe that the bodies of thousands of men lie a few leagues to the west, already stripped and laid out for the gravediggers in that vast open-air morgue on the plains of Höchstadt.

There will be no such honour for Bucephalus and the multitude of horses lost during the battle. The strictest orders have been given that no soldier touches them for fear of infection. Within days the stench rising up from this stretch of land will become unbearable. However, Mr Barker is confident that by then the wounded will all have been transported to the general hospital that the Duke of Marlborough has established fifty leagues to the north.

'Whatever the outcome, the captain doesn't want us to travel with the unit to Nördlingen,' Elen says.

'Why ever not?'

'He's concerned that Ned Harley is still abroad. If we go to Nördlingen, we will be easy to find and the captain is not yet well enough to defend us.'

Sarah frowns. 'Us?' she says. 'By that, I assume you mean the captain and yourself.'

'I do.'

'Elen, my dear, let us sit down for a few moments.'

'I don't want to sit down. The sun is high in the sky, it is already past midday. I'm sure the operation is completed by now.'

'No. I need you to sit down.'

'I know what you are going to say.'

'No, you do not.'

Sarah sinks down onto the meadow, patting the grass next to her to encourage Elen to follow suit. When Elen looks down at her friend, she feels a jolt of anxiety, for Sarah looks grave.

'Whatever is the matter?' she says. 'Why do you look so anxious?'

'I have something bad to tell you about your captain.' Elen is filled with a black dread.

'He's sicker than at first we thought?' she says, grabbing at Sarah's hand. 'He bleeds inside and you could not bear to tell me?'

'No, it's not that,' Sarah says, drawing her down to sit.

'What then?'

Sarah reaches into the pocket of her apron and takes something out. At first Elen thinks she holds a jewel because as the sun glances across it, it shines with the brilliant light of a diamond. Sarah passes the keepsake across to her, watching Elen's face with an earnest expression.

Elen lays it on the palm of her hand. It is a miniature portrait, surrounded by a halo of brilliants. It depicts not a face, but a single eye, painted in exquisite detail. The delicate arch of the brow and the single lock of golden hair, leaves her in no doubt that the eye depicted is that of a woman. The colour of the iris is the softest grey, paler than the feathers of a pigeon, but the eye's expression speaks of a sophisticated sexuality.

'Whose lover's eye is this?' she says sharply, although she already knows.

Sarah presses her lips together.

'The captain's?' Elen says.

Sarah nods.

'Where did you get it?' Elen says, diverting her shock at seeing the image on to Sarah for having it in her possession.

'It was in the pocket of his justacorps.'

'You went through his pockets?' Elen says, fury building in her chest.

'Of course I did. I wanted to make sure no valuables had been left behind when Mr Barker took him away.'

'Oh, is that so? You expect me to believe that? You were looting. You are no better than Ned Harley.'

Sarah listens to Elen's cruel words with that irritating look of pity on her face. 'You can rail and shout at me as much as you like, Elen. It is not I with whom you are furious.'

'It most certainly is.'

Unperturbed, Sarah looks out across the water.

Hot with anger, Elen glares at her friend's profile but Sarah maintains a sad and tranquil expression as she gazes into the middle distance. With no resistance to fight against, Elen feels her rage abating and a creeping sense of doom slipping in to take its place.

She looks at the keepsake in her hand. The wanton eye stares back at her. With shaking fingers, she turns the jewel over. The reverse is engraved with a bluebell and the initials A and C.

'I know the bluebell signifies everlasting love,' Sarah says, although she still gazes out across the water. 'I imagine the A stands for the lady you mentioned to me, Lady Arabella.'

When Elen speaks her voice is curiously high. 'The captain's first name is Crispin.'

Sarah turns to face her, reaching out to take her hand. Meekly, Elen lets her. 'I am so sorry, my dear.'

They sit together in silence, listening to the sounds of the lake, the purr of wind through the sedge and the plop of a fish breaking the surface of the water. After a few minutes Elen gives a deep sigh and says, 'It doesn't change anything.'

'I think it probably does. It's unlikely he would carry such a token into battle with him if he did not intend returning to her.'

Elen looks away to dash a tear from her eye. Throughout all her waking dreams, she never allowed herself to imagine a real life with Mordiford. She may have imagined quitting the fields and the dairy to take on the role of governess or teacher but a countess? Organising the social running of Duntisbourne? That was a ludicrous notion.

She has allowed herself to live for the day, to dream of the next step she would take in their developing intimacy. She imagined she would be satisfied and at peace if she only knew he felt the same, but from the moment he threw that kiss to her as she drove away all those months ago, it ceased to be enough. She began to dream of his embrace, certain it would leave her fulfilled and calm. She slept in his arms the night before and still she yearns for more.

As if she can read her thoughts, Sarah says, 'Desire is like an itching fleabite – the more you scratch, the worse it gets.'

'That's a crude analogy,' she says. Sarah shrugs and stays silent. Elen studies the initials. She hears a family of ducks quarrelling on the opposite bank. Eventually she says, 'What am I to do?'

'Do you want to know what you should do or what you could do?'

'I don't think I know any more.'

'Then I will start with what you should do. You should make your way to England as swiftly as possible, go back to your family and put this behind you as a great adventure.'

Elen shakes her head and cries vehemently, 'I cannot leave him and I cannot forget him.'

'Of course you can't, but time will round the corners of your pain and one day, maybe many summers in the future, you will see him riding out on the estate. Then you'll reflect on these brief months when you had a loving connection and the memory will bring you happiness.'

'That could never make me happy.'

'How can you possibly know, Elen? Passion of every kind has only so much energy, whether it is love, or grief, or revenge. It's difficult to keep it fresh and keen for longer than a few years.'

'Just a year together would be enough,' she says in despair.

Sarah squeezes her hand and continues, 'As time passes, passion cannot help but change. Occasionally it becomes an obsession which can eat into any man's heart, but for the rest of us, we lay the fervour aside as a memory – a thought quite stripped of any emotion.'

Elen cannot imagine such an outcome, and shakes her head. 'I cannot bear to stifle a flame so recently lit.'

Sarah takes a deep breath and lets it out with a sigh. 'Then you could indulge it, give yourself to him, swive away until the lust is spent...' Sarah raises a finger of warning. 'If you take that path, one day, many summers from now, you will see him riding out on the estate and all you will remember is the way your love faltered and how the affair died.'

'I would not.'

'Oh, yes, you would. You would remember the missed meetings, the disappointments, the angry words, the pain of the captain putting his real life – perhaps his real family – before you. Eventually you would know that the occasional moments of joy are not worth the days and months of unhappiness. You will part as bitter enemies.'

'If the path of love is so bleak, why are you still with Mr Barker?'

'Oh, my dear, that is a quite different situation. Of course the frantic lust that nabbed us when we first clapped eyes on each other was quite worn out after a few years of furious swiving but we were able to replace it with real love and true affection.'

'What I feel for the captain is real love.'

'No, it is not. At the moment you are mad with the feeling of love. That's not real love at all. It may turn into real love, but not unless he can take you as his wife in the eyes of God and society.'

'That is so false. Love is not about convention.'

'But traditions exist because real love survives in them, otherwise we'd never marry. We'd take what we wanted, whenever we wanted it and we'd live in a fever of lust or misery. It'd be a terrible life of extremes.'

'I cannot give him up. I'll live each day as it comes. If I have to suffer pain in the end, it will be worth it because I cannot do otherwise.'

Elen gets to her feet and stalks off across the meadows in the direction of the barns, grinding the keepsake into the palm of her hand as she walks.

The heat unsteadies the air. Sarah's words blister in her mind, but soon they are replaced by an even greater anxiety. If Mordiford rode into battle with that keepsake in his pocket, he must indeed have affections for Lady Arabella. It is this thought, above all others, which causes her the greatest pain, and yet she cannot believe it to be true. Whatever feelings he had for that sophisticated lady back in England, they cannot compare to the emotions Elen has shared with him. She has seen him at his worst and loves him still.

–

The barns are a good half hour walk from the lake. By the time they appear on the horizon, Elen is burning up. The sun has heated her bones, her shoulders, her skull. Her chemise presses between her legs, holding her back, the fabric cracking in the dry heat as she strides along. She breaks into a run, lifting her skirt free of her ankles. As she nears, sounds of distress reach her ears. In alarm, she rushes into the barn.

Mr Barker looks up from his work with a frown on his face. She freezes, appalled that in her anguish she has done the very thing Mordiford begged her not to do. Mr Barker twitches the head of a bloody saw in the direction of the stable.

'All done, Miss Griffiths,' he says cheerfully, before returning to his work on the struggling patient before him.

Elen runs out and across the yard, tripping on the rough cobbles. When she enters the stables she is momentarily blinded by the sudden gloom. She creeps across the hay and swings herself into the stall where Mordiford lay that morning.

There he is, pale and weak. As her eyes become accustomed to the shadows, she sees that Mr Barker has not relieved him of his leg, and calming herself, she comes towards him.

Mordiford opens his eyes as if he senses her, for she has made no noise at all. He smiles wearily and holds his hand out to her. 'There you are,' he says, his voice deep and ragged. 'Come to me, my angel.'

She takes his hand, hot and damp from his ordeal. She kneels beside him, lays her face against his chest and listens until she hears his heart beating strong and true. In the quiet of the stable, she lets her silent tears moisten the linen of his shirt beneath her cheek.

Chapter 2

With the campaign season almost at its end, the Duke of Marlborough's army march towards Landau to support the Margrave of Baden in his siege. It was said that once the fortress fell, Marlborough would establish a good position in the Moselle valley for the following year and then quit for England.

Elen, Dr Argyll and the Barkers volunteered to stay behind at the barns with the intention of following on to the hospital at Nördlingen, as soon as the rest of the wounded were pronounced fit enough for the journey.

In pairs or in groups, some on foot if they could walk, others on transport when it became available, the wounded moved on. The lime pits were filled in, the bloodied straw burned and the Prussian surgeons bidden farewell. As the days passed the collection of buildings along the highway to Donauwörth began to look less like a field hospital and more like a farm again.

Elen is tired of this devastated countryside and the flat, featureless plains. She wants to walk through the Lugg valley, climb over the flat stones of the river and watch the trout. Whenever an ox cart of soldiers departs, Elen goes down to the roadside to see her brave charges off, silently sending her love back to her family with them. Some of the soldiers will convalesce over the winter and return in the spring to fight again with the Duke of Marlborough, others will be obliged to quit the army for good due to their injuries, but each one of those young faces, who cheer as they wave her goodbye, have had the good fortune to survive and embark on their journey home.

The news for the captain is not so good.

'I cannot understand it,' Dr Argyll says. 'I thought the countryside at this time of year teemed with flies. Yet not a single one will do me the service of laying a few eggs in that man's wound.'

The day has been fine and dry and Elen is taking her supper in the yard with the doctor, the surgeon and his wife. Mr Barker sucks at his teeth and says, 'He should have let me have the damned thing away. If we wait much longer, he will lose more than his leg.'

'You cannot take his leg now when he has suffered so much to keep it,' Elen says.

Mr Barker shrugs and takes another piece of bread. 'I had a sergeant's wife who was nurse on one of my wards,' he says, tearing the bread with his fingers and wagging the crust at Elen. 'She snagged her thumb and caught an infection. She delayed and by the time she let me relieve her of the thumb, the sluff had reached the hand. She delayed again and when the hand came off, the sluff reappeared in the stump, but she refused another operation, and in consequence she died.'

'Mr Barker! Watch that tongue of yours,' his wife says, nodding her head in Elen's direction.

'Sooner rather than later, is all I say,' Mr Barker concludes.

'Another day,' Dr Argyll says. 'Let us wait until tomorrow evening before we make a decision.'

A gloomy silence descends and Elen watches a swallow dive above the barn's roof. 'Perhaps there is a reason the flies are not interested in the stable,' Elen says.

'Flies are always interested in stables.'

'There have been no animals in there for weeks,' she says, 'and all the other soldiers have moved on. It is as far away from the camp garbage and the latrines as it can be. Perhaps the flies,

300

roundabout, have too much to glut on. Those charnel fields are only a few leagues way.'

The medical men ponder her theory.

'She could be right,' Dr Argyll says. 'There would be little harm in moving the captain closer to where the kitchen waste is piled.'

'Dump him down by the latrines, why don't you?' Mr Barker says. 'There is a swarm of the little blighters round there.'

'I'm not certain a fly who spends time around the latrines is quite the right fellow to lay a handful of eggs in a wound,' the doctor says.

Elen pushes her bowl of beef and potatoes away uneaten. Despite all she has experienced, she loathes the idea of using maggots. She trusts Dr Argyll's judgement, but finds it hard to believe that a creature so associated with decay could bring any succour to the captain, however, she is acutely aware that he is rapidly becoming very sick and that his leg is causing him a great deal of pain.

Once supper is finished, the doctor and the surgeon organise a couple of orderlies to move the captain across to a small hay barn a hundred yards away from the farm building, out in the meadows. Elen makes him as comfortable as she can. He is listless with fever and alcohol, drifting in and out of sleep. Much of the waste has been flung into a tributary, which runs along the boundary of the grassland. The stream's flow has not been sufficient to keep it clear and the waste has formed a dam, creating a small lake of foul slurry.

Dr Argyll opens the barn's hay shutters to let the evening air in. 'The brook is black with flies,' he says, looking out across the darkening field, 'and the wind is blowing up from that direction.' He turns to Elen and says, 'This is a capital idea, Miss Griffiths.'

The light is failing fast. Elen busies herself lighting a lamp, which she carries over to where the captain lies, his eyes closed. But when the doctor takes it from her hand and holds it over Mordiford's leg, she sees his buoyant mood ebb.

301

Elen stares at the wound in the captain's shin, running her eyes down to his ankle and over the mottled flesh across his high instep. She sees a look pass between the two medical men. When Mr Barker has examined the wound, Dr Argyll hangs the lantern on a nail in the beam and makes the smallest movement of his head, a nod of invitation towards the door, meant only for the surgeon. Mr Barker follows the physician and Elen creeps to the end of the stall to catch their words.

Mr Barker paces slowly, head dropped, speaking at the ground. 'The sluff has begun,' he says. 'When I pressed the edge of the wound I felt it crackling beneath the skin. I'm sorry, Argyll, but surely you could smell the corruption.' The doctor nods. 'The leg must come off.' Elen presses her cheek against the wall, the rough planks still warm from a day of hot sun. She feels such a rush of grief. It is the confirmation of all her fears. For days she has known his fever is rising. She's caught the scent of pears on his breath, not an unpleasant smell, but she knows it means his body is battling the evil miasmas.

'Can it wait until the morning?' Dr Argyll says.

'No longer,' Mr Barker replies gravely.

Elen waits, poised to flit out of sight when the doctor turns, but he remains gazing out across the fields. He draws himself up and inhales. When he turns back, she doesn't hide. He has arranged his face into a mask of reassurance, which is not wholly successful.

'Ah, Miss Griffiths,' he says. 'I shall send an orderly down presently to sit with you and the patient for the night.'

'No, thank you, sir. I need no help this evening.'

'You have everything you need?'

'I have, sir.'

'Very well. Good night, Miss Griffiths.'

When she turns, Mordiford is watching her, his eyes bright with fever. His gaze never leaves her face as she walks back from the door towards him. 'It seems my poor leg has lost the battle,' he says.

'I didn't think you heard.'

'I heard.'

He rolls his head away. She reaches across to move the hair from his forehead. When he feels her touch, he takes her hand and presses it to his lips. He sighs heavily. 'Soon there will be little left of me for you to nurse.'

'There will be more than enough of a man left for me to care for.'

He gazes up at her with such a look of despair it makes her throat ache. She must not cry. If one tear falls she will sob herself dry. He must not see how she suffers when his ordeal is so much worse. Her eyes begin to burn, the muscles around her mouth begin to stretch. She is not up to the task.

She says, 'I must quit you for a second.' She manages a coy look, hoping he will assume she needs to relieve herself.

Indeed she does. As she walks away from him towards the door, her face is instantly soaked, the torrent of tears hot and salty, pouring down her cheeks, over her lips, which are already snarled in silent misery. She flees into the dusk, knowing that she must control herself if she is to be any help to Mordiford through this long and terrible night.

–

With sobs catching her breath, Elen flings herself onto the ground, muffling the sound of her grief in the sweet-smelling grass. As she cries, she prays. At first silently, but when she gains some control, she kneels and presses her hands together, looking up at the darkening sky above her head.

'Dear God, take me. He has suffered enough. Let him heal and be well. Let him live. If I have to live in this world without him, I am dead anyway, so take me.'

The wind soughs through the meadow. In her mind the gusts are like the breath of God sweeping across the land to answer her prayers and heal Mordiford. She lowers her eyes towards the horizon. There's a movement in the shadows beneath the hedge. The tears in her eyes distort the image. Something is prowling. She blinks her tears away.

A figure moves stealthily across the field towards her, stooped like an animal. When it is almost upon her, it rises up from the ground. The face is mired in blood, the hair stiff with clay and the eyes look like two black nails hammered into the skull. Satan incarnate has been sent as God's angel to take her in payment for the life of the man she loves.

Chapter 3

Elen braces herself, expecting a blow. It does not come. She gets unsteadily to her feet, her temporary insanity gone. Not the devil incarnate. Ned Harley. She feels no fear, seeing him standing before her. Her prayer has strengthened her. He looks thin, defeated. He is no longer the swaggering, cunning fox who sniffed her out at Friedberg. And she is no longer the meek, frightened lamb.

He casts his eyes down and says, 'I come upon you, kneeling before me. Yet it is I who should throw myself to the ground and beg for your forgiveness.'

It is difficult to read his expression by the weak light of the moon, but there is a slyness behind his plea. She takes a step back, checks over her shoulder. Should she make a break for the barns?

Ned reaches out a hand towards her. 'Help me.'

He drops to the ground, grasping at her hem as he kneels. She pulls away and he lets the fabric stream between his fingers before falling forward onto all fours and creeping towards her.

'I cannot help you,' she says, backing away.

'You must help me. I starve. Wherever I go, I am hounded and hunted. I cannot find my way home. I fled west but found myself retreating with the French. The first time I spoke, they knocked me around the head. I barely escaped with my life. I lay low for days, until hunger forced me to find food, but the locals thought me French and beat me again. I have nowhere else to go.'

He crouches before her, his body heaving, his shoulders slumped and penitent. She remembers him proud and handsome, and an echo of the feeling she once had for him seeps into her heart. He is so cowed, his bind is so desperate that despite herself, she cannot completely reject him.

She sighs deeply and says, 'Go up to the barns. Tell all this to the doctor. He may take pity on your plight.'

'He does not share your compassion. He will not help me.'

His fawning ignites a flash of irritation in her and she says, 'Is that surprising after the way you served me?'

'Do you imagine a single night has passed when I have not regretted my foolish and terrible behaviour towards you?'

'When? Back at Duntisbourne? Or later, when you tried to force yourself on me in Friedberg?'

'I know I have been weak. My baser instincts are easily tempted, but look at me. See how I suffer for my past wrong doings. I am full of remorse.'

'And what of your attack on Captain Mordiford?'

'Captain Mordiford? Oh, may God have mercy upon me. Surely he was not that horseman who charged me after the battle as if to kill me. If I had known, I would have stayed my hand... but I had to defend myself.'

'You cannot expect me to believe these lies. You knew it was he. He called out his name and you smote him as he lay trapped beneath his horse.'

A thought seems to strike him and, forgetting his chastened tone, he says abruptly, 'Mordiford lives?'

'You give yourself away,' she cries. 'You tried to end his life.'

Still on all fours, he drops his head like a wounded beast and begins to weep, but instead of wringing sympathy from her, the sound is so exaggerated she feels embarrassed for him. She can hardly stand to watch his performance.

'I am a wretched beast,' he wails between sobs, shaking his matted hair. As he moans and whimpers, he drags himself towards her as if he is using the last few ounces of strength in his body. 'Take pity on me, Miss Griffiths, for I am truly sorry for my sins.' He reaches up towards her like a drowning man lunging for a piece of flotsam.

If I get the wretched man to his feet, she thinks, I can end this performance. She leans forward, takes his hand.

'Oh, thank you, thank you, Miss Griffiths,' he says.

The next moment he snatches at her ankle and fells her with a swift tug. She puts a hand back to break her fall. The sharp edge of a stone nicks the skin of her palm. He crawls swiftly over her prone body, crouches above her, his fists pinning her shoulders to the ground. 'Ha!' he says triumphantly. 'Now I have you.'

What a fool she is to have trusted him. Now, she cannot move her shoulders but she can move her hands. Her fingers find the edge of the stone. She balls it into her fist, snaps her arm up and strikes him on the temple.

It tosses his head to one side but does not throw him off. He shakes his head, spinning gobbets of blood onto her, then roars in her face, his breath foul. As the roar abates, he snarls and growls from deep within his chest.

She thinks: he will sink his teeth into my face and tear my flesh from my throat.

Her knees are free. She jerks one up, smashing it between his straddled legs with a crunching velocity. He buckles. She shoves him, scrabbling away as he rolls back, his fists clasped between his legs.

'You vixen,' he yells.

She's on her feet again. Which way to run? If she sprints towards the barns, Mordiford is unprotected in the hut. If she runs to him, Ned will follow. The captain cannot save her, cannot save himself.

Her hesitation costs her dear. Ned is up. Her skirts, her wretched skirts. Without them she may outrun him over the longer distance to the barns and rouse the others but there's no time. She must dash for the sanctuary of the hut where

Mordiford lies, perhaps reach it before Ned, shut the doors, bar him out.

Ned lumbers over the grass towards her. She snatches up her skirts, running for the deep shadows behind the hut. She can work her way round to the entrance in the blackness. The land rises steeply. The eavesdrop of the hay barn is chocked with weeds. Brambles clutch at her clothing and tear at her legs.

She pushes on. Her skin throbs, pierced by nettles that pepper her hands and arms. She reaches the corner of the hut and stops, listening. She can't hear him in the eavesdrop, but he's out there, waiting for her.

Slowly she peers around the corner of the hut. The feeble light from the lamp within spills from the doorway, illuminating a semi-circle of caked mud at the entrance. She makes a dash towards it.

A column of blackness breaks from the shadows and rushes towards her. She grabs hold of the door, swinging it shut. Ned rams the planking with his shoulder, knocking her into the hay and muck inside. She can just see Mordiford. He tries to sit up, his face deathly white, streaming with fever. Ned is on her again, grabbing, hurting. Mordiford is struggling off the stretcher. He has his good leg on the ground. He is reaching towards his kit, which lies beside him.

Ned has her by the hair, and is wrenching and pulling at her. The hang-sword rattles as Mordiford fights to free it from the scabbard. He takes his full weight on his leg and bellows out in pain as he falls, clattering to the ground.

Ned snaps his head round. 'Well, good evening, my lord,' he pants, dragging at Elen's hair. 'A little busy just now. I will attend to you as soon as I can, sir. I have unfinished business here first.'

Elen lashes around in the dust of the floor, trying to sit up. The roots of her hair scream with white pain. She is pinioned, locked, can't move her head to see Mordiford. All she can see is Ned: the bloodshot eyes, the crazed, rugged cut across his temple, oozing with fresh blood.

His shirt is ripped and open. How can he be so strong when his body is cadaverously thin? It is his rage. His rage makes him super human. Suddenly Ned releases her hair but instantly his hand is on her throat. She tugs at his fingers. Her heels drum and push against the floor. His nails bite into her skin.

The other hand is pulling her skirt up, his nails scraping her flesh, his fingers gripping her thigh, dragging aside her chemise. His hold on her neck tightens. She can no longer breathe. She gargles, desperately trying to force out a breath. Her lungs will burst. She can hear her own blood thumping in her ears.

Mordiford's shouts come to her, muffled as if she's being held underwater. She stares up at Ned. Let me breathe. Blackness is coming, pushing in around the edge of her vision. Everything is stretching, bowing. She thinks, I am dying... she thinks, thank God, this terror will end.

Suddenly the pressure on her neck stops. She takes a huge gulp of air. Ned is still on her, but he is sitting up, staring down at his stomach, his face crumpled in a baffled frown.

She follows his gaze. He has something in his hands. He holds it so delicately. When he uncurls his fingers, they run with blood and there, in the palm of his hand, is the bloodied tip of a sword.

He opens his mouth to speak. Blood wells up behind his teeth, breaches them and pours down his chin. He coughs, showering her with blood, then sinks backwards, onto his heels. Slowly his body deflates. His torso sags, his head lolls forward. He does not fall but she knows he is dead.

She smears at the blood on her face, trying to sweep it from her eyes. The iron tang on her lips makes her gag. She slides her legs free of Ned's weight.

Mordiford is on the floor, motionless. The arm that drove the blade into Ned's back is thrown wide. He is dead. She struggles towards him, gathering his head up into her arms. Deathly pale, eyes closed. She presses her fingers into the side of his throat. Nothing. She can feel nothing.

And then… yes, the smallest flutter. And again. Her head sinks onto his and she begins to rock. He lives. They both live. They are invincible. Now they can sleep, sleep in the muck and dust of the floor. Together they can sleep.

Chapter 4

Something is irritating her face, making her lip twitch. Elen snaps awake, dashing the fly away. A brilliant shaft of early morning sun cuts through the planking of the door, momentarily blinding her. She shifts her head, yawns, and then it all floods back in.

She looks down at Mordiford who lies with his head on her lap. As he sleeps, the muscles of his face wince and frown. Waves of pain must be piercing his dreams. Her eyes move down to the wound on his leg. It is black with flies.

Instinctively she sits forward to brush them away. Then she sees Ned. Even in death he kneels, his head hanging down to his chest, his hands resting on his lap, palms up. If not for the handle of the sword buried in his back, he could be praying. She sees the sunburn on his neck, a rim of pale skin along the hairline. He looks so normal, she shudders – it is as if he might at any moment murmur 'Amen', and turn to face her.

She hears voices. The door to the hut opens wide, flooding it with sunshine, the sudden rush of morning air sending the flies droning up in a tumbling cloud.

'Good grief!' Dr Argyll says. 'What horrors have occurred here?'

Mr Barker pushes past him and hurries over to where she lies with Mordiford.

'He is alive,' she says.

Mr Barker looks down at Mordiford, reaching out to touch him. Mordiford wakes with a start. The surgeon's eyes dart back to Elen's torn clothing, up to the finger marks on her neck. He takes her hand, turns it this way and that, tracing the scratches with his finger. He looks angry, furious. 'Are you all right, my dear?'

'I think so.'

He helps Mordiford into a sitting position to release her. Mordiford is groggy, disorientated. She pulls the hem of her dress down as she slides free.

Mr Barker continues to stare. He has seen the marks on her legs, the deep bruising; the tears in the hem of her chemise. His breathing quickens. Elen struggles to her feet. Everything about her is stiff, everything is sore. The nettle stings bubble her flesh, tingling and burning as if a flame has passed over them.

Dr Argyll moves across to where Ned Harley kneels. He catches sight of the sword and looks up at Elen, a frown on his face. She says nothing. The doctor puts a hand on Ned's shoulder. Stiff with death, Ned topples sideways, his head striking the floor with a sickening crack, making the doctor step back. Mr Barker turns, getting to his feet.

'This poor devil is certainly not all right,' Dr Argyll says. He does not know him, Elen thinks suddenly. Ned is so changed, the doctor has not recognised him.

'What in God's name happened?' Mr Barker says to her. 'How was this man killed?'

'I was attacked. The captain saved my life – and my honour.'

Mr Barker nods his head and purses his lips. His expression is one of pity, sympathy but something else. Embarrassment, yes, that's it. He thinks he knows the details and doesn't want to dwell on them, doesn't want to ask. He reaches out and gives her elbow a comforting squeeze.

She looks over at Dr Argyll. He has crouched down, peering into the face of the corpse. He stands slowly, wiping his hand with a kerchief and inspecting his fingers as if he fears the pollution of death may still cling to them. He will not look at her. She reads the fractional narrowing of Mr Barker's eyes.

'There is doubt on your face, sir,' the surgeon says.

She feels an odd fear, not in her, but over there, in the body lying stiffly on the floor. There's a watery looseness in her knees, a horrible sensation that perhaps Ned would not have raped her, would not have killed her, and yet he is dead. She looks at Mordiford for support, but he lies against a stook of corn, barely conscious.

'Not doubt. Anxiety perhaps,' Dr Argyll says.

'What anxieties can you have?' Mr Barker says. The doctor jerks his head towards the door. Mr Barker frowns, moves nearer to the doctor who leans in, and says in a quiet voice, 'Should we not be concerned that a crime has been committed here?'

She turns away, she does not want to hear, but Mr Barker has not mastered the whisper.

'Of course we should,' she hears him say. 'Miss Griffiths' skirts and stockings are filthy and torn. There's bruising on her neck and thighs, where some hand has grasped her. That alone tells us much of last night's story. Attacks of this sort have long been a favoured form of retribution for enemy soldiers for centuries.'

'I was not referring to...' and the doctor swallows the word. She does not hear it.

'Then to what precisely do you refer?'

Dr Argyll drops his head. 'Murder.'

'Holy Mary mother of God, Argyll,' Mr Barker hisses back. 'What point are you trying to make? A vagrant, probably a French deserter, finds an unguarded dwelling and goes in looking for food. Instead he finds a wounded man and an attractive young woman. He takes his revenge.'

She can stand it no longer. She has to speak.

'That is no vagrant,' she says. Both men turn. Dr Argyll looks guilty for being overheard, Mr Barker does not. 'He's not French either, Mr Barker. He's a private in the English army and I know the man.'

'You do?'

'His name is Ned Harley.'

Dr Argyll looks back at the crumpled body in astonishment. 'Ned Harley?' he says. 'Surely not.'

'Who?' Mr Barker says with some impatience.

'He was footman to the Earl of Duntisbourne and valet to Captain Mordiford,' Elen says. 'I'm afraid both myself and the captain had plenty of reasons to want him dead.'

The men fall silent. Mr Barker takes a handful of almonds from his waistcoat pocket and chews them thoughtfully.

'Well,' he says presently. 'I imagine we will hear a full account of the night's events by and by. I cannot imagine for a moment that either of you planned or executed a brilliant murder. This was clearly self-defence.' He turns to the doctor. 'Look, Argyll. Tens of thousands of men have died in the last month. One more is not going to make a difference.'

'Supposing the orderlies make trouble for them?' Dr Argyll says. Finally he looks Elen full in the face and adds, 'I am sorry, my dear. I make no judgement here. It is a worry, nothing more.'

'Then we will keep the true identity of this man a secret between us,' Mr Barker says. 'Let us encourage the orderlies and privates who remain to believe my initial summing up of the situation.'

'We must make sure he carries nothing on him that could lead to an identification. No clue in his clothing or distinguishing marks,' Dr Argyll says.

Elen remembers the undercroft that crisp winter's morning, Ned drawing his shirt up to show her his well-muscled abdomen. She is swept with a muddy emotion. Not fear of exposure – all she has to do is wait for the doctor to remember too. No, that is not what sullies her. It is her shame that she lusted after a man who proved to be so utterly vile.

'He did have an anatomical peculiarity,' Dr Argyll says. Mr Barker groans. Dr Argyll continues, 'He was swaddled as a child. He had no navel.'

Elen thinks grimly, Ned may not have had one in life but he certainly has one now. She cannot say it, cannot explain

314

how, from the moment she saw the tip of the sword in his hand, she felt relief. It was as if God had punished him for that superstitious belief in his own invincibility.

Mr Barker rolls his eyes heavenward, shakes his head. He takes a pace over to the body and leans forwards, peering down. 'We must examine him to make absolutely certain,' he says. 'But from the angle of the sword, I would say we have nothing to worry about. The orderlies can take him down to the Danube and fling him in with the rest of the dead.'

She almost protests. She stops herself. Everything she fervently hoped for has come to pass. And there it is again, that tang of disgrace, crawling up her tongue.

Mr Barker's next statement startles her like a gush of cold water. 'Come, we must get Captain Mordiford up to the main barn and remove that leg with immediate haste.'

Elen feels the same helpless horror as when Ned had his hand on her throat. Mr Barker must slash and saw at a leg already agonisingly painful, every nerve fibre grazed and seared with pain from weeks of suffering. She cannot be there. She must be there. She must let Mordiford crush her fingers in his agony, let him sink his teeth into her arm. She must hold him as his body bucks and quivers under the saw.

Mr Barker has fetched the stretcher from the manger and put it on the floor next to Mordiford. She comes forward to help them lift him. She kneels down, laying a hand on Mordiford's shoulder. He is drowsy with fever but he looks up at her. An understanding passes between them.

'Stay your hand, Mr Barker,' Dr Argyll says, pushing them both aside and peering down at the wound on the captain's leg. 'See! It crawls with maggots.'

She looks at the leg and flinches. Patches of white have bloomed in the crater of the captain's wound. It is as if a handful of seed has been sprinkled onto the glistening tissues, each tiny white seed pleating and straightening.

'We cannot delay a moment longer,' Mr Barker says. 'Look at him. He is too sick to keep this leg, maggots or no maggots.'

'Surely, sir, he is too weak to lose it and live,' Elen says.

The surgeon considers the dilemma and begins to nod slowly. 'You may be right.'

The hay rustles as Mordiford moves. 'Could I trouble you,' he says, 'for a draught of water or am I to die of thirst before any of your theories have been proven?'

His voice is weak but his words make her want to laugh out loud and say: there gentlemen – proof, if proof were needed, that Captain Mordiford is, without question, an exceptional man.

'Yes, of course,' Dr Argyll says. 'Miss Griffiths, are you up to the task of drawing some fresh water for the captain?'

'I am, sir.'

'Before you visit the well, please send a couple of orderlies down here with as much haste as possible. We must get Captain Mordiford away from this foetid shack as soon as we can.'

As she gets to her feet, the captain twists his body, feebly trying to reach his wound. The doctor intervenes, laying a steadying hand on his arm.

'Let me at it,' Mordiford says. 'It itches abominably.'

'Your saviours have arrived, sir. You must leave them to do their work. It seems Harley's corrupting influence has served you well on this score at least. Without a doubt, the presence of his cadaver has been instrumental in drawing the flies inside.'

'Sir,' she says urgently to the doctor, 'we must never speak his name again.'

'I stand corrected. You are right, Miss Griffiths. It must be assumed he was a French deserter chancing his luck. No one else will know his identity.'

'There are no secrets between Mrs Barker and myself,' says the surgeon, and Elen is glad of it. She would not want to keep a secret from Sarah.

'She must be the only other person to know the truth of what occurred here last night,' she says.

'It is agreed. Now, my dear...' The surgeon takes her by the elbow and leads her to the door. Once outside he says, 'I want you to have no worries about the consequences of this terrible night. While the doctor and I ensure the anonymity of the deceased, I urge you to speak to Mrs Barker. Should you have sustained any injuries of a...' The surgeon pauses and clears his throat. '...of an intimate nature following your ordeal, Mrs Barker is the woman to help.'

'You must not trouble yourself on that score, Mr Barker. The captain despatched my attacker before anything truly unpleasant occurred.'

'Ah, that is such a relief.' Mr Barker's face broadens and splits into a wide grin. 'Capital. Excellent news. Now, hurry along my dear. The doctor and I have a small task to perform.'

—

When Elen returns with the water and the orderlies, Harley is lying on his back. The sword has been removed and where his shirt gapes open, she sees a black and bloodied hole in the centre of his abdomen.

She remembers looking on that line of dark hair that marked the middle of his torso, remembers pressing her fingers on the skin where the hair swirled and thickened. She remembers the heady scent of cloves that rose up from his skin when she came close and she grieves, not for Ned, but for the days when men were whole and healthy, clean and free from wounds.

As the orderlies heave the body from the floor, the limbs sagging loosely in their sockets, she turns away. Despite all that has passed, she does not want her mind branded with the image of a bloodied corpse where once there had been a dangerous beauty.

Chapter 5

'It is most important that the wound does not dry until all the dead flesh has been devoured,' the doctor says to Elen before turning his attention to Mordiford who has been settled in an upstairs room of the farm cottage for the past few days. 'I know you are feeling weak, sir, but we must hurry on to Nördlingen as soon as we are able. When the wind is from the west, you can smell the stench from the battlefield. It is quite overpowering. It will only worsen during the next few weeks. Besides, the Barkers and ourselves must go where we are needed.'

'I am actually feeling a deal stronger,' Mordiford says. 'I have slept quite soundly for most of the day.' He smiles up at Elen. He has lost that deathly pallor and those deep, dark rings beneath his eyes.

'That is good,' the doctor says. 'It means the wound has already been cleared of some of the poison.'

'Is it not painful?' she says.

'Painful?' the captain says. 'The whole leg is damnably painful, but perhaps a little less than before. But the devils irritate and itch. I have to use all my willpower not to knock them away. Lift that gauze, Argyll. I want to see them at work.'

'I would not advise it, sir,' she says.

'You think me qualmish? Last winter I watched my whole body bubble and erupt. Do you imagine I will be unsettled to see these fellows at work?'

The doctor shrugs then bends to peel back the moistened dressing. Several of the maggots have attached themselves to the fabric and drop, white and wriggling in their blindness, onto the bed.

The wound scintillates as the maggots move within. She longs to snatch the pitcher from the floor and jet a stream of clean water deep into the cavity to knock them away.

Mordiford cranes forward, the narrowing of his eyes betraying anxiety despite his own robust championing of his curiosity. He stares down at the deep crater in his shin and his face blanches. 'Damn the bloody rood,' he says. 'That is the most...'

'Incredible sight,' the doctor interjects with enthusiasm. 'Already the wound is free from the sickly smell of death,' he says, pressing a cautious finger onto the edge of the gaping ulcer. 'The surrounding skin no longer crackles with gas. The maggots will swell as they feed. By the time they pupate, I'll be bound we shall see the most beautiful, pink and healthy tissue.'

Dr Argyll bends forward, his nose inches from the wound and inhales deeply. 'Aah, as sweet as a peach,' he says. 'Mr Barker's excellent work on the operating table has been abetted by these capital little creatures.'

Dr Argyll moistens the gauze in the pitcher on the floor. Before he lays the fabric back over the wound, he retrieves the fallen maggots and drops them back onto Mordiford's leg. 'Now, can I fetch you a little supper, sir?' he says cheerfully.

The captain swallows twice in quick succession before answering, 'Perhaps I shall wait a few minutes longer.'

'That was foolish,' Elen says after the doctor has left.

'Maybe. I own it was not the sight I expected. But it looks so unlike a part of me that it is more bearable than my imagination. Why do you smile so?'

'You have reminded me of the night you found the looking glass.'

'Ah, that. I remember that night well, as I do all the nights you sat with me.' He lays his head back and smiles. 'I know I spent my days baiting you...'

'You were trying to drive me away for the best of reasons.'

'Not always, I think.'

'You do not mean that.'

'There were times when your flawless complexion and implacable patience filled me with resentment.'

'Do you have to remember the past with such remorseless accuracy? I prefer to think your behaviour sprung from concern.'

The captain shrugs. 'Do you? I hope so, but I was only just rising to the surface back then. A man cannot turn himself around on a farthing.'

She wonders how completely he has turned himself around. The keepsake still rests in her pocket. She knows she should ask him to explain why he carries it with him, but the very thought makes her heart drum. She is not prepared for the wrong answer.

If she has no intention of challenging him, she should return it to his pocket forthwith. Is she waiting to see if he misses it? Every day that passes when he does not search for it should reassure her that it means nothing to him, but instead her insecurity strengthens. Sooner or later she is bound to speak.

Mordiford has shown a courage that she lacks. He dreaded what he would see in the looking glass when he had the pox, and again just now, beneath the gauze covering his leg, but still he acknowledges that his imagination may be worse than reality. She must make the same leap of faith or her imagination will poison the well of understanding between them.

The day has been hot and sultry. All the windows of the building are thrown open, but instead of cooling the rooms, the panting heat has stolen in and sucked moisture from the walls, making the air thick and heavy.

Swallows scream and dive in the yard below, feasting on a banquet of insects, which tumble in the sweltering air. The rich smell of wood smoke drifts in through the windows from the cooking fires. Now that evening is falling, the sky has become overcast and a breeze begins to flicker the leaves of the poplars along the margin of the yard, which flash white as they twist. A barely perceptible rumble in the low hills to the north accompanies the wind and makes the dogs out in the meadow bark. 'Could that be cannon fire?' she says.

'I think not. Thunder, I should imagine.'

'I hope we have rain.'

'Run away with me.'

Another rumble rolls in the distance. She stares back at him, unsure if she has heard him correctly. Although his eyes glow as if a blue light shines behind them, his smile confuses her. She has seen that smile before. She knows what it heralds. She goes over to the window and looks out at the darkening sky. Without turning she says, 'You must be recovering well to begin teasing me again.'

'I am not teasing you.'

'You are, sir.'

She hears him sigh. 'Elen, Elen. I can call you Elen, can I not?'

'If you wish.'

'I have called you Elen in my mind for so many months. Does it sound so strange to you?'

'A little.'

'How do you address me in your thoughts?'

'Mordiford, always Mordiford.' She turns away from the window and back to face him, her heart bumping beneath her rib cage. When he sees her expression, a hesitant frown passes across his brow.

She takes a deep breath to steady herself and says, 'And how does Lady Arabella address you?'

Mordiford pushes himself higher up in the bed and stares at her. 'How did we get here?' he says presently. When she does not reply, he sighs and says, 'She calls me Crispin, as a matter of fact, a name I cannot abide, for it is one favoured by my father.'

'Why do you not tell her that you dislike it so?'

'Because I have not communicated with her for many months.'

'But she is clearly never far from your thoughts.'

A gust of wind blows a dead leaf in through the window and rattles it across the floorboards.

'This is a curious game, Miss Griffiths.'

'It is no game, sir.'

'A minute ago I imagined we had an understanding with one another.'

'I understand you very well.'

'Then you have the advantage.'

'I know you have feelings for Lady Arabella.'

Mordiford shakes his head as if to clear it. 'Feelings of affection towards a friend, nothing more.'

She reaches into her pocket and retrieves the keepsake, closing her hand around it and holding it to her chest. 'I have something here which proves that to be a lie,' she says.

Mordiford pushes himself higher and peers forward. 'I cannot see what you have.'

'Something you carried into battle.'

'Something you stole from my pocket?'

'No. Sarah handed it to me, she meant it as a warning to me.'

'A warning? A warning of what?'

'That you still have feelings for another.'

Mordiford gives an impatient sigh and sinks back on his pillows. 'I do not have feelings for another.'

'I know you lie,' she says, brandishing her closed fist towards him.

'Then come here and show me. For pity's sake, I cannot come to you.'

She cannot tell if he is genuinely ignorant or intentionally disingenuous.

'If you have feelings for none other, what is the explanation for this?' she says, thrusting the keepsake at him.

He strains to sit further forward. 'Bring it here,' he says. 'I still cannot see it.' She steps forward and recognition registers in his expression. He reaches out to take it from the palm of her hand. 'Oh, that,' he says. 'It is a pretty thing. I had quite forgot it.'

She expected a number of reactions – a denial perhaps or an angry defence at being caught out. With neither to parry, she is at a loss as to what to say next. Another growl of thunder comes through the open window.

'Why do you carry it?' she says.

'Because it was given to me.' He turns the jewel over in his fingers, studying it with a half-smile on his face, before laying it on the table at the side of the bed and looking up at her. 'I see by your expression, that we have some kind of worriment here.'

'Worriment? Now you do mean to antagonise me, sir.'

'I do not.'

'You carry into battle a keepsake popularly called a lover's eye.'

He looks back at her with confused amusement on his face as if he thinks she may be mocking him. 'I have said already, I had quite forgot it. Arabella had it made for me and sent it as a parting gift. It is perhaps a little mawkish and sentimental, but it was kindly meant and I am glad that I have not lost it.'

'Glad?'

His expression darkens and, as if in concord with his mood, the clouds rolling in from the fields beyond the window flash momentarily to herald the approaching thunder.

'I have no stomach for a fight,' he says. Another thunderclap rises to a crescendo, excusing her the need to reply. As the noise grumbles away across the distant hills, Mordiford says, 'But I shall ask you again, how did we arrive at this? I had a notion to begin a conversation on quite a different subject altogether.'

'Oh, I am sure you did.'

'I meant to tell you that when I am well enough to quit Nördlingen, I thought to stay on the Continent through the winter. I had hoped I could persuade you to stay with me. I had a notion to travel to the Low Countries and enjoy a simple life free from duty in order to replenish our spirits in readiness for next season's campaign. Instead, we end up like two fighting cocks squabbling over a nothing.'

'It is not a nothing to me. You ask me to run away with you and yet you will not tell me the feelings you have for another.'

'I thought I had. She gave me a gift. It was a kindness. I am glad I have not lost it.'

'Why do you keep repeating the same words?'

'Because you keep asking the same question.'

'You are being intentionally obtuse.'

'That is where our opinions differ. I believe I am being as clear as crystal.'

'Have you no idea what words I want you to say?'

'I have not or I would say them,' he replies with rising exasperation. 'Come, tell me what they are so that I may recite them and put an end to this oppressive atmosphere, which apparently needs more than a good storm of rain to clear it away.'

They are cut short by the arrival of Sarah with a tray of food.

'My, but it's hot up here,' she says. 'There you are, captain, beef and potatoes, as usual.'

'Take it back down to feed another, Sarah. I have quite lost my appetite.'

Elen takes the opportunity to quit the room and hurries down the narrow staircase, tears springing into her eyes. She crosses the yard and paces out into the meadow, breathing the freshened air while the grasses buck and ripple around her. The first speck of rain plops onto her shoulder, another taps on her hand. She turns her face up to the lowering sky and lets the drops cool her skin as the wind snaps her hair across her eyes.

Why can she not be at peace? She had been so certain that their increasing closeness would bring nothing but joy. Instead she seems destined to follow the path Sarah mapped out, that of an unhappy future. She thought her life would lack for nothing if the captain lived, but every time a prayer is answered, a demon waits in the wings with another trial to test her contentment.

'Damn you, Mordiford,' she shouts above another roll of thunder, but as the sound tumbles away, so does some of her anger. Damn him for what? For wanting to run away with her? No, not that. She damns him because she wants to possess all of him, his past as well as his future, and she knows she cannot.

Chapter 6

'Elen,' Sarah calls. 'What are you doing out there? Come back under cover. You'll be drenched to the skin.'

As the rain quickens her friend hastens towards her, throwing a shawl around herself. 'Whatever's the matter?' she cries above the tempest.

'Sarah, I have been so foolish.'

'That's allowed. Getting soaked and catching your death isn't.' Sarah tosses the shawl across both their heads and, grasping Elen by the shoulders, pulls her in a stumbling run towards the nearest shelter, a lean-to at the entrance of the yard.

'Oh, but we need this rain. That is powerful cool,' Sarah says, shaking the droplets off the shawl and running her hands through her hair.

She sits down on one of the piled logs before threading an arm around Elen's elbow and pulling her closer, as she is inclined to do. 'You poor little pigsney. You look as miserable as a wet bee. Tell me how he has vexed you.'

The rain clatters on the shingled roof, the torrent pouring from the eaves with such force that it throws up a fine mist, blurring the other buildings around the yard.

Elen gives her account of the recent argument. Her friend considers the information for a few moments, then says, 'Men are simple creatures. They're not the same as us.'

'Of course they are. Men love, do they not?'

'Yes, but the things that drive them are not the same. For a woman, kinship is the single most essential thing in life – her lover, her family, her friends, her children. These matter

326

to a man, but other things come first – honour, position, respect. You and I, we know the language of kinship. Men don't. They're good at other languages that we sometimes find impossible to understand. You can't expect a man to say the words that a woman would say.'

'How then can I know his feelings?'

'By his actions.' Sarah squeezes her arm. 'I wasn't there, I didn't hear what passed between you, but it sounds to me as if he wasn't being crafty. He was being straightforward and honest.'

'He refused to say he cared nothing for the keepsake.'

'Do you want him to scoff at this Arabella behind her back simply because she has feelings for him? Should he belittle her gift so you can feel better about yourself?'

'No. Of course that's not what I want,' she says, although she does not wholly mean it.

'I am glad of it, for a man who's cruel about his past is likely to remain unchanged in the future.'

'You support his evasions.'

'Are you so certain that's what they were?'

'I don't know any more.' She looks out at the drumming rain. 'What would you do?'

'I would say sorry.'

'But I did nothing wrong.'

'And it wouldn't surprise me a jot if he was sat up in that room, watching the rain and thinking just the same.' She pats Elen's hand before releasing her arm. 'Look Elen, this is a minor skirmish to what lies ahead. You told me you were taking each day as it comes, and yet, here you are, fretting about a future that may or may not be.'

'He wants me to stay with him on the Continent when he is well again.'

Sarah sighs. 'That would be very foolish. Look at how tonight has pained you. You think he's the love of your life but you don't truly know him.'

'I do. I've seen him at his lowest. Surely there is no better way to understand another person than to know them at their worst.'

'But your stations have been skewed, first by the pox, and now by his injuries. You're his carer and protector. By all the laws of nature, these two duties should fall to the man.'

'That's not true. Twice he has come to my rescue.'

'Which proves my point. Both times, although he was sick, the urge to protect you was too strong to resist. The rest of the time, he has had to surrender his power to you. You've taken the position that he, as a man, needs to have. Until he is strong again and you're both free of these unnatural restraints, you can't judge how things between you will be.'

'It will be months before he is truly fit and no longer dependent. What am I supposed to do now?'

'There is no point, I suppose, in telling you to go home?' Elen shakes her head. 'Then all you can do is make friends again for the time being, but I beg you, be careful. I see powerful troubles ahead.'

The storm is skirting the hills to the east; the time between the blaze of lightning and the crack of the thunder lengthening as the boiling clouds hurry past. Over the drumming of the rain Elen hears shouting. She listens more carefully. Someone is whooping and cheering in the distance.

Sarah also hears it and is on her feet in an instant, peering through the mist rising up from the sodden ground.

'Oh, Mr Barker – this will not do,' she says, but her expression is one of impish amusement. 'Cover your eyes, Elen. I'm afraid my darling Mr Barker has his own special way of celebrating the arrival of the rain.'

As the torrent begins to ease a little, Elen can just make out the pale figure of the surgeon gambolling around in the puddles of water on the other side of the yard, his arms stretched up towards the sky. The sight of a forty-year-old man dancing around like a child would have been singular enough in its own right, but Mr Barker is as naked as the day he was born.

His wife dashes through the rain towards him, her hair streaming out behind her like a pennant. On hearing her approach, he rushes across and sweeps her into his arms, spinning her around. Sarah pummels him playfully on the shoulders until he drops her, then she wraps her shawl around his waist, knotting it fast to cover his modesty.

'You are the most ridiculous clown, Mr Barker,' she says, panting from her exertion.

'And you are the most wonderful woman, Mrs Barker.'

Elen leaves them to their celebrations and creeps upstairs to the upper room, expecting to find Mordiford asleep. He is not. The sound of the Barker's laughter comes up to them through the window.

'How do they manage to be so happy when the world is full of pain?' he says.

'I have depressed you with my foolishness.'

'Quite the reverse. I am naturally full of the black humour. It is you alone that balances me. You are spring to my autumn, winter to my summer fire, yet still I drag you down.'

'It seems I am quite capable of doing that all by myself.'

'Draw up that stool. Come and sit beside me.' She does as he asks and he reaches out for her hand. 'Has the storm passed?'

'It has.'

'I am glad.'

'And I am sorry.'

'No, I will not have it,' he says. 'You and I, we have been through much together. Harley's death was a most singular and violent experience. It will be burned on our memories for the rest of time. Perhaps to divert ourselves, we squabble over a trinket.' He smiles wearily and looks at the keepsake lying on the table. 'What would you have me do with it?'

'Keep it,' she says. 'It is a pretty thing.'

Mordiford frowns at her then shakes his head. 'The mind of a woman is a truly perplexing thing,' he says.

'Now you truly are baiting me, sir.'

'Indeed I am.'

Chapter 7

October 1704

The storm moved on, and gradually, over the next few weeks, so did the wounded, until the only patient remaining was Captain Mordiford. Each day Elen expects to be told to start loading up the carts for the journey to Nördlingen. Instead she and Sarah take trips in the pony and trap to buy food from the nearby homesteads, loyal to the triumphant allies. Each evening Mr Barker and Dr Argyll reassure one another that tomorrow they will break camp, move on up the line, and throw themselves into their medical work again.

Captain Mordiford is the focus of their delay. As he grows stronger, she knows that his is not the only wound healing in the enchanted tranquillity of the farm amongst the cornfields. Mr Barker fills his days constructing a complicated splint from wood and leather. 'Give me another week,' he tells her, 'and I think I may be able to get the captain upright.'

Dr Argyll checks his patient early each morning before leaving Elen in charge for the day and setting off into the countryside with an insect net and a notebook. Lately the captain has been sleeping in the lower rooms of the farmhouse so that he can be easily moved outdoors in the daytime. Elen suspects Sarah's cautious hand in the arrangements for it means they are seldom alone together, but her friend's vigilance only increases their understanding. When Sarah settles down after lunch with her bodice loosened, basking like a cat in the sun, Mordiford clasps Elen's hand or twists a curl of her hair around his fingers.

'See,' he whispers, his eye on the surgeon's wife. 'This lock is a living thing. I tie it in a knot thus and when I release the end, quite unaided, it uncoils itself like a serpent.'

In company, Elen feels his eyes on her. When she catches Mordiford's glance, the flutter in her stomach is so violent it feels as if she has swallowed a bowl of butterflies. At night she fights sleep for as long as she can, playing her waking dreams in her head. In those dreams the finger that twists the curl of hair, strokes her cheek, slips down to the nape of her neck and beyond.

She imagines the roughness of Mordiford's hand running over the smoothness of her skin, knowing that despite her innocence, he could conjure a wantonness from her that would leave her with no shame at all. She longs for time to pass and free Mordiford from the restraints of his injury, but at the same time, she wants these sun-filled days to last forever.

One evening this merry band is eating supper round a makeshift table set up under an old grapevine, which has spent the latter part of the summer bursting free from a ramshackle frame. They dine on smoked sausage, fresh eggs bought from local villagers and bread baked in the outdoor oven. Wine is in plentiful supply and Elen enjoys the freedom of a few glasses in the evening.

Mordiford sits opposite her, his leg, now free of maggots and healing well, supported on a bench to the side. She drains her tumbler and Mordiford reaches with difficulty across the table towards the pitcher. She is about to save him the trouble when Sarah places a restraining hand on her wrist below the table.

'What is it?' Elen says, thinking for a moment that Sarah disapproves of her drinking.

'The wine is always sweeter from a man's hand, my dear,' Sarah replies, giving her a good-humoured wink before sliding her gaze over to the captain. Elen watches the wine trickle into her glass, lets her eyes travel up to his hand on the neck of the pitcher. How dark that hand would look lain on the white skin of her stomach, her thigh, her... She inhales quickly and smells the perfume from the waxy flowers on a tree nearby. Mordiford sits back, keeping his eyes down, until the other three are chattering loudly over one another, then he looks across at her.

He has never been more handsome. The food and rest has filled out his cheeks and smoothed away the frown of pain that used to crease his brow. The pits on his face have faded as his skin has browned, which in turn has made the blue of his eyes glow all the more vividly.

'We have been leaving you outdoors to toast for too long I think, captain,' Sarah says, jerking Elen away from her thoughts. 'You have gone as brown as a peasant.'

'And you have gone as red as a tomato,' he says.

'But a tomato does not have such gorgeous freckles across its nose,' Mr Barker says, kissing the article in question.

'Red hair may mean red skin all summer long,' Sarah says, 'but in the winter I have a face so pale I could pass as a countess.'

'I find it hard to imagine that,' Mordiford says with the shadow of a wink at Elen.

'And I find it impossible to imagine you as an earl, which one day you shall be. What sort of earl will you make, do you think?'

Elen stares down at her plate. She doesn't want to imagine what sort of earl he would make. She wonders if this is part of Sarah's plan, to remind her of the hopelessness of her affections. Mordiford picks up a piece of bread and tugs it apart. He replies, 'Nothing like my father.'

Elen feels a sense of relief. He also wants to stop the conversation dead, but Sarah, her face flushed with sun and wine, gives no quarter. 'Come now, that is no reply. What a capital sight it would be to see you spruced up like the Duke of Marlborough, all wig and perfect manners.'

Elen does not see the Duke of Marlborough — she sees the Earl of Duntisbourne in his finery, the tang of corruption on his breath, tobacco on his hands, the sickly scent of rose water coming from his clothes.

'I care nothing for life at Court,' Mordiford says bitterly. 'It is a hellish place of gossip and manipulation and there is none so fiendish as your namesake, Sarah Churchill, the Duke of Marlborough's wife herself, when it comes to that.'

'So I've heard,' Sarah says with a flash of her eyes to encourage him to tell more.

The captain will not be led. Instead he says, 'I can assure you when my father decides to do me the great service of finally meeting his maker, I have no intention of taking up where he left off.'

Elen gives Sarah a warning look but she returns it with a cussed stare. 'You cannot throw your responsibility so carelessly aside,' Sarah says. 'There is no choice for a man such as you.'

'There is always a choice. My grandfather ran the estates in a very different way. He loved Duntisbourne as a great piece of real Wales where people toiled and cared for the land, not as some pleasure palace for the wicked to indulge their sinful practices away from the prying eyes of Court. My grandfather never entertained and he never curried favour. He took care of the land so that he could pass it on replenished. The tragedy is that he passed it on to my father.'

Elen thinks, I could easily fit in to such a life. If Sarah is pushing the conversation to warn me, she has done the exact opposite.

'Ah,' Sarah says to the table in general, 'the captain means to live as a gentleman farmer with all the charm of a recluse.'

'It is not such a poor notion,' he says. 'But enough of this. I am a soldier now. By the time Marlborough has brought France to her knees, I may never have to return to England.'

'What can you mean?' Elen says, frowning at him.

'As you well know, it is the custom for senior officers to lead their men forward from the front,' he says, avoiding her eye and addressing the others. 'Our exposed position claims a far higher proportion of death and injury than among the regular soldier.'

'You are not wrong,' Mr Barker says. 'Losses among the officers at Schellenberg alone were devastating, and that was merely a skirmish. Forty high-ranking officers lost their lives that day.'

'You can be sure the higher I climb, the more likely it is that I may never have to face the prospect of becoming earl.' Elen stares across at him, willing him to return her gaze, but he does not.

'Heavens above,' Sarah says, 'does the thought of becoming earl appal you so much that you'd rather die on a field of battle than return to your estates?'

'The countryside around here is very different from the Welsh marches,' Elen says desperately to turn the conversation. 'Where I grew up, it was all small valleys and compact little hills, whereas here they have these vast, open plains and big skies. You have travelled to many exciting places, Dr Argyll, have you not? What would you say was the most impressive country you have seen?'

'That is a most difficult question to answer,' Dr Argyll says. 'I have always been a great lover of Europe, but often it is the very strangeness of a place that impresses. I suppose if I have to make a choice it would be Dekhan in India. That place impressed and horrified me in equal measure.'

'India?' Mr Barker says. 'That is a far-flung spot.'

As the conversation meanders off down this different route, Elen looks back at Mordiford, still playing with his bread, his mood morose. Slowly he raises his eyes. With a swift glance to his side to ensure that the attention of the others is no longer on him, he mouths a faint 'thank you', then closes his eyes in a lazy blink of bliss as a smile of secret understanding spreads across his lips.

Chapter 8

As dusk creeps in earlier each evening, Elen knows this paradise is nearing an end. The others seem to feel it too – Mr Barker announces the splint is ready and Dr Argyll loses interest in the insects out in the meadow.

Elen is woken one morning by the sound of a cart. A local driver waits in the yard with a high-sided wagon pulled by two oxen. He has been sent to transport them to Nördlingen as soon as possible. He hands her a message for the surgeon. The order is more in the form of a request, but Mr Barker and the doctor are in agreement that their brief furlough has reached an end. As Elen helps to load the wagon, she notices that the swallows are massing, preening and chattering, also readying themselves to leave, and she feels a terrible melancholy.

Although the bulk of their equipment left weeks ago with the army and convalescing soldiers, by the time the ox cart has been loaded, there is no space for the captain to sit now that his leg is immobilised in Mr Barker's excellent splint.

'Let me travel in the malbruch,' the captain says, pointing at the two-wheeled trap, which has been left behind by the army. 'The pony is quite docile enough for Miss Griffiths to handle and we shall follow directly behind.'

Sarah is about to raise an objection, but Mr Barker and the doctor say this a capital solution. 'If we set off within the hour,' Dr Argyll says, 'we should cover the distance to Nördlingen easily before nightfall – but keep us well within view, Miss Griffiths. The route is straightforward, but I would hate you to get lost.'

'I would love you to get lost,' Mordiford murmurs as Elen settles the last few bags around him on the platform of the malbruch.

'Hush! The others will hear and you shall end up with Mr Barker as your driver.'

'It is an excellent notion though, is it not? Once we are in Nördlingen, there will be precious little opportunity for us to be alone. Make sure you have stowed bread and wine. Let us at least mark the end of this oasis of happiness with a picnic supper before we arrive at the city walls.'

'They will not leave me unchaperoned.'

'We have our chaperone...' and Mordiford taps the wood of his splint. 'Even the suspicious Sarah cannot imagine I could wreak much havoc encased in this. I am as safe as a hobbled horse.'

Elen hesitates, glancing over her shoulder, but Mordiford continues, 'I warrant I am not much of a companion. Indeed, throughout our whole acquaintance you have hardly known me stood on two legs.' She smiles despite herself. He grasps her hand and says urgently, 'Please, I beg you. Will you not agree to spend one evening alone in the company of this melancholic soldier with a plooked face and crooked leg?'

She leans forward and whispers, 'With all my heart.'

Mordiford lies back in the cart and smiles up at the heavens.

In fact, they do not leave much before noon. For the early part of the journey, the convoy travels through open countryside. The crops near to where the battle was fought have been left to spoil, but as they move north, the scars of war lessen.

Men are out in the meadows, mowing with long scythes while women stook the corn. They break the journey after a couple of hours to rest the animals and eat some luncheon. The captain shuffles around on his good leg, aided by a stout support that the surgeon has made for him, slipping pieces of sausage and cheese into his pockets when no one is looking.

'How is that leg faring?' Mr Barker says.

'Sound as a bell, but my rump feels punched to a board after a couple of hours in that cart.'

'This army life has made you crude, sir,' Elen says.

'It is the company, I am afraid, Miss Griffiths. You know what these medical men are like.'

The journey resumes. Sarah, who had spent the first part of the drive peering over her shoulder to check the pony and cart, settles herself on top of a pile of bedding, facing backwards. From this new perch she gives Elen a coy wave and a good-natured look of warning. Within minutes however, the combination of hot sun, wine at luncheon and the rocking of the ox cart has a somnolent effect on the surgeon's wife. She loosens the lacing on her bodice, snuggles deeper into the pile of linen, and is soon fast asleep.

By late afternoon, the convoy has entered the dappled shade of a woodland. The track meanders around outcrops of rock and dense vegetation and it is not very long before Elen begins to lose sight of the ox cart. Momentarily it appears, only to vanish again, as it drops down an incline or turns another corner on the twisting track. The jingling of the tack and clanging of the cooking pots becomes fainter until soon they are barely audible.

'Very sound work,' Mordiford says quietly behind her. He has pulled himself sideways on the platform of the cart to watch the track ahead. 'I believe you have lost them altogether.' She turns and he smiles raffishly at her. 'There,' he says. 'Take that track on the right. Let's see where it leads.'

'We will get lost.'

'It is no matter. The evening is fine, the woods are deserted, I have pockets full of provisions and I see you have managed to stow enough wine to slosh a whole company of men.'

The pony plods her way between the trees but after ten minutes of travelling, she pricks up her ears and begins to move with renewed focus.

'She seems to know where she's going,' Mordiford says as the cart rattles and jumps between the potholes. Elen hears the hollow cry of a water bird echoing through the trees and all of a sudden, the cart breaks into a large clearing filled with a tranquil body of water, edged all around by a fringe of rustling reeds.

The pony trots across the shingle and drops her head into the water, her lips breaking the glass-like surface into rippling rings, which gently rock the rafts of lily pads.

'She was thirsty,' Elen says.

'She was inspired. She has found an enchanted lake for us.' Mordiford pulls himself a little higher behind her. 'Elen, is this not the most perfect place for us to be? Help me down. We must set up camp for the night.'

'The night?' she says, coming round to the back of the trap. 'I thought we were stopping for a picnic supper before going on to Nördlingen.'

Mordiford has pulled himself to the edge of the platform, his body twisted so that the splint is supported as his good leg swings over the edge. He reaches out and holds her gently by both hands.

'That was before we found this. I had imagined a field beside the track, a few stolen hours, not this beautiful haven, tucked away in this bewitching wood.' He gazes up at the canopy of trees above their heads. 'It is like a cathedral of green, the boughs arching over to protect us. Elen, Elen, surely this was meant to be. Let me have this one night with you under the stars, let me lie with you in my arms as I have lain so many times in my dreams.'

She feels giddy with desire but Mordiford misreads her hesitation. He crosses his finger on her lips as if he fears her argument will steer him away from his plan. 'I promise you on my honour that nothing will pass that you need ever regret in the future. Even were I free of this elaborate mechanism that Mr Barker has bolted to my leg like a crusader's chastity belt, I would not take advantage of you. My single purpose in life is to be in concord with you, in everything we say and do.' A cautious smile opens up his face and he says, 'You want us to stay, do you not?'

'I do – you must know that I do.'

It takes a good half hour to unbridle the pony, rub her down and give her a bucket of oats for her supper. As Elen works, Mordiford hobbles around the margin of the lake, gathering firewood under one arm and laboriously limping back with small loads to the spot he has chosen beneath the boughs of a sweet chestnut tree. The evening is warm and balmy, the surface of lake disturbed only by the scudding water boatmen and the occasional fish rising to the surface to claim an insect. A column of gnats climb and fall along the margin of the water, the sinking sun illuminating them as it drops towards the horizon of trees.

By the time the fire is lit and crackling merrily, the sun has sunk out of sight, but its last rays shine through the vegetation on the opposite bank of the lake, bathing the shore in an olive glow. They dine on smoked sausage and bread which they skewer on sharpened sticks and toast in the fire. Food has never tasted so good nor wine so sweet. They talk in hushed tones, not wanting to bring dissonance to this peaceful place. As darkness falls and a slender moon rises above the trees, they sit before the glow of the embers in companionable silence.

'Is there not something intensely sensual about the heat?' Mordiford says unexpectedly. 'I sometimes wonder if it is that which so seduces me, but then I remember how my heart burned with fire for you when we journeyed over the cracked ice of Radnorshire, and I know it is nothing to do with the seasons.'

She does not answer for she does not want to break the spell that has fallen on them. Instead, she leans against his body resting her head on his shoulder.

'But heat is seductive,' he says presently. 'Even the country-side cannot help but respond. It builds itself up and when it can no longer stand the pressure, it bursts its clouds and thunders around the hills, flashing lightning in its ecstasy.'

339

He twists to face her, his eyes reflecting the light of the fire. 'So it will be between you and me.' He reaches out and draws her hands towards his chest where he clasps them against his heart. 'In the heat of summer the smells are stronger, every touch is vibrant and trembling. I want to slip my skin and curl myself around you. I want our bodies to slide against one another until we are as close as two human beings can be. I want to be locked within you, surrounded by you, flowing into you.'

'Stop. I beg you,' she says. 'You promised I would be safe. How can I be safe when you say words to me that move me as intensely as if you were making violent love to me?'

He lifts her hand to his mouth and kisses her fingers one by one.

'How dearly I wish I could,' he says, drawing her towards him.

As they kiss, she clutches at his shoulder to anchor herself for she is gripped by a sense of profound disorientation. Slowly, he lies down, drawing her across his body.

'You are as light as the finest goose down,' he murmurs in her ear, his breath on her neck sending spasms of pleasure through her. His hair is fragranced with the spice of wood smoke and his skin smells of fresh water, but beneath the clear, mineral scent throbs a musk as strong as the blossom that filled the nights at the farm.

She wants to sate herself on him. She hardly knows how, so intense is the longing as he caresses her hair and lets his lips slip wet across hers. His shirt has fallen open, her bodice has loosened. As their skin presses against one another, she thinks she will go mad. She knows that had he been fit and free from the splint, she would be powerless to stop him. In fact, he would be powerless to stop her.

Chapter 9

Elen wakes at dawn. Mordiford sleeps, one arm encompassing her shoulders, the other lying heavy across her waist. She feels the regular rise and fall of his rib cage, his face resting on her hair. All around them she hears the chatter of birds in the trees, the knocking of wings on water as birds take flight from the surface of the lake.

Carefully, she slides her arm back to raise herself onto her elbow. She wants to gaze on his sleeping face. He stirs as she moves, shifting his body a little and turning his head away. She studies the generous sculpt of his mouth. The fingers of his hand twitch as he sleeps and she wonders why she has never noticed how beautiful a hand it is. The skin across the back is burnished a golden brown from his days in the sun, here and there, a flat freckle lies as companion to a dipped white scar where once a pox had been. This is the hand that cupped her cheek to draw her in, the stout fingernails that ran tenderly across the skin on the inside of her arm. These thoughts alone reignite the passion she felt the night before and she knows she cannot heed Sarah's advice.

She must run away with him, stay on the Continent until he is well. They can live as man and wife for as long as possible. When it is no longer possible, she will sacrifice herself and release him. She would rather face that agony than never experience the ecstasy a true union with him could bring.

She stands up and walks down the shingle to look out across the lake. A mist rises from the water, light tendrils playing along the surface. It flows in the opposite direction to the puffs of seed heads, drifting by, drawing her eye along the margin of bulrushes on the opposite bank. Suddenly a jolt of horror makes the tips of her fingers tingle with fear.

A figure stands motionless in the mist, staring across at her, hunched and brooding. A terrible chill runs through her. For one appalling moment she fancies it is the spirit of Ned Harley, come to exact a supernatural revenge. But then the mist thins revealing a heron.

Her fear subsides, but still she watches the bird with a stifling prescience of doom. The bird's stooped back and sickle-sharp beak remind her powerfully of the grim reaper. The black eye stares unblinkingly across at her, lifeless but intense in its unwavering glare.

Slowly it steps nearer to the edge of the water. She wants to shoo it away, to make it take flight and remove its malevolent presence from this beautiful place. The bird seems to respond to her movement by tipping its head and elongating its neck. She thinks it is about to fly but suddenly it stabs down with incredible velocity. The sound of a high-pitched and terrible scream echoes around the trees. A tiny rabbit is thrashing around in its beak.

Mordiford wakes with a start and tries to struggle to his feet. The screams of the kit increase in pitch. The heron tosses it and catches it again by the paw. Still it twists violently. Still it screams. Elen rushes back to Mordiford and grasps him by his shoulders. 'You've got to stop it,' she says. 'It will die.'

'It is dead already,' he says.

'It is not. Still it screams.'

'But it will die before we reach it. There is nothing we can do.' He holds her head, his hands over her ears, and cradles her face against his chest, muffling the screams. By the time they stop she is sobbing against him.

'It is over now, my darling one,' he says, raising her face.

On the other side of the lake the heron, its throat disfigured by the body of the poor kit, stares back at her impassively before taking a leggy step into the water, followed by another as it insolently picks its way through the shallows at the foot of the tributary.

'There,' Mordiford says, 'he is moving off now. It is all done.'

'It was horrible, horrible.' Still she clings to him. 'It is a premonition, a warning,' she says.

'Hush, my darling girl. It is nature, nothing more or less.' He strokes the hair away from her face, kissing her gently but the magic has been shattered. As if by a mutual consent, they silently gather their things and make ready to leave.

When the pony is harnessed and the malbruch loaded, she helps Mordiford up onto the platform. Before he pushes himself towards the back, he takes her face in his hands. 'Are you sad because we are leaving?'

'I'm afraid, Mordiford.'

'There is nothing to be afraid of any more.'

As the pony picks her way back towards the main track, Elen feels the chill of autumn in the air. Dew beads the webs that the spiders have thrown between the trees. The track is littered with fallen leaves. She can hear Mordiford humming a little tune to himself but she does not feel the same good cheer. The end of the summer always produces a wistful melancholy in her but this is different. She is gripped by a sense of loss and foreboding that confuses her.

After nearly two hours of travelling, the traffic along the route increases. They overtake carts laden with harvest bounty, and in the distance, she sees the towers of a city breaking the skyline.

'That must be Nördlingen ahead. I think we are nearly there,' she calls behind.

Mordiford reaches through the back of the driver's bench and weaves his fingers between hers. 'How cold your hand is,' he says. 'Stop the cart for a little while and let me warm it for you.'

'We should not. I am already anxious of the reception that awaits us.'

343

'I would gladly face court marshal and flogging if I could spend another night with you by that lake.'

'I was thinking of far worse than a flogging – Sarah.'

Mordiford chuckles and flings himself back onto the luggage.

'Were we really there?' he says. 'Did we really do all those things? I am amazed. Stunned. You are shining in me.'

—

As the malbruch nears the city, the weather begins to change. Clouds mass along the horizon and a chill wind shakes the loose oilcloths covering the luggage.

'It looks like rain,' Elen says. 'You had better cover yourself or you will be soaked to the skin before we make it to Nördlingen.' Mordiford tugs the oilcloths across himself, pushing one forward for Elen. She pulls it over her head as the first few spots of rain begin to patter onto the cart. Before long a fine drizzle is falling, muddying the potholes and blurring the distant landscape.

Ahead on the road, she notices a lone horseman coming in their direction. He slows as he reaches each of the vehicles travelling towards the city, peering at the passengers and exchanging a few words with the occupants before raising his hat with a bow of thanks and moving on to the next cart.

As he nears, she recognises the uniform of a dragoon. 'There's a soldier riding this way,' she says.

'That is of little surprise.'

'He is a dragoon.'

Mordiford grasps the back of the driver's bench and hauls himself higher, squinting into the rain. 'He is a horseman – from Wood's Regiment by the looks of it. I cannot quite recognise his face yet.' Mordiford raises his tricorn above the cart and waves it over Elen's head. 'I see him now. It is Lieutenant Adair. I know him well.'

The dragoon spurs his horse into a canter and comes alongside the malbruch.

'Captain Mordiford,' he says, 'we have been waiting over a day for your arrival.'

'And you do not have to wait another minute, for here I am. How far to the city?'

'Less than half an hour but you must hurry. News has arrived from England and I have been sent out to search for you.'

'News? What news?'

'I know not, sir. I have been riding this stretch of road hourly for the last day in the hope of finding you. All I have been told is that I must escort you to the city hospital with immediate haste.'

'Very well, Lieutenant. Lead on and we shall follow.'

Lieutenant Adair spurs his horse back in the direction he has come, shouting at vehicles to make way. Elen slaps the reins onto the pony's rump and trots after the dragoon, her anxiety from this morning increasing in her chest.

'What can it be?' Mordiford calls over the rattle of the cart. 'Does Marlborough need reinforcements sent to Landau to support the Margrave? The duke clearly has a highly inflated confidence in Dr Argyll's skills if he imagines I am already fit enough to ride out and join him. But, no, it cannot be that. Adair says that news has come from England.'

'We will find out soon enough.'

Presently they pass into the shadow of the city gates. Within the city walls, houses rise on either side, four, sometimes five storeys high. Their steeply sloped roofs are covered in red tiles, the gable ends elaborately stepped and decorated. The cart rumbles over the flint cobbles, the pony's hooves echoing between the buildings.

Up ahead she sees Lieutenant Adair dismount in front of a large, stone hospital building and hurry inside. By the time their wagon reaches the entrance, Dr Argyll has come out and is waiting in some degree of agitation.

'Good heavens, child,' he cries, grabbing hold of the pony's bridle. 'Where have you been? We have been searching up and down the country for you.'

Before she has an opportunity to reply there is a commotion at the entrance to the building. A small crowd push out into the rain and a voice calls, 'Has the earl arrived? Is he here? Let me through.'

As the people part, a vision of pale cream taffeta topped with a travelling cloak of the softest dove grey stands out between the drab taupe of the crowd. A delicately dressed girl rushes past Elen, the hem of her gown soaking up the mud from the street, the fur-trimmed hood of her cape falling back as she picks her way hurriedly to the back of the cart with a rustle of stiff underskirts.

Her hair is blonde and piled up at the nape of her neck, the escaping ringlets bobbing as she moves. If she had deigned to glance her way, Elen knew her eyes would be pale grey, matching the colour of the lover's eye on Mordiford's jewelled keepsake.

'Crispin! Oh, is it really you?'

'Arabella? What in the world are you doing here?' he says, pushing the oilskins away and hauling himself to the edge of the cart. Arabella reaches up and clasps his hands.

'Your father, it is your father, Crispin. I have brought you the most awful and tragic news. Your father is dead this long month past. I have been sent to bring you home.'

Chapter 10

'You girl, follow my coachman,' the dowager countess says, taking a cologne-soaked kerchief momentarily from her face. 'He will show you the way to the townhouse.'

Lady Ludlow is a stout woman dressed all in black with a silk tricorn hat over a mantilla of lace and ribbon, and a velvet cape long enough to cover her shoulders, but short enough to show the heavily embroidered sleeves and copious quantity of lace at her elbows. She makes up for her lack of height with the carriage of her head, her nose held high, her mouth pinched and her beady eyes staring haughtily up at Elen, waiting for her to obey her command.

Dr Argyll steps in front of Lady Arabella's mother. 'Lady Ludlow, this girl is not a driver, she is one of my nurses.'

'A nurse?' Lady Ludlow covers her nose with the kerchief and says, 'Well, I never. What a draggle tail.'

'That's as may be, but she has been charged with the care of Captain Mordiford.'

'I think you mean Lord Duntisbourne.'

'I mean...' The doctor takes a deep breath to steady himself. '...that I need Miss Griffiths here at the hospital. I cannot spare her to follow you to your quarters. I would also recommend that the captain is brought inside the hospital, so that we may see all is well with his wound after his journey.'

'What a nonsense! I cannot have my future son-in-law spend a single minute in that house of death and disease. It is all arranged. The Countess von Oettingen has gifted their townhouse to us until arrangements for the return journey are

347

completed. Lord Duntisbourne will be far more comfortable there. You can follow on and minister to him when he is settled. Get down, girl. Connelly, take her place and hurry up, we are all soaking here.'

'We have supplies of our own on the malbruch, my lady,' Dr Agyll says stubbornly.

'I will send them back in the morning.'

By now a small gaggle of onlookers have gathered around the trap. Elen is helped down by a footman who climbs up to take her place. However hard she tries to peer over the heads of the throng, she can no longer see Mordiford.

As the pony turns, the crowd surges forward. Lady Ludlow shoves and shoulders her way through and the press of people move off down the narrow street, leaving Elen and the doctor standing alone in the rain.

'What a frightful woman,' the doctor says. 'I must apologise, Miss Griffiths, for my somewhat snappish welcome. Lady Ludlow has been here since early morning. She is most provoking company, particularly when all she can do is sneer. Come along, now. You can dry off in the kitchen. Now that is over, we can get on with some luncheon.'

—

Sarah is busy at the range. When she sees Elen, she drops her spoon in the pot and clasps her to her bosom. 'Goodness me, you are shivering with cold,' she says. She rubs Elen's hands to bring the blood back, then draws a stool close to the range and presses her down.

'Go and find Mr Barker, would you, Dr Argyll? Tell him that his luncheon is ready.'

'He'll be along shortly,' the doctor says, pulling out a chair to sit upon.

Sarah makes a small shooing gesture at the doctor and purses her lips.

'Oh… I see,' Dr Argyll says, getting up hastily from the seat. 'Yes, of course. I shall go and find Mr Barker.' The doctor scuttles off down the passage, leaving the two women alone.

'I was so worried about you,' Sarah says.

'Please do not scold me. I could not bear it.'

'Of course I'm not going to scold you. I was afraid for you. Those women were waiting in the city when we arrived. The mother is the most ghastly harridan, the daughter a weedy milksop of a thing. I wanted to warn you, prepare you.'

'You could not have.' Elen gives an ironic laugh. 'I suppose at least their arrival will ensure I follow your advice.'

'I think it's a little late for that,' Sarah says meaningfully.

'Not at all. The captain has behaved perfectly honourably towards me.'

'I still think it is a little late.'

Elen gives Sarah a fatalistic smile. 'I only wish I had had the opportunity to fall completely.'

Sarah bellows with relieved laughter. 'That's the spirit. A few more months of hard work out here, then back home with the doctor to see that family of yours, which you must be sorely missing.'

'I am.'

Elen is determined to hide her distress for it would reveal that she imagined a future with Mordiford. The sight of Lady Arabella gliding through the filthy street has forcefully demonstrated to her how foolish a notion it was. She could not hope to match that level of elegance and sophistication.

She does not doubt the captain believed all the strong feelings he expressed the night before, but his passions were fanned by the extraordinary circumstances of these past few months. Once Mordiford returns to his former life, how can his affections be strong enough to overcome such a contrast in their social stations?

She quickly resolves to face her loss with the same fortitude that Mordiford has shown throughout all his trials. She cannot be his lover, but she will not become his guilt. She must find a way to be glad for him in her heart and rejoice that she earned his regard.

Half an hour or so later, Mr Barker and the doctor tentatively peer into the kitchen. Seeing Elen hard at work, helping Sarah, they relax and take their place at the table.

'Well,' Dr Argyll says, 'this is a turn up for the books. I had quite forgot over the past few months that the captain was anything more than a regular soldier, so pleasant a young man he has become. He will be sorely missed.'

'Was his father an elderly man?' Mr Barker asks.

'Not at all.'

'Have you divined what took his life so early?'

'It was the pox without a doubt,' the doctor says, dropping his voice. 'And I do not mean the red plague. He succumbed to a different kind of pox altogether. The French disease.'

Ah, thinks Elen, the doctor has known it all along.

'The Great Pretender,' the surgeon says.

'Very much your province, Mr Barker.'

'Indeed. I cannot imagine the earl consulted you about the treatment.'

'No, indeed,' Dr Argyll replies. 'However, his increasing madness left me in little doubt that whichever barber surgeon in London he consulted, he left it too late for mercury treatment to be effective.'

'Why is it called the Great Pretender?' Elen says.

'Because often the first symptoms resolve themselves,' Dr Argyll says. 'The ulcers and pustules heal, but months, sometimes years later, new and different symptoms appear – aching limbs which may be mistaken for gout, fever which may be mistaken for influenza, and the most feared and terrible manifestation of all – insanity.'

She ponders this for a few moments, then says, 'Which explains the earl's extraordinary and depraved behaviour of late.'

'It does, but more likely his natural tendency to that kind of behaviour is the reason he acquired the affliction.'

'A night with Venus, a lifetime with mercury,' Mr Barker says.

Chapter 11

Throughout the afternoon Elen uses industry as a salve, but as evening approaches, the effort of keeping her sadness at bay is wearing her out. She dearly wishes she could mourn her loss in solitude.

'I think I shall take a stroll through the town,' she says to Sarah.

'Let me grab my shawl and I'll come with you.'

'I shall be perfectly safe. Plenty of people are still abroad and I would value a few minutes of solitary reflection.'

Sarah nods her understanding and Elen sets off into the rain-washed streets. They are no longer littered with the stinking guts of fish and chickens left by the market stalls; the poor have carried any edible detritus away. All that remains is straw filthy with mud, which will scatter in the night when the wind blows along the empty streets or be swept away the following morning by brooms and sluices of water.

Elen passes a lamplighter working down the street, climbing up his propped ladder, offering the taper up to the wick beneath the glass dome which blooms, bathing his face in golden light. At first she ambles along with little purpose, relieved to be alone. She attracts little attention, for her head is draped with a thick shawl and her gait is that of an old woman. Her misery seems to have drained her of her youth.

As she slinks along in the shadows of the tall houses, she pauses to stare into the blackened windows of one of the shops. Staring back at her, she sees a pitiful figure with a shrunken and drawn face. A split second later she realises it is her own reflection.

She has been walking for twenty minutes when the sound of revelry reaches her. Ahead the yellow light of a tavern shines onto the wet pavements. It seems a popular drinking haunt, for a crowd has spilled out, sheltering from the fine drizzle beneath the green awnings that jut from the front of the building. Among the babble of foreign tongues she catches a few halting words in English and sees two soldiers, chatting to a couple of attractive young women and making a reasonable flint of being understood in French.

She has no idea what possesses her, but she crosses the street and joins the group. 'Excuse me, sir,' she says to one of the soldiers, 'are your companions inhabitants of this town?'

'Indeed they are.'

'Would you be good enough to ask them if they know the whereabouts of the townhouse of the Countess von Oettingen?'

One of the women frowns and shakes her head but her friend thinks about it a little longer before stepping into the street, pointing this way and that. She then makes an extravagant gesture with her hands, chattering in French all the while to the soldier.

'She says you must follow the street down to where it turns left,' the soldier says. 'Then make a right some time after that. Apparently the house is easy to find because it sits in the centre of the street, which splits either side around it. She says the house is white and has Flemish decorations on it. There is also something painted on the wall but I have no knowledge of the word, miss.'

His companion tries to explain again, but it is hopeless. Elen thanks them and leaves them to their amused confusion. She had not planned to hunt out the countess's house, but now she is heading towards it, she feels comforted. She has no intention of seeking an audience with Mordiford but the rhythms of their lives have been linked for so long, she feels sure that if she could picture where he is, it would make her pain easier to tolerate.

The house is impossible to miss. It fills one complete side of a small square, the crow-stepped gables rising up five storeys, each window framed with buttercup-yellow shutters. The feature to which the woman referred is, in fact, an elaborate sundial, decorating the front of the building.

Light spills out from the ground floor windows and, like a moth to a candle, Elen finds herself drawn through the dusk of the street towards the glow. Servants are visible, moving through the rooms. The curtains have not yet been drawn.

Her heart thumps in her chest.

Mordiford is standing in one of the rooms with his back to a vast fireplace. He looks strong and well. His face is freshly shaved and in the looking glass behind him, she can see that his hair has been neatly queued and tied in a maroon ribbon. He is dressed in scarlet justacorps and has cast aside the bulky walking aid that the surgeon constructed, replacing it with an elegant stick on which he leans. He is talking to someone, but she cannot see whom it is because the listener is seated out of sight of the window.

Like a wraith, she drifts nearer, her eyes fixed on the dumb show before her. As she nears, she can see Mordiford's earnest expression, the gestures he makes with his free hand as he speaks. She cannot hear the words but she can read the language of his body.

The conversation is intense. Eventually he pauses. The seated figure rises and comes into view, her head bent. Mordiford moves forward and catches Lady Arabella by the arm. Still she looks down until he reaches out and raises her chin gently with the knuckle of his hand.

Elen staggers back into the shadows, turns and hastens away. As she hurries through the dark streets, the tears she has kept at bay for so long, pour down her face, forced out, not only by her grief, but by anger at herself for being so foolish.

She has spied on him and she has been punished. The image of Mordiford on the point of kissing another woman will be burned into the back of her eyes for all eternity. How she wishes she could tear them from her head.

–

Cold and wet, Elen goes in through the back door of the hospital and slips up to the tiny room under the eaves, which is to be her room for the next few weeks. She climbs onto the bed, opens the shutters and struggles with the catch of the window. It opens with a patter of rust and, leaning on the lintel, she looks up into the night sky.

The blue hulls of rainclouds pass silently over the city. At this very hour, the previous night she lay next to Mordiford in the sure and certain knowledge that their destinies had joined them together and that no man could tear them asunder. Yet the man who has now torn them apart is Mordiford himself.

A gale of laughter rises up from the street, mocking her stupidity. She shuts the window with a slam, throwing herself onto the bed, her damp cloak still around her. Had she learned nothing from her brush with Ned Harley? Is she destined to misjudge every man in the future for whom she holds strong feelings? Her emotions swing from despair to utter bafflement. She was so certain this time that her judgement was sound. Having discovered it is not, she has lost faith, not only in Mordiford, but also in herself.

Elen lies still, listening to the dripping of the rain and the distant voices of the town. On the stairs the wood creaks. There is a tentative tapping on the door.

'Elen?' Sarah calls softly. 'Are you awake?'

She sits upright on the bed, pressing the backs of her fingers onto the skin below her eyes in a futile attempt to soothe the swelling. She peels off her cloak and leaves it on the bed behind her.

'I am,' she says, wearily getting to her feet and taking the single step required to reach the latch.

'The captain is here. He asks, will you come down and speak with him?'

'I am not certain that I shall.'

Sarah gives the door a light push and slips into the room. 'He has put himself to great inconvenience to return here this evening.'

'I did not ask him to.'

'Elen,' Sarah says, 'do not be so cold hearted. We five have become such friends of late. The captain is downstairs in the kitchen with Mr Barker and Dr Argyll. He looks quite the English gentleman – but still he laughs and jokes with us as though we are all the same.' Elen feels a fresh pang of loss for the man she thought she knew. 'He is most insistent. He does not wish to quit the Continent until he has had the opportunity to speak with you.'

'I know what he has come to say. I do not want to hear it.'

'How can you know unless you come down? Please, Elen. Do not make me disappoint him. His manner is bluff, but I can see that he is troubled at heart and much distracted.'

Despite her anger, this last piece of information weakens her resolve. She curses her heart for holding on to love when it should be filled with antipathy. She wishes she could delight in the thought of his unhappiness but she cannot.

'Very well,' she says. 'I will come down presently.'

Either Sarah or the captain have conspired with the assembled company to let her have a private audience, because the minute she appears in the kitchen, there is a degree of hearty assurances of industry as the Barkers and Dr Argyll quit the room. So clumsy is their flight and so poor their excuses that had her heart not been so heavy, she would have laughed at their ineptitude. As it is, their exit is sufficiently contrived to make her feel all the more awkward.

The captain struggles to his feet, grasping hold of the table until he regains his balance. Having done so, the smile that was on his face when she entered the room melts away. He looks at her fixedly but she does not know why. Is it pity, regret? Or does he want to commit one last image of her to memory before they part?

Presently he speaks. 'Miss Griffiths, I apologise for calling at this late hour. I see by your expression that my visit is inconvenient.'

'Unexpected, sir.'

'Is that so?' He looks perplexed and pauses for a moment, casting his eyes down to the floor. 'Perhaps I should have waited until the morning,' he says as if speaking to himself. He looks up at her and says, 'Events have moved so swiftly and so unexpectedly that I...' He pauses again before adding, 'My father is dead.'

'I know, sir.'

'A month gone by. And all that time, when I thought of him, which I grant was not often, he no longer walked this earth. Is that not the strangest thing?' He pauses, waiting for a reply, but when none comes he presses on. 'How old were you when your mother passed away?'

So incongruous is the direction of the conversation that she shakes her head as if to clear it. 'It was during my sixteenth summer, sir.'

'And your grief was keen?'

'Acutely,' she says, frowning.

'And in those sixteen years that you knew and assuredly loved your mother, did you have any regrets?'

'Of course. That she was taken from us so soon.'

'I mean, did you feel remorseful in any way after her passing? Had you left anything unsaid, any kindness to her not given?'

'Not a one,' she replies, her frown so severe now that her head begins to ache.

'Then you are lucky indeed. I imagined my father's passing would give me not a moment's discomfort. I was mistaken, for however serious his shortcomings, I find now...' Here he stops again, his eyes cast to the ground. '...that I loved him.'

She stares at him, quite at a loss. He looks up, and seeing her incomprehension says, 'You see, my grief is not as yours was when you were a child. You had the privilege of a sorrow so pure I imagine it was like a sharp knife cutting deep but clean, and sooner healed.'

'It is presumptuous of you to imagine another's pain, sir.'

'Yes, perhaps it is. All I know is that my grief is nothing like that. I am torn and muddied inside, full of regret that the opportunity to understand, perhaps in time to forgive, has been ripped away from me. I thought I had years ahead to unravel the mystery of the man whose blood I carry in my veins this very day.'

'We must all find our own path to peace when someone who has filled our lives is taken from us, sir,' she replies coldly.

He narrows his eyes and says, 'Something is very much amiss here, I think.' When she does not reply he continues, 'I hurried over to see you this evening because I needed your gentle council to help me with my pain.'

'If your leg is causing you pain, I suggest you sit, sir.'

Mordiford looks as startled as if she has struck him. 'Miss Griffiths, you mock me. How has this barrier risen between us?'

A great wave of frustration wells up inside her. In a tone she imagines he cannot mistake, she says, 'With the arrival of Lady Arabella.'

'I see. Yes, indeed. That was also a great shock. However, it has distilled my thoughts and led me to make a firm and definite decision. Having made it, I came with as much haste as I could to tell you.'

'I do not wish to hear it.'

Mordiford stares at her, his face riven with anxiety and despair. 'I think I understand. You judge me for my actions this evening.'

'Of course I do.'

'I accept I have caused great pain to a person whom I have always held in high regard.'

The despair that she has felt all evening swiftly turns to anger. 'That, I suppose, does you some credit,' she manages to say.

'I am glad you think so. You see, were I to turn away from what I know to be right, I would only add to the intolerable burden of regret that I already bear. I know absolutely and unequivocally that I cannot fulfil my duties here or at home unless...' He sighs again and stares up at the ceiling. '...unless I marry.'

By now she feels such a fury towards him, this revelation hardly rocks her. Her anger has created an emotional distance between them. She pities his dilemma yet feels no compassion for his struggle. The more he talks, the greater is her belief that he has come to seek her blessing. She cannot give it. Far better that had he quit the Continent without a word than come this evening to extract an absolution from her.

'What would you have counselled me to do?' Mordiford continues. 'To falsely tie someone to me if I knew I could not offer her the life she had come to expect?'

'I cannot answer this, sir,' she says. 'It is cruel of you to expect me to.'

'Cruel? Then I am quite lost. I am without a compass.' Grasping his stick, he limps across to the fireplace where he hangs onto the chimneypiece staring morosely into the fire. 'How poorly I have judged everything. I mistook the pity you felt for me as love, the care you poured on me as devotion. I had thought myself renewed by my hardships and worthy of your regard. I see now it was my conceit rearing its ugly head again in a different guise.'

'Your conceit, sir, is to come from the arms of one woman and seek the approval of another.'

Mordiford starts like a spooked stallion and swings round. 'What's that you say?'

'I walked down through the town. I found the house where you stayed. I watched you. I saw you with Lady Arabella.'

'When we were locked in a brutal conversation?'

'Brutal? That was not the word I would have chosen, having seen you lift her chin as a prelude to a kiss.'

'A kiss?' Mordiford says in disbelief. 'A kiss?' He repeats. 'In all innocence, no kiss has passed this evening between myself and Lady Arabella.' His stares at her, his face working as if he struggles to recollect the scene, until understanding lightens his brow and laughing quietly, he says, 'Clearly you did not stay to see the tableau through.'

'I could not stand to.'

'If you had, you would have seen that by raising her chin, I forced her to look me in the eye so that I could be sure she understood the strength of my convictions.'

'To marry her.'

His forehead puckers with incredulity.

'No! A thousand times, no. God damn it, Miss Griffiths! Are the words I have been speaking for the past ten minutes coming out of my mouth in Flemish for you to so misunderstand me?'

'I understand you completely, sir.'

'No, you do not. I told Lady Arabella that I could not face the task ahead of me without the woman who has been my saviour, the woman who has bewitched me, body and soul. That person stands before me now.'

She rocks as if caught by a gust of wind. She fumbles at the edge of a table to steady herself.

'And still she speaks not,' Mordiford cries out.

'And Lady Arabella?' she manages to say.

'Lady Arabella finally accepted my words as truth.'

'Her mother?'

'Ah, the mother was not so easily convinced. However, they embark for England tomorrow. That part complete, I summoned a carriage. I came immediately with news I foolishly imagined would bring joy to your heart.'

She covers her face with her hands, the happiness she should be feeling overwhelmed by chagrin, filling her with a misery of the acutest kind.

'I have made a terrible mistake,' she says, unable to look at him.

'It appears it is I myself who is most in the wrong. I imagined that the honourable way to act was to tell Lady Arabella of my decision before I came to you. You are angry with me for speaking plainly to her.'

'I am not. I imagined the heart you must break was mine own.'

'Never.' He says this with such vigour she knows her foolishness has made him angry. 'How little you must think of me to imagine that I could spend such a night with you and cast you aside the very next day.'

'I beg you, sir. Do not raise your voice at me.'

'Do not raise my voice? What else am I to do when you will not understand me?' He strikes the floor with the ferrule of his stick, his shoulders heaving, his knuckles white where he grips the head of the cane.

Still staring into the fire, he continues in a calmer voice, 'My only anxiety was that my new station would test your affections and make you believe you must forsake all you have loved back in Wales for the passion you have found here. I was ready to challenge that view and promise you that having lived our lives beyond convention these past nine months, we could continue to do the same.'

'Oh, Mordiford,' she whispers, dropping her head in shame. 'I am sorry. Can you find it in your heart to forgive me for so doubting you?'

She hears him sigh. Presently he says, 'I am not so sure that I can.'

His words freeze her heart. Slowly she raises her head and looks at him.

He has turned to face her but he no longer looks angry. His head is tilted to one side. He gazes at her with such intensity his eyes have never seemed so blue. 'I might forgive this folly...' He pauses before taking a faltering step towards her and gathering her fingers into his hand, '...if your foolishness extends to accepting the hand of this clumsy soldier who loves you with all the truth imaginable.'

'You mean the soldier with the plooked face and the crooked leg?'

'The very one.'

She hesitates, unable to resist a mimic of his earlier tease, but she knows from the warmth of his eyes and his smile that at this moment he will not be gulled.

Chapter 12

December 1704

Two whole months have passed since that evening of joy and celebration in the kitchen at the hospital in Nördlingen. Elen survived the copious quantities of alcohol pressed on her by the Barkers to celebrate the news. She survived a tearful parting with Mordiford the following day, secure in the knowledge that he returned to Wales, not only to sort out his affairs, but also to seek permission from her father for her hand in marriage. She too survived the gruelling journey back to The Hague and the difficult sea crossing, much lengthened by the autumn storms.

It was not until Elen arrived in London in the company of the Barkers and Dr Argyll that her worries crept up on her. Elen felt the cold clutch of reality when they stopped at The Black Swan in Holborn and Sarah pulled her into her bosom, saying, 'Come the spring, Mr Barker and myself will hasten across the borders of Wales and see you – that's if the Countess of Duntisbourne ain't too grand to receive a surgeon's wife.'

She had filled the past months with thoughts of how her life would change, but the exact details remained hazy. When she thought about the passion of their final union, she imagined it occurring in the bed in the sealed chamber where she first learned to love Mordiford, not in a grand bedroom in the private apartments. When she thought of eating in company, she imagined Mordiford breaking bread with her family at their table. She could not imagine eating at the dining table in the south wing with Mr Antrobus, bending stiffly to serve her.

As the stagecoach laboriously ate up the leagues from London to Wales, the doctor regales their fellow passengers with stories of the Duke of Marlborough's glorious victory. Elen only half listens, her mind filled with concerns that, once plunged into a life she was never born to live, she will fail, and Mordiford's love for her will falter.

She comforts herself with the notion that their love has been strong enough to overcome the most terrible trials. At other times she has believed those trials were easy compared to a union that society at large would find impossible to accept. And by the time she glimpses the red earth of the Welsh marches through the window of the coach, her dread has moved onto a fear of living at Duntisbourne Hall. The place holds so many horrors for her. Even without them, she cannot imagine living in that cold and forbidding building, thronged with the ghosts of the past, her days filled with the tedium of a life without labour or purpose.

—

Elen wakes with a start. It is noon and they have arrived at the Three Cocks Inn on the Hereford to Brecon Road where they are to be met, according to her latest communication from Mordiford.

The doctor helps her down from the coach and starts bidding farewell to his admiring audience who begin to head across the muddy courtyard in search of food and drink. Elen wonders if they too should partake of a little refreshment before continuing. The east wind whips around her as she waits for her bag to be unloaded. As the coach moves away towards the stables, she recognises a trap standing in the courtyard. It is the very one that Mordiford used to drive her over to Presteigne on the night he rescued her from the Knights of St Sebastian.

The doctor bustles her into the inn. The atmosphere is thick with pipe smoke and the smell of bodies. The doctor peers into the bar room and catches the eye of the landlord.

'A driver from Duntisbourne awaits us,' the doctor says.

'That's right, sir. I'll let him know you're here.' He disappears into the crowd.

Elen takes a deep breath – this is the first contact with a servant from the hall. Does he know she is betrothed to his master? And how will he feel when he realises who she is, the dairymaid who nursed the viscount in the winter?

Here he comes now, his tricorn already on his head, tipped down so that she cannot see his face. He isn't wearing livery. Instead he is dressed in a frockcoat of dun-coloured wool over a simple waistcoat and brown breeches. She has time to wonder if Mordiford has banned formality among the servants, when the man raises his head and she finds herself looking into a pair of the clearest blue eyes.

Mordiford snatches his tricorn from his head, tucking it under his arm. Taking her fingers, he presses them to his lips.

'Good heavens above,' Dr Argyll says taken aback. 'Is that you, Captain Mordiford?' He stops abruptly, momentarily lost for words before adding, 'What on earth am I saying? I mean, Lord Duntisbourne.'

Oh, no, she thinks. I cannot call him that – he will always be Mordiford to me. The landlord overhears and hurries across, wiping his hands on his apron and touching his forehead with a knuckle.

'Lord Duntisbourne? I had no idea, no idea at all,' he says, looking Mordiford up and down, before his drinker's face flushes an even deeper crimson. 'Come on through, my lord, into the parlour.'

Mordiford claps his hand on the man's shoulder and says, 'Your ale is just as fine in the bar room but we must away now, thank you. These two fine people have been travelling for weeks and are looking forward to sleeping in their own beds tonight.' He gives Elen a jaunty wink, which makes her blush almost as brightly as the landlord.

As they walk across the courtyard, she notices he no longer uses a stick although he walks with a dip to the left, lifting the knee of his injured leg a little higher to swing the foot forward.

'I think you quite meant to trick us, my lord,' the doctor says, 'coming in disguise like this.' She is cheered by the doctor's lack of deference; happy that the easy friendship they developed in Bavaria has not been damaged by the passage of time.

'Disguise? This is no disguise. Do you not remember? I told you all in Donauwörth that I have no ambitions to ape my father's life, and most certainly not his style,' Mordiford says, pressing a coin into the hand of the boy helping with the bags before climbing up onto the wooden seat of the trap, helping his left leg up with his hand. 'Come along,' he says, holding out a hand of invitation. 'Three of us can squeeze on here.' Elen is sandwiched between Mordiford and Dr Argyll.

Although the wind is keen, the sun breaks out from behind the scudding clouds and bathes the winter landscape in golden light. The track is dry and they make good progress.

She wants to slide her arm into the crook of Mordiford's elbow, but feels she cannot with the doctor sitting beside her. She wishes that, like the doctor, she could slip back to the easy manner they shared the last time they were in one another's company, but she feels a crippling shyness and does not know how to overcome it.

She thinks, all will be well once we leave the doctor at his front door – but the next stop will be Duntisbourne Hall, where all will not be well. She steals a look at Mordiford's profile and sees the corners of his mouth twitch, then begin to smile. He looks down at her, his expression one of supressed excitement. Yes, all will be well, she thinks taking a deep breath. Somehow, all will be well.

They reach the doctor's house by mid-afternoon, refusing the refreshments pressed on them by Mrs Argyll and bid the doctor farewell. As the trap turns the corner and the doctor's house disappears from sight, Mordiford hauls on the reins, tosses them down and gathers her up in his arms.

'Elen, my darling Elen. I thought my old temper was going to rise and make me fling the doctor from the trap so that I could hold you in my arms.' He sweeps her hair from her face, his gaze darting from her eyes to the tip of her nose, to her lips and back again. 'This precious, precious face. You have returned to me and I am the happiest of men. But we must hurry if we are to make it back to Duntisbourne before nightfall.'

'And to the dairy,' she adds. He doesn't reply but there's a rascally glint in his eye.

'I thought you could dine with me first,' he says. 'Your father is only expecting you in general.'

The sun is dipping in the sky by the time the trap enters the estate. Elen sees the chimneys of the hall above the trees, and feels a pall of anxiety squeezing the happiness out of her heart. She does not want to dine at the hall. She wants to sit down to supper with Mordiford at the rough pine table in the kitchen, surrounded by her family who love her.

To her surprise, Mordiford guides the pony onto the path to the right, which leads away from the hall. 'Surely,' she says, 'you're not playing your father's silly game of taking a round-about route to the entrance, just to show the hall at its best, are you?'

'I think it is too lovely an evening to head there just yet,' he says and she frowns at him. Whatever is he planning? It is surely too cold for a picnic.

On they trot, up through the woodland and out onto the fields high above the hall to the west of the estate. How lovely, she thinks, we will pass Maes yr Haf and, as they break free of the woods, there it is, tucked away at the top of a gentle valley, the stones of the handsome house glowing like amber in the low winter sun.

'My mother loved that farmhouse,' she says.

'I know she did. Your father told me when I went and asked for your hand in marriage.'

'Was he not exceedingly surprised?'

'He was, and not a little worried, but I talked to him of my plans for the land, my determination to honour the debts left by my father and make Duntisbourne a great estate once more. I reminded him that his own marriage was a powerful example to follow and he talked a deal about the happiness he found with your mother. She must have been a woman of extraordinary good taste as well – Maes yr Haf is one of the prettiest houses on the estate.' He gives her the most tremendous smile. He looks as if he is about to burst out laughing or fling his hat into the air and whoop with joy.

'Whatever is the matter with you this afternoon, sir?' she says.

'I am overjoyed to see you,' he says, slapping the reins across the pony's rump as the trap speeds towards the large farmhouse.

Elen gives up trying to read his mood and returns to admiring the proportions of the building ahead with its bay windows and stone mullions.

As they near, the front door opens. A figure comes out and stands beneath the portico. Two tall young men join him, then a girl steps forward, holding a child by the hand, and Elen gasps – it is her family.

'Why is Tad here?' she says as the trap rattles towards them.

'They have come to dine with the mistress of the house,' Mordiford says mischievously.

'The mistress of the house? Who, pray, is she?'

'Her name is Elen Griffiths and soon she will be the wife of this simple farmer who has no interest or desire to live in that gloomy mausoleum by the lake.'

'You do not mean to live in the hall?' Elen says.

'I cannot, even if I wanted it. My father has left too many debts. No, it has been quite shut up and I have found employment for the staff elsewhere on the estate. I have taken the best books from the library and spent the last month creating one here – for you – a safe haven where you can read after we have worked side by side in the fields. This is to be our home, my darling Elen. We will farm and fill this house with children and laughter.'

So, as the sun sets over the winter landscape, Elen embraces her father and her sisters, shakes her brothers by the hand (for they are far too grown now for hugs) and links her arm through Mordiford's. Together they enter the house that once stole the heart of her mother.

Author's Note

I grew up in a medical family. This gave me a lifelong interest in disease but also made me a career hypochondriac. Researching things I might actually get is a dangerous exercise for my over-active imagination but smallpox, which was eventually eradicated from the human population in the 1970s, fascinated me and fitted the themes of suffering and rebirth that I wanted this story to embody.

Smallpox was a devastating disease, extremely contagious with a high mortality rate and no respect for rank or wealth. Those who survived were often left severely scarred but at least they could never get smallpox again. This immunity was understood in 1704, but the Chinese process of giving healthy people the living virus, known as variolation, was only just reaching the western world. However, it was well-known that people who caught cowpox were immune to smallpox, hence the old-English saying that something was 'as smooth as a milk maid's skin'. (It was not until 1796 that Edward Jenner decided to test this observation, publishing his treatise *On the Origin of the Vaccine Inoculation*, the word 'vaccine' coming from the Latin 'vacca' meaning cow.) I had found the perfect way of plucking Elen from the comfort of her father's hearth and placing her in the Gothic setting of Duntisbourne Hall.

Duntisbourne Hall was inspired by my time working at Blenheim Palace, a magnificent English Baroque stately home in Oxfordshire. It was a 'gift from a grateful nation', bequeathed by Queen Anne to John Churchill, 1st Duke of Marlborough for winning the Battle of Blenheim in 1704, a key turning point in the War of Spanish Succession. At Blenheim Palace, I worked in a room tucked away above the great courtyard and accessed not only by a wide staircase on one side, but also by a narrow stone spiral staircase hidden behind a door in the central office. Like Duntisbourne Hall, in winter Blenheim was draughty, cold and spooky but it was also breathtakingly magnificent. The incredible tapestries in the staterooms show various battles in the War of Spanish Succession, but many of the visiting public assume they show the Napoleonic Wars a century later.

The more I learned about the Duke of Marlborough, the more surprised I became that his extraordinary achievements had always been overshadowed by the Duke of Wellington's 1815 victory against Napoleon. When Marlborough beat the French at the Battle of Blenheim in 1704, it changed the balance of power in Europe more profoundly than Wellington's later victory at the Battle of Waterloo.

I think one of the reasons Waterloo eclipses Blenheim is because the politics behind the War of Spanish Succession are complicated. Spain's childless King Carlos II died in 1700, perversely leaving his throne to the grandson of the French King Louis XIV. This gave France an extraordinary extension of influence and power because at that time, Spain had extensive territories in Italy, Belgium, the Netherlands and the Americas as well as controlling the slave trade from West Africa.

England formed a Grand Alliance with Austria and Holland to protect their territory and trading rights against the French. Queen Anne chose the handsome, cunning and charming John Churchill, 1st Duke of Marlborough as Captain-General and Commander-in-Chief of her army on the Continent, giving him authority over the Dutch troops as well as the English, Scottish, Welsh, Irish, German, Danish and Swiss soldiers. In 1702 the Franco-Bavarian forces had broken the barrier fortresses, which protected the Dutch Republic from the French, and the following year, other Franco–Bavarian victories directly threatened Vienna. When the 1704 campaign 'season' began (winter weather caused havoc for soldiers on campaign, so the season started in the spring and ended in the autumn, with troops returning home for the winter months), Marlborough was determined to stop the French at all costs.

I have had the privilege of reading John Churchill's personal correspondence held now by the British Library. He cared deeply about his soldiers, making sure they were 'well paid and well shod', and that fresh saddles, boots and food were sent ahead up the lines during the long march to the Danube. He was one of the first commanders to organise the wounded, setting up dressing stations and hospitals such as the one at Nördlingen. However, these were nothing like the arrangements today. There was no formal army medical corps on campaign, and wives, camp followers and barber surgeons did the work when and where they were needed.

Dr Argyll's initial antipathy towards Mr Barker was standard at this time and can be traced right back to the 12th century when the clergy, who at that time acted as both physicians and surgeons, were banned from dealing with blood. Barbers, who traditionally worked in the monasteries, keeping the monks clean-shaven, took over all blood-related work such as tooth extraction, minor operations and bloodletting. The striped barber's pole symbolises the stick the patient held in their hand during this procedure, the brass ball at the top of the pole symbolises the bowl used for collecting the blood or for holding leeches. After treatment the bandages were washed and wrapped around the pole to dry, giving it the traditional striped pattern.

The Black Plague had a devastating effect on the number of university-trained physicians (those with a doctorate) and in 1540, Henry VIII united the Company of the Barbers and the Fellowship of Surgeons with a royal decree, the Company of Barber Surgeons, to alleviate the shortages. (Even today, a hospital doctor loses his or her 'Dr' title and becomes 'Mr', 'Mrs', 'Ms' or 'Miss' once he or she has acquired higher surgical qualifications.)

Mr Barker mentions Ambroise Paré. Originally apprenticed to a barber, this famous Frenchman accompanied the French army and pioneered a number of innovative treatments such as the application of egg yolk, oil of roses and turpentine used by Elen on amputated limbs. When Paré's book *Les Oeuvres* was published in 1575, his ideas spread across Europe and respect for surgeons began to build until, in 1745, the surgeons finally dissolved their centuries-old partnership with the barbers to become the well-respected profession they are today.

Despite these advances, surgery at the Battle of Blenheim was basic, bloody and agonising. It's almost impossible for us nowadays to understand how soldiers withstood the pain of pre-anaesthetic surgery. Perhaps the courage that made them brave in battle helped them face the pain of their wounds. In one account, I read a gunner had an arm and both damaged legs amputated in a single session but was found the following day, propped up on his remaining elbow, calmly smoking his pipe. Another soldier refused to be helped to a transport cart after having his leg amputated, preferring to hop over to it under his own steam and it was not unknown for soldiers to chat with the surgeon as he worked. All the same, Mr Barker's speed would have been much appreciated and remained vital to a soldier's survival – the longer the operation took, the less likely the patient was to survive. Occasionally that speed was at the expense of the fingers of a surgeon's assistant.

Another reason for the soldiers' bravery may well have been the attitude to suffering at this time. It was seen as a strengthener to the soul and most surgeons operating in a pre-anaesthetic era believed it was a vital stimulant necessary for keeping the patient alive. They even delayed the administration of opiates and alcohol, viewing unconsciousness as a danger to the patient. It is interesting to reflect that the fear of pain in the modern world is every bit as acute despite advances in anesthesia, perhaps because we no longer view it as character forming. The only modern equivalent I can think of is when exercising or doing weight training. Knowing that pain is essential to improvement makes it easier to bear.

Maggots had been used to aid wound healing for centuries. My mother came across it when she was nursing during WWII and there has recently been a resurgence of interest in their use. Not only do the maggots clear away dead tissue, they secrete enzymes that fight infection.

When Mordiford told Elen that he was 'full of the black humour,' he was referring to the theory of the four humours, which dominated medical practice right up until the 19th century. It was based on the teachings of Hippocrates and Galen who believed that the body was composed of four liquids – blood, phlegm, black bile and yellow bile. These in turn were associated with the air, water, earth and fire as well as with the seasons. When these humours were balanced, a person was healthy in body and mind, but when they went out of balance, disease and sickness were the result. Bloodletting was used if the body contained an excess of blood, and other popular ways of restoring balance included enemas, laxatives, emetics and blistering of the skin. This story is set at the dawn of the Age of Enlightenment, a time when philosophers and intellects began to question these long-held beliefs, using scepticism and careful observation to formulate alternative hypotheses. Dr Argyll embodies this open-minded attitude to the treatment of his patients.

This novel is of course fiction but much of it is based on fact. The Duke of Marlborough did suffer from migraines – he described his periodic violent headaches in his letters to his wife. This gave me the opportunity to bring Dr Argyll and Elen to his side and the ergotamine that the doctor prescribed is still used in migraine medicines today.

The description of the Battle of Blenheim comes from many sources, one of the most fascinating being the first-hand accounts written by two soldiers that fought during the campaign, Captain Robert Parker, Royal Regiment of Foot of Ireland and the Count of Mérode-Westerloo, Field Marshal of the Holy Roman Empire in *Military Memoirs of Marlborough's Campaigns 1702-1712*, edited by David Chandler. I also depended heavily on James Falkner's *Great and Glorious Days* and George Malcolm Thomson's *The First Churchill*, as well as the first volume of Winston Churchill's biography of his forebear, *Marlborough, His Life and Times*. Winston wrote this majestic biography of his ancestor so that his extraordinary achievements would not be forgotten — I hope this story reignites an interest in the man who some believe was the greatest commander in British military history.

Acknowledgements

I started this novel during my MA at Oxford Brookes and owe a huge debt of thanks to my fellow alumni who work-shopped chunks of it during our tutorials, along with my inspirational tutor, James Hawes who had such faith in the story, and Sarah Dunant for her candid appraisal of the original battle scenes. I must thank in particular the special writing chums that I made there, Mandy Robotham and Izzy Brown who still have the patience to read and comment on my writing.

A massive thank you to Rebecca Smith who gave me invaluable advice about bringing this unusual era of history to life. Thanks also to Louise Cullen and Canelo Publishing for adding the story to their list and producing such a fabulous cover, as well as Elizabeth Woabank for her forensic editing of the manuscript.

I owe a huge debt of thanks, as always, to my wonderful agent, Giles Milburn who may not be a super-fan of scheming valets, but continues to back my writing career to the hilt as well as throwing incredible Christmas parties.

I thank all the members of my immediate family for their unstinting support and encouragement including Sam, Tamsin, Katie-Jane and Tom, but in particular Ben who, as a writer himself, has to chew the fat of plot problems with me more than the rest. The exception is my husband, Chris who is always willing to listen, read and comment and who, despite claiming to be the most unromantic man in the south of England, has a particular soft spot for this story.